DAJA blinked. She had thought the shelf on
a level with her own eyes was empty last time.
Yet here was a half-melted female figure with a
loop on the back, as if it were a pendant. Silver
gleamed through cracked gilt. Daja stared at it,
a memory stirring at the back of her mind like
the gleam of silver. She had seen that figure
hung around someone's neck. Goosebumps
prowled her arms and her spine. Something
was not right here.

North Fortress

Odaga

Alakur

Central Fortress

Kadasep

Least Fortress

Bazniuz

Shield

Airgi

Pearl Coast

The SYTH

Less Ship-quarter

Greater Shipquarter

Suroth-Gate

0   ½   I   2 miles

© 2002 Ian Schoenherr

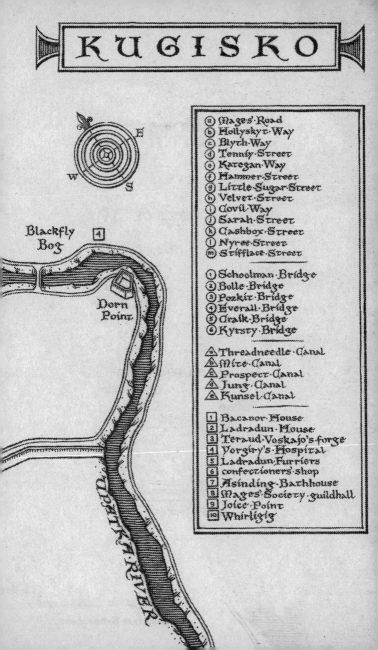

KUGISKO

a. Mages' Road
b. Hollysky't Way
c. Blyth Way
d. Tenniy Street
e. Karegan Way
f. Hammer Street
g. Little Sugar Street
h. Velvet Street
i. Covil Way
j. Sarah Street
k. Cashbox Street
l. Nyree Street
m. Stifflace Street

1. Schoolman Bridge
2. Bolle Bridge
3. Pozkir Bridge
4. Everall Bridge
5. Craik Bridge
6. Kytsty Bridge

△ Threadneedle Canal
△ Mite Canal
△ Prospect Canal
△ Jung Canal
△ Kunsel Canal

1. Bacanor House
2. Ladradun House
3. Teraud Voskajo's forge
4. Yorgiry's Hospital
5. Ladradun Furriers
6. Confectioners' shop
7. Asinding Bathhouse
8. Mages' Society guildhall
9. Joice Point
10. Whirligig

Blackfly Bog

4

Dorn Point

UPATKA RIVER

POINT

Enter the Circle of Magic

TAMORA PIERCE

The Circle Opens

Cold Fire

POINT

SCHOLASTIC INC.

New York Toronto London Auckland Sydney
Mexico City New Delhi Hong Kong Buenos Aires

TO THE FIREFIGHTERS, POLICEMEN, RESCUE WORKERS
AND MEDICAL PERSONNEL OF NEW YORK CITY,
OUR TRUEST HEROES IN OUR DARKEST TIME

ISBN-13: 978-0-590-39656-1
ISBN-10: 0-590-39656-0

12 11 10 9 8 7 6 5 4 3 2 1   7 8 9 10 11 12/0

Printed in the U.S.A.   01

First Scholastic paperback printing, March 2003

Book design by Elizabeth Parisi

The text type was set in Adobe Caslon.

In the city of Kugisko, in Namorn:

Niamara Bancanor, twelve and sometimes too helpful in Daja Kisubo's opinion, gripped Daja's left hand and elbow. They stood on one edge of a broad circle of ice where the Bancanors docked their household boats in the summer. Now, in the month of Snow Moon, eight weeks before the solstice holiday called Longnight, it was a place to skate, with benches and heaped banks of snow at the sides to protect those less able to stop than experts like Nia. For all her fourteen years, Daja was as much a beginner at this as any three-year-old. She wouldn't have agreed to these lessons, wanting to protect her dignity, but after three weeks of watching the Namornese zip up and down the city's frozen canals, she had realized it was time to learn how to skate, dignity or no.

"Are you ready?" asked Nia. The cold air made dark roses bloom on her creamy brown cheeks and lent extra sparkle to her brown eyes.

Daja took a deep breath. "Not really," she said with resignation. "Let's go."

"One," counted Nia, "two, three."

On three Nia and Daja thrust with their left legs against ice smoothed each night by convict crews who performed that service for the entire city. Daja glided forward, knees wobbling, ankles wobbling, belly wobbling.

"Right, push!" cried Nia, gripping Daja's arm. Two right skates thrust against the ice. Left and right, left and right, they maneuvered across the length of the boat basin. Daja fought to stay upright. She knew her body was set wrong: while she didn't skate, years of training in staff combat told her that she was not at all centered. It was like trying to balance on a pair of knife blades. Who thought of this mad form of travel in the first place? And why had no one locked them up before they passed their dangerous ideas on to others?

She didn't want to think of the picture she made, though she'd bet it was hilarious. Five feet, eight inches tall, she towered over Nia by four inches. Where Nia was slender, Daja was big-shouldered and blocky, muscled from years of work as a metalsmith. She was a much darker brown than Nia and the other Bancanor children, whose mother was light brown and whose father was white. Daja's face and mouth were broad. Her large brown eyes — when she was not trying to learn to skate — were steady. She wore her springy black hair in a multitude of long, thin braids. Today she had pulled them into a horse-tail tied with an orange scarf; she wore no fur-lined hat as Nia did, because she had her own way to keep her head warm. Her clothes were in the style worn by Namornese men: a long-skirted coat of heavy wool over a slightly shorter indoor coat, a full-sleeved and high-collared shirt, baggy trousers, and calf-high boots to which the skates were strapped.

"See, this isn't so bad," Nia said as they reached the entrance of the boat basin. "Soon it will be as easy as breathing. Now turn . . ." She swept Daja around until they faced the stair to the rear courtyard, across the small basin. "Ready, left, push," Nia coaxed. Daja obeyed.

Left, right, left, right, they slowly made their way across the ice. Servants coming and going from the house and outbuildings watched and hid grins. Like Nia, they had spent their lives here on the southeastern edge of the Syth. For those who could not afford horses and sleighs in winter, ice skates were necessary. They were a quick way around a city sprawled over various islands in waters that were frozen solid from mid-Blood Moon to late Seed Moon.

By the time Nia turned Daja again, the older girl was starting to get the idea. The trick was to rock as she stroked, using alternate legs to push. If she brought her legs together, sooner or later she would stop moving. Skates, when not in motion, had an ugly tendency to make the wearer fall over.

Nia guided her back to the end of the boat basin, where

it passed under a street bridge to enter the canal beyond. Without stopping, she moved Daja onto a course that circled the ice instead of halving it. Three times they went around, Daja feeling stronger and more confident with each turn. It was not so different from being aboard a ship, in a cold way. She enjoyed it so much that she didn't realize that Nia had let go of her. She skated two yards alone before she noticed. Then she made the mistake of looking for her partner. Her knees and ankles wobbled. She frantically tried to recapture the rhythm, managing three strokes of the skates before her feet hit the basin's edge. Daja went face-first into heaped snow.

She sank a foot before Nia pulled her out. Laughing, the girl apologized. "I thought you were doing so well that you'd just keep —"

Daja straightened, bobbling. Nia had gone abruptly silent. A moment later Daja realized the servants had also stopped moving. Everyone stared at the place where she had fallen.

Daja sighed. Her Namornese hosts had told her that she had adjusted wonderfully to their northern winter. She had not mentioned that her mage talents included the ability to control her body warmth by drawing heat from other sources. As a result, her very warm body had melted her precise shape into the snow, down to each finger on her gloves. The snow that had iced her face when she fell was melting down the front of her coat.

"Can Frostpine do that?" asked Nia, putting her own gloved hand into the hand-shape Daja had burned into the snow. Daja's teacher, a great mage dedicated to the service of the Fire gods, was the reason they were spending the winter in Bancanor House. Nia's parents were old friends from the time before Frostpine took his vows.

"No," Daja replied. "Even if you have the same magic as someone else, it shows in different ways." It would require too much explanation, or she would have added that *she* wouldn't have this ability if she had not spent months with her magic intertwined with that of three other young mages. Though Daja and her foster-siblings had finally straightened their powers out, they still carried traces of what the others could do. Daja's ability to draw warmth and see magic came to her courtesy of a weather-mage.

"Well," Nia said, determinedly cheerful. "Let's try again."

The lesson went forward. Daja caught the rhythm and managed two circuits of the basin before they decided to stop. Back into the house they went, shedding their winter gear and skates in the long, enclosed area called the slush room. Afterward they followed the halls that made the outbuildings part of the house to reach the kitchen.

Daja accepted a mug of hot cider from one of the maids. She sat near one of the small hearths, where her jeweler's tools and a task that she *could* handle awaited her. No servant would ask a great mage like Frostpine to mend their bits of jewelry. Daja was fair game; they thought she was a student, willing and skilled. The whispers that she too might be a great mage had not come as far north as Namorn.

Daja enjoyed the work. She liked to sit here doing small repairs, breathing the scents of spices and cooking meat, and listening to servants and vendors chatter in Namornese. Before she had mastered the strange tongue, her travels with Frostpine in the empire of Namorn had been lonely. It was wonderful to know what people actually said.

She touched the necklace the cook, Anyussa, had given her. Daja's left hand bore a kind of brass half-mitt that covered the palm and the back; strips passed between her fingers to connect them. As flexible as her body, the brass shone bright against her dark skin. The magic in the living metal told Daja that the necklace was gilt on silver — expensive for a servant, even one so well paid as Matazi Bancanor's head cook, but Matazi herself would turn up her nose at it.

Daja laid the gilt metal rope straight on the table. She didn't touch her pliers. Gilt was tricky stuff on which to apply any force: badly worked, it would flake off to expose the metal underneath.

She needed to warm it a bit. Turning, Daja reached toward the hearth and called a seed of fire to her. It swerved around the two cooks who worked there: Anyussa was watching Nia's identical twin Jorality, or Jory, stir a green sauce. Jory saw the fire seed go by and grinned at Daja, then shifted nervously from foot to foot as Anyussa inspected her work.

"Now look — you rushed. It's gone lumpy," the woman said, lifting a few green clumps in a spoon. "That's the ruin of any sauce. If you don't stir enough, or let your attention wander, or add flour too fast, it lumps, and it's ruined." Anyussa turned to chide a footman who had dropped a basket of kindling.

Daja was about to tell the glum Jory it was just a green sauce for fish, not a disaster, when a silver tendril of magic leaped from Jory into the sauce-pot. The girl stirred it in with a trembling hand. Daja stared. She and Frostpine had lived here for two months. No one had mentioned that any of the Bancanor children, the twins or their younger brother and sister, had power.

Anyussa returned to Jory. Daja watched the cook. Had the woman seen Jory's small magic?

Anyussa dipped her spoon again. "I tell young girls, you cannot rush —" She fell silent as she raised her spoon and turned it to spill the sauce back into the pot. A long, smooth, green ribbon flowed neatly down, without a lump in sight. "But I was *sure* . . ."

As Daja repaired the necklace and mended cracks in the gilt, Anyussa drew out smooth spoonful after smooth spoonful. She tasted the sauce and poured it into a dish: no lumps. When a baker's apprentice came to argue with

Anyussa over a bill, Daja slid over the bench to sit close to Jory. The girl regarded the bowl with a puzzled frown.

"You know," Daja said quietly, "if you can find a way to fix that spell to a powder or liquid, you could sell it. Cooks everywhere will sing your praises."

Jory blinked at her. She had Nia's large brown eyes and slender nose, set in a face the color of brown honey, a shade lighter than her southern mother's. She was lively, smile-mouthed, and a handful — her twin, Nia, was the quiet one. Her chief beauty (and Nia's) was the masses of gold-brown crinkled hair that fell to her waist. "What spell?" she asked Daja.

Daja smiled. "What spell? You unlumped your sauce. I can see magic — it's no good telling me you didn't spell that pot." She inspected Jory's face, and frowned. The twins weren't hard to read. "You didn't know?"

"I don't have magic," Jory insisted. "Papa and Mama had magic-sniffers at me and Nia when we were two, and again when we were five. Not a whiff." She grinned at Daja. "Maybe it was a spark. Things glitter in here all the time."

Daja got to her feet and draped her coat over her arm. Anyone who saw magic would glimpse it all around this kitchen. There were runes to keep out rats and mice, spells in the hearthstones to keep a few embers alive until someone rebuilt the fires, and a spice cupboard magically built to keep its expensive, imported contents fresh.

"You would know," Daja said. "If you do figure out what you did, you should write it down."

"Oh, Anyussa just scraped from the bottom or something," Jory said airily. "She wants everything perfect —"

"Fire!" someone yelled outside. "Fire in the alley! Fire brigade, turn out!" Jory fled, Daja assumed to warn her mother and the housekeeper. The kitchen help streamed outside.

Daja put her coat down and followed them, wondering what "fire brigade" meant. She was surprised that Anyussa had allowed everyone to run off to gawk — the woman was fair, but strict. When she reached the courtyard Daja discovered her mistake in thinking the servants had come to watch. A line of kitchen helpers stretched between the well and the alley off the rear courtyard; they passed buckets of water out the rear gate. Another line of people led from the large pile of sand kept for use on icy paths. They passed buckets of sand the same way.

Daja followed the full buckets into the alley. The efficient assembly stretched down its length to the nearby blaze, an abandoned stable behind Moykep House. Daja viewed it with an intelligent eye, since fire was mixed into her power. The stable was gone, that was certain. The closest buildings might be in danger, but it seemed this strange local efficiency covered that as well. Men stood on every roof that might be at risk, soaking shingles with water, keeping an eye out for jumping flames or wads of burning debris.

Daja was impressed twice over. Since her arrival in Namorn, she'd found it hard to feel safe in cities that were almost entirely wood. Here only the nobility and the empire built in stone. Apparently she did not worry alone. Someone was teaching Kugiskans organized ways to battle fires.

"How did this happen?" she asked Anyussa, who stood beside her. "Most places, they have sloppy lines and hardly anyone ever thinks of the neighbors' roofs but the neighbors."

"We got lucky," Anyussa replied. She was a fortyish white woman with brown eyes, sharp cheekbones, and a full, passionate mouth. Unlike many northern women, she left her hair brown rather than dye it fashionably blonde, and wore it pinned in a coil. "Bennat Ladradun, the man who trained us to fight fires, studied with the fire-mage, Pawel Godsforge."

Daja whistled. Everyone who dealt with such things knew of the great Godsforge, whose home was tucked among mountain springs and geysers in the northwest corner of the Namornese empire. "Ladradun is a mage?" She recognized his name: the Ladraduns lived nearby.

"Not *Ravvot* Bennat," Anyussa replied, using the Namornese term for "Master." "But he said there was plenty for even a non-mage to learn, and he learned it.

When he came home, he talked the city council into allowing him to train districts in Godsforge's firefighting methods. Then he talked some of the island councils into granting funds and people to train. It paid off. It's been two years since a house burned to the ground here on Kadasep. He —"

Suddenly people in the stableyard were shouting. Above the adult voices rose the thin screams of children. Daja left Anyussa and raced toward the stable, realizing someone must be caught inside. She gathered her power in case she had to do something in a hurry.

In the stableyard, people stood as close as they dared to the entrance of the burning building, full buckets in hand. Their eyes were wide in soot-streaked faces, glued to that dark opening ringed in flame.

Someone went in, Daja thought. They're waiting for him to come out. She was reaching with her magic, prepared to hold back the fire, when a bulky, awkward, gray shape came out of the smoke-filled entrance at a dead run. Behind the shape overtaxed roofbeams groaned and collapsed. The stable roof caved in, sending gouts of flame blasting out the doorway to clutch and release the gray shape. Daja saw a clump of burning straw shoot up through the hole in the roof, swirling in the column of hot air released by the fire. The brisk Snow Moon winds seized it and dragged it higher, toward the main house.

Daja raised her right hand and snapped her fingers,

calling with her power. The clump of fire came to her, collapsing until it was a tidy globe that rested on her palm. Holding it before her face, she asked, "What am I going to do with you?"

She looked at the gray shape. Firefighters pulled the water-soaked blanket away to reveal a large, sodden white man with two boys no older than eight or ten. He carried one over a shoulder, one under an arm.

Daja's throat went tight with emotion. There was no glimmer of magic to this fellow who had nearly been buried in the stable. With only a wet blanket for protection he had plunged into flames to save those boys. He'd come close to dying: one breath more and that burning roof would have dropped on his head.

This was a true hero, a non-mage who saved lives because he had to, not because he could protect himself with magic. He was a tall man in his early thirties, coatless; his wool shirt was covered in soot marks and scorches. His russet wool trousers were also fire-marked. He appeared to have forgotten his wriggling burdens as he stared at Daja and her fire seed with deep blue eyes.

The firefighters tugged on the boys. Recalled to himself, the tall man released them and grimaced. He shook his left hand: it was crimson and blistered with a serious burn. The boys were coughing, the result of their exposure to smoke. Their rescuer eyed them with a frown as a firefighter wrapped linen around his burned hand. "Which of you set it?" he demanded.

A woman in a maid's cap and white apron was offering the boys a ladle of water to drink. She dropped the ladle at the blue-eyed man's words. *"Set?"* she cried.

"His fault, Mama," one croaked, pointing to the other. "He spilt the lamp."

"You said we could play up there!" cried his companion, before a series of coughs left him wheezing.

The maid grabbed each lad by an ear and towed them into the main house. Daja shook her head over the folly of the young and glanced at the burning stable. The firefighters had given up. They simply kept back and watched for more flying debris. They also edged away from Daja, their eyes on the white-hot fire globe in her hand.

"If you don't want people to be nervous with you, don't do things that make them nervous," Frostpine had advised after they'd been on the road a week. "Or do things they won't notice. You've been spoiled, living at Winding Circle. There everyone's used to magic. Outside, making things act differently than normal turns people jumpy."

Daja didn't like to make people jumpy. She covered her fireball with one hand.

"How did you manage that?" The boys' rescuer walked over to Daja, cradling his wrapped left hand. "You called it. *Viynain"* — Namornese for "a male mage" — "Godsforge had that trick, except in ribbons, not balls." He thrust his right hand at Daja. "Bennat Ladradun," he said. Even covered with soot and scorch-marks he was a comfortable-looking man, with the soft, big body of a well-broken-in armchair. His broad cheeks were each punctuated with a mole, one high, one low. His nose was fleshy and pointed; his flyaway curls were reddish brown and losing ground on top of his head. Someone came up with a dry blanket to wrap around him: his clothes were soaked by the blanket he'd worn into the stable.

Daja had to uncover her fireball to shake his hand. "Daja Kisubo," she replied. "You were brave to go in there."

"No, I just didn't think," Bennat replied absently. "If I had, I'd have known better. The roof was about to go." He turned her offered hand palm up and closed his fingers around it. "Not even hot," he remarked. "A little warm, that's all." He let Daja go. "You're one of the smith-mages, am I right? The pair staying with Kol and Matazi?"

Daja nodded. "The Bancanors' cook says you teach Kugisko to fight fires."

Bennat smiled, his thin mouth tucked into ironic corners. "I teach parts of Kugisko, bit by bit, kicking and screaming," he replied as he inspected the fireball. He held his hand over it and snatched it back. "Well, *that's* hot, at least. *Viynain* Godsforge wore spelled gloves so he wouldn't get burned when he worked with flame. Why doesn't the fire bother you?"

"It's magic," she told him quietly. "One of the first things we learn."

He shook his head. "My whole year with Godsforge, only two of our mages learned to hold fire, and they couldn't manage something that hot. What are you going to do with it?"

Daja shrugged and tossed it back to the stable. It vanished in the flames. "Did the blanket really help in there?" she wanted to know.

The man wandered over to a barrel set beside the far wall and sat on it. Daja followed him. "The trick's in guessing how long you have before the fire sucks the damp out," he explained. "I hoped it was wet enough that I could reach the loft, grab our fireflies, and get out. It helped knowing where they were — we saw them, in the window over the door. If I'd had to search, I might be a little charred now." Looking at the burning stable, he shook his head. "I told the Moykeps six months ago they ought to pull this thing down. It was an accident waiting to happen."

"This whole *city's* an accident waiting to happen," Daja said with feeling. "All these wooden houses — it's mad-brained, that's what."

Bennat looked at her and smiled. "That's right — you're from the south. Somebody told me you were. Wood's cheap in this part of the country — we've got more forests than we know what to do with. And families moving into the city, they want something that reminds them of home."

"Wood," Daja said, shaking her head in disgust.

"You get used to it," Bennat said. "There's real craftsmanship in the carvings on the roofs and doors and porches. And the builders use different kinds of log, to contrast colors and textures in the wood."

"Here I thought they just built these places any old way," Daja admitted. "It never occurred to me they used different woods on purpose." She realized she was being rude. "I'm sorry. It's not my place to criticize your home."

Bennat chuckled, then began to cough. One of the women firefighters came to offer him a flask. Bennat took it and drank, coughing between sips. At last the coughs stilled. He returned the flask. "Thanks," he told the woman after he wiped his mouth on his sleeve. Looking at Daja he asked, "So do you fight fires?"

Daja smiled crookedly. She wasn't sure that he would term sucking a forest fire through her body to douse it in a glacier as firefighting. "Mostly I just handle it in the forge," she replied. "I know a trick or two — there's always the risk of little fires starting in forges or inns — but I almost never use them."

"I'd like to hear about them sometime," Bennat told her. "Anyone who balls up fire and holds it probably knows more about how it works than I do." He lurched to his feet, cleared his throat, and sighed. "I'd better check the outposts, make sure no other wads of debris went flying." He offered Daja his hand. "Thanks for the help."

Daja shook hands. As she walked back to Bancanor House, she eyed the firefighters. They kept watch over the stable as it burned low, but they were relaxed and joking. The worst was over. The stable was gone, but two boys were still alive, and nothing else had caught fire, because Bennat Ladradun had trained these people well. That was far more impressive in this firetrap city than *her* ability to handle flames.

When the staff returned to the Bancanor kitchens, Daja returned Anyussa's repaired necklace. Then she collected her coat and climbed the servants' stairs to her room.

Her excitement over the fire and Bennat's rescue of the children vanished, leaving ashes in its wake. Homesickness swept over Daja as she walked into her Namornese room with its ornately carved mantel, its high bed heaped with feather-stuffed comforters, its heavily shuttered windows, and the riot of colors in its thick carpet and drapes.

All these things reminded her that she was not at home in Emelan, at Winding Circle temple with its stucco buildings, simple furniture, and many gardens. She was far from the Pebbled Sea, and she couldn't expect to meet her three foster-siblings or their teachers around the next corner. There was plenty to see and do as she traveled, plenty of occasions for excitement, activity, even fun. But every time strong emotions faded, she longed for her foster-family. No one else would talk to her of fashions, constellations, diseases, skin creams, staff fighting, or the art of miniature trees. She even missed their dog Little Bear, big, galumphing, drooling animal that he was.

Even if she went back now, the others weren't there. Sandry lived with her great-uncle, Duke Vedris of Emelan, in Summersea. She had given her room away, she'd written Daja, to a terrified novice thread-mage. The last time Daja had heard from Briar, their lone foster-brother, he and his teacher Rosethorn were on their way east. They might not return for two years. Tris and her teacher Niko had gone so far south that Daja fully expected them to return from the north.

It was Frostpine's idea to travel as well, to show Daja the ways of other smiths. She knew it was in part to take her mind off the absence of Briar and Tris. It was also true that she had learned a great deal in smithies that ranged from tiny crossroad places where the specialty was horseshoes, to elegant goldsmiths' forges where she learned to put designs composed of tiny gold balls on metal. Here in Kugisko she studied with Teraud Voskajo, who Frostpine called the greatest ironsmith he knew. It seemed unfair that she had to go so far to learn so much. At least they had settled for now in a comfortable place. They were not wander-mages here. They were honored guests of the head of Kugisko's Goldsmiths' Guild, which controlled the city's banks.

She wished she could have this learning *and* her Emelan family. A break from her foster-siblings had been a fine thing at first. After mingling their powers, they had kept a magical bond that allowed them to know what the others thought and felt. When they'd left Emelan Daja had thought she could go months, perhaps a year, without knowing three other people inside and out, as they knew her. She had lasted two whole weeks, she thought ruefully.

One thought brightened her mood: she'd had a nice talk with Bennat Ladradun. A sensible talk, about useful things. Smiling at this simple pleasure, Daja hung up her indoor coat. Bennat had mentioned something that tweaked her imagination: gloves spelled so the wearer might handle fire. Could *she* make gloves that someone with no magic might use? If such gloves could be made, what about an entire suit? With a fireproof suit, someone like Bennat wouldn't have to rely on the scant protection of a water-soaked blanket.

She thought until she realized that she daydreamed with no purpose. She set the ideas for gloves and suit to heat in the back of her mind and turned to her current project: matching jewelry sets for each of the Bancanor women, even eight-year-old Peigi. For Kol and his five-year-old son Eidart she had already created matching gold neck rings and wrist cuffs, jewelry favored by Namornese men. They were her Longnight presents, her thanks to this openhearted family.

Daja labored over her gifts, shaping the women's jewelry to be as fine and ornate as lace. The cost of the gold was nothing. The strange, unique pieces she made with the excess living metal she took off her hand daily — if she let it go unchecked, she would be coated in it by now — had made Daja wealthy.

She was shaping a sign of health when someone rapped on her door. "It's open," she called, twitching a nearby piece of cloth over her work to hide it.

Jory danced in, followed by her twin. Nia sat beside Daja, while Jory wandered the room, chattering. "Anyussa says cook-mages study from books. They put spells on sauces and draw symbols on pots and pans. They shape magic signs in bread, and strengthen herbs and spices to use in spells. They can make people fall in love with a cup of tea, except they'd get caught and arrested for magicking people without permission. She said Olennika Potcracker, who used to be the empress's personal cook, was so powerful that if someone put poison in the empress's food? It all turned green."

Daja crossed her arms and waited for Jory to get to her point. It was a tactic Daja had learned over the last two months.

"*And* Anyussa says cook-mages are found by magic-sniffers and they all get a license from the Mages' Society here or a medallion from Lightsbridge University or Winding Circle that says they're proper mages and have read all the right books, just like Olennika Potcracker." Jory plumped herself down on a footstool. "So I couldn't be a mage like that. The magic-sniffers said we weren't mages. Twice. It's in Papa's family, but not in us."

Daja touched the medallion she wore under her clothes. Frostpine had made one for each of the four at Discipline Cottage eighteen months before, and given them out at a supper attended by them and their teachers. The front of each pendant had the student's name and that of her or his chief teacher inscribed on the outer edges. A symbol for that student's magic was at the center; Daja's was a hammer over flames. On the other side of the medallion was the spiral symbol for Winding Circle, where they had studied.

The medallions were spelled so that usually the wearers forgot them unless someone asked them to prove they were accredited mages. Winding Circle's mage council had granted the medallions the four had earned only after Frostpine promised to ensure they didn't brag about a credential that most mages studied for years to get. He didn't tell the council that the four weren't likely to brag — the council would not have believed it. Sandry wore her medallion like her nobility: it was so much a part of her that she rarely thought about it. Briar might once have used it to boast, but no longer. Tris wanted the world to forget how powerful her magic was. For Daja the forgetting spell was useless. Not only did her own power tell her what she wore, but the disguising spells on the medallions were Frostpine's, whose magic she knew as well as her own.

For now, she saw no point in telling Jory that as an

accredited mage, she knew more about magic than Anyussa. Instead Daja told the girl, "There's another kind of mage, not as common as the ones who train with the Mages' Society or at Lightsbridge. We see a lot of them at Winding Circle. They use magic that's *already* in things, rather than adding magic to something. It's called ambient magic. You can make it stronger, or bigger, or more accurate, with book studies, but you still draw on magic that's already there. Everything has some magic in it." She looked at Nia. "I suppose you like cooking too? Though I hardly ever see you in the kitchens."

Nia shook her head.

Jory replied, "She won't go near a hearth. She's afraid of fire."

Nia glared at Jory. "You would be, too, if you had any sense," she informed her twin.

The house clock chimed the hour.

Jory and Nia looked at each other. "Music lessons!" they yelped, and tumbled out the door.

Daja uncovered her necklace and went back to work.

After a couple of hours' labor, Daja realized she was stiff. A walk might clear the cobwebs from her skull. Down the servants' stair she went, bypassing the kitchen and its enticing smells, following the corridors that connected the buildings until she reached the slush room. Properly clothed, she wandered out into the waning afternoon and the alley. The rear gate to Moykep House was still open, the trampled and sooty ground around it frozen into ruts and holes. Daja looked in. A tall, rumpled figure in a heavy sheepskin coat wandered through the remains of the stable, kicking apart any large clumps of charred matter. Bennat Ladradun was checking for hidden blazes that might find something to burn if the wind picked up.

Entering the courtyard, Daja threw her power out ahead of her, feeling for heat. "There's nothing warm left," she told him. "I just checked."

The big man smiled. "Another useful skill, *Viymese* Daja," he said, using the Namornese word for a female mage. He walked carefully across the burned-out mess until he reached her. Places where the firefighters had used water were frozen, making the footing treacherous. As he spread his arms for balance, Daja saw a neatly wrapped bandage on his left hand.

"You got scorched," she said, pointing to it.

He made a face. "Not too badly. There was a piece of wood in the way when I went to get those boys. I knocked it aside, but the blanket slipped and I hit it with my bare hand. The healer says when I take this off, day after tomorrow, I won't even have a scar." Changing the subject, he remarked, "I'm surprised you're not studying with Godsforge. I don't know if you've heard of him —" He slipped on the edge of the building.

Daja instantly steadied him. "I have," she said, releasing

23

him as he got his footing. "I'm a smith, really — fire for its own sake doesn't much interest me. All I know about fire comes from my magic. I know *you* studied with him."

Bennat shook his head. "We think we're such a worldly city, but really, we're just a collection of villages. Gossip flows quicker than air here. Did they tell you about my birthmarks?"

Daja grinned up at him. "I don't know how they missed that," she replied. She had already discovered that most Kadasep Island residents knew her name and Frostpine's, why they had come to Kugisko, and where they lived. "If you don't mind my asking, why study with a fire-mage if you've no magic yourself?"

"Because he knew how fires burn with different materials, and how to fight them," the man replied. "Things even someone like me could learn. Things like when you're in a burning building, touch a closed door first. If it's hot, you won't like what happens if you open it."

Daja raised her eyebrows in a silent question.

He answered: "Opening the door, you give the fire inside a burst of air. It blasts out and cooks the person in the doorway."

Daja whistled softly. "I'll remember that. And it makes sense. We use a bellows in the forge to pump air into the fire to make it burn hotter. What else did you learn?"

"How to know if a fire was deliberately set," he explained.

"And wind patterns, the use of sand in winter . . ." He stared at the ruins, hands stuffed in his coat pockets. "One time there was a barn that had to be destroyed, so he set fire to it. Then he threw a shield over us, so we could stand in the middle of the barn and watch how the fire burned, along the floor, up the walls, into the loft. It was like a carpet of fire blossoms rippling over our heads." He glanced at Daja. "I'm sorry. People tell me that I just rattle on."

"No, no, I'm interested!" Daja protested. "The only time I ever saw anything like that was during this forest fire. Even then, what I saw didn't ripple or anything. I pulled it through me. All I saw was streaks." She realized what she must sound like, and hung her head. "I'm not boasting. It really did happen."

"Oh, I believe you," said Bennat, his eyes blazing with excitement. "What I would give to see that!"

Daja grinned at him. "At the time I wished I hadn't, but it wasn't like I had a choice. I would have died if my foster-brother and -sisters and Frostpine hadn't helped with their magic. And I didn't exactly come away unscathed." She rubbed her thumb against the metal under her left glove. Yes, it was useful. Yes, she now made living metal creations that rich people bought at high prices. She had also seen revulsion on the faces of those who touched her hand and found warm metal, or those who saw her peeling the excess from her flesh. She'd also suffered infections when the metal caught on something and pulled away part of her skin. She shook off those memories. "Did you learn about forest fires from Godsforge?" she asked her companion.

"Enough that I prefer city fires," Bennat said with a grimace. "Or at least, I prefer city fires if I have trained people to fight them. Godsforge had us out in the woods digging firebreaks one time, and the fire jumped the break. Without him to protect us . . ." He shrugged. "He said that once a really big forest fire gets going, it can't be stopped until it rains or it consumes all the forest it can get."

They were moving out through the Moykep gate, into the alley. "It's true," Daja said. "At least, Niko — Niklaren Goldeye, he was one of our teachers — he said that about lots of things, storms, forest fires, tidal waves. They reach a point of strength, and even the most powerful mages can't stop them. The best you can do is shift them."

He'd come to a halt, and was staring at her. "You studied with Niklaren *Goldeye?*"

It was Daja's turn to shrug. "He's the one who saw my magic, and taught us to control what we had. Mostly he was my sister Tris's teacher, though." She made a face. "They were well suited — always with their noses in books."

Bennat laughed and offered his hand. "I enjoyed talking with you, Daja Kisubo. I hope we can do it again."

Daja took his hand. "Thank you, *Ravvot* Ladradun. It's nice to talk to someone who doesn't just think a fire's for use or putting out."

"Call me Ben," he told her. "And I know what you mean. To most people fire's a means to an end, or it's a monster. They don't realize it has moods just like the Syth, or the skies."

"No, they don't," agreed Daja.

They stood in the frozen alley for a moment, smiling at each other, sharing that understanding of fire and its shapes. Then Ben sighed. "I really should go home," he said. "Mother will have fits when she sees my clothes. What can you do?" He wandered down the alley toward Ladradun House, hands thrust once more in his coat pockets.

Daja watched him go. She had thought that once children were grown, they didn't have to worry about a parent's wrath. Maybe it was different when the grown child came to live under a parent's roof once again.

The wind threw a fistful of sleet into her face. She turned and hurried back to Bancanor House.

2

On her return to Bancanor House, Daja went to Frostpine's room and knocked on the door. Invited in, she found her teacher beside his fire, seated so close to it that the snow-damp hem of his red wool habit steamed gently. He was a tall black man in his late forties, lean and ropy with muscle, full-lipped and eagle-nosed. His bald crown gleamed in the firelight. Daja often thought that it was sheer defiance of his baldness that made Frostpine grow long, wild, bushy hair on the sides of his head: today he had pulled it back and tied it with a thong. The discipline he'd forced onto this hair emphasized his equally wild and bushy beard.

Frostpine had gold coins in each hand when she came in. He walked them through his long fingers, turning them over as they traveled. "Close the door, you're letting in a draft," he ordered, tossing a coin to Daja. "I just got back from riding and I'm *cold*."

"You'll set yourself on fire if you move any closer to the hearth," she informed him as she took the chair beside his.

"Then I'll die warm," Frostpine said, glum-faced. "What do you think of that?" He pointed to the coin Daja held.

"What must I think?" she asked, holding it in her palm. "It's an argib." She named the standard coin of the empire. "A gold argib, with that awful portrait of the empress on the front."

"It's a fake," he said.

Daja was indignant. "And wouldn't I tell —" she began to say.

Frostpine leaned over and traced a sign on the coin she held. Daja immediately knew she held a brass counterfeit. "You never taught me how to do that," she accused him. "How could I not know it was false?"

"Because you weren't thinking about the possibility of a counterfeit, and because it's the best such spell I've ever seen," he said. "Thank Hakkoi of the Fire and the Forge that the chief of the magistrate's mages guessed something was wrong and asked me to take a closer look. It took me two hours to sort through the illusions on it."

Daja whistled, impressed. "Faking gold so even I couldn't tell it wasn't real? That's serious."

"The governor wants me to work on this along with Heluda — Heluda Salt, the magistrate's mage who called me in." Frostpine sighed. "We have to see not only who's doing this, but how many fakes are in circulation. And we have to do it quietly."

"I should think so!" Daja was born a Trader, a people whose many clans bought, transported, and sold goods over a large part of the world. Trader babies got wooden teething toys carved like the main coins for the countries where their families traded. For ten years Daja's life had been about trade and money. She knew what happened when people found that the coins on which they depended were false. Currency would plummet. No one would buy or sell anything in gold, perhaps not even in copper or silver, until it was proved that no more fakes remained. Such a crisis could result in a government's fall, or even in war, as well as instant poverty for entire populations. "What about the silver argib?" Daja asked.

"Safe," Frostpine said. "Whoever did this concentrated on gold — this method would never work on silver. We may have caught the counterfeit early enough to make a difference. I went through half of what's in the governor's treasury, and only found ten fakes so far. We need to catch who's doing it, of course. And any friends he may have. You might not see much of me for a while."

"You're sure you can catch him?" Daja asked.

Frostpine smiled. "I handle enough of his fakes and I'll sniff him out like a hound."

"You said that when someone was filching your tools

back home," she said ruthlessly. "It took you all winter to find him."

Frostpine's dark eyes flashed. "I didn't know I was looking for a *child*," he said tartly. "I suspected dark plots by — oh, you have no respect for me."

Daja grinned. "I have plenty of respect for you. Truly. I swear it."

Frostpine slouched in his chair. "Time was when students didn't mock their teachers. They did as they were told and said, 'Yes sir,' and 'No, sir.'"

"That nobleman in Olart who wanted you as his teacher — *he* was respectful," Daja said innocently. "He 'sir-ed' you across the realm and back. You called him a, a 'cake-mouthed ninny dressed as a peahen.' *And* you told him memorizing runes and chants did not make him a smith-mage. We had to sleep in someone's barn that night."

"Is it *my* fault he disliked criticism?" Frostpine wanted to know. He put another log on the fire.

As he returned to his chair Daja said, "About students and teachers . . . I think Jory has cook magic."

Frostpine raised heavy brows. "You *think?*"

Daja shrugged. "I was in the kitchen while she was making a sauce. Anyussa said it was lumpy. When she got distracted, Jory did some" — Daja twiddled her fingers to indicate magic — "on it, and the next time Anyussa checked, no lumps. I saw the magic pass from Jory into the pot. And she sees the spells in that kitchen, though she just thinks it's flashes of light at the corner of her eyes."

"She's an ambient mage?" Frostpine asked.

"Has to be," Daja replied. "She and Nia told me they were tested by magic-sniffers twice, and they didn't find a thing."

"Well, if one twin has magic, both do." Frostpine stretched his booted feet toward the fire. "That's always the case with twins. The power takes different paths — it seems to be shaped by their personalities and what happens in their lives. Have you a sense for what Nia's magic might be?"

Daja shook her head. "I have no idea."

Frostpine smoothed his beard. "Then you need a testing device. Something to help you find out the kind and the strength of magic a person might have," he said. "There are all varieties — mirrors, globes, crystals. I knew a paint-mage who spelled a clear oil so that when the one she tested put his hand to canvas, a picture of his power, or her power, grew out of it. Beautiful work," he remarked, and sighed. "I was consumed with envy."

"So let Kol and Matazi just take Nia to a magic-sniffer and tell him to look harder," Daja replied. "I have projects of my own to do." Living metal gloves for a hero, one who didn't have magic to shield him, she thought but didn't say.

Frostpine inspected his nails. "I suppose we *could* get a

magic-finder and explain things." His voice was suspiciously mild. "Things like the Bancanors heard Nia *has* power, but the discovering-mage couldn't tell them what it is."

Daja glared at him. "You're needling me," she accused.

"What'll be worse is when the magic-finder works out the magic Nia has and sends her back to you for instruction." Frostpine seemed to need to ensure that each of his fingernails was clean. "I doubt it would help her confidence in you to know you needed someone else to explain what to teach her."

Daja sat bolt upright. "*I'm* not teaching anybody. And I'm not letting a strange mage tell me anything."

"That much is my fault," Frostpine said, putting yet another log on the fire. He held out his hand and raised it an inch in the air. Flames spread over the fresh wood in a leap, making it burn quickly. "I didn't think we'd have to deal with this for years, but the gods like to make a man feel unprepared, so the wisewomen say."

Daja drummed her fingers on the arm of her chair. "Stop dancing around it," she said. "I hate it when you take a year to walk a mile."

"As the discoverer of their magic, you *have* to teach them," Frostpine explained. "I did mention the rules, when you got the medallion. Part of the price you pay for it" — he pointed to the spot on her chest where it lay under her clothes — "is that when you find a new mage, you serve in a teacher's place until a proper one of the same kind of power is found. Sandry wrote you, didn't she? To say she had a student?"

Daja nodded slowly. "I thought she was being silly, telling me she had to make spells up for this Pacon, or however he calls himself, because there aren't any other lone dance-mages. And I'm as bad off as she is — I don't know anything about cooking for Jory, or whatever Nia has. I can't do it!"

"Don't panic," Frostpine said firmly. "Cook-mages, at least, are as common as salt. Magic-sniffers who can see and identify ambient magic aren't common, but the Mages' Society keeps a list of those who can do it. Chances are, once you know what kind of magic Nia has, you'll be able to find a teacher with her magic as easily as you'll be able to find a cook-mage for Jory. In the meantime, start teaching them to meditate. If Jory's magic is popping out without her knowledge, Nia's can't be far behind. They need to learn to control it sooner rather than later."

The hall clock chimed. It was time to change clothes for supper. Daja levered herself out of her chair. "I *have* to do all this?" she asked, pleading with him. "Run all over the city for magic-sniffers and teachers and all?"

"Since you don't want to make a testing device of your own to tell you what Nia has, I suppose you do," Frostpine replied. "And you must tell Kol and Matazi. They'll be pleased."

"Would *you* be?" Daja asked, shoving her hands into her breeches pockets.

"Now there's an odd question," Frostpine said. He had returned to walking the false coins over and under his fingers. "Aren't you happy you're a mage?"

"Sometimes," Daja said as she went to the door. In her mind's eye she saw herself, adrift in a wash of ship wreckage, straining to reach a floating box filled with life-giving supplies. "And then remember that I learned about my power after my entire family drowned and I got declared an outcast. I wonder sometimes if magic really *is* a good thing."

Frostpine looked up at her with a smile. "Well, it was a good thing for *me* that you came along," he said. "That should count for something."

Daja went back to her room, feeling decidedly grumpy. For one thing, changing clothes for the evening meal was the kind of folly practiced by people who had too many clothes they didn't have to wash. Since it was the custom in wealthy houses Daja changed her garments, but it chafed her spirit.

More than the clothes, though, Frostpine's information irked her. It was bad enough that she must teach — she was *busy,* after all. Just going to a mage she didn't know to find out what exactly she must teach was somehow worse. She felt as if she had been challenged to do something, and had failed.

The magical testing methods Frostpine had mentioned involved seeing. She had studied something of the kind a couple of years ago. Tris's teacher, Niko, whose specialty was seeing-magic of all kinds and who taught the four general magic, decided they ought to know how to scry, or to see things that took place in the past, the present, and sometimes the future. Those mages with any talent for it easily saw the present in their scrying devices. Some even glimpsed the past. Occasionally they saw bits of the future, but because the future changed from moment to moment as the present did, those bits were rarely useful.

So Niko had given the four of them a choice of crystals, mirrors, even bowls, which showed images when filled with water or oil. He then tried to teach them different ways to call visions to their chosen devices. Tris was the only one who could do it every time, but she had trouble seeing anything that interested her. Scrying was such a will-o'-the-wisp magic that Briar and Sandry had given up in disgust. The best luck that Daja ever had with it was when she looked for things in a small bowl of her living metal: that was how she had discovered that a kitchen boy was taking Frostpine's tools. It wasn't reliable: one bump of the bowl and the image was gone, never to be recaptured. In the end she had discarded the metal she'd used in the bowl. It continued to flicker with images long after she gave up scrying, and she couldn't use the metal for anything else.

Daja stopped changing into supper clothes halfway and

sat at her worktable, pulling a slate and a piece of chalk toward her. What if she created a living metal mirror? That would be more stable than a bowl; she could use it over and over. She could take what Niko had taught them and shape the mirror to reflect a precise image of someone's magic. She scribbled hurried notes. If she remembered everything properly, she had all she would need in this room.

Excited — she would show Frostpine! — she opened the trunk at the foot of her bed. It was covered in leather and secured with leather straps, with the emblem of Daja's own House Kisubo burned into every side. This was a *suraku,* a survival box that seafarers packed with food and water against the possibility of shipwreck. The contents of this one had kept Daja alive until Niko had found her. It was her chief treasure and all that remained of her drowned family, so it was only natural that she turn it into her mage's kit. Inside the copper-lined box she kept magical tools, herbs, oils, and metal samples in small bottles and jars, corked, sealed, and tucked into padded trays. Daja selected tiny vials of mercury and of saffron oil, a slender hollow glass tube, a silver disk as wide as her hand was long, and an engraving tool. These she placed on her worktable.

Next she opened the big jar that took up half of the *suraku's* interior. Its contents gleamed the bright silvery gold of brass. She had started filling it with excess pieces of the metal that continued to grow on her left hand. Later, as she found uses for it, she added brass scraps and drops of her own blood to the jar's contents: within a day the scraps would soften and blend, giving her a good-sized container of living metal whenever she needed it. Living metal creations had made her rich at fourteen: it was good she'd found a way to create more without having to wait for it to grow out of her flesh. Now she took a bowl and dipped it full, then set it on the table.

Beside the door was her Trader's staff. The wood was five feet of solid ebony, capped in brass on the top end and iron on the butt. On the cap she had engraved or inlaid signs in wire, telling her story to anyone who read Trader symbols. Here was her survival of the sinking of her family's ship; her time as an outcast; her rescue of a Trader caravan during a forest fire; the end of her outcast status; and her present life as a mage with whom Traders could buy and sell in honor.

It was also very useful for defending herself, as Traders had done for centuries, and for creating circles of protection. Extending her power through the ebony, Daja drew a circle around her worktable, leaving herself plenty of room. Once done, she leaned her staff against her chair and closed her eyes, sliding into the core of her power. She raised a barrier until she was enclosed in a silvery bubble that would allow no scrap of her power to leak out. In her second year as a mage, she had learned the hard way that an incomplete circle resulted in the most interesting kinds of damage wherever her power met someone else's magic.

Her protective globe completed, she opened her eyes and smiled. She liked to be enveloped by her magic. As a very young girl she'd had a favorite blanket that made her feel warm and safe. Her protections seemed much like the blanket, though she had never told anyone that.

Now she was ready. Daja sat down and reached for her silver disk.

Leaving her room with her completed mirror in hand, Daja heard her belly complain. Passing the hall clock downstairs, she saw why: it was two hours after supper. The family and Frostpine would be in the book room.

When she walked in, everyone turned to stare at her. Of the four Bancanor children only the twins were present, Nia tatting lace, Jory reading a book on the hearth. Frostpine, Kolborn Bancanor, and his wife Matazidah, or Matazi, were all there, Frostpine as close to the fire as he could manage. Kol and Matazi were in their favorite chairs near a table where a tea service already sat.

"Daja, we missed you at supper," Matazi said, ringing the bell for a maid. "You must be starving." She was a beauty who never seemed aware of her looks, a quality she had passed on to the twins. Her skin, the color of coffee well lightened with cream, was perfect; her eyes large and dark over a slim nose, and reddened lips, the lower slightly fuller than the upper. She wore her handfuls of dark, crinkly hair pinned up in coils, accented by the topaz drops that hung in her ears. She was dressed in Namornese fashion in a long, sleeveless tunic dress of cinnamon-colored wool with embroidered lilies around the hem and tiny gold buttons that went from collarbone to shoe. Under it Matazi wore a cream-colored undergown with full sleeves and a band collar, trimmed with gold ribbon. Daja fixed the details of her outfit in her mind: Sandry always liked to hear about the latest fashions, and the entire city looked to Matazi for colors and styles.

When a maid answered the bell, Matazi asked her to bring a tray for Daja. The maid bobbed a curtsey and left as Nia offered tea to Daja. With an inner sigh, Daja accepted. Even after three months in Namorn, two in this house, she still was not used to the idea of tea served in a glass cup with a wrought silver base.

"More tea, Frostpine?" Matazi inquired. He passed his glass to her and got a full one in return. From a dish on the table at his side he took a lump of sugar, set it in front of his teeth, and drank his tea by straining it through the sugar. Daja watched him do it with a shudder. He liked to practice the customs of the country they were in, and the Namornese drank their tea either that way or by straining it through a mouthful of cherry preserves. Daja didn't care if it was rude not to follow the custom: she hadn't eaten the baked sheep's head in Karang, either.

Jory bounced up to a sitting position. "Were you doing

something magical, Daja? Frostpine said you were doing something magical. He said he could tell."

Daja sat down hard in a cushioned chair, clutching her tea glass to keep it from splashing. Suddenly her knees had gone watery. Her work had taken more out of her than she'd expected — missing supper hadn't helped. "Yes, I was," she told Jory. "And of course Frostpine could tell. He's my teacher." Holding her glass with both hands to steady it, she drank her tea. By the time she finished, the maid arrived with a large supper tray. As she caught a whiff of its contents, her stomach gave a growl that everyone could hear.

"Daja can tell you what she did after she eats," Kol Bancanor told Jory as the maid put dishes and utensils on a small table beside Daja's chair. Daja wasn't about to argue. She started with the soup, spooning it up eagerly.

"I hear you had a fire in the alley today," Frostpine remarked.

"A small affair. We've grown very casual about these things, thanks to Ben Ladradun. He's drilled all Kadasep Island in what to do," said Kol. He was a tall, broad-shouldered, easygoing man with a lean face and very sharp blue eyes. He wore his brown-blonde hair combed straight back. He dressed well because Matazi, a former seamstress, saw to it, but there was little trim on his plain brown wool coat and breeches or on his white, full-sleeved shirt. His boots were polished to a glossy finish, to the credit of the bootboy, not because Kol took an interest. He told Frostpine, "Three years ago, four, maybe five houses would have caught from that one mishap. Now our people walk around clapping one another on the back and saying 'That wasn't so bad.'"

"So this fellow, Ben — ?" asked Frostpine.

"Bennat Ladradun," Kol supplied.

"Ladradun did the island a favor," remarked Frostpine.

Kol nodded. "Other islands, too. Over the last two years he's been training firefighters and getting the island councils to clean up obvious fire hazards."

"It was a wonderful thing, to draw out of such devastation," Matazi said, sipping her tea. Daja had been relieved to see that the mistress of Bancanor House drank tea like a normal person, without sweet stuff smeared all over her teeth. "Only think, he lost his home, his wife, and his children. They feared for his sanity. He was absolutely shattered. And then off he goes to Godsforge —"

Frostpine raised his heavy brows. "The fire-mage?"

Kol nodded. "Ben studied with him for two years. Then he came back to Ladradun House like a man on fire, if you'll excuse the expression. He talked, wheedled, bullied, all to get funds and firefighters to train. He's changing how we approach fires. Other Namornese cities send people here to study his methods." He shook his head. "Awe-inspiring. Heroic, even without the people he's saved with his own two hands. If he sees smoke, he's there as fast as he can move."

Daja listened as she ate. For the thousandth time she wondered what these three were like when they had first become friends. Kol and Frostpine had roomed together for three years in the capital of Bihan, studying the goldsmith's craft. They had met the beautiful seamstress at the same time, and Kol had courted and married her after her affair with Frostpine ended. Only on their arrival in Namorn did Matazi learn that the copper-counting student she had married was the heir to one of the wealthiest merchant families in Namorn. Through that and the years that followed they had stayed in touch with Frostpine, and convinced him and his student to stay with them over their winter in the north.

Daja looked at the plates and bowl before her. She had cleaned them all. When she sat back with a sigh, all eyes turned to her.

"*Now* will you say what you were doing?" Jory demanded.

"Jorality, manners," warned Matazi.

Jory rolled her eyes. "*Please* say what you were doing?"

Kol frowned at her. "I believe your mother meant that you should give Daja a moment to take a breath."

Daja looked at Frostpine. "You could start," she offered.

Frostpine shook his head. "No halfways," he informed her. "Talking to the family is part of the responsibility."

Daja scowled at Frostpine, who dipped up a spoonful of jam. Before she actually saw him drink tea through it, she turned to Kol and Matazi. "Jory used magic today." Since she couldn't think of a delicate way to deliver the tidings, Daja chose to just say it. "Not a charm or a chant, something she'd buy from a street seller or a shop. This was her own, coming from her. She took the lumps out of a green sauce she was making. And Frostpine says if one twin has magic, so has the other."

"But I *told* you," Jory began.

"We've had magic-sniffers at both of them, twice," Matazi protested. She refilled Daja's empty tea glass.

"Thank you," Daja told her. "Jory's what we call an —"

"Ambient mage," said Kol with a nod. "Taking the magic that's already in things and turning them to her own use." He grinned at Daja. "You don't live with a mage for three years without learning a thing or two."

"Ambient magic isn't always easy to see," Daja explained to Matazi. "You have to look for it in a particular way. Since I can't tell what Nia's got, I made a mirror to use as a scrying device. That's why I missed supper."

"Excuse me," Nia asked as Daja took a swallow from her fresh glass of tea, "but — scrying?"

"Seeing," Frostpine told her. "Mirrors, crystal balls, bowls of water — it depends on the mage, but all of them work for most people."

"Here's the mirror I made to test for magic." Daja fished

it out of her belt pouch and held it up for them to see. The disk was edged in living metal and covered with it on the back; runes for seeing and magic were carefully etched into the rim. The mercury she'd used to wake the silver to its magical potential was covered over with her power and made solid, making it safe for those who were not metal-mages to touch it.

Frostpine extended a hand. Daja put her mirror in it. When he looked at the surface, white light blazed out, star-tling everyone. "Very good," Frostpine said with approval. "A nice, neat, thorough job."

"May I?" asked Matazi, holding out her hand for the mirror.

Daja nodded and Frostpine handed the mirror over. As Matazi looked at it, Daja went behind her to watch over her shoulder. All the mirror revealed was Matazi's own lovely features. When she returned the mirror, Daja offered it to Kol, who shook his head.

"Nia," Daja said, beckoning. Jory would be so busy talk-ing about her power that Nia might leave unnoticed. She was good at that. Daja had yet to decide if Jory did such things deliberately to help her shyer twin get away, or if Nia was the only one to see that Jory's speeches left her time to escape. Whichever it was, Nia would not slip out this time.

Reluctantly, Daja's skating teacher came forward. Unlike Jory that evening she wore a single braid that harnessed most of the wavy masses of her hair. She didn't share her twin's affection for glittering bracelets and beaded hair ornaments, though she wore a copper wristlet that had obviously come from the south, and tiny pearl earrings. Jory liked bright colors and plenty of intricate embroidery on her blouses and hemlines; Nia kept her clothes plain.

"Must I?" she asked Daja, looking at the mirror as if it would bite.

"Magic has to be used, and trained, the minute it starts to appear," Daja told her gently. "Otherwise you won't be able to control it later. Remember I told you about my foster-sister Tris, the weather-mage?" Both twins nodded. Daja continued, "Her magic wasn't recognized for years, and it kept breaking away from her. She actually made it hail indoors once. I know I saw Jory use magic, whatever Anyussa said." She glanced at Jory, who grinned. "That means *you* have it, and if you don't get it under control, it could turn on you."

Nia shook her head, but she took the mirror, and looked into it. Faint light, sparkling like opals, raced around the mirror's rim, making the runes shimmer. Watching over Nia's shoulder, Daja saw flickering images of tables, a pile of wooden buttons, hands wielding a plane to smooth wood flat, inlaid boxes, a pot of stain, and Nia's face behind it all, her dark eyes wide in shock.

Frostpine gripped Daja's shoulder warmly for a moment and let go. "Carpentry, Niamara," he said. "Your power moves through shaped wood. Aren't you glad there's a reason you like whittling so much?"

Nia's face had a look of mingled confusion and pleasure. "Yes," she whispered, then thrust the mirror into Daja's hands and clung to her mother. Kol and Matazi exchanged looks.

"My turn," Jory said, bouncing up and down.

Opal fire darted around the rim, just as it had for Nia. Looking over Jory's shoulder, Daja saw what she expected to see: pots on hearth-fires, spices being measured, busy hands working dough, all reflected with Jory's face in the mirror.

"Cooking and carpentry," remarked Kol. "Well. Don't look so glum, Nia. This could make you girls more sought-after marriage choices."

"It'll make *Jory* more sought-after," said Nia. "Families *want* cook-mages for their sons. What house will want a bride covered in sawdust?"

"A wise one," Matazi said, kissing Nia's head. "I can think of three ship-building clans who will give their eye-teeth for a bride who can sense woodrot."

"Ship-builders?" Nia asked, her face brightening a little.

"Ship-builders," Kol said firmly. "Including old Domanus Moykep. I don't believe he's arranged matches for his youngest son's boys."

Nia blushed and hid her face against her mother's

shoulder. Daja wasn't surprised that the Bancanors were already looking around for good matches for their twins: northern girls were married at fifteen or sixteen, and negotiations between wealthy families took years to complete. She was surprised to find Nia liked one of the rowdy teenaged boys who lived down the alley — she would have expected Nia to hide the moment a boy so much as addressed her.

Looking at Daja, Kol asked, "What comes next?"

"I'll need to find what mages are here in the twins' specialties. Each twin will do best with a teacher who has the same magic that she does," replied Daja. "And Frostpine says I'd best start showing them how to meditate, so they can get to know their magic and control it."

"Oh, *splendid*," moaned Jory. "*More* lessons."

Daja ignored her. "I'll need a regular time for meditation every day," she told the twins' parents.

Matazi thought for a moment, tapping her cheek with a graceful finger. "I'll change the dancing master to the hour after midday," she said at last. "You can have his time in the late afternoon to meditate — will that suit?"

Daja nodded.

"These mages," Kol asked, a wicked glint in his eye, "what kinds of fees will they charge? Will I get a two-for-one discount, since they're twins?"

"*Papa*," cried the girls, rolling their eyes in exasperation.

"Just like a banker, always thinking about money," said

Frostpine with a grin. "Just keep in mind how much bigger a bride-price you'll get for mage-wives. The lessons are an investment." He drained his tea glass and continued more seriously. "As for fees, if a potential teacher got a credential from Lightsbridge or Winding Circle, he won't charge a fee. Teaching is what graduates of those schools do to repay their masters for their own training. You want graduates. They have broader learning than someone who only has a Mages' Society license."

Matazi nodded. "I'll draw up a list," she said. "Those I don't know, Anyussa or the housekeeper will." She looked at her daughters. "Well, you two are always full of surprises. Off to bed with you."

The twins kissed their parents and raced toward the stairs. Jory wondered aloud if she really *could* make and sell a charm to take the lumps from sauces and gravies, as Daja had jokingly suggested earlier. Daja shook her head, thinking, Merchants' daughters to the bone.

Kol, Matazi, Frostpine, and Daja sat once more. Daja ran her finger around the mirror's rim. She was trying to decide if it could be used for other things than magic-seeing when Matazi said, "This isn't from *my* side of the family." Daja looked up to see Matazi shake her head, her smile half-amused, half-rueful.

"No, it's mine," Kol said tiredly as he poured himself a fresh glass of tea. "That's why we called in magic-sniffers twice," he explained to Frostpine and Daja. "We have cousins at Lightsbridge now, and one who graduated from there. There's an uncle in Dancruan who's a cook-mage. My great-grandfather was a carpentry-mage. So they come by it honestly." He and Matazi exchanged a troubled glance.

"Most parents would be happy, with such an opportunity for their girls," Frostpine remarked softly.

Kol said, "It complicates things."

"Two families who expressed an interest in the girls will turn mages down flat," added Matazi. "Many people think that mage-wives are far too independent and unpredictable. Yes, we'll replace Nia's candidates with ship-builder clans, but we'll have to start talks all over again. Namornese marriages take years to arrange."

"We have time," Kol said. "We're not remotely ready to let them go. And I know that Nia has an eye on that Moykep boy. We'll need to see how she feels in a couple of years before we finalize anything. The Moykeps will reduce what they want as her dowry since she does have carpentry magic."

"All of this is nothing you have to worry about, though," Matazi told Daja with a smile. "I feel like we're imposing on you, asking you to choose their teachers, but I'd feel better leaving that to a mage."

Daja covered a yawn. She was exhausted. "I have a responsibility to them," she told Matazi. "To them, I suppose, and to my own teachers. If you could make up a list of possible instructors?"

"We'll have it for you by breakfast," Kol promised.

"If you'll excuse me, then." Daja got to her feet and tucked the mirror into her belt purse.

"Good night, Daja." Frostpine reached out and gripped her wrist. Through their shared magic he told her silently, *You did good work here tonight, with the girls and with Kol and Matazi.*

She smiled at him shyly. A compliment of that kind from him was worth cherishing. "Good night," she said, and kissed his bald crown.

3

The next day was Watersday: people traditionally spent it in worship and relaxation. Daja knew she would find no teachers doing business that day. She wouldn't be teaching, either, with the Bancanors visiting first the temple where they worshipped, then family members scattered all over the city. Daja reminded Kol that the twins had to begin to meditate, only to see him shake his head. "It's Mother's sixtieth birthday," he explained with regret. "If we aren't there all afternoon and well into the night, she will be quite unhappy."

Daja winced. Once she'd overheard one of Kol's mother's scolds. She didn't want to witness the results of another, or subject anyone else to it. The older women of Namorn were famous for their power over their families, and for their tempers.

With the Bancanors gone the big house was quiet. All but a very few of the servants left to worship, visit their own kin, and run personal errands. Frostpine was absent, chasing his counterfeiter. Daja tried skating on her own, now that she could fall as much as she liked without anyone to see her, but grew discouraged after her fifth landing on her back. Stripping off her skates, she went to her room and spent the rest of the day working on her Longnight gifts.

At breakfast the next day, Sunday, Matazi gave Daja the promised list of Kugiskan mages versed in carpentry or cookery magic. "I've also assigned you a sleigh and driver for all this," she told Daja. "You've only been here for two months, and some of these places are out of the way. Do you know our footman Serg? He'll be waiting outside — just send word to the housekeeper when you're ready to go."

Daja thanked Matazi with a rueful inner sigh. It would be so much easier if she could skate. Or perhaps it wouldn't, she thought as she looked the list over. She hadn't the least idea of where most of these streets were.

When she walked out of the house, Trader staff in hand, her medallion gleaming against her sheepskin coat, a young man in the yellow-trimmed brown livery of Bancanor House jumped down from the driver's seat of the small sleigh in the front courtyard. "*Viymese* Daja, good morning!" he said. Serg was in his late teens, an efficient young man with a long, cheerful face and light brown hair that hung to his shoulders. Despite the flakes of snow that drifted slowly from the sky, he wore his sturdy, quilted wool coat open. It revealed a band-collared tunic shirt that fastened near the right shoulder, favored wear for eastern Namornese. This garment was a cheery red like his full trousers. He wore cowhide boots lined with fur, and carried leather gloves, also fur-lined, thrust into his belt. *"Ravvi"* — Namornese for "Mistress" — "Matazidah has asked me to take my orders from you." He had the Kugisko accent that Daja liked so much, one that made each word sound like a particularly tasty piece of cheese. "Where do we go?" he asked.

Daja consulted her list. "Nyree Street," she told him as she climbed into the sleigh.

Serg took the driver's seat. He clucked to his horses, snapped the whip well over their heads, and guided them out the open main gate onto Blyth Street with the ease of long practice.

Walking into the large, prosperous, busy woodworking establishment that belonged to Camoc Oakborn, wood-mage, Daja felt ridiculous, a child in adult clothes pretend-ing to be a mage. How was she supposed to convince this man that she was any judge of who had magic and who did not? Her palm was sweaty where she gripped the ebony of her staff; her mouth was paper dry.

Standing inside the door, she eyed her surroundings. This was no single-mage operation, or even the average carpenter's workshop: this was a major business, employing dozens of men and women. They smoothed wood with planes, made and repaired barrels, wagons, sleds, sledges, and even small boats for the canals in summer. From the nearby stairwell Daja heard the sounds of hammers and saws: more carpentry was done on the upper stories.

She was gathering her courage to ask one of the busy workers where she might find the master when someone called, "You! Mage!"

She looked toward the source of the voice. A tall, raw-boned white man with curly hair turning from red to gray advanced on her. His bushy eyebrows formed caves in which pale-blue eyes fixed on her. He wore a full-sleeved shirt under his leather apron, and baggy trousers covered with wood dust and shavings.

"Nobody's ever come through this door so grained with magic as you," he informed Daja in a rough voice. He stopped in front of her and leaned down to squint at the medallion on her coat front. "Well, that makes sense, at least. Forgive me, but —" He touched Daja's medallion with a finger tipped in the silvery light that was magic in the working.

Daja, also used to this, closed her eyes just in time as her medallion flared hot white. All around her she heard the exclamations of the others in the shop. Master Camoc had used his own power to make sure Daja's medallion was genuine, with the usual results.

"It's real," the mage said gruffly. "You're very young for it, you know."

Daja opened her eyes and looked up into his. "I do know," she said quietly. Was he going to be one of the mages who resented her because she had achieved a status most student mages gained only in their twenties?

He was not. He extended his bony hand. "Camoc Oakborn, wood- and carpentry-mage."

Daja gave the answer courtesy demanded as she shook hands. "Daja Kisubo, smith-mage. Might I have a moment, *Viynain* Oakborn? I promise I won't keep you from your work long."

"Over here," he said, and led her to a quiet corner of the shop. Seeing that the other people in the room were staring, he barked, "Isn't there work to be done?"

Everyone immediately turned back to their tasks.

Camoc leaned against the wall in the corner. "How may I be of service, Daja Kisubo?"

Daja took a breath. "At the present time my teacher, Dedicate Frostpine of Winding Circle temple, and I are guests in Bancanor House. I recently discovered that Kolborn and Matazi Bancanor's twin daughters have ambient magic. Niamara's is with carpentry. I am talking to the best wood-mages in the city, to see if they are taking on students. If they are agreeable, I would bring Nia another day to choose who she would study with."

Camoc rubbed his chin. "Well, you can see I've students and apprentices both, mage and non-mage. Another won't disrupt things. Will the chit work?"

Daja frowned, not sure what he meant. "Nia's loved wood all her life, as I understand it. She wants to learn."

Camoc sighed. "She wants to learn *now*," he said. "If an older mage might give you some advice . . . ?"

"Of course, sir," Daja replied, confused.

"Kolborn Bancanor's oldest daughter, one of them. Lived in luxury all her life, has tutors that come and go with the fashions — young Daja, I've seen dozens of these children of the rich. They putter and learn just enough to amuse themselves, but they haven't the taste for real *work*, not like you and I know it." He nodded at her staff. "Now, if she were Trader get, I wouldn't even question it, not that Traders let their mage-children study with outsiders. But Traders understand the value of time and teaching. I'll take her on if she likes, but I guarantee she'll learn a trick or two and then weary of it."

Daja stiffened. "I don't believe that of either of the girls," she told Camoc.

He smiled at her in that understanding, patronizing way some adults had, a smile that said the younger person was entitled to her ideas, however silly. "Well, I'll be honest with you — if she did study here, chances are she'd study at first under one of my journeymen. This is a big shop — I've people working on the second and third floors as well as this one. We do everything from miniature work to what you see down here. All of my journeymen who are mages know the basics, and most of them have taught. So she wouldn't be learning from me, though I'd keep an eye on things. That's how the bigger shops do it."

Daja nodded. The smith who was teaching her the fine points of cast and wrought iron, though he was no mage, worked in much the same way, placing new apprentices with journeymen for their basic instruction. "The final decision would be Nia's, in any case," she replied.

"Bring her around, if you like," he said, pushing himself away from the wall. "If she's so inclined, I'll take her on. You can find me here any day but Watersday, unless I'm called out by someone who can afford my time. Do you attend any of the Mages' Society gatherings?" he asked.

"Not yet," Daja replied. "Frostpine's mentioned it once or twice."

"We only meet in the winter — too much to do the rest of the year. You and your teacher should stop by sometime. We're always interested in the work that's being done in the south." He offered Daja his hand in farewell, and returned her grip with his own firm one. "May I see your list of possible teachers?" he asked.

Daja drew it out of her coat pocket and handed it to him.

He read it over, humming softly. "Forget Ashstaff," he counseled Daja. "Since that third heart attack she's barely working magic enough to whittle with. She won't be taking any more students on in this life. And I'd advise against Beechbranch. He's a little too liberal with the switch when he's been drinking, and lately he drinks constantly." He passed the list back to Daja.

She took it, confused. First he talked down to her and

spoke ill of a girl he didn't know, then he was helpful. Or maybe he was just a gruff person, one with a good heart who didn't know when his words stung. "Thank you, Master Camoc. I appreciate knowing that."

"First student?" he asked, walking her to the door.

Daja nodded.

"And you feel like you're in over your head."

Daja smiled up at him as he opened the door for her. "Yes, actually, I do."

Camoc gave her a wintery smile of his own. "We all do. Believe me or not, you grow accustomed. Good day."

Daja thanked him again and walked out into the icy air. Serg, chatting with a girl who carried a tray of hot buns, immediately came to help Daja into the sleigh. She settled back, still a little dazed by Camoc's brisk but, in the end, kind treatment. The question was, of course, would he be as kind to Nia, given his prejudice against the rich?

Well, Nia might not even like the man as a teacher.

"*Viymese* Daja?" asked Serg from the driver's seat. "Where shall we go next?"

Daja checked the list and called out their destination. Each meeting followed the pattern of this first one, more or less, in shops that sported ten and twenty students, mages and non-mages, and in houses and shops where mages had one or two students, or in a few cases, none. Some were willing to take on new students; others weren't. All tested Daja's medallion before they would believe she was a mage.

Unlike Daja, Serg knew the city well. Not only was he expert at dodging horses and other sleighs, but he also knew small side streets that cut weary minutes from their travels over Kadasep, Airgi, Bazniuz, Odaga, and First Fortress Island. He also seemed to know most of the young women who worked in the houses and shops along the way.

The sky was turning indigo as they turned back toward Bancanor House on Kadasp Island. Nights came early this far north, so late in the year, and Daja had to be there in time for the girls' first meditation lesson. The city's lamp-lighters were already out, going from lamp to lamp along the main streets and bridges. In another week, Serg told Daja as they drove across Bazniuz Island, the city would hold the ceremony when the great-lights, giant oil lamps backed by polished metal reflectors, were set aflame for the first time that winter. They would be needed as the city entered a night that would last until the month of Carp Moon.

"Is that one of them?" Daja asked Serg, pointing to an orange bloom up ahead. They were driving west on Velvet Street, on their way to the bridge over Prospect Canal.

Serg muttered what Daja suspected was a curse. "It's a fire, *Viymese* Daja. This is Shopgirl District — boarding-houses for girls and women mostly. We'll pass it."

He was right about the fire, though not their ability to pass. The fire was just off Velvet Street, which was blocked with sleighs and those on foot who'd come to watch. Serg halted the sleigh. Daja, concerned, got out and walked through the crowd, using shoulders and elbows to make room. When she came into the open, she found herself just to one side of a line of well-trained firefighters who passed buckets of water to the fire and back from the nearest well.

Ahead she saw Ben Ladradun emerge from the house, a sodden blanket over his head and around the woman he carried in his arms. He handed her to waiting friends, then turned to direct the bucket brigade to douse a flaming chunk of shingles that had dropped into the street. As he stripped off his blanket, he bellowed orders for those assigned to keep watch over the crowd, directing them to back up and force the crowd farther back from the building. People came to him for orders and left him at a brisk trot, no sign of fear in their faces, only determination and tension.

They get that feeling from him, Daja realized, awed by Ben's command of the situation. He's not frightened, so they aren't.

One woman near Daja, her hair falling into her eyes, nearly dropped a water bucket. Serg, who had followed Daja, took her place in the line as Daja helped the woman to pin her coils of hair out of her face.

"All our things," the woman told Daja, trying not to weep. "I hope everyone got out. If I hadn't been sick I would still be at the shop —"

A shriek split the air, yanking all eyes to the third floor of the narrow building. A girl, framed in an open window, waved frantic hands. Daja saw the problem instantly — most of the first floor was on fire. Ben had escaped just before the blaze covered the front door. He and his fire brigade would know the house was finished. Now they spent all their efforts to protect the nearby buildings. A handful of women and possessions on the icy street testified that the firefighters had carried a great deal out of this place before they'd given up.

"Yorgiry save us, that's Gruzha!" cried Daja's companion, clinging to her arm. "She's blind — she can't get out alone!"

Daja looked at Ben. He stared up at the third floor of the house, his lips moving — in prayer or in calculation, Daja wasn't sure. He's going to try it, Daja realized. He's going to go in there after her. She stripped off her coat with trembling hands, removed her medallion, and stuffed it into one of her pockets before she folded the coat and handed it to the woman beside her.

"Would you hold this, please?" she asked. The woman took it without looking away from the girl in the open window. Her own lips moved as she prayed.

Ben waved some firefighters up. They ran in with a canvas sheet, trying to get as close to the house as they could, under that window, so they might catch the girl if she jumped. Daja knew they would never get near enough. Ben would go if she didn't hurry.

She yanked off her boots, stockings, and belt, putting them on top of her coat in the woman's arms. That was enough: the clothes she still wore were made by Sandry to resist flames. Knowing what she was about to do, Daja swallowed, her mouth suddenly dry. She had passed through fire once, four years ago. It had not been fun. Combined with powerful magic, it had stripped her naked, burned her old Trader staff, left her with strange metal on one hand, and filled her with a kind of pain so wonderful she hoped never to feel that way again. Pain should be one thing, she knew, exhilaration another. At least, she thought they were supposed to be different, most of the time.

She strode up to Ben and grabbed his arm. He looked at her, about to pull out of her grip, then frowned. "Daja?"

Speaking to this man as she would speak to one of her Winding Circle teachers, Daja said, "I think I can get her."

His reaction made her heart pound. He grabbed a bucket of water from one person, a blanket from another, and soaked the blanket thoroughly. Briskly he rolled it into a small bundle. "Are you ready?" he asked.

Daja nodded, mute with admiration. No going on about her youth, no refusal: he accepted her on her own terms. How many adults did that?

Ben thrust the rolled-up blanket into her hands and led her through the lines of firefighters. He stopped five yards from the blazing door and looked down at her. "I imagine you can be killed like anyone else if the roof or floors collapse." Daja nodded; he continued briskly. "Don't be a fool. If your hear beams groan, *get out of there*. Understand?"

Daja nodded and ran through the front door, which hung off its hinges. The firefighters had hacked it to pieces to get inside.

A quick look around told her that the hall floors and the stairs were still intact, a minor miracle. Instead the fire busily gobbled the contents of the rooms on either side and reached for those side rooms on the upper floors. Someone, or several someones, had spelled the halls and stairs with charms against fire, so people could still escape when the house burned. Those charms shone pale silver in Daja's magical vision as they fought to hold their ground against the eager flames. Soon the fire would get so big that it would overwhelm these spells as avalanches did snowballs.

The fire puzzled Daja as she ran to the stairs and began to climb. Why hadn't the blaze consumed this entire ground floor, not just the rooms on either side? The spells were no match for it. Had it come up from the cellar? If so, it should have worked its way forward or back from its starting point, sweeping along to burn everything in its path. Upstairs, she saw the rooms on either side were burning, but again the hall floor was barely touched. It was as if the fire had begun on each side of the house, which made it no accident.

When she reached the third story, she heard the girl called Gruzha coughing in the front room. Daja ran through her open door. "Gruzha, come on! We're getting out of here!"

The blind girl whirled away from the window, hands before her, questing. "Who is it? Who are you?" She coughed helplessly.

"Not important," Daja said, and hacked a puff of smoke from her own throat. As a by-product of fire, smoke wasn't as dangerous to her as it was to others, but it was an annoyance that would clog her lungs until she got rid of it. "Cover as much of you as you can with this." She handed the girl the wet blanket.

"My birds!" Gruzha cried.

Daja saw the cage in the corner. "Leave them!" she snapped.

The girl opened her mouth, then shut it, and swallowed hard. Tears ran down her sooty cheeks, leaving pale tracks.

If she had argued, Daja might have abandoned the birds. Instead Gruzha's mute acceptance twisted Daja's heart. As Gruzha draped the wet wool over her head, Daja seized the cage by its wire handle and laid her hand flat on top. Her power coursed through thin wire bars, wrapping cage and terrified occupants in her magic, holding air inside, fire outside. Gripping the cage in one hand, Daja took Gruzha's blanket in the other. "Can you stay right behind me?" Daja shouted at the area where the girl's ear must be.

The sodden wool cocoon nodded. Gruzha stuck a hand out; Daja pulled Gruzha's free arm around her own waist.

Carefully she led the way down the hall. The blaze had

reached this floor; it mumbled cheerfully in the rooms around the stairwell. Daja thrust it back first, then the flames that began to test the stair itself. In a tunnel of fire they descended to the ground floor.

Daja stretched her power through the kitchen and beyond, seeking a better escape route. There was none: the fire had reached the storeroom at the back of the house. She felt it feed on exploding jars of oil. The rear half of the building was in flames. It was the front door or nothing.

She wrapped Gruzha's hands around her waist, feeling the sodden blanket soak the back of her shirt and trousers. Daja set the birds' cage at her feet, then beckoned to streamers of rippling flame. The fire came eagerly, curling around her arms, sniffing at her clothes. Daja gripped its strands firmly before it found the less-protected girl at her back.

The ceiling above them groaned.

Swiftly Daja wove fiery strands, shaping the blaze as a tube made of flame net. When she thrust the tube wide and high between her and the door, it pushed away the flames in walls and ceiling to open a path. Only a handful of fiery tendrils reached through holes in the net to threaten the two girls. Daja picked up the cage in her left hand and walked forward. She used her right hand to weave escaping bits of flame into the net over her head, to make it stronger and tighter.

The ceiling collapsed. The roof of her tunnel sagged.

Clumps of plaster dropped through two wide spaces in her net, but the rest of it held the weight of the upper floor.

The front door was still an opening filled with a sheet of fire. That part fought her, strengthened by the wind outside, but Daja was in no mood to be nice. She was willing to let this fire continue because someone had invited it here, but it could not be allowed to delay her.

She gripped cords of fire in the door and began to weave again, pulling flame-threads tight, yanking them ruthlessly into a fiery square. Once done, she thrust it ahead of her like a shield. It bulged out through the doorway, bubblelike.

Daja felt the blaze surge. Under her, the floor sagged.

She turned, bent, then thrust up from her knees, draping Gruzha over her shoulder. With the other girl's head and feet just inches from the flames, Daja strode outside with her and the birdcage. As they crossed the threshold, the floor where they had stood dropped into the cellar with a roar.

Outside Daja helped Gruzha to stand and released her fire weavings in the house. The flames returned to their meal.

Ben waved some women forward. They wept as they took the wet blanket off Gruzha and wrapped her in a dry one, patting her head, face, and arms as if they couldn't believe she was real. As they did they backed away from Daja, taking the blind girl with them. Daja sighed and held out the birds' cage, reclaiming the silvery protective shield she had put on it. The finches began to chatter in tiny voices as a woman carefully took the cage.

Daja looked down. Her shirt and breeches, overcome by more fire than they were spelled against, were crumbling on her body. Firefighters and those in the crowd backed away, just as Gruzha's friends had.

"Very admirable," Ben snapped at the onlookers, striding toward the woman who still held Daja's belongings. He snatched them from her hands; the woman then fled into the crowd. Ben turned to Daja and offered the girl her boots and stockings. Daja pulled on the boots, shaking her head at the stockings: they were too much trouble to put on now. Her clothes fell away in flakes as she straightened. By the time Ben shook out her coat and wrapped it around her, she wore only a breastband and loincloth. The harsh wet air raised goosebumps all over her and made her teeth chatter. She dragged more warmth into herself from the house until her teeth stopped clacking.

"I'd see you home myself, but I'm not done here." Ben glanced at the burning house, then scanned the crowd. "Is there a hired sleigh about —"

Daja pointed wordlessly at Serg, who had left his place in the line of firefighters to come for her.

Ben looked at him. "Serg, isn't it? You're in one of the Kadasep brigades."

The footman nodded, gingerly offering his arm to Daja.

"Get her home," Ben said. "If you've any hot, sweet tea, give her some. Forgive me for rushing off." He strode over to a neighboring house, shouting to those on the roof and pointing to a cluster of shingles that had started to burn.

Daja looked at Serg and at the offered arm: it shook. He gulped and tried a quivering mockery of the smile he'd given so readily that morning. "There are side streets we can follow to Everall Bridge," he told her.

Daja waved the arm aside and followed him back to the sleigh. Everyone moved away; whispers preceded them. They'll get over it, she told herself as Serg helped her into the sleigh. They always do. Eventually.

Later, when all the gawkers had scattered to their homes, he returned to inspect the remains of the boarding-house. He checked them thoroughly, breaking open large clumps in case embers still burned at their hearts, but the true fire had gone. His bones ached, warning of snow on the way. If any hidden fire pockets remained, they would soon be dead, covered with snow and ice.

Sythuthan, but she had been glorious to watch! As much as it burned him to see her go where he could not, it had been wonderful to see her in action. To watch the fire bend and reshape itself to her liking. She had gone up the steps and through the flame-wreathed door as she might walk into her own house. Flames slid from her clothes, her hair, her skin. In that moment alone she was a beauty and a terror, this stocky, brown-skinned girl with her calm, thoughtful eyes and her fistfuls of thin braids.

He and the watchers had waited as the blind girl screamed — how was he supposed to know she was home? — for someone to help her. Then the blind girl turned from her window, and was gone. The crowd had moaned. Had the wench heard Daja? Or had the fire caught her?

The second floor was well and truly burning by then. Flames spurted through the third floor windows at the sides of the house. He'd done such a fine job of shaping this fire, starting on both sides of the basement. It had raced first up the side walls, as he'd wanted. He'd left an escape path clear in case anyone remained inside, because he did try to cover all possibilities. He'd honestly thought he was being overcareful, that no one was there when he'd lit the wicks in their lamps of oil. He'd heard nothing as he'd prowled the cellar and the ground floor. If he'd heard anyone, he would have left the place alone. Nobody was supposed to die, particularly not some blind shopgirl, but the firefighters had to be tested. They had to prove themselves, not on some tame fire, in a building that was scheduled for destruction, but on a real fire with lives and property to worry them.

Somewhere inside the house as it burned, after Daja had

gone in, he'd heard the crash of wood and plaster. Ceilings had started to drop.

Then, a miracle. The flames around the front door bulged out, away from the house, like a sail in a strong wind. Suddenly the bubble they formed popped, tearing the sheet of fire into long streamers. At the center of the streamers stood Daja Kisubo, a blanket-muffled body over one shoulder, a cage in her hand.

A cage?

Daja walked out of the building. The body was the blind girl, still very much alive. And Daja carried a cage full of finches, of all things.

The sight of the birds made his heart twist. He hadn't wanted to kill any animals, especially none so harmless as finches.

Daja put the girl on her feet. Behind her the streamers of fire turned back into the doorway, released to finish their meal of wood and cloth, oils and glass.

The idiots in the crowd shrank away from Daja. They ought to flinch from a goddess like her. They weren't fit to kiss her bare feet as she stood there in the icy mud, offering the birdcage to anyone who would take it.

Why was she here, in Kugisko, now? Had she come for him, to make him her servant, or her priest?

He would have to see. He would have to find out if she was worth his service. She might not even *be* a goddess, just another self-satisfied mage. And wasn't it funny, at his age, to fall in a kind of love with a teenaged girl barefoot in the mud, her clothes blackened and crumbling, her dark skin gleaming with sweat? Whatever she was, he would love her until they died.

4

Muffled giggles and whispers woke Daja in the morning, when she would have liked more sleep. She sat up in bed: Nia and Jory, halfway across her floor, jumped back a step. They were dressed to go outdoors.

"What do you think you're doing?" Daja asked in her most forbidding tone. "You're only supposed to come in when I'm here." She always put work materials away after an early mishap in which the youngest Bancanor, inspecting her things, had turned his hand bright yellow, but there was always a chance the children could find trouble with items she couldn't put away.

"But you *are* here," Nia replied.

"I was asleep. That's not here, here." Even to a tired Daja that didn't sound rational. "What do you want?"

"There's the teacher thing today, yes?" asked Jory reasonably. "And meditation after you get back, even if it's still light. You'll never learn how to skate this way."

Daja looked at them with horror. "Skate? Now? Before breakfast?"

"It's a good time," Nia assured her. "We'll have the basin to ourselves. And you have to practice till you're used to it."

Daja glowered, though she knew they were right. "Who's teaching who here?" she demanded. When she saw the twins were about to reply, she hastily put up a hand. "Never mind. I'll meet you in the slush room." They stared at her, unmoving; Daja sighed. "I have to clean my teeth and dress, don't I?"

They walked to the door. Nia was opening it when Jory squeaked and dug into a pocket. "This came for you last night," she said, depositing a sealed note on Daja's worktable. "From Ladradun House." She followed Nia out.

Daja flung off her blankets and got up. She would deal with the note later, when she remembered how to think. "First thing in the morning — no, it's not *even* morning," she grumbled. The water in her pitcher was cold. She set her palms on the pitcher's sides, calling warmth until the ice on the water melted and she could clean her teeth and rinse her mouth without shrieking from cold.

When they left the house, Daja shook her head with dismay. It was dawn on the rooftops of the city, but on the level of the boat basin and the canals it was still shadowy. "I can't see what I'm doing," she complained. Nia ran into a shed for torches.

"Sometime we'll take you night skating," Jory promised

as she and Daja sat on a bench to don their skates. "On Longnight everyone carries a torch or a lantern and skates around the city, and people have stalls where they sell tea and hot cider and winter cakes. Everyone skates till dawn — that's how the sun finds its way back to us in the dark. And there's singing, and baked apples, and hot pies."

Nia returned with lit torches, set them in sockets around the basin, then put on her own skates. She and Jory stood and glided to the center of the ice.

"Come on," Nia urged the seated Daja. "Let's see how much you remember."

Daja grimaced and tried to stand. Her feet went out from under her; she resumed her seat on the bench, hard.

"Dig in with the end of one skate," Jory advised. "Or you keep moving."

Daja accepted this advice and managed to stand. She then yanked the toe of her skate from the ice and shot across the basin, arms windmilling. Nia and Jory slid out of her path. Two-thirds of the way across Daja's feet kept going, but the rest of her did not. She landed on her back, staring at the pearly dawn sky.

Jory and Nia, stifling giggles, hauled her up.

Bruised and ready for more sleep, Daja sat down to breakfast in the busy kitchen, where no one would try to converse with her. She was nearly done when she remembered the note from Ladradun House: she'd thrust it into

75

her pocket on leaving her room. Opening it, she checked the signature: *Bennat Ladradun*. She remembered his help the night before, his cool direction of the fire brigade, and smiled. He must have been exhausted, yet he'd made time to send this.

Daja picked her way carefully through his handwriting. Ben's letters slanted this way and that; the lines staggered across the page like drunken men. The loops of his y's looked like claws. Weren't tutors supposed to ensure that the sons of rich families had decent penmanship? Briar's handwriting was clearer after only six months of study. Of course, Briar's teacher had threatened him with death if he mislabeled her bottles. Perhaps Ben needed a teacher like Dedicate Rosethorn.

> *Dear* Viymese *Daja,*
> *I would like to talk to you about the fire last night, if you would be so kind. I will not take much of your time. I will be at Ladradun House tomorrow until noon if you would visit me there, or I will call on you when you say it is convenient.*
>
> *My thanks, Ben Ladradun*

Daja folded the note. Maybe she would mention her idea for living metal gloves to him. And she would like to see the home of a true hero. How many of those was she likely to meet?

Kugisko's nobles built their Pearl Coast homes in stone; so did the imperial governor. In the city, all but a very few built their large houses out of wood: it was a point of pride, a willful separation from the nobility. Bancanor House and Ladradun House were both samples of Namornese wood-work. The houses sported enclosed porches that ran around the sides to the rear, ornately carved roofpieces, window, and door frames. Both were three stories tall, their work-shops, chicken coops, and stables enclosed and connected to the rear of the main structure so that no one had to go outside during the bitter winter storms.

Ladradun House was larger than Bancanor House, its windows curtained with brightly embroidered drapes dis-played through expensive glass windows. Steps, window frames, and shutters were vividly painted to distract people from Namorn's long gray winters. Soon after Daja's arrival, the twins had given her a tour of the neighborhood, explaining that roof and window carvings showed the family's occupation. At Ladradun House Daja saw bears, otters, lynx, hares, and beavers in the carvings, a proclama-tion of the family's fur business.

A maidservant let Daja in and led her to Ben's study. The woman dressed in the band-collared, tunic-length blouse and long skirts of the Namornese, but unlike most, she sported no colorful embroideries. As Daja followed her they passed two other servants, a man and a woman, whose clothes were just as drab. Namornese fashion was to dress servants in matching clothes, or liveries, but Matazi had given her people a choice of three bright colors for their indoor clothes, and let them decorate with embroidery as they wished. Daja wondered if the Ladradun servants were depressed by such dull garments.

The maid admitted her to a room containing a wooden table heaped with books and papers. Books were stuffed into shelves on the walls; more books filled a cupboard beside the window. The curtains were blue, as was the small rug on the floor. The room was cold, with no fire burning in the stove. The maid left Daja there.

Daja settled herself in a chair to wait. There were drawings on the walls, but little else in the way of decoration. On her arrival in Namorn she'd found the clutter of designs, carvings, and vividly dyed and embroidered cloth annoying. Now she was in a house that had stripped most of that away, and she missed it.

She was shaking her head at her folly when the maid returned with a tea tray. The girl set the tray on a corner of the table nearest Daja and filled a tea glass before she scuttled out again.

Daja sipped her tea. It was watery: the third or fourth

brewing from these leaves, not the first. Did they think she was a servant? If she were here as a Trader, to do business, she would have left. Pebbled Sea hospitality dictated food, tea, and a comfortable setting, articles as important as the business discussed. Tea like this was a slap in the face.

"Daja, hello, hello." Ben Ladradun walked in, making the room feel cramped. He seemed taller indoors than he had out. "You're good to come, and so quickly. I thought you might be exhausted — we can really talk another time. . . ."

"No, I'm fine," Daja said. "Truly, I am, *Ravvot* Ladradun."

"Ben, remember. *Ravvot* Ladradun is who I am to the people at my business. I prefer to think about business as little as possible." He poured himself tea, put a sugar lump in his teeth, and tried to swallow. He made a face and went to the door. Leaning out, he called, "I want *my* tea, Yulanny." He turned back to Daja, running a big hand over the unruly curls on top of his head. "She didn't realize that you're an important guest. They get in trouble if they brew fresh tea for someone who isn't merchant class. . . . Where are you from exactly? I don't think anyone mentioned it."

"I lived four years at Winding Circle temple in Emelan, where Frostpine's a Dedicate," said Daja, looking up at him. She wished he would sit. "Before that, I was a Trader on the Pebbled Sea."

To her relief — her neck was getting sore — he crouched

to start a fire in his stove. "As I understand it, if you're a Trader, you're one for life."

"People can leave," Daja said. "Some do, usually for love. I was made *trangshi* — outcast — when my family's ship sank and I was the only one who lived."

"And now you're a smith-mage." He added wood until a healthy blaze was going.

Daja nodded, then realized he couldn't see it. "So they tell me," she replied. "I keep thinking I haven't learned nearly enough."

He asked her other things, about her travels, about the metals she had studied. Once the maid brought fresh tea, Ben poured for Daja and himself. Settling into his chair, he cradled his steaming glass in his hands. His left hand was unbandaged now, with newly healed skin bright pink on its back. "How do you do it?" he wanted to know. "I told you Godsforge couldn't handle fire, though he could shape it. He made creatures for the local children on holidays. They loved his fire butterflies and dragons. But he could never have walked into a burning building like you did and come out unscathed."

"I don't know how I can do it and others can't," Daja replied. "Though Frostpine can, too."

"And you can see, even inside the flames?" Ben asked.

Daja nodded. "Just as clear as you see me."

Ben set his glass down, turning the metal base in his fingers. He took a deep breath, like a man about to dive into the sea, then asked. "Did you see anything odd inside the boardinghouse? Anything unusual?"

Daja thought, Of course. He's probably seen hundreds of fires. He'd notice this one was not typical. "I think the fire was set," she told him.

He frowned. "I was afraid of that," he commented softly. "I'd hoped I was wrong." He coughed and sipped his tea. "Why do *you* think it was set?"

Daja stared at the hearth-fire, picturing the burning house in her mind. "On the ground floor, everything to the right of the hall and everything to the left was burning. The hall and stairs were spelled against fire, but the spells weren't *that* good." She drank her tea, registering the stronger taste. "Accident fires run outward from one place. By the time this one reached those spells, it should have been big enough to roll over them." Ben nodded. She continued, "That hall should have been on fire, too. I think it was started, maybe in the cellar, along each side of the house. That's why the hall and stairs weren't burning — the fire hadn't reached them yet."

Ben sighed. "I think you're right. I noticed each side was going up first, along the length of the building. It just looked wrong."

"Have there been other suspicious fires lately?" Daja asked.

Ben smiled crookedly. "No. We lost a warehouse a couple of months ago, but that wasn't suspicious. And there

weren't any big fires all summer, which is our worst season."
He shook his head. "I've heard some broth-brains claim
we've made the city so safe that the fire-spirits have left us."

Daja made a face. "People aren't all that clever, mostly,
are they?"

"*Someone's* clever," Ben reminded her. "Someone arranged
that fire like artists arrange paints."

"Have you any idea who?" Daja wanted to know. "What
kind of monster would burn a girl to death?"

Ben actually flinched. "Please don't say that," he asked.
"We came too close there. If you hadn't arrived —"

"You would have found a way," Daja interrupted. "I
know you would have."

"I'm honored, but you overestimate me," Ben told her.
"Did you see anyone — odd — watching the fire?"

It was Daja's turn to smile crookedly. "I haven't been
here long enough to know what's normal and what isn't,"
she admitted. "So, should I take this to the magistrates? Tell
them the fire was set?"

"I'll go," Ben replied. "They may call at Bancanor House
to ask you for details, though I doubt it. Magistrate's mages
tend to rely on their spells more than the words and ideas
of mere human beings." He sighed. "I'll nose around and
ask some questions of my own. Luckily I know Bazniuz
Island well. My — my family and I lived there."

Daja looked down. She wanted to say something proper,
something that wouldn't stir up painful feelings for this

man she admired. In the end she could only think of the commonplace: "I am sorry for your loss. I heard how you came to study all this in the first place."

Ben picked up a small oval painting on the worktable, and held it out for Daja to examine. "Kofrinna — my wife," he explained as Daja accepted it. It showed a blandly pretty young woman with dark eyes and a timid smile. "Not a day goes by that I don't miss her and our children." He looked away.

"I'm sorry," Daja said, putting the portrait on his desk. "I didn't mean to —"

"Actually I'm glad you mentioned her," he said. "No one talks to me about her or the little ones. I —"

The door opened without a preceding knock. Daja turned to see the newcomer, a hard-faced woman about five feet, five inches tall. She wore a plain undergown of cream-colored wool without a speck of embroidery. Her overgown was brown wool with black braid trim around the hem, collar, and sleeve openings, secured down the front by plain black buttons. Her head veil was cream-colored linen, the round hat pinned on top of her veil as brown and unremarkable as her dress. They covered hair that had been dyed blonde in the Namornese style so often it looked like straw. Hers was a hard, tight face, with lines that bracketed a broad, unsmiling mouth and short nose. Tiny pupils that never expanded were at the center of her pale gray-green eyes.

The eager, intense Ben Daja had been talking to was gone. In his place was a large, awkward man whose body was as stiff as his voice when he said, "Mother. Allow me to introduce *Viymese* Daja Kisubo. Daja, this is my mother, *Ravvi* Morrachane Ladradun."

Morrachane looked at Daja and sniffed, as if she didn't believe Daja had a proper claim to a mage's title. "Good morning, *Viymese*. I would like to speak to my son." She turned to go, then hesitated and looked at Daja again. "You are the one who stays with the Bancanors?"

Daja, who did not like the way that Morrachane had sniffed at her, gave only a tiny bow of agreement.

Morrachane's lips moved: the corners turned up; the wrinkles on either side of her mouth deepened. It took Daja a moment to realize that Morrachane was smiling. It took another moment to wonder at the kind of person Morrachane was, that a smile looked so alien on her face. "You are staying with my young friends Niamara and Jorality, then. Pray give them my greetings."

Daja gave another bow in reply. It spoke well of the woman that she liked Daja's friends, but not well enough to make Daja forget the change her arrival had worked on Ben.

"Would you be so good as to tell them I found that book of lace patterns I told them about?" asked Ben's mother. "They had asked to see it."

"Yes, of course," Daja replied.

Morrachane's smile, such as it was, evaporated. "Bennat," she commanded and walked out.

Ben looked at Daja, patches of red embarrassment marking his broad cheeks. "Please excuse me," he said and followed his mother, pulling the door shut behind him. It slid open an inch, enough that Daja could hear their conversation.

Ben said quietly, "Mother, that was rude."

"Why are you here?" Morrachane demanded. She didn't seem to care if anyone heard. "You've frittered nearly three days away on this nonsense. No doubt our clerks are robbing us blind while you chat with this southern wench."

"Mother, Daja is a mage and deserves respect!" Ben still kept his voice low.

"Only by dint of bedding with that 'teacher' of hers, I'm sure. Those with magic have no morals. I would never expose *my* daughters to such people as Kol and Matazi have done. And you shouldn't be lolling about with her."

Daja felt like a knot of embarrassment tied around a ball of fury. As a Trader she was used to the hate of non-Trader *kaqs*. In those days, like every Trader, she told herself that this was the jealousy of the inferior. She didn't think that about non-Traders any more, though for Morrachane Ladradun she would make an exception.

She went to the window to put distance between herself and the door as Morrachane continued to scold Ben. Half the city thinks he's the most wonderful thing since window glass, Daja thought. And this dried-up codfish of a woman treats him like an idiot. How can she not see how good he is?

She noticed something in the corner, tucked between the window and a bookcase. It was a six-foot-tall section of shelves, nearly invisible to the rest of the room. Each shelf held an assortment of objects, all scented faintly with smoke. Here was a metal soldier, top half perfect, the bottom half melted smooth. She touched it with her brass-gloved hand and saw a room with toys scattered everywhere, the carpet and hangings in flames. Women in nightdresses ran out with screaming children in their arms. Daja jerked her hand away.

Here was a half-burned book; there a molten piece of glass. There were nearly fifty things, all marked by fire. The one that made the hair stand on Daja's arms was the skeleton of a hand, each bone threaded on wire to keep its original position, a molten glob of gold around the wedding ring finger. She did not touch the gold.

"Mementoes," Ben said. Daja spun — she hadn't heard him return. "Every fire where I manage to make a difference, keep it from being a complete disaster, I like a reminder," he continued. "In case I get to thinking I'm not worth much."

Daja looked at him. He was still red with humiliation.

"I apologize for my mother," he added hesitantly. "She's — very strong-minded. She made us rich after my father lost our fortune. Anyway, she sometimes forgets what she says or does isn't . . . polite. Every business deal is a crisis for her."

He looked worn down. He half-killed himself on that fire last night, making sure everyone did as they should, even worrying about me, Daja thought angrily. He should be in bed, resting, and she orders him out to look at account books and shipping bills.

Daja couldn't give him any rest, but she could help him avoid more burns like the one that scarred his left hand. She had meant to think about the project some more before she spoke, but she wanted to cheer him up now. "Would you like a pair of gloves — well, gauntlets, ending about here" — she tapped her elbow — "to shield your hands from flames?"

His eyes widened; he rubbed his left hand. "Are you joking? You can do that?"

"I work with a kind of living metal." She rubbed her own left hand; his eyes went to it. "I did an artificial leg with it once — well, me, Frostpine, and my foster-brother and -sisters. I've been working with it since — the living metal, not artificial legs. I mean, maybe I could do a leg now. I haven't tried."

Ben's mouth twitched; there was humor in his eyes. "For the first time since we've met, you sound like a fourteen-year-old," he pointed out. "I can't make head nor tail of what you're saying."

Daja smiled and went back to her chair. She sipped her

tea: it was cold. "Never mind the leg. The important thing is, I can make gloves for you." She didn't want to mention the suit yet. That was more complicated than gloves, and would require a great deal of planning, if it could be done at all. "Have you paper or a slate?" she asked. "I need to know how long your arms are — a tracing will do."

Daja left Ladradun House with the paper in a roll under her arm as Serg brought the sleigh around from the Ladradun stable. After tucking the paper under the front seat where it would be safe, Daja glanced up at the house. Morrachane's unwelcoming face watched her from a window. The woman grimaced and turned away.

"Kaq," Daja muttered in Trader-talk.

"Where do we go now, *Viymese?*" asked Serg.

Daja shoved Morrachane from her mind and consulted her list of possible mage-teachers. "Little Sugar Street," she directed.

Once she had spoken to the last mages on her list, Daja and Serg returned to Bancanor House just before the hour when Daja was to teach meditation. Daja didn't want to leave that for another day. The last of Sandry's letters to arrive before winter closed the roads south had described the mess her student made because she hadn't pressed him to learn to control his power. Daja thought no one at Bancanor House would appreciate being left to hang in midair, or worse.

She found Nia in Kol's study, inspecting her father's set of ebony and cherry chessmen one by one. "I don't know what carpenter's magic even is," she told Daja. "I know this is well polished, and the clothes on the pieces are shaped to make the grain of the wood look like cloth, but that isn't magic."

After thinking about her own studies and those of her friends, Daja said, "A lot of magic is just everyday practical. No matter what power you have, how it gets used centers on the same things, mostly. People always like magic to protect them from fire, from thieves. Magic gets used for medicine and business." She leaned against Kol's desk, looking at Nia. The girl was alert and intent. She wants this, Daja thought. Even if it's not what people expect of wealthy girls, she wants it.

Daja fiddled with her Trader's staff, her constant companion. Odd, that she'd always thought of the brass cap and what it said about her, never about the ebony that ran between the metal-covered ends. "What kind of wood is this?" she asked Nia, though she knew the answer.

"Ebony," Nia replied instantly. "Expensive and hard. Used for furniture, inlays — it's imported from the south."

"When Traders give their children their first staff, they tell us ebony's magical use is for protection. Well, what do carpenters make for protection?" Daja asked. "You can spell ebony inlays on a baby's cradle, to keep it from harm. You could place spells against fire in ebony thresholds in one of your father's banks. It would have to be very powerful, because some things, like a really big fire —" She stopped, thinking of the boardinghouse fire and the spells that battled the flames. She blinked, shook off the memory, and continued, "Some things have more power than you. Still, you can keep the bank from catching fire because someone knocked over a candle."

Nia's eyes were wide. "Really?"

"In time," Daja said. "It depends on the strength of your power and on your education. You need practice, and a teacher, and control — which means meditation. Let's start on that. Do you know where Jory is?"

Nia closed her eyes for a moment. Then she opened them. "Book room," she said, leading the way.

"Why did you do that?" Daja asked, curious. "Why close your eyes?"

"Oh, it's because we're twins," Nia said. "It's not magical, though. We know some other twins, and they do it, too. Usually Jory and I know where the other one is. If something big happens, we can tell. When Jory broke her arm falling off the stable roof, I knew it, even though I was at market with Mama."

Jory was in the book room, as Nia had said, poring over recipes. "Why would anyone want to peel a thousand walnuts?" she demanded as Daja and Nia came in. "Do they mean the shell, or the brown skin over the nut meat? Where could you even *get* a thousand walnuts?"

"I don't know and I'm not interested," replied Daja. "Come on. You won't learn to meditate reading walnut recipes."

"Oh, that," Jory said, closing her book. "What is meditation, anyway? Is it boring?"

"Come do it and find out," Daja told her firmly. "Where can we be undisturbed?"

The twins looked at each other and shrugged simultaneously. "The schoolroom, I suppose," Jory said. "Nobody's there at this hour."

Daja followed them up to the schoolroom, on the third floor with the twins' bedrooms and the nursery where Peigi and Eidart slept. The floor was silent: the younger Bancanors were no doubt out somewhere with their nursemaids.

Inside the schoolroom, the twins watched as Daja used her staff to draw a protective circle big enough for the three of them. Leaving a foot of it open, she beckoned for them to come through and sit.

"I'll get my dress dirty," they chorused, looking at the floor with disdain. They looked at each other and grinned: they often echoed each other.

Daja leaned on her staff and waited. The twins pointed out the silvery magic of the flat circle to one another. That answered something for Daja: she knew Jory had glimpsed the kitchen spells, and now she also knew that Nia could see magic. It wasn't a common gift, though it made life easier for those who had it.

When the novelty of the circle wore off, Jory sighed. "Do we have to do this? It's late. I've been at lessons *forever* — can't I have time to myself? I'll get splinters on the floor. And I'm hungry."

Daja waited. She didn't expect Nia to be a problem, but Jory would be, given a chance. She had to learn now that she couldn't get around Daja as she did others. Their situation was only temporary, but if Daja had to teach at all, she would teach as if it mattered.

Nia sat first, her skirts tucked neatly around her. Jory continued to stare at Daja. Finally Nia tugged Jory's orange skirt. "Stop it," she told her twin. "I don't think she's interested."

Once Jory settled, Daja said, "I'm not." She closed the circle, then sat on the floor and raised her protections until they were enclosed inside a perfect magical bubble.

Next she told the girls, "Meditation teaches you to control your power. To control it, you have to find it, so that's where we'll start. First step. Take a long, deep breath. Count to seven as you do it. Then . . ." She continued instructions on proper breathing, words she could repeat in her sleep. As she spoke she watched their faces. What was going on behind those similar, yet different, eyes? "Let's try it. Sit up straight." The girls' backs were straighter than Daja's, the result of hours with etiquette teachers. "Breathe as I count. Breathe in." She counted as automatically as she'd described the breathing, letting them get familiar with this easiest part of the exercise. After about ten minutes she let her voice grow quieter, until she finally counted only in her own mind. The twins kept pace even without hearing her.

"Very good," Daja told them softly. "As you breathe, empty your mind of thoughts. Forget everything. This might take time, but try. As I count, let your thoughts flow away as if you empty them from a pitcher. Ready? One . . ."

She knew once she told them to empty their minds, they would think of anything and everything. Each time they lost track of the count, Daja corrected them and started over. She had restarted five times when Jory complained, "This is boring."

"Quiet. Listen inside your mind," Daja said firmly. "One. Two. Three . . ."

"I can't help it. I keep thinking about things." It was Jory again. "There's a crick in my neck."

"Shake it out and start over. Be quiet inside, *Ravvikki* Jorality," Daja ordered, using the Namornese word for "Miss," knowing she sounded as dry as the twins' other teachers. The girls responded instinctively to the schoolteacher voice, straightening backs and shoulders, composing their faces.

Daja counted through another three rounds of in, hold, out, hold, before Jory scrambled to her feet. "I have a cramp!" she told Daja, massaging her calf. "This is a silly way to sit!"

"Jory, would you *please* hush?" demanded Nia. "I almost had it!"

"Mouse turds," Jory retorted. "You didn't almost have anything."

"Sit in a way you're comfortable," Daja ordered. "I'm not letting you out of the circle until you really try, and not just for a moment or two."

"Then why don't I just —"Turning, Jory walked straight at the protective barrier. She struck the curved dome head-first. Her hair stood on end, clinging to the magical bubble, and Jory's knees buckled. She dropped to the floor, pulling her long hair free.

"Sit comfortably," Daja said as Jory tried to pat her hair down. "You make this harder when you fuss."

Jory sat with her knees bent to one side. She soon developed cramps in the arms she used to support herself, and switched to the other side. That arm went to sleep. Next she stretched out on the ground. By then the looks Nia gave her had gone from impatient to murderous. Daja was even starting to feel cross.

When the clock struck downstairs, they all sighed with relief. Daja reached over to rub out a handspan of her circle. As the barriers collapsed, she drew her power back into herself. "Come back here tomorrow, and we'll do it again."

Jory groaned.

It occurred to Daja that Jory would fight her until Daja made it clear that she was in charge. Now she walked over to stand between Jory and the door, leaning on her staff as she stared into Jory's eyes. "Maybe you could go all your life with magic just making a little trouble for you because you never got the discipline," she said, her voice so quiet that the twins had to lean closer to hear. "Maybe," Daja told them. "And maybe your magic will break loose and cause a disaster. It happens. Will you behave, or do I speak with your parents?"

Jory pouted. "I'll behave," she said at last.

"Here. Tomorrow. Same time." Daja stood aside, letting the twins dash away to change clothes. To the empty room she murmured, "That could have gone better." She rubbed her head. The trouble with meditation was that it was harder to talk about it than it was to do, and she was not the best talker. Why couldn't Briar, or Tris, teach the twins?

The thought made her smile. Briar would end by tacking Jory to the floor with thorny vines. Tris would have the girl so terrified that Jory would be able to think of nothing, including the control of her power.

Yawning, she descended the stairs to wash up for supper. If only she could show them that cool, bright place she went to when she meditated. Then she wouldn't have to worry — unless the places the twins carried within themselves looked and felt completely different. She had to match them up with proper teachers. Then Jory would be someone else's headache.

In the hope that Frostpine could advise her, she checked

his room. It was dark and chilly: in all likelihood he was out on his investigation. Daja sighed, then fed warmth to the hearthstones. They would hold it for hours, heating the room until the servants came to build the night's fire. Then she went to change.

When the supper bell chimed, Daja opened her door to find the twins. They wore supper clothes; their masses of hair were neatly combed, Nia's braided, Jory's tied back with a broad ribbon. "What about teachers?" Jory asked. "Did you find one?"

Daja looked down to hide her smile. So Jory at least hadn't enjoyed her teaching, either. "I found several," she replied when she could keep her face straight. She followed them to the stairs. "Now we have to meet those who will take a student. You have to pick the one who seems right for you."

"But Mama picks our teachers," Jory argued as she rattled down the stairs.

"Well, this is different," Daja told her bouncing back.

"If Daja says you are to choose, you are to choose," Matazi informed her daughters when they asked about it over supper.

Kol nodded agreement. "Around here, we leave mage things to mages. When can you start taking them to these teachers?" he asked.

Daja looked at the twins. "Tomorrow."

"You'll have Serg to drive you for the day," said Matazi. "You two, pay attention, and *think* before you choose. You can't just go changing teachers whenever you like. Jorality, are you listening?"

Jory exhaled a tremendous sigh. *"Mama,"* she complained.

"Your mother is right," Kol added firmly. "No trying this one, or that one, and deciding you want someone else in a month. These are busy people. They're good enough to offer to teach you, and you will be good enough to treat it seriously."

Jory stuck out her chin and met her father's level gaze. Immediately the chin retreated; she looked down. Very quietly she replied, "I will, Papa."

5

The following morning Daja was awake when she heard giggles and the click of the door-latch; she was rarely caught by surprise the same way twice. She sat up and glared at the twins when they came in. "Do you find this amusing?" she inquired.

"But we're doing it for you," said Jory at her most innocent.

"If this is revenge for my revealing you have magic, it's working," Daja informed them. She tossed her covers aside and tried to get out of bed. After the previous day's skating lesson she had gone stiff with pain in places she hadn't known she could hurt. Muscles heavy with years of smacking things with hammers ached as if she'd picked one up only a day ago. Her back was one large bruise.

"It didn't hurt *me* that bad," Nia commented as Daja hobbled to her water pitcher.

Jory suggested, "Maybe you didn't fall as much."

"I don't think it's that she fell more." Nia sounded as if

she were genuinely trying to be helpful. "Maybe Daja hit harder, because there's so much of her to hit."

Daja turned to glare at them. "Unless you want to spend the winter stuck in ice to your knees, you will go downstairs and wait for me."

"How can we get stuck in ice?" Jory demanded as Nia towed her from the room.

"She'll melt it under us and let it freeze," Nia replied as they closed Daja's door.

Daja stared at herself in her looking-glass. "If this is how old people feel, I don't like it," she told her reflection. "I don't have to do this. Plenty of other people walk. They don't have to skate." And they take forever to go anyplace, a treacherous part of her brain replied.

Somehow she dressed and tottered downstairs. When she emerged from the house in her winter clothes, her skates over one sore shoulder, she saw the twins had set out fresh torches and were skating as gracefully as birds, swooping and curving, spinning and gliding backward, the metal blades on their feet winking in the torchlight.

Oh, thought Daja with a sigh of longing. *That's* why I want to learn.

She was a big, strong girl, not graceful like her foster-mother Lark, not elegant like Matazi Bancanor. Usually she liked to be big and strong: it helped her to handle iron, brass, and bronze. Still, now and then she wanted a little elegance, like the day she found that most boys preferred smaller, more delicate girls, or the day Teraud had shown her iron worked like lace. The skaters on Kugisko's canals made her think that perhaps she could be elegant for a time with her own body. She wanted to try, at least.

She got down to the bench and put her skates on. As the twins glided to a halt to watch, Daja stood. This time she dug in with the toe of one skate until she felt steady. Then she pushed off, freeing the dug-in toe at the same moment. She stroked down with that skate next, gliding into the center of the ice. Feeling the smoothness of her motion, its *grace,* Daja got excited. Her next stroke was a little too enthusiastic. She flew across the basin and slammed into a frozen snowbank, face-first.

"Ow," she said. Her nose was mashed flat.

The twins pulled her to her feet. I *want* to learn this, Daja told herself grimly. She pushed off again, gliding to the center of the basin.

After breakfast Nia and Jory rushed out of the house and clambered into Serg's waiting sleigh. Once the girls were in place, Daja used her staff to climb in.

"You walk like an old woman," Serg remarked, confused. "But you were fine yesterday."

"It's the ice-skating," Jory informed him. "She's trying really hard."

"And *you* are really trying," Daja said, trying to get comfortable on the padded seat. She glanced up at the sky: fat snowflakes drifted down in a slow dance. "I hope this doesn't get too bad."

"It won't," Nia replied. "The weather-mage's crier comes every morning. Today's supposed to be just snowfall like this. It'll build up, but not too badly."

"At least, it won't if the weather-mage is right. Most of the time they are," Jory contributed.

"Do not borrow trouble, *Ravvikki*," Serg told Jory. "*Viymese* Daja, I await orders."

"Camoc Oakborn," began Daja.

"Nyree Street," replied Serg. He clucked to the horses and drove out the main gate with easy grace.

Once they arrived, an apprentice ushered Daja and the girls into Camoc Oakborn's large shop, then went to find the master. They didn't have long to wait before Camoc joined them. "*Viymese* Daja," he said with a nod. He looked at Nia. "This is the girl you spoke of?"

"Niamara Bancanor, this is *Viynain* Camoc Oakborn," Daja said giving him the Namornese title for a mage. As Nia curtsied, Daja added, "And this is her sister Jorality." Jory curtsied as well. "Jory doesn't share Nia's magic, *Viynain* Camoc."

"I see that," he said. "Come along, then, *Ravvikki* Niamara. I'll give you the tour." He led Daja and the twins around the shop, identifying for Nia what was being made. He took a moment to inspect each of his people's work before he moved on. Nia looked at everything with wide and shining eyes, breathing the scents of paint and wood shavings as if they were perfume. By the time they reached the second floor, her dark and practical gown had acquired a coat of sawdust and a variety of wood shavings. Her creamy brown cheeks were flushed.

She belongs here, Daja realized. Remembering her misgivings when she'd met Camoc, she added, Or someplace like it.

On the next floor carpenters toiled over everything from tables to beds. Jory was bored by then; Daja sent her out to buy hot cider and wait with Serg at the sleigh.

Daja toiled up more steps behind Camoc and Nia, who remained spellbound by her surroundings. The third floor was for delicate work: inlays on fancy boxes, end tables, and cupboards, parts for looms and spinning wheels, even a dollhouse in the east Namornese style.

"Most places are smaller," Camoc explained to Nia. "I don't specialize, so instead of running from shop to shop all day, I put it all under one roof, and climb stairs to keep my figure." He smiled ruefully at Daja. To the girl he said, "About half my people are woodcraft-mages, as I told *Viymese* Daja. All are specialists. If you choose to study here, one of the senior mage-students will teach you at first. I don't really handle beginners. Arnen would be your tutor."

He pointed out a bespectacled young man of medium height and neatly trimmed brown hair and beard. He was intent on shaping a wooden tree that flattened on top to become a table: Daja saw magic follow his hands in glowing silver ropes, his power sinking into the wood. It was carved and stained to make it resemble a century tree from the south, twisted and gnarled from long, very slow growth.

"Arnen's good with beginners," Camoc said. "I have to let him get one of these fancy pieces out of his system now and then. The rest of the time he makes the best barrels and axle-trees money can buy. Those barrels hold anything, and his axle-trees never break."

Looking at Arnen's tree, Daja marveled at the mind that could jump from barrels and wagons to something so beautiful. Arnen reminded her of Briar, who went from weeding temple fields to shaping miniature trees, not just to fit them for magic, but because there was loveliness in the tree itself.

Camoc opened a door onto a classroom much like the one in Bancanor House. There were no maps on the walls. Desks were replaced by long tables and work benches. A case of books lined one side wall; a large slate was hung on another. On it someone had written the magical runes for strength: flexible strength, hard strength, endurance.

A collection of wooden cubes about the size of Daja's fist sat on a table. Camoc stirred them with knobby fingers. "Come here, girl," he ordered. "Let's see what you know."

Nia walked over, her eyes on the blocks rather than on Camoc's face. She pulled one away from the others. "Yellow pine," she murmured.

"Speak up," the man ordered. "What use does it have?"

Nia cleared her throat. "Shelves," she said. "Porches, house walls —"

"Pick something else," Camoc ordered.

Nia pulled a second block from the collection. "Maple," she announced. "Musical instruments, shelves, stairs, interior trim —"

"Next," ordered Camoc.

She went through most of the pile, unable to name only a few pieces. Daja saw that Nia had learned a great deal already, haunting carpenters' shops near her home. She reminded Daja of all the time she'd spent as a child, handling every piece of metal her family's ship had carried.

What happened to ambient mages who never found teachers? Did they even know what they were missing? The thought made Daja shudder. She dragged her attention back to Camoc and Nia. The wood-mage was asking her to name a series of carpenter's tools and their uses. Daja sat and waited.

Finally Camoc looked at Daja. "She knows more than I expected," he told her. "I know you've other mages to see before she decides —"

"Please, I don't want to see anyone else," Nia said, her voice quiet again. "I'll stay here."

"You're better off meeting other carpentry-mages. Different carpentry-mages," Camoc insisted. "Smaller shops, not as many people trooping in and out."

"But I like that it's big," Nia said, almost whispering. "There's all kinds of things to do here."

"May I talk to Nia a moment?" Daja asked Camoc. He nodded, and went out into the shop. Daja turned to the girl. "Nia, not all teachers work the same. Some are easygoing, some strict. You won't even be studying with Camoc at first, but his student. Tell me why you don't want to see anyone else."

"You have Jory to settle," Nia explained. "And I like it here." She brushed at a streak of sawdust on her gown. It clung to her stubbornly. "It's . . . homey."

Daja grimaced. Too often Nia put her twin first. "Never mind Jory. Let's visit some other carpentry-mages."

Nia shook her head. "You said I could pick. Well, I have." She looked at Daja with flashing eyes. "I've been in other wood-mages' shops, you know. This is the best, and now I know why, because my magic's here."

Daja scratched her head and grimaced as she yanked a loop from one of her many braids. She didn't like it — she wasn't sure that she liked Camoc — but Nia was the one who had to live with the choice. If Camoc or his assistant Arnen had been handsome and charming, she might have forced Nia to meet other teachers. The girl wouldn't be the first twelve-year-old to fall for a handsome face. When Daja thought of the healer-mage student she'd fallen for two years ago, she felt her cheeks warm. She had mooned over the fellow for months. But Nia didn't show signs of a sudden infatuation, and Daja had only a feeling that Camoc might be too hard on her. It wasn't enough.

She would do better to let time decide. Nia might well change her mind. If that happened, Daja was fairly certain she could get Matazi and Kol to let Nia change teachers. They should know how uncertain anything involved with magic was.

She took Nia out to Camoc, who introduced her to Arnen. About to go, Daja hesitated. "Nia, how will you get home? Have you money for a guest-sleigh, or —"

"I'll skate home. There are always lawkeepers on the canals — I'll be fine," Nia insisted.

"Excuse me, *Viymese* —" That was Arnen. He spoke as quietly as Nia did.

Daja looked at him. "What can I do for you?"

Arnen glanced at Camoc, then pushed his spectacles up on his nose. "It's about meditation. Most of us started with other mages, and we already know it."

"Impossible to meditate here," Camoc said brusquely. "Too much noise. Can you take that part of it?"

"It really is noisy," Arnen told Nia apologetically. She nodded, too shy to speak.

Daja wanted to object, but suddenly she could hear her grandmother's voice. "Shirkers are half-*kaq*," that fierce old lady told her grandchildren. "Traders take the burden they are given."

She had been given this burden. It wasn't shirking to find teachers with the twins' own skills, but if those teachers asked Daja to help, she would be a shirker to refuse. "We'll meditate at home," she told the men and Nia. "We've already started, anyway." She did her best to seem happy about it, though her inner self was demanding to know how she was to work on her own projects if she had to nursemaid the twins. She stepped on that self hard. Nia would hear any touch of impatience in Daja's voice. The minute she did, she would fade away like a ghost, learning nothing properly from anyone. Daja ran her right thumb over her brass glove. "We'll practice tonight, when we get home," she told Nia, who nodded.

When Daja left Camoc's, she was astounded to see Morrachane Ladradun, elegant in a sable-trimmed coat and hat, in the sleigh with Jory. There was liking and affection in the face that was so harsh when Daja had met her. Jory said something, and the woman actually laughed.

She must have been pretty once, Daja thought. My mother was right — if you keep making the same nasty face, one day your face will set in that expression.

"Daja," Jory said eagerly, waving. "Daja, come meet Aunt Morrachane." She grimaced and added, "Sorry. *Ravvi* Morrachane Ladradun. Aunt Morrachane —"

"I have met *Ravvikki* Daja," said Morrachane with a nod. "I understand you have brought the twins wonderful news. You are to be a cook-mage," she said with a smile, cupping Jory's cheek in one gloved hand. "Houses will scramble to offer marriages for you and my little Nia. But where is she?" Morrachane asked Daja. "Jory said she was inside with you."

Daja ran her fingers over the living metal on her left hand and silently listed the various coins used in Bihan. Normally she disliked the title *Viymese*. She felt nothing like the acknowledged mage it proclaimed, yet it irked her that Morrachane would not use it.

Jory was unaware of Daja's tension and Morrachane's snub. "She won't keep us waiting forever, will she?" asked Nia's twin. "We've other boring carpenters to see —"

"Actually, Nia wants to stay here," Daja told Jory.

"She does?" Jory asked, surprised. "But she hasn't met any of the others!"

"One moment," said Morrachane with a frown that looked easier for her face than smiles. "Nia *chose?*"

"Isn't it fun?" Jory asked eagerly. "We never get to pick our teachers, but Daja says we have to."

Morrachane patted Jory's arm, but her pale green eyes with their tiny pupils were fixed on Daja. "I know you like the freedom, dear one, but adults" — was Daja imagining it, or had Morrachane emphasized the word? — "know more of the world. Surely it is up to your parents to decide."

"Nia's mad to pick the first place she sees," Jory added. "Is she serious? She doesn't rush into things. She's not like me."

"She says she's certain," replied Daja, speaking to Jory.

"*Viynain* Oakborn said she ought to meet others, too, but her mind's made up."

"She likes it here, then," Jory said firmly, smoothing the robe over her lap. "Good. No more boring carpenters!"

"I cannot believe Matazi Bancanor consented to this," Morrachane said flatly. "Someone like *Viynain* Breechbranch, with his selective shop, would be far more appropriate for a well-bred girl than this hurlyburly place."

Daja was not temperamental. She certainly wasn't like her foster-sister Tris, who went up like explosive boom-dust if anyone disagreed with her, or even like Sandry, who sprang to battle the moment she thought someone was treated badly. There was something about Morrachane that swiftly got under Daja's skin, stirring her to unexpected surges of temper. She toyed with melting the woman's gold coat-buttons and her elegant ruby-and-gold earrings, but knew such a petty revenge was beneath her. She imagined it briefly as she considered and discarded a number of sharp replies. Finally she said, "I thank you for your interest, but I have discussed these matters with *Ravvot* and *Ravvi* Bancanor, and with my own teacher, the great mage Frost-pine. This is how it is done."

"Then it is done foolishly, without thought for the student's good," Morrachane said flatly. "What order is there when children are not guided by the advice of their parents? Family is sacred. To encourage young people to ignore the family's needs —"

"But we aren't, Aunt Morrachane, really!" Jory laid a placating hand on the older woman's arm. "It's just this one thing, and Mama and Papa worked out the list of teachers. They have medallions and things that say they teach as well as work magic. And it's so much fun to decide something for ourselves."

"There!" snapped Morrachane. "You see? Already it begins."

Daja's knuckles were creaking, so tightly were her hands clenched in her coat pockets. The living metal bit into her flesh, squeezed by her working muscles. In the end, she did something she had always sworn she would never try. She could almost hear Dedicate Crane, the most snobbish mage at Winding Circle, talking as she spoke. "Forgive me, *Ravvi* Ladradun," she said, gathering an invisible robe of arrogance around herself as she stood straighter, "but we speak of things magical, which may only be understood by adepts. Nia has discovered something within these walls which calls to the source of her power. It cannot be safely ignored. However incredible it seems to those without magic, it is a thing that any mage will know." She turned to Serg, who was pretending not to eavesdrop. "Let us seek out a teacher for *Ravvikki* Jorality." To Morrachane she added, "Will you excuse us? The moment power is revealed, a teacher must be found quickly, or tragedy may result."

Morrachane sighed. Her face was briefly wistful as she

kissed Jory's cheek. "Tell your sister I am sorry I did not get to say hello."

Jory kissed Morrachane's cheek in return. "She'll be sorry, too, Aunt Morrachane."

The older woman climbed out of the sleigh. Her nod to Daja was barely polite. "Good day to you."

Daja nodded, then climbed into the sleigh. In her normal voice she said, "Little Sugar Street, please, Serg." As he set the horses forward, Daja looked back. A sleigh with the Ladradun insignia was drawing up before Morrachane.

Jory, who had remained straight-faced through Daja's speech, collapsed into giggles. "I'm sorry," she said when she caught her breath, "but you should have heard yourself. What was that? Is it really so drastic to find us teachers?"

"That was what Briar calls snooty mage jabber," Daja replied with a rueful smile. After two months, the Bancanors were all familiar with Daja's foster-family. "I shouldn't have done it, really."

"Oh, that's all right," Jory said. "Aunt Morrachane's sweet to me and Nia, and to Eidart and Peigine when she sees them, but she isn't very nice to other people."

"Is she really your aunt?" Daja asked. She couldn't imagine the Bancanor family tree sprouting any fruit like Morrachane.

"No," Jory replied, flouncing to get comfortable. "But we call her that. I think she misses Ben's children, so she adopted us. She likes it when we call her Aunt. She says it makes her feel like we're really family."

And that is a good thing? Daja wondered as Serg wove the sleigh through crowded streets. I'd as soon be related to a shark. Sooner.

Daja had planned to stop for midday at some point, but she had reckoned without the cook-mages they visited. Each offered Daja and Jory tea and refreshments; Namornese hospitality meant that Serg too was fed. By the time the sun dipped below the western roofs, they had visited all of the cooking-mages on Daja's list. Jory had chosen none of them.

"What about Inagru?" Daja asked. "Only has two other students, bakes for the governor's castle, does the Goldsmith's Guild suppers . . ."

Jory shook her head.

"*Viymese* Valerian," Serg suggested wearily. "Nobles' banquets only. Jars of summer vegetables with magic for strength, health, peace, love. I should eat at his table."

Jory shook her head.

"We've met the best cook-mages in Kugisko," Daja reminded her. "You saw this list. Your mother approved every name on it. I don't —"

"There's one I didn't mention," Jory said without meeting Daja's eyes. "Mother didn't list her because she's said not to take students. But we don't know till we ask, right?"

Daja labored against a feeling of ill-usage. Jory had arranged things so that by the time she mentioned this person, Daja would be too exhausted to object. Worse, her maneuver worked. Daja just wanted to see this mage and get it over with. "Who?" she demanded.

"Olennika Potcracker," Jory whispered. "In Blackfly Bog."

"I am doomed," announced Serg, shoulders drooping. "*Ravvot* Kolborn will use my blood to strengthen his gold and make my skull into a chalice."

"Papa won't put blood in gold," said Jory. "It wouldn't be good for it."

Don't reason with him, Daja thought wearily to herself. You'll just make the fit last longer.

"Or I will be killed in Blackfly Bog by dangerous men for my clothes and the pretty horses," Serg moaned.

Daja sighed. "Blackfly Bog?" she asked Jory.

"Not *in* Blackfly Bog," Jory said, glaring at Serg. "On the river, across Kyrsty Bridge. Beside the Yorgiry Hospital. It's patrolled by lawkeepers, Serg. It's perfectly safe."

Serg straightened his shoulders and back. "If we die, I blame you," he replied with dignity. He set the horses forward.

Daja turned to Jory. "You could have mentioned this earlier," she pointed out.

"I thought maybe I'd want one of the others," Jory mumbled.

"Hmpf," snorted Daja as the sleigh hissed through the few inches of snow on the streets. "In Oti Bookkeeper's accounts it says that the thing you put off doing is the thing you pay for the most."

"Who is Oti Bookkeeper?" asked Serg over one shoulder.

"The headwoman of the gods, just as Trader Koma is headman," Daja explained. "At least, they are to my people. In the beyond, after you die, Trader weighs your life in his gold scales, and Bookkeeper writes down what you owe."

"I thought you followed the Living Circle, like Frostpine," remarked Jory.

Daja shook her head. "I pay alms to Mila of the Grain, goddess of the north, for using metal ores and wood, and to Hakkoi the Smith, god of the south, for the learning I get," she explained, watching the sky go dark. She felt drowsy and peaceful with the arrival of night. "That's good manners, to pay what you owe to your adopted family's gods."

Lamplighters now roamed the streets, tending the lamps that the wealthy paid for so there was light at intersections. Indoor lamps cast a foggy glow through windows covered by horn or oiled paper, or scattered rays of light through expensive bull's-eye glass panes.

Serg guided the sleigh deftly. The lawkeepers were changing their watch, their white-painted sleighs dropping fresh keepers at their posts and picking up those who were done for the day. People rode in sleighs and on horseback, on their way to homes or entertainments. Once Serg had to move aside as a nobleman's sleigh shot down the center of the street.

"Tell me about this Potcracker," suggested Daja as Serg waited for an intersection to clear. "You've mentioned her before."

Jory studied her gloved hands. "She was the Empress's personal cook. They had others that she oversaw, but Potcracker fixed everything for the high table herself. No matter what people used, if someone tried to poison anything that she made? The food would turn green and it would roll to the one who sent the poison. Anybody the Empress sent Potcracker's food to, enemies, nations she wanted to make alliances with, most times they'd do what she wanted."

She fell silent as they turned onto Cashbox Street, the route to Kyrsty Bridge. "I don't believe the palace is in Blackfly Bog," Daja said when it seemed as if Jory had forgotten her in her consideration of Potcracker's achievements.

"Oh! Oh, no — somebody pushed her into the Syth, so these nobles who meant to poison the Empress could do it. The Syth, in Wolf Moon! Can you imagine? Except she lived." Jory sighed with admiration. "She had a vision. She said the goddess Yorgiry came to her, and said there were more important things to do than cook veal with truffles and thyme for people too ignorant to like the taste."

"She did?" asked Daja, startled. She supposed that gods

could do as they wished, but visiting their worshippers seemed very irregular.

"She did!" insisted Jory. "Well, she does in that play, *The Cook's Vision*. The Skuretty girls told me the story when they visited last. Anyway, Potcracker gave up being the Empress's cook."

The sleigh glided into Kyrsty Bridge, which arched high over the river-canal they called North Upatka. Before them shone the sullen lights of a truly poor district. To their right lay the frozen section that in warmer months was called the Whirligig, where the Upatka River split to surround the islands and feed their canals. A small beacon tower stood on an island of rocks at the Whirligig's heart, lighting the ice for skaters.

To the southeast of the Whirligig was the river's main stem, flowing past the governor's palace on Dorn Point. On the heights of the river's southern shore were the nobles' estates. Their walls, built of pale marble, gave the place its mocking name: the Pearl Coast.

As they drove off the bridge onto a road that followed the riverbank, Jory continued her story. "Potcracker got the Empress to give her a huge amount of money to set up hospital kitchens that also serve the poor, and the Empress made the nobles give her money, too. Potcracker built kitchens in five cities, but she mostly works . . . there." Jory pointed.

Above the wall that guarded the back of a four-story

building ahead of them, lanterns blazed. The building's shuttered windows were closed tight against the dark and cold. Piers jutted into the frozen river, where ships could unload cargo in summer. Sleighs now stood in a line that led through the gate closest to their road.

Daja looked at the place and smiled. Runes for health and protection were written around each door and window she could see, glowing magically bright.

"Yorgiry's Hospital, and its cookhouse," Jory said, bouncing with eagerness.

Daja, about to tell her that slaving to feed the poor would not be as gloriously heroic as she seemed to think, changed her mind. A taste of the real world wouldn't hurt Jory in the least.

Together Daja and Jory walked around a line of people carrying fresh loads of supplies into the hospital's immense cookhouse. Once inside, a billow of mixed scents — fresh bread, steamed barley, stewing meat — enfolded the two girls. Daja could also see that Jory noticed the silver gleam of runes and protective spells against uncontrolled fire, rats, mice, and mold: they were inscribed on the ceiling, every set of doors, the walls, even the floor. Somewhere to their right Daja heard the regular thump of bread being kneaded. Closing her eyes, she thought she could be at Winding Circle's great kitchen, where a cook-mage named Gorse ruled and no one came away hungry.

Someone cursed in Namornese. Daja's illusion evaporated. Gorse also never fixed millet and bacon soup, a Kugisko favorite with a distinctive smell. Even with those differences between kitchens, something edgy inside her relaxed. She was not a cook-mage, but she knew the feel of a kitchen-mage's realm. This was a good place to be.

"Don't stand there steam-struck," a sharp voice said. A bag of flour came at Daja's chest; she caught it. "Take it to the cellar."

Daja looked into black, snapping eyes. They were set in an olive-skinned white face crowned with masses of carelessly pinned hair as soft and as shadowy as dark wool. The woman's face was square-jawed and straight-mouthed, divided at the center by a strong nose. Under a full white apron she dressed like a respectable housekeeper in brown wool with a plain band collar. The sleeves were rolled away from forearms nearly as muscular as Daja's own.

"If you leave it on the floor down there I'll put you in a soup!" the woman called as Daja followed the other laden workers through a door at the kitchen's rear. "I could feed a whole ward on you!"

Looking behind her as she descended the stairs, Daja saw that Jory had been pressed into service with a bag of onions. Serg, behind her, toted a bag of rice.

He shrugged when he saw Daja. "They say, they tend horses and sleigh and nobody eats before supplies are brought down. I do not want sick people to starve."

They made three more trips to the cellar storeroom, the last with the burden of an entire dead pig, wrapped in canvas. Daja was ready to go home after that. Instead she found herself seated at a long table, a roll in one hand, thick stew in a bowl in front of her, a plate with parsnips in beef broth beside that. Someone passed her a cup of milk. She had believed she was stuffed on cook-mages' treats, but this food smelled so good. And of course she ought to taste what they'd given her to be polite. By the time she had finished tasting, her bowl and plate were empty, her roll crumbs.

"At least you know you need to eat with a body like yours," said that sharp voice. Daja looked at its owner, who now sat across from her. "At court I saw girls with big frames, big muscles, eat like birds, faint, get sick, die. The Duke of Eileag's youngest daughter starved herself to death. Don't fight the body the gods send you, I told them, but did they listen?" The woman reached over and grasped Daja's wrist, thrusting back her coat and shirt sleeves. "Good arms. Blacksmith arms." She transferred her grip to Daja's fingers. "Who are you, blacksmith? I am Olennika."

"Daja Kisubo," she replied, returning the friendly squeeze of the fingers before the cook-mage released her. "From Emelan. I'm here with my teacher, *Viynain* Frostpine. This is Jorality Bancanor. He's Serg."

"Bancanor?" Olennika raised straight black eyebrows. "You are a long way from Kadasep, Bancanor's daughter."

Jory was so overwhelmed by awe for this great mage that she was speechless. The girl stared at Olennika, transfixed.

"See that door?" Olennika flapped a hand toward a door set in the wall across from their table. "Bring to me an ounce of truffles, three saffron threads, a tablespoon of dill chopped coarse, a ginger root, a tablespoon of parsley, and a tablespoon of tarragon. There are trays and bowls there, and any tools you need." She handed Jory a large, iron key. "Go," she ordered.

Jory went.

Daja said, "We are looking for a teacher for her." Somehow she knew that she didn't have to tell this woman about Jory's power.

"There are plenty of cook-mages closer to Kadasep," Olennika commented. She beckoned to a girl who carried a teapot and a tray of handleless cups.

No glasses here, Daja thought with satisfaction as the girl served them. "I know. We've seen them today." Daja held the filled cup under her nose and inhaled. Even the steam was refreshing. "Jory wanted to come here. She wasn't sure you take students."

"Almost never," Olennika said. "That is my personal workroom, where I have sent her. No labels. If she is serious, she will know the things I have requested. I do not think the master of the Goldsmiths' Guild will let his daughter study in Blackfly Bog. We do fine cooking maybe four times a year, when the hospital feeds the rich to get money from them. The rest of the time we cook for the sick and the poor. Quantity, no fancy spices or elaborate creations. She ought to study with Valerian."

"*Ravvikki* Jory doesn't want him," Serg said gloomily.

Olennika looked Daja over. "What is your interest, Kisubo?" she asked. "How is it a southern mage takes Bancanor's daughter to see teachers?"

"You know I'm a mage?" Daja asked. Then she winced at the folly of her question. Olennika had already shown that she recognized Jory's power.

Olennika smiled one-sidedly. "I have a nose, girl," she replied. "The *ravvikki* is a spearmint plant, crushed in the hand. You — you are a bed of it, half an acre at least, rolled on by a herd of horses. Why are you here?"

Daja explained. By the time she finished, Jory had returned with a tray full of tiny dishes and plates. Each had something in them. She set the tray down, wiped her hands on her skirts, grimaced, and brushed the places where she'd wiped her hands.

"Don't fidget," Olennika ordered, poking a finger through the contents of the dishes. Jory froze.

"Put everything back as you found it." As Jory left, Olennika faced Daja. "I suppose she is not to be all day with one teacher. I suppose she studies music, and dancing, and books."

Daja nodded. She was impressed by Olennika's brisk handling of Jory. It would be good for the girl to study here. The soft-spoken Inagru hadn't seemed up to Jory's bouts of enthusiasm. "She can stay as long as you wish for a week," Daja explained. "But then it's mornings. As she advances, I think her family can be persuaded to let her stay longer. They're sensible people."

"If you say so." Olennika got to her feet. "Time to start cooking for the morning," she said. She looked tired. When Jory returned Olennika told her, "We will have a trial. Come tomorrow ready to work."

Jory squeaked and flung her arms around Olennika's neck. She gulped, released the woman, then spun giddily for a moment. Taking a deep breath to get herself under control, she ran to fetch their coats.

Olennika watched her. "She will be my student in a week, or she will be happy to study with Inagru or Valerian," she said with a firm nod. "We shall see." She turned to Daja and smiled ruefully. "There is one thing," she began.

Someone dropped several pots on the floor. Everyone flinched at the clatter.

Daja's heart sank, but she could see the problem. "Meditation?" she asked.

Olennika nodded. "Even in my workroom there is no quiet. People come and go in the cellar, in the attics, from the hospital. Will you —"

It was Daja's turn to smile ruefully. She knew what she had to say; she just didn't like it. "Yes, of course."

"It will be best if she meditates before she comes here," Olennika said as Jory returned with the coats. "She will be good for nothing but sleep when she gets home. Be here by the second hour of the morning," she told Jory, then turned to answer an undercook's question.

At Bancanor House, rather than leave the girls at the front door, Serg drove the sleigh into the courtyard next to the boat basin. A stablehand took charge of it and the horses as Daja, Jory, and Serg trudged into the house. Inside they found that supper had been served and cleared away. Daja and Jory went on to the book room, where Kol, Matazi, and Nia sat and read. Jory told them about Olennika: Matazi and Kol took the news well, though they exchanged a glance when Jory announced where her new lessons would be held.

Daja looked at the yawning Nia, then at the clock. "We need to do meditation," she said.

"Now?" Jory whined. She glanced at her mother: Matazi raised both elegant eyebrows, a look that dared Jory to continue as she had started. Jory looked down.

"Now," Daja said. She asked the twins' parents, "It's just an hour. Will you be awake?"

"Certainly," Kol said. "I want to finish this book, and my womenfolk keep interrupting."

"Papa!" Nia cried. Matazi gently kicked her husband.

Daja grinned and towed the girls out of the room. If she ever married, she hoped she would have as much fun at it as Kol and Matazi seemed to.

They returned to the schoolroom. Finding it dark, Daja

went to one of the hall lamps, pinched off its flame, and carried it back to light the lamps. Next she drew her circle with her staff. Once that was done, the twins inside with her, she raised her protections to enclose them once more.

"Could you work magic without your staff?" Jory wanted to know when Daja finished.

"Mages always have staves in the stories," added Nia. "Remember the story of Deliellen Stormwalker, raising her staff to part the waters of the Syth?"

"We could make it fashionable, perhaps." Jory's voice lacked confidence. "Slender, with a jewel for a knob, or ribbons tied to it." She brightened. "We could learn to fight with them, like the apprentice boys do!"

"I don't want to fight anybody," protested Nia.

Daja leaned on her staff and waited for them to be quiet. Jory sighed. The twins took their seats on the floor. Only when they were ready did Daja take her own place, laying her staff on her crossed legs.

"No, you do not need a staff," she informed them. "I carry one anyway, so I put it to use. Think, both of you! How many mages today did you see carrying staves?"

The twins hung their heads. "We didn't realize," Nia said sheepishly.

"Well, you're mage-students now. You'd better start realizing. Enough. Close your eyes and breath. One . . ." She continued the count until they had the rhythm, then stopped counting aloud. Inside the heart of her own power she saw the ragged silver flares that shot away from each of the twins. They flickered more than they had the day before. Even yesterday's spotty meditation had strengthened their uncontrolled power.

The moment Jory first shifted and opened her mouth, Daja poked her with her staff. Jory inhaled to speak again; Daja raised her brows. She hoped she said as much with the gesture as Matazi did. Jory looked at the floor with a scowl and took up the breathing again. Nia shook her head once, impatiently, but continued to breathe to the silent count.

When Jory inched an ankle out from under the opposite leg, Daja poked her. Jory scowled and bounced one knee impatiently. Daja poked her again.

"Stop it, Jory!" snapped Nia. "I'm trying to do this!"

"So am I!" Jory snapped back. "But it's hard and it gives my legs cramps and I'm bored!"

"If you quit wanting exciting things to happen for long enough to really pay attention, you wouldn't *get* bored!" retorted her twin.

Daja watched with interest. Only around outsiders did Nia huddle down like a mouse. It had taken her a week to get comfortable with Frostpine and Daja, while Jory had been in and out of their rooms not an hour after they'd arrived.

"I suppose *you* aren't bored?" demanded Jory of Nia.

"No, I'm not!" replied Nia. "Or I'm almost not, but I thought I felt something, and you ruined it!"

Now Daja poked both of them with her staff. When they turned accusing eyes on her, she said, "I can work a whole day with little sleep. Can you? Because the longer you fight, the longer we sit here." Grumbling, the twins settled down, Jory sitting with her feet to one side, Nia cross-legged. They closed their eyes and began again. Daja fell into her own meditations, letting herself drift, free of thought. She set about housekeeping, collecting strands of magic that slipped from her central store, tidying up as she would tidy a forge at day's end. Suddenly a light snore brought her to full attention. Both twins had gone to sleep.

Their day had been hard; Daja thought they all had done as well as they could. She nudged them awake with her staff and rubbed out part of her circle, gathering its magic back into her. "Meet me here, tomorrow morning, half an hour past dawn," she said. "Before breakfast."

"But if we did it tonight," protested Nia, interrupting herself with a yawn.

"No," Daja said firmly. "Tonight was fiddling and fussing. We didn't get anything important done, not the way we need to do it. Here, tomorrow."

"But skating . . ." Jory protested wearily.

Daja sighed. For a moment just that morning she'd felt as if she flew. "Meditation is more important right now," she informed the twins. "You need to control your power. Meditation is the only way. Good night."

She watched them stumble out of the schoolroom,

frowning as she rubbed her brass mitt. She had more problems than just the cancellation of skating. This form of meditation wouldn't serve for Jory. She was too active, too used to movement.

"You have two ways to make the deal," Daja's father had taught his children. Lessons in Trader ways were held on deck; they all worked at ship's chores — mending fish nets, sewing canvas, winding rope, polishing brass — as they listened. "You can make it your way, proving to the customer you are wonderful, wise, powerful, and right. Then the customer either buys once and never again, or he doesn't buy. Or you can invite the customer, hear his troubles, soothe his fears, show understanding, and he buys. Your way or his way. Your way, you feel superior all the way back to your clan's house with a begging bowl in your hand. His way, and he brings his children to buy from you next time."

She could force Jory to meditate in the way that would plainly work for Nia, the way that had worked for Daja and her three friends. If she kept to that, she might lose Jory by turning what should be the most comfortable way to manage her power into a chore. It would be like clipping a bird's wings before she learned to fly.

She owed Jory better than that. She owed her own teachers better than that.

It suddenly occurred to her to wonder what projects Frostpine had set aside to teach her, when she walked into his forge. What important magics had Lark and Rosethorn put off, to watch over four very different young mages? And Niko, who had worked the most with their meditation, what had he given up? People had constantly mentioned their surprise that the rootless Niklaren Goldeye had spent four whole years in one place, after only staying a year in others. He'd given up four years, to ground Daja and her friends in their command over their power, and to teach Tris. None of them had ever questioned it.

So there was the lesson of mage-teachers, if Daja wanted to learn it. Teaching was more important than personal objectives. Teaching was a serious debt that could only be repaid by correct teaching of new mages.

Deep in thought, Daja blew out the lamps. There were other ways to meditate. Maybe it was time to try one of those.

About to enter her own room, she remembered that Kol and Matazi wanted to talk with her. Still thinking, Daja went downstairs.

"Sit," Matazi ordered when she joined them. "You look exhausted. Here." She poured Daja some tea.

Kol put aside his book and leaned forward, propping his elbows on his knees. "How safe is Potcracker's kitchen?"

"It's not actually in the slums," Daja said, sitting back in her chair. "It's part of the hospital, with a log wall between it and the Bog itself. I saw lawkeepers everywhere, and there are wards and spells laid all over the place for safety, good ones."

"I know the hospital," Matazi said. "We contribute to it. Potcracker has a tremendous reputation. I'd just always heard she didn't take students."

But she did when faced with one, Daja realized. Just like Frostpine and Niko and Lark and Rosethorn. "I like this Olennika," she told the Bancanors. "If she agrees to keep Jory, I think it will be very good." Daja hesitated, then decided to be honest. "Jory surprised me. Olennika didn't make any bones about it, Jory will work hard, not at wonderful, wizardly things, but at plain cooking. And Jory didn't flinch. I think better of her for it, though I have to take some of that good feeling off for her dropping Potcracker on me at the last minute after we'd been all over town."

"What about this Oakborn fellow?" Kol inquired. "Nia's teacher?"

Again Daja had to think. The answer she came to was the one she owed to these people. "I'm not sure. She's shy, and he doesn't like wealthy people. If she was to study directly with him, I would have said no. I doubt he's patient. But Camoc's placing her with his senior student, Arnen. He may be all right."

"Will you keep an eye on Nia?" asked Matazi, putting her hand on Daja's. "I called her little Shadow, before she became a young lady and too dignified for such things.

She'll hide in the shadows and not say a peep if something bothers her."

"I'll keep watch," Daja promised. "I'm still their meditation teacher, for one thing." In response to their curious looks she explained, "Both Camoc and Olennika have huge shops — plenty of noise and distractions. I don't know how they think straight in all that. They asked if I'd keep with the twins on meditation, and I agreed."

"We can find someone else," Kol suggested. "You're our guest, not the girls' tutor."

Daja could still get out of it, keep her time all to herself . . . no. Her teachers had not shirked their duty to new mages, and neither must she. And she owed the twins a personal debt for their skating lessons; she had to repay that to balance the books. She cupped her hand over her mouth to hide a yawn. Tea or no, she was nearly asleep on her feet. "No, I discovered them, they're my responsibility. Besides, I'm not going anywhere before spring." She fought another yawn and got to her feet. "Forgive me. I'm tired."

Kol and Matazi stood when she did, and offered their hands. Daja looked at those outstretched palms, then at the owners, confused. Kol said, "We owe you more than we can say. You found something in our girls everyone else missed, something that could have made them unhappy."

"We know it's work for you, and you have your own studies," Matazi added. "If we can ever thank you properly . . ."

Daja felt ashamed that she had ever resented her obligation to Nia and Jory. This whole family had taken her in as if she shared their blood. They gave freely; she must do the same. She clasped each offered hand. "See if you feel that way come spring, after a winter together." She returned the pressure of their fingers and released them, touched by their thanks.

Before she went to bed, Daja wrote a note and left it for a servant to carry to Ladradun House in the morning. The next day she was to work iron with the smith Teraud. If she finished early enough, she wanted to start fitting Ben for those gloves.

The First Dedicate of the Fire temple, the temple of justice, law, and combat, was a weathered, lean white man with short red hair that stuck out at all angles, and a short red beard. He had a way of talking that sounded like a shower of nails being poured into a metal bucket. Once a general, he'd taken the name Skyfire when he dedicated himself to the temple. That night Daja dreamed about Skyfire's form of meditation. In her dream she was back in the practice yard used by the Fire temple's warriors. The day was summery, the yard so dry that dust rose like smoke from the ground and from the practice clothes of everyone present.

Daja panted as she circled Dedicate Skyfire, her staff in her hands. He was old, but he was quicker than eels. She hurt all over from the quick punishing raps he gave her when he thought her attention had strayed. "Stop waiting for me to strike here or there," he barked. His dark blue eyes blazed through the coat of dust on his face. Sweat tracks marked it like a tribal mask, even in his short red beard. "Stop trying to think. Don't expect anything — expect everything. Be open to its approach? Empty your head, or I'll crack it so the thoughts run out. You aren't a girl, with a staff, on two legs, any more than I am a creaky old man who shouldn't be able to touch you. I can't touch movement. Be movement. Be air. Be nothing."

He lunged. Daja blinked, half-hypnotized by his words, half in the quiet place she found when meditating. She blocked him and waited for his next try. He moved. She stayed as she was and waited to hear what came next. After five minutes of hard work when he scored few touches, he called a halt.

"But this is meditating, only we're moving," she panted, bracing her hands on her knees. She felt wonderful.

"That's all it should be. I never could sit on my behind and count myself silly," Skyfire replied breathlessly. "I meditate this way."

The dream was with her when she opened her eyes. She was smiling. Her classes with Skyfire after that day had been very different. She thought Jory would like the tough old man.

Daja rolled stiffly out of bed — she would have to find

another time to skate if they were to meditate at this hour — cleaned up, and dressed. She had seen wooden poles in a room off the passage between the stables and the pantry. Taking the back stairs, she bypassed the kitchen — she hated to see a kitchen dark and fireless. A little exploration brought her to the room where old chairs, tables, and other things were stored in case of need.

The poles were stacked in a corner. They were smooth stakes about five feet long, probably used to replace handles in mops and brooms when the old ones wore out. All were smoothed down, so she didn't have to worry about splinters; all were made of sound wood, so she didn't have to worry about them breaking in mid-strike. They were absurdly light after her own staff, but her own comfort was not the point.

Daja had chosen three when she heard a woman scream. She dropped her poles and headed toward the screams at a dead run, imagining fire, assassins, rats . . .

She burst into the kitchen. Anyussa the cook and Varesha the housekeeper, half-dressed, arrived from the servants' quarters as she did. A maid cowered against one of the long tables, still screaming. As Varesha and Anyussa converged on her, she pointed at the great fireplace, burst into tears, and hid her face in her hands.

Daja had been wrong to expect a cold and lifeless kitchen. The sheer size of the fire that roared in the hearth told her it had burned long enough to make the room deliciously warm. At the heart of the blaze sat Frostpine, his back to the room, legs crossed, hands palm-up on his knees, eyes closed. He was so deep in meditation that he hadn't even heard the maid's screams. His masses of hair and beard fluttered in the flames' caress. His clothes for the day were neatly folded on a stool placed beside the hearth.

Daja's mouth twitched.

Noise made her turn. More people had reached the kitchen, most still wearing night clothes. Anyussa and the housekeeper, standing with the hysterical maid between them, drew close to stare. Jory and Nia must have galloped down from the third floor. They peered around the maids, eyes wide. Footmen arrived in nightshirts, demanding to know what the fuss was about.

Daja's mouth twitched again. She sternly forbade herself to smile and walked over to the hearth. She wasn't sure if her shirt was one of Sandry's. To be safe — she thought one naked mage was all this household could stand — she put her hands palm to palm, and pulled them apart. The flames between her and Frostpine split neatly. Leaning in, she laid her palm on his shoulder. Through their common magic she said, *Come back*.

Frostpine twisted to glare at her. "What?" he demanded. "Can't a man meditate?"

"I thought you did that in your room," she said. "Frostpine, you're naked."

"Naked and *warm*," he said with a scowl. He hitched

himself around until he faced Daja, doing it so expertly that he hardly disturbed the wood stacked around him. "I can't get a decent fire going up there, the hearth's too small. I thought I'd do everyone a favor and start the fire here."

"Did you tell anyone?" Daja inquired.

"I meant to be gone by the time —" Frostpine looked past Daja to see his wide-eyed audience. "Hakkoi and Shurri," he grumbled. "I just wanted to get warm."

"Why didn't you put up a folding screen? Or let someone know?" Daja asked. "Then maybe the whole house would still be asleep right now."

"You'd think they never saw a naked man before," Frostpine grumbled. He crouched, then stepped carefully out of the blaze without scattering wood or ashes. He then used a poker to shove the burning wood in until it covered the place where he'd sat. Once done, he set the poker aside and began to dress.

The maid was still sobbing. Other servants were backing out of the kitchen. This wasn't the magecraft they knew, a matter of potions, signs, and charms. They were unnerved. Only Anyussa was unshaken. She looked Frostpine over, hands on hips, a crooked smile on her lips. "My cousin says mages are eunuchs. I wish he were here right now. Do you want breakfast?" she asked Frostpine as he put on his habit.

He grinned. "I'm ravenous," he admitted. "And for the first time since I came here I feel warm."

Daja shook her head and went back to collect her poles.

In spite of the morning's disturbance and their reluctance the night before, Jory and Nia were in the schoolroom when Daja arrived. No fires were lit in the hearth: wool dresses and stockings or no, the twins' breaths steamed on the chilly air.

"I can't sit like this," Jory informed Daja. The twins were shivering. "We'll freeze."

"You're not sitting," Daja said. She tossed a pole to Nia, who caught it easily, and another to Jory, who nearly dropped hers. She placed her own pole against the wall.

"I thought you said we wouldn't have staffs," Nia said, running her hands over her pole.

"You won't need a staff as a mage," Daja replied. "You —"

"Does he always sit in fires naked?" asked Jory. "Are we going to learn how to do that? And why'd he pick the name Frostpine if he hates being cold?"

Daja had asked him the same thing, as they huddled in a mountain travelers' hostel during a late summer blizzard. To Jory she repeated his answer: "He said he hadn't thought cold got so *very* cold, and he thought frostpines must be pretty trees. Neither of you will be sitting naked in any fires."

Nia shuddered. "Oh, please!" she whispered. "I have nightmares about fire!"

Daja patted her shoulder. "Once your magic's under control, you'll feel less like you're actually made of wood," she said gently. "You'll be able to seal yourself off from your magic. The dreams will stop then. Now," she said before they could interrupt again, "we'll start with some easy first moves with the staff."

"But how —" Jory began.

"Just do as I say," Daja told the girl sternly. Jory nodded, mute.

She didn't mean to make fighters out of them, but if she was going to do this, she ought to do it properly. Otherwise her next dream of Skyfire might end as he trounced her for slipshod teaching. She taught the girls how to properly grip the staff and how to stand to keep their balance. Then she showed them th. high strike and its defense, the high block, the body strike and its defense the body block, and the low strike and block. Next she gave them a sequence, high, middle, low. Jory struck first as Nia blocked; after they had done five sets, Daja switched them so Nia struck Jory's blocks. They didn't hit hard. It was more important at this point to hit and block correctly. They repeated the sequences over and over until both girls showed beads of sweat at the temples. As they got more confident, they picked up speed.

Jory began to hit too hard. Nia shrank a little at each blow. When it was her turn to strike, she tapped Jory just as she had at first. When Jory became striker again, she was impatient. She brought her high strike down with all her strength behind it. Nia cringed. As Jory launched her middle strike, Daja thrust her own pole in and knocked Jory's staff aside. Nia backed up.

"Keep control of your feelings," Daja told Jory. "You can't get excited. You have to pull that in. And you can't shrink away," she told Nia. "Keep the rhythm going. Don't worry about anything but doing the same moves over and over."

"But I hate to hit, and I hate being hit," protested Nia. "Why can't we meditate like before?"

"I hated *that*," Jory told her. To Daja she said, "I'll be good. Just do the things, and hit nicely, and not get excited."

"Pay attention to the pattern and to the way your body works," Daja said. "That's all. Nobody's going to hurt you, Nia. This is just a pattern, like the breathing, only with all of your body. All right, you strike, Jory blocks, high, middle, low, then switch. Begin."

They obeyed, striking and blocking slowly, as they had at first. Little by little they relaxed. Daja watched carefully, noting when they began to speed up. Jory started to grin. Faster they went. Jory hit harder; Nia began to flinch. Then, as Nia struck high, Jory blocked and swung a middle strike at her sister's ribcage. Daja, expecting it, slid her own pole in, hooked Jory's, and sent it flying. After another lecture to Jory about emotions, Daja started the twins a third time. It was no good; after a minute she saw that Nia didn't believe her sister's promise to control herself. She flinched every time Jory struck her, even though she blocked Jory.

When the breakfast bell rang, the twins looked at Daja. She held out her hand for their poles. Nia thrust hers at Daja and fled. Jory gave her pole up reluctantly. "I'd get better," she told Daja. "Only I suppose you'll want to go back to the boring way now." She ran out of the schoolroom.

Daja chose not to eat with the family. A burned scent in the air told her that breakfast cooked by a half-terrified staff was something she could give up. Instead she dressed for the outdoors, picked up her real staff and the satchel that held her tracings of Ben's hands, and set out for Teraud's smithy. Halfway down Tenniy Street an old woman made almost perfectly round by skirts and shawls sold dumplings from a cart. Daja bought herself breakfast there and strolled on, turning her problem over in her mind.

Nia liked to sit and meditate. Jory concentrated best when she was moving. No matter how many times Daja put those facts into the forge to heat, they always came out in the same shape.

That's magic for you, she thought gloomily. One part glory, one part fun, and one part polishing the brightwork till your back and your knees and your hands all ache.

Then she chuckled. Sometimes her old seafaring life

broke into her thoughts at the oddest moments. She also took the lesson. Brightwork got ruined by rust without plenty of scrubbing. The twins would never get the best out of their power if Daja was a lazy teacher. Work was work: it had to be done right.

7

If Teraud Voskajo was not the ugliest white man Daja had ever met, she had mercifully forgotten the uglier man's appearance. Stringy brown hair barely covered his blocky head. Dark eyes peered out from under a shelf of brow. His nose was mashed; a slab of chin jutted out beneath a thin mouth. His arms were mallets of muscle and bone. He was six-and-a-half feet tall.

Every child in the neighborhood knew the man who looked like a monster would do anything, from rescue kites to give coins for sweets. Girls told him their love troubles; young men asked his advice on dealing with their fathers. He was a leader of the smith's guild in Namorn and knew more of working iron than even Frostpine. He was not a mage.

He had been delighted to give Daja forge-time in exchange for her assistance with some of his projects. With him she studied fine ironwork, shaping metal into lacelike forms: between the Syth and the Pebbled Sea, Teraud was the best at it. As a successful master smith Teraud supervised nearly twenty apprentices and journeymen in his massive Hammer Street forge.

Before she entered Teraud's, Daja took a moment to look at the canvas-covered sleigh in the courtyard. The sleigh belonged to Kugisko's governor. It was a glory of brasswork, enamel paint, and gilt moldings. All it required was runners; those were nearly finished. Today she and Teraud would harden the long metal pieces that would be shaped to create two silvery, elegant lengths of metal that would cut through ice and snow. If all went well, they could temper the steel the next day, and fit the runners the day after.

Once inside, she laid her Trader's staff against the wall of the coatroom, then hung her satchel and outer coat over it to hide the telltale brass head from view. While none of Teraud's people had spoken against Traders, it was silly to flaunt her people's best-known symbol. She stuffed her scarf, gloves, and knit hat into her coat and worked off her fur-lined boots, replacing those with leather shoes.

"You ready to work?" Teraud stood in the doorway, tying on his leather apron. His family had been miners in the hard lands north of the Syth; he had still not shed the accent after thirty years on its southern shore. "Teaching didn't wear you out?"

Daja grinned as she found her own leather apron. "How does anybody have a private life on this island, the way servants gossip?"

Teraud chuckled as he led the way to his forge. "The whole *city* prob'ly knows you teaching dose girls by now," he teased. "Our servants are good at da gossip."

Between stretches when the metal heated to the proper brownish yellow shade for hardening and Teraud checked his apprentices and journeymen, Daja worked on the iron rods she used for so much of her own work. That morning she took extra care, shaping her rods with her power as much as her drawing tongs. These would be the foundation of Ben's gloves.

The morning flew past. Daja was startled when Teraud's wife called them to midday. She stowed her tools as the journeymen and apprentices headed for the dining room in a fast-moving herd.

Once inside, apprentices at one long table and journeymen, Teraud, and Daja at another, everyone fell on their loaded plates. Unlike plenty of masters, Teraud made sure his people were well fed. He'd once told Daja it was just self-interest — happy workers meant better work.

The meal was half-over when a maid showed in a boy who carried a sealed sheet of parchment. She pointed Daja out. As he approached, Daja saw he wore the Ladradun insignia on the shoulder of his threadbare gray coat. He was trying not to stare at the laden table. Mutely he offered his message to her.

She took it and signed for him to wait, digging in her pocket for a silver argib as a tip. He looked half-starved.

She hoped he'd buy himself something to eat before he returned home.

"Better read dat careful, make sure you don't need to send back no answer," Teraud advised her. He speared a thick slice of roast pork with one hand as he scooped up two slabs of bread with the other. He dropped the meat onto one piece of bread, capped it with the other, and thrust the whole at the boy. "My wife cooks too much," he growled. "Eat before it goes bad."

The boy didn't need encouragement. He clutched the offering with both hands and took a huge bite. Daja slowly cracked the seal and read the few lines of Ben's note. It was his answer to her request for a time to fit him for the gloves. If it wasn't too late when she finished at Teraud's, he wrote, she could find him at the Ladradun warehouses on Bazniuz Island, at the joining of Cashbox Street and Covil Way.

She read it three times before the boy finished what he'd been given and accepted a second bread-and-meat slab from Teraud. Then she gave the messenger her argib and said, "Tell *Ravvot* Ladradun I will see him later this afternoon."

The boy nodded, still chewing, and trotted away. Teraud's wife Nushenya came over, shaking her head. "The way that woman stints on food, you'd think every grain of wheat was taken from her own children," she said to her husband. "She whips them, you know. The servants. The island council fines her — she doesn't care." She glared at the journeymen, openly eavesdropping. "Don't think any of *you* ae too big for a whipping. I saw that vegetable plate! A vegetable plate goes back half-empty at supper and we serve what you turn away instead of meat tomorrow!"

Daja ducked her head to hide a smile as the diners, male and female alike, dug into eggplant and carrots.

"Somet'ing's not right at dat house," Teraud commented as he sat back and dug at his teeth with a toothpick. "Morrachane's half crazy."

Daja put her fork down. "But what about Ben? He's all right isn't he?"

"He's a hero," insisted a young journeywoman. "That carriage shop on Rider Street would have burned last winter —"

"The hat shop on Stifflace Lane," someone else put in.

"Emperor Noodles," called a girl apprentice.

"If you can talk you can work," Teraud said. Apprentices and journeymen left the tables to wash up and walk around a bit before they returned to their tasks. Only Daja remained with Teraud at the table. His wife joined them with sturdy mugs of honeyed tea. She was from Capchen, where tea was drunk in the way Daja expected it to be drunk. She too sat with her husband, willing to let the maids clear the tables.

"Call me a grumpy old man wit' a nose full a soot and a copper-coated tongue," Teraud said over his toothpick. "To hear da world tell it, Ben Ladradun's de only good dat family ever gave Kugisko." He shook his blocky head. "Me? If somet'ing like a fire took my joy" — he engulfed his wife's hand with one of his own — "I wouldn't go hunting da t'ing dat took my sweetheart and my children." He sighed and looked into his mug, then drained it.

Daja followed him back into the main forge. Ben's intense focus on fire didn't seem odd to her. She had seen Tris destroy part of a fleet because those who sailed with it had murdered her cousin. Sandry had battled her terror of the dark to keep her friends alive. Briar had plunged into death rather than let go of his beloved teacher. Dreadful events, in her experience, led people to do extraordinary things. It made sense to her that Ben would devote his life to a war on fire. Maybe Teraud just didn't know the kind of people she did.

It was mid-afternoon when Daja left Teraud's forge, staff in hand, a bundle of slender iron rods and her rolled parchment tracings of Ben's hands in her satchel. Outside it seemed warmer than it had that morning. Despite there being two more hours until sunset, the light was going. Masses of clouds like fat gray moonstones slid by overhead, their edges fuzzy and soft. After weeks in the mountains and months in the north, Daja knew snow clouds. These looked serious.

With her satchel over her shoulder, Daja strode briskly along Kategan Way, testing the ground with her staff where she suspected hard ice lay under the snow, and dodging sleighs and riders. She could risk her life to cross to Bazniuz on foot, or she could risk her life to hire a sleigh: they all seemed to be driven by madmen. *I have* to practice skating, she thought as a sleigh hurled slush on her boots and coat. *I don't care how much I ache, it will be worth it.*

She did take in the vividly painted storefronts and fences along the way. Color was a Namornese obsession. Roofs were trimmed in yellow, scarlet, emerald green. Outside walls were blue, red, pink, and orange. Doors were bright enough to startle. It was hard to believe that Sandry, whose taste in color was perfect, was half-Namornese.

By the time Daja stepped onto Bazniuz Island, the lamplighters were out. As she walked down Sarah Street, shopgirls and boys left their businesses for the walk home. When she turned north on Cashbox Street, fat snowflakes began to drift idly through the air, as if they toured the city.

Reaching Ladradun Furriers, Daja halted. The property included most of the block on which it stood, expensive on the islands that made up half of Kugisko. The sprawling wooden complex of buildings marked with the Ladradun emblem included a large warehouse, a furrier's shop, a workshop from which men and women dressed like common laborers streamed, a courtyard where men put covers on wagons against the snow, and the charred remains of a second warehouse. For a moment she had the fanciful idea that the fire gods were vexed, to visit a man who dedicated his life to destroying their work. She made a face and shook the idea from her head: that was Tris's or Sandry's kind of addled, imaginative thinking, not hers.

The shop that fronted on Cashbox Street was a haunt for the rich. Luxuriant pelts were draped in its many-paned window, an invitation for buyers to come and touch. That polished cedar door, inlaid with ebony and white pine, was not for the likes of Daja. She walked around the corner. Beside the courtyard gate was an ordinary door and a sign: LADRADUN FURS: TRADESMEN ONLY. She entered that way.

Inside was a typical clerks' office: long, tilted desks and benches for seats. Account books lined a wall. Lamps with brass reflectors supplied light for those who kept the company's records. A hearth on one wall was the only supply of heat; the amount it gave off was meager. Everyone, even the chief clerks, wore outdoor coats.

The messenger who had come to Teraud's sat by the door, whittling a stick into kindling. He jumped to his feet when he saw her. "*Viymese* Daja, *Ravvot* Ladradun's expecting you," he greeted her. "This way."

"A moment." Daja bent to tug at her boot, as if it had twisted on her foot. She thrust deep into the ground with her power, passing through stone and watery mush, then granite, until she reached the earth's hot lifeblood of molten stone.

Straightening her other boot, she called the heat up to her, letting it pass through the wooden floors sheathed in her magic to keep the boards from catching fire. Opening her right hand she spread her fingers. Warmth streamed through her to settle into any metal in the clerks' office that could hold it: the heavy iron grate, the andirons and pokers of the hearth, the empty metal coal bucket, and the brass lamp reflectors. She gave the metal just enough heat to warm the air without changing the metal's color. The workers might not realize they were more comfortable, but she knew. It was her slap at Morrachane's copper-clutching fingers.

She cut the flow of heat and let the rest fall into the molten rock again. One second more she waited, to ensure the metal in the office would not burn the wood around it. She had done something here. Content, she straightened and stamped her feet, as if to make sure her boots were comfortable. "I see you had a building fire outside," she commented as she followed her guide down the hall to the rear offices.

"A month ago. It wasn't serious." He stopped at a closed door and faced Daja, swallowing hard. "*Viymese*, you gave me too much money." He held out a silver coin. "You being foreign, maybe you don't know — the likes of me gets a copper argib, not a silver. If we gets anything."

Daja smiled. "I bet that honest streak pinches you, doesn't it?" she asked. She couldn't imagine Briar correcting anyone about such a mistake. "Don't be silly," she added. "You had to skate around two islands, both ways. Someday when you have a bit extra, give it to one who needs it."

The boy shook his head. "And I always heard southerners are tightfisted. Griantein shine on your winter, *Viymese*," he said, naming the Namornese god of light and warmth. He rapped on the door, then opened it. "*Ravvot* Ladradun, *Viymese* Kisubo is here." He bowed Daja into the room, then returned to the clerks.

"Daja, welcome," said Ben. His office was crammed with a large desk, account books in cases, maps on a worktable, and pigeonhole shelves into which rolled pieces of paper were thrust. One wall backed a large cupboard. The wall beside his desk was covered with large slates that looked to be shipping schedules. A corner stove threw off a small amount of heat, enough that he didn't wear his outer coat. He did wear his indoor coat buttoned all the way up. Somehow she didn't think he was that much warmer than his clerks.

She reached again for the earth's heat, letting it spread from her this time in a pool of warmth. She doubted the ability of the stove to hold what she could bring to it. Testing it with her power, she saw the joint weldings were cheap work that only fused the edges of the attached pieces. Moreover, the iron sides were uneven in thickness. It was better to radiate the heat from her own body.

As the air warmed, Daja shed her outer coat, rested her staff against the wall, and opened her satchel on the worktable. She watched Ben from the corner of one eye. In this room, with its inkwells, slates, books, and stacks of patterns on heavy parchment, the hulking Ben seemed like a bear in a pit, resigned to having starved dogs dropped in to harry him. The contrast with his behavior at the boardinghouse fire pinched her heart. He ought to be outside, facing danger head on, not trapped with clerks and furriers.

"You won't be comfortable," Ben warned as she doffed her inner coat. Despite his words, he'd begun to fiddle with his own collar buttons. "We get a daily allowance of coal for the stoves, and I'm out." He tried a smile. "Mother says people get lazy if they're too warm."

He took Daja's inner coat from her hands and folded it neatly before he set it on his desk. "I spoke to the magistrates' mages about the boardinghouse fire, by the way. They say they'll look into it, when they have time. Of course, a fire in Shopgirl District isn't at the top of their list of priorities."

Daja, remembering the counterfeiting case that *was* at the top of their list, and its potential for national disaster, nodded.

Ben unbuttoned his coat. "What do you need me to do? It must be about to snow — it's warmer in here, don't you think?"

Daja took the metal rods from her satchel. That afternoon she had cut them to fit the lengths shown in her tracings of Ben's arms. "It *is* snowing," she told him. "Could you make a clear spot on your desk?"

He shifted stacks of paper and accounting books. When he finished, Daja had him sit with his arms flat on the desk. "I thought you'd just mold them on me like clay, or maybe sew cloth gloves?" Ben asked.

Daja shook her head. "I need to make a metal form, like a dressmaker would use, only for gloves," she explained. "And I have to be sure of all the dimensions in your hands and arms. Otherwise you'll be fighting the gloves to hold things when all your mind should be on the fire."

Ben commented, "So when I have to push burning material aside, I won't cook the back of my hand again."

"Exactly," Daja replied. She positioned two rods on either side of his forearms, leaving room for him to wear the gloves over his outdoor coat. Taking the elbow and wrist rods, she channeled the earth's heat up through a sheath of magic to shield the wood around her. She used it to warm her rods to the point where she could handle them like clay. It was tricky work. She had to add enough heat to the elbow and wrist rings both to make them curve around his joints, and to fuse them to the side rods, all without burning the man or his clothes.

"Raise your forearms until they're straight up, palms facing out," she said quietly. Ben obeyed, lifting his hands. Now Daja closed the elbow and wrist rings, heating them until the ends merged without a seam.

As Ben sat patiently, she added rod after rod to the

forearm model, heating the ends and molding them around the rings. He remained silent and steady, a rare virtue. She'd had to stop using Briar as a model for this kind of thing because his ability to sit still was limited unless he worked his own magic. Then he had a tree's patience.

"Do you need a rest?" she asked when the forearm and wrist segments were finished. "Move your arms?"

"I'm fine." Ben said. "It's soothing, in a way. You're much better than the maid who fits my clothes. She chatters about silly things until I want to scream. What happens next?"

"I do the same thing, but with your hands. That's trickier," she explained, warming the shorter rods. "I have to work around the joints, so there are lots of little pieces to fit. Don't worry, this is just the boring part. The finished gloves will feel like your own skin." The short pieces for the palms were ready. As she began to attach them to each wrist ring, she said, "I saw that burned-out warehouse on my way in."

"That," he replied contemptuously. "It happened a month ago. Losing it was a blessing. It just held old furnishings and nonsense. I would have cleaned it out years past, but Mother saves everything. Mind, this was the first fire we'd had in the city since spring." He smiled ruefully. "You'd think I'd be glad for a summer without fires, but . . ." He shook his head.

"You keep waiting for the black ship to dock," suggested Daja, working away.

"Black ship?" asked Ben.

"Sorry — a Trader thing. A ship with black sails carries bad news," she explained.

"That's a vivid image. A black ship — I'll have to remember that. Yes, I suppose I was waiting for it. Expecting it, really, only it never came. And the longer we went between fires, the lazier the people I was training to fight them got. It was maddening."

Daja nodded, most of her attention on her work. In a corner of her mind not fixed on her creation, she thought it a pity that a man couldn't take up firefighting as employment. Ben's heart wasn't in trade. And Teraud was right, a little: it *was* odd that Ben had gotten entangled with the thing that had destroyed his early life.

"May I ask something?" he inquired as she checked the gaps between her framework and his body. Living metal didn't stretch. If she didn't leave plenty of room for clothes, he'd have to remove his coat to use the gloves against some fire and risk freezing outdoors some bitter night.

Daja nodded.

Ben tapped one metal-framed arm against the brass on her left hand, making it clink. "How did that happen? Doesn't it hurt you?"

"Oh, that," she murmured, stretching a thumb ring gently. "Remember the fire I told you I was in? I was holding my staff with that hand and the cap melted all over it. I guess it mixed with the magic my friends and I were using, and, well, there it is. Now that I'm accustomed to it, I don't mind. You should see my foster-brother's hands. *They're* strange. He tried to tattoo them with plant dyes, and now ink plants bloom and grow all over his hands." She eased each form off, setting them on the desk while Ben rubbed his hands and arms. "My thanks. You were very patient."

Ben smiled. "It's all to my benefit, after all. Surely my sitting for a short time isn't too high a price to pay."

Daja stowed her materials and the iron sleeve forms in her satchel, pulled on her coats, and picked up her staff. "I'll send word when I have something to show you."

Ben shrugged on his outdoor coat and lit a spill from his stove. In the outer hall he used it to light a lantern by the door. He took it from its hook. "I'll walk you to the street. Are you hiring a sleigh to go home?"

Daja smiled. "I'd as soon jump off a bridge. Besides, I like walking in the snow."

Ben frowned. "It's a long walk, Daja." Together they went into the courtyard. "Why don't you wait until Mother comes from shopping, and ride with us?"

The thought of sharing a sleigh with the sour-faced Morrachane made Daja shudder. To change the subject without offending Ben, she glanced at the mess of the burned warehouse. "May I take a look?"

Ben obligingly led the way through snow that fell in fat, steady flakes. "I could hardly believe it when it happened," Ben remarked. "The place went up like a torch. Usually most of the ground floor walls are left, but not this time."

The wreckage inside the huge, cluttered rectangular pit that was the cellar of the old warehouse was nearly two feet deep in accumulated snow.

Daja sighed and hunkered down with her staff against one shoulder. She was annoyed at having to deal yet again with Namornese winter. In civilized places winter arrived as rains, obscuring the ground only if the water collected into a pond. She called a burst of heat up, jamming it through her outstretched, spread fingers to blanket the ruin. This heat-wash was far quicker than those she'd used in the Ladradun offices, and far hotter. She didn't hear Ben's soft gasp as the snow within the walls of the ruined building shrank, collapsed in on itself, and trickled away, melted completely.

"That's better," Daja commented with satisfaction. She stood. "Now we can see. May I have your lantern a minute?"

Ben handed it over. Daja opened it and took a pinch of flame, then closed the lantern and returned it to him. She let the pinch of fire roll into her palm, then called again on the earth's heat. Her fire seed bloomed to brighten the entire courtyard. She held her hand out before her to see the wreckage clearly now that she had cleared it of snow. The hole in the ground showed the remains of charred floors at its edges. Inside fragments of the outer walls she could decipher the way the upper floors had dropped through the lower ones until everything came to a stop in the cellar. At the very rear of the pit she discovered a gaping hole.

"What's that?" she asked, pointing to it.

Ben squinted to see what she meant. "It's a loading tunnel," he explained. "All the canal-side businesses have them. In the summer the boats tie up in front of the tunnels, and the hands can then carry supplies right into storerooms and warehouses."

"Very tidy," said Daja, impressed. "Were the doors to the canal open last month?"

"Yes," Ben replied with a puzzled frown. "We keep them open all winter, or the freezing in the ground warps, even breaks them. Why?"

"It's the key to how the warehouse burned so fast," she explained, walking around the wreckage to get a closer view of the open tunnel. Sure enough, she felt a cold draft rising from it.

He stared at her. Even the bright light she held didn't bleach his features enough to hide that he was plainly startled. "How do you know that?" he asked.

"It comes of being a smith." Daja let the seed of fire sink into her palm. It made her hand glow orange, lit from within, until she thrust it into the ground. She forgot to sheath it in her power: the instant the unguarded heat entered the earth, the snow melted and she sank into slush to her ankles. Daja climbed out of the puddle with a sigh and shook her booted feet off.

"We pump air with the bellows through a channel under

the fire. That makes it even hotter, and that's why this place" — she pointed to the shadowy depths of the ruined warehouse with her staff — "went up so thoroughly." She walked back to him. "How did it start? Was it deliberately set? All this is too perfect to be an accident."

Ben shrugged "Why go to so much trouble for a worthless building? I assumed some beggar got in there to sleep out of the wind, and his cookfire or candle set it burning by accident. Frankly, I didn't care. I've been after Mother for years to pull that firetrap down. At least it gave my local firefighters a chance to use their training, after months of no fires at all."

Daja nodded, impressed. That was so like him to worry that, without chances to work, his people might not be ready for a true disaster. Only Ben would think that more important than the loss of a second-rate warehouse.

A gust of wind made him shiver. Here she was, keeping this man out in the cold. "I'd best be going," she told him.

"I wish you would wait for Mother," he complained. "It's on —"

"Ben!" a hard voice cried, interrupting. "Lamps are lit in the cutting room with no one there!" Morrachane Ladradun walked out of Ben's office — Daja guessed she had entered through the store on Cashbox Street. "Where are the Dancruan accounts? And your office is far too warm."

If Morrachane had a mirror, thought Daja, it had to be

metal. Silvered glass would break every time Ben's mother showed that face to it. As it was, Daja bet the metal had to be flattened at regular intervals. Continued exposure to Morrachane's face would warp the best metal from time to time.

Ben sighed faintly and went to his mother. Daja followed.

"Who is with you?" demanded the older woman. She peered through the swirling snow at Daja. "Oh. *Ravvikki* Kisubo."

"*Ravvi* Ladradun." Daja said with minimum politeness. Even that was for Ben, not for this unpleasant female who refused to call her by her mage title. "I was just going."

"Daja, wait and leave with us," Ben said. "We have plenty of room, and it's a miserable night."

Morrachane's lips crept upwards at the ends. Daja winced. She had forgotten — happily — the unfortunate results of Morrachane's attempts to smile. "I am happy to offer a ride to the twins' friend," she informed Daja. "Particularly the one who revealed their magical talents. I always suspected it, of course, but having no familial ties, I couldn't very well get them examined by a better mage than those the Bancanors hired."

Daja opened her mouth to reply to the implied insult to Kol and Matazi, then closed it again. The mark of a born Trader was to know when persuasion and discussion were useless. Instead she bowed to Ben, then to Morrachane. "I thank you, but I've been at the forge all day. I need the walk. Good night to you both." Rather than risk Ben arguing with her, she walked briskly to the gate on the street.

In her wake she heard Morrachane tell her son, "It's just as well. I want to review those accounts from the capital."

8

Outside the Ladradun gate lamps burned, marking the edges of the road in the snow. Daja trudged down Sarah Street, looking around her. She didn't care what Frostpine said: she loved freshly fallen snow, the way it clung to trees, fences, and ornamental carvings, softening even the jingle of sleighbells, muffling the clop of horses and the sounds of people going home. She loved the way it danced in the air, shaping globes of light around the lamps, swirling in and out of patterns. In the mountains between the Syth and Emelan snow was untouchable, hard, and deadly. Here people trudged through it, swept it, rode through its cutains and streamers, played with it. It made the busy Kugiskans into friendly people. Everyone she passed wished her a good evening, or smiled and said things like, "A foot or two by morning, at least!" Daja answered them with smiles and nods. She didn't know enough about this white element to predict how much would come down before sunrise.

She heard bells approach behind her and moved close to the lamp-posts to give the sleigh plenty of room to pass. She kept her head down, hoping the vehicle coming up on her wasn't the Ladraduns'.

"*Viymese* Daja?" a familiar voice called. "Is that you?"

She turned as the Bancanor sleigh, Serg at the reins, drew up by her. Behind Serg Daja saw a lump of quilts and furs that had to be Jory.

"Why are you afoot?" Serg demanded, reining up. "Get in. You'll freeze."

Daja climbed up beside him rather than disturb the girl. They drove on in friendly silence until they turned into the back courtyard at Bancanor House. A stable hand emerged from the snow to take the sleigh as Serg scooped Jory off the seat, blankets, furs, and all. He carried her into the slush room, Daja behind him.

After hanging up their own coats and boots, they unwound the sleepy Jory. She had ash on one cheek and flour on another; her apron was splashed with some kind of red sauce, and a gluey substance clung to the end of her braid. "She says Anyussa's a good teacher," Jory told Daja drowsily as they went into the kitchen. "She said I don't have to unlearn things."

In the kitchen they saw Frostpine at one of the tables. He worked his way through a bowl of soup as he talked to Anyussa. Nia sat across from them, whittling buttons. Other members of the household were gathered there, some with sewing in their hands, others giving pots and boots a thorough polish, still more just gossiping.

"What's going on?" Jory asked, sliding onto the bench next to her twin. "Why's everybody in here?"

On of the maids opened the door that led to the family's part of the house. They heard a clear, commanding female voice: "— the day that one of *my* granddaughters would be spending any more time in Blackfly Bog than she might need to drop off a basket for the poor —" The maid shut the door again.

"Oh," said Daja with a wince. She had forgotten this was the night that Kol's mother came for her once-a-week meal with her son and his wife.

"'Beware the matriarchs of Namorn,'" Frostpine said, quoting a proverb, "'for they are queens without crowns.'"

Daja grimaced. *If Morrachane's a queen, it's of pijule fakol,* she thought, placing Ben's mother in the worst of the Trader afterlives, reserved for those who did not pay their debts.

Frostpine eyed Daja. "You look all nice and rosy with the cold," he remarked. "I suppose you're going to tell me this weather isn't so bad."

He looked so miserable that she went over and kissed his head. "I won't say any such thing," she promised him. Instead she laid her fingers under his beard, where she could feel the pulse in his neck veins. Slowly, carefully, she let heat trickle into his body to warm his blood.

Frostpine sighed his gratitude. "Not that the food hasn't thawed me out wonderfully," he told Anyussa, who smiled.

"Or that you're practically sitting in the kitchen fire," Daja added, feeling its heat on her back. She asked Nia, "How did it go, your first day?"

Nia held up a wooden rod the width of Daja's thumbnail, and gestured to a small saw, carving knives, sanding paper, and a heap of buttons and sawdust before her. "Arnen showed me how to make buttons," she said with a shrug. "I'm to work on them at home, and he'll check every week to see how many I do."

Daja grinned. "Smith apprentices get nails," she said. "I used to think they start you on boring things so you'll be half-crazy by the time they show you anything real. We have meditation in the morning, first thing. Don't forget."

Nia's eyes fell. "No, I won't." She reapplied herself to her buttons.

"Don't make plans for Sunday night," Frostpine told Daja. "We're invited to the Kugisko Mages' Society's first winter festival. Our fellow mages would like to make our acquaintance."

Daja grimaced. She hated parties. "How can I say no to the Kugisko mages?" With a nod to everyone, she went up to her room by the servants' stair, to keep out of Kol's mother's way.

*　　*　　*

In the morning Jory awaited her in the schoolroom, staff in hand, her breath steaming on the air as she bounced eagerly. Nia was absent.

"Where is she?" Daja asked.

"I don't know," replied Jory with a shrug. "Do we need her? She's just going to jump anyway, she won't really hit."

"You both have to learn to meditate," Daja reminded her, leaning her broom-handle staff against the wall. "Refusal isn't a choice you get." She had an uncomfortable feeling that she knew what she had to do. The prospect made her grumpy. She had come to Namorn to *learn*, not to teach. "Tell me where to find her."

Jory shrugged again. "By the time I got dressed she was gone."

Daja crossed her arms over her chest. "You know where she is."

Jory shook her head.

"You're not fooling me," Daja told the younger girl. "Nia knew where *you* were, the other day."

"She's the only one who can do that," Jory said blithely. "I can't."

Daja sighed. She supposed that closing ranks against outsiders did well for the twins. "Don't lie to me again," she recommended. "I've been lied to by an expert. Compared to Briar, you're as obvious as a cow in a mud puddle."

Jory set her mouth stubbornly.

It was too early for a contest of wills. "All right," Daja

said. She went to the hearth, which had yet to be cleaned, picked up a piece of charcoal, then beckoned Jory close to one of the walls. "Face that wall and hold your staff in the high block position," she ordered.

Jory obeyed. Daja adjusted the girl's hands, the angle of her staff, and her stance. Once they met Daja's requirements, she used the charcoal to mark the positions of the upper and lower end of the staff on the wall and the placement of Jory's feet on the floor. Moving the girl an arm's length to the side, she marked the correct positions for the middle block on the wall and the floor, then marked them for the low block.

"The housekeeper will have a fit when she sees those," Jory said, more interested than sullen now.

"Send her to me. Your hands in the right position?" Daja checked the placement of Jory's hands on her staff. "Hold it just like that." She yanked up heat from the roaring kitchen fire two stories below through her body and into her hand. Then she pinched the staff with her thumb and forefinger, burning the wood to show Jory where to grip. The girl yelped when she felt the heat and saw the wood char, but she held still.

Daja returned her borrowed warmth to the kitchen, but kept enough to answer a question. He hand was still hot enough to burn cloth, if not wood. She laid it over one of Jory's hands. The girl smiled. "That's warm!" she exclaimed. "Do the other one?"

Daja folded her hand around Jory's cold fingers and summoned more heat, enough to boil water. Jory grinned.

"Well, you'll never need potholders," Daja remarked. "Have you ever lifted a hot kettle with your hands?"

"Are you joking?" asked the girl. "Nobody lets me do *anything* that might scar my hands. Grandmother even gets cross if she sees me wash vegetables — she says my hands will get chapped, and nobody will believe I come from a good home."

Daja smiled. "Well, my hand is hot enough to burn, and all you noticed was that it was warm. You can pick up hot pots without fear. I can't speak for what will happen to your skin when you wash things. Now, I want you to practice ten high blocks with your staff, feet and hands *on the marks.* Then ten middle blocks, then ten low. When you're done, if I'm not back, start over and keep practicing. I'm going to find Nia." She went to the door.

"But I thought you would teach me fighting with this!" cried Jory. "I don't want to sit in a circle and think of nothing and try not to scratch any itches. I *hate* that!"

"Practice your blocks," Daja said firmly. "Over and over, with everything just as we marked it."

"How can I learn anything like that?" Jory complained.

"By repeating basic movements over and over, you learn them throughout your body. That's the first step. Get moving. We'll talk about meditation some more after Nia joins us."

Jory moved into high block position. "You won't find her."

"And adults say young people these days don't know anything," Daja retorted, shaking her head. "If only those adults knew that *you*, Jorality Bancanor, know everything, why, they'd hope for the future."

Daja had thought it might come to this, which was why she had her new scrying mirror in her belt pouch. She took it out and cleared her mind of everything, even the sounds Jory made as she practiced high blocks. Daja recalled her sense of Nia, then breathed onto the mirror. Her breath condensed on the metal, then slowly evaporated. When it was clear again, Daja saw Nia in the wood room where she had originally found their staffs.

Tucking the mirror into her pouch, Daja trotted downstairs.

She found Nia yawning as she inspected a handful of wooden buttons. They dropped from the girl's fingers when Daja walked in. "I won't do it!" Nia cried. She knelt, scrambling for the wooden rounds. "That isn't meditating! Nobody ever talks about hitting when they meditate!"

"Then they haven't met Dedicate Skyfire," Daja said, picking up a button that rested against her foot. "You can't decide you hate it after just one try."

"Yes, I can," Nia said, her chin thrust out mulishly as she glared up at Daja. "I hated it even before we were done. I'm not Jory! She always gets excited, and she starts hitting, and she's always sorry after, but that doesn't make my fingers

not hurt, and I liked the other way, the sitting and counting — why are you looking at me like that?"

"I just wanted to see how long you would make that
sentence last," Daja admitted. "I honestly don't think you
meant to stop before breakfast."

Nia stared at Daja for a long moment, plainly baffled.
Finally she said, "You aren't really *like* anyone else, are you?"

Daja smiled. "I am, but I don't think you'd be comfortable
around the people I'm like." She sobered again. She knew
where this was leading, and her own heart was in rebellion.
She wanted more time to herself, not less, to work on Ben's
gloves and maybe even a suit for him to firewalk in. It's not
like I *wanted* to be a teacher, she told herself.

"Children in Capchen want the same things you do,"
her Aunt Hulweme used to say. "They can have them,
because they're only *kaqs*. Our children don't get the things
kaqs get, so now you decide. Are you a Trader, or are you a
kaq?"

"Are you sure you don't want to try the staff?" Daja asked,
though she knew the answer. "It's like dancing lessons, only
different."

Nia's eyes filled with tears. "I'm sorry I'm a coward," she
said, and sniffed.

Daja sighed. "You're not a coward," she told her second
student gently. "You just don't know what you're brave at."

"I'm a coward," Nia insisted, tears running down her
cheeks. She wiped her eyes on her sleeve. "Jory says I'm

always squeaking and jumping, I always hide, I don't argue . . ."

It bothered Daja to talk so long to a kneeling girl. She knelt and helped to gather buttons. "The bravest person I know is afraid of the dark. She sleeps with a night lamp always, but if her friends are threatened? She suddenly thinks she's a bear twelve feet tall and attacks whoever scared her friends. There are all kinds of courage. You'll find yours." She felt a sigh rise in her chest and swallowed it. Nia felt bad enough: Daja would not let the girl think that she was unhappy to teach her. "Though looking for courage when Jory gets worked up doesn't seem useful. We'll go back to the meditation we tried first."

Nia stopped gathering buttons and frowned. "But Jory. She wiggles until I just want to scream."

"I'll use this hour of the day for Jory's meditation," Daja said, offering Nia a handful of buttons. "You and I will meditate the hour before supper."

"And I can breathe, and count, and sit, and not get hit with things?" Nia asked, suspicious. "We'll be quiet?"

"Quiet as mice," Daja said. Remembering her first nights sleeping aboard her family's ship, she corrected herself: "Quieter, actually."

With Nia reassured, Daja left to rejoin Jory. She glanced into the kitchen on her way to the back stair. The main hearth fire roared, sending heat throughout the house. Anyussa was rolling out dough for the dumplings called *pirozhi* as Frostpine stirred a pot of buckwheat kasha cooked with milk and spices. Anyussa laughed at something he said and looked at him in a decidedly flirtatious manner.

Daja smiled and walked on. She liked the brisk, irritable cook much better, knowing that Anyussa had it in her to like Frostpine.

"Well?" Jory demanded when Daja reached the schoolroom. "You couldn't find her, could you? I didn't think you would." Her hair was popping out of its braid; her cheeks were red, testimony that she had been exercising.

"Nia and I made other arrangements," said Daja as she picked up her own broom-handle staff. "We'll meditate in the afternoons. You and I will go on meeting here at this hour."

"How does learning to fight with a staff help me get my magic under control?" asked Jory nervously as Daja spun her light staff hand over hand, moving out into the center of the room.

"We've got all winter to thrash it out," Daja told her. "See, the idea is, you get so used to those three blocks and those three strikes that your body will move, but your mind will be free. Then it doesn't matter if someone tries to hit you. You'll be at your center, within your spirit and your magic. That's when you start to learn control, where you pull your magic in or let it out as you need. But for now —" She struck high at Jory, who blocked just in time. Daja went immediately to the middle strike, then the low strike, slowly enough that the girl saw the blows coming and blocked them. They continued to trade blocks and strikes, so preoccupied that when the clock chimed the first hour of the day, both jumped.

"Right here, tomorrow," Daja said. Jory nodded and ran to dress for the outdoors. She was due to leave for Blackfly Bog in half an hour.

Daja leaned on her broom-handle staff, barely winded. It would take longer to teach Jory to grip her magic this way, but she knew they now steered the right course. She also knew she was right to give the twins separate lessons, though she was less happy about that. Still, they were both good girls and they did want to learn. Daja could appreciate that. And she had liked trading blows with Jory. She missed her practices at the temple, and Jory had a natural talent for it. Maybe once the younger girl learned to control her power, she might also like to study more combat techniques. That was something Daja could look forward to.

After breakfast she spent the morning in her room, working on her fireproof gloves. First she molded living metal as southern bakers shaped flatbread, tossing rounds from hand to hand until they reached the proper thickness. As she worked the stuff, she sent her magic through it, calling on the power of its birth. Then she had dragged a forest fire through her flesh, which had included a hand covered by the molten brass cap of her staff. This metal would be able to endure fires that intense. She also imagined how Ben would use the living metal gloves — to knock burning debris aside as he had at the fire when they'd met, to lift flaming beams out of his way, to grasp hot metal to shift it. She filled the living metal with her idea of Ben as she'd first seen him, laden with two boys he'd carried from an inferno just in time. When she finished, these gloves would happily do whatever Ben asked of them.

Once she set a piece of living metal on a glove form, she carried the form to the window and stuck it outside. The wind blew hard off the Syth, trying to yank her creation from her grasp without success. With the living metal strip cold enough to hold to the iron form, not drip through the openings between the rods, Daja added the next strip, molding it in place and pressing its edges against the cold section until they blended seamlessly. Then she took the form back to the window.

She finished one glove by the time the clock struck noon, and went down to take her meal with the kitchen staff. About to return upstairs, she realized she needed physical activity. Handling living metal was more an exercise of power than work for her body. She went into the slush room and looked outside. People had been moving snow all day after the two-foot-deep fall during the night, the Bancanor servants among them. Not only were the paths around the house clear, but the ice of the boat basin was too.

Daja looked out under the street bridge, where the boat

basin opened on the canal. Convict work gangs were hard at work, smoothing the broad strip of ice. Skaters used the ice they had cleared.

If I want to skate the canal, I have to practice, Daja told herself. She went to the slush room and put on her outdoor clothes, then went to the boat basin to skate.

When she returned to her room, she felt ten feet tall. She had learned how to turn while still in motion, and she had not fallen once. While she had been telling Jory that her body had to learn movements so well that she didn't have to think about them, Daja's own body had done a bit of learning of its own.

She felt so good that work on the second glove went even more quickly than it had that morning. She finished just as the maids came upstairs to light the lamps. Nia would be home from Camoc's soon.

With both forms covered, Daja tied heavy cords to their inner iron frames, opened one of her windows, and hung the forms outside. The night's cold would set the liquid metal. In the morning she'd remove the iron forms and complete the magic that would keep the gloves in that shape forever.

Pleased with her day's work, Daja leaned out the open window. Snow lay thick on the rooftops, in heaps on either side of Blyth Street and Prospect Canal, but there was less than she'd seen that morning or even at midday. People who lived with heavy snows found plenty of ways to handle it, Daja had learned. Servants worked almost as long and as hard as convicts to clear courtyards and walks so that nothing kept their wealthy masters and mistresses from the day's business. Convicts labored on snow removal in huge crews, shivering in rags and shackles. Daja felt no pity for them. They were criminals and deserved their lot.

She scooped up a handful of snow: it melted almost instantly. She had raised her personal heat the moment she'd opened the shutters. Daja let it drain back through her until her skin held only normal warmth. This time when she gathered snow, it didn't melt away before she could eat it. She loved the taste of clean, crisp snow.

She was working on her jewelry when she heard the clatter of footsteps on the back stair. "Daja!" Nia cried. "I'm home!"

Daja put her work aside, collected her Trader's staff, and joined her student. "How did it go today?" she asked as she and Nia climbed to the schoolroom.

Nia held up a cloth bag. Wooden rods in three shades — pale oak, chestnut, and ebony — poked out of it. "More buttons," she said. "By the time I'm done, no one will have to make any more for decades. Maybe even a century."

"That's how I felt about nails," Daja told her as she opened the schoolroom door. "It's amazing how many of such things people use though."

Nia shed her bag and coat and sat on the floor. As Daja drew the circle around them with her staff, she realized she was glad to have this quiet girl to herself for a while. Smiling, she took her own place and enclosed them in a bubble of magic.

In the morning, after a round of staff practice with Jory and a good breakfast, Daja returned to her room and brought her gloves in from outside. Carefully she slipped her fingers between the living metal and the iron forms, then worked the forms out of their gleaming yellow sheaths.

At last she set the iron aside and put her creations on. The gloves were much too big, of course, since they were made to Ben's measure. The cold inside the metal made her flesh ache.

She took the gloves off rather than call heat to warm her arms. She didn't want heat near the gloves yet. First she had to embed signs in metal around the cuffs, runes shaped from lead for stability and copper for flexibility. Then she would cover the gloves inside and out with a liquid spelled for more flexibility and stability, and for strength. Only when that was done could they be safely warmed.

Dreaming of fire suits as she wondered how in the Trader's name she would create that much living metal, Daja set the gloves upright on their bases. They looked like golden hands grasping for the next rung of an invisible ladder. She went to her *suraku* and collected her materials. On her way back to her worktable she froze. The gloves were collapsing in on themselves, returning to their original, thick syrup consistency.

"Pavao!" cried Daja. *"Pavao, pavao, pavao!"* With all her work and with the magic she had used in their shaping, they should have kept that form for a day at least! Their collapse, while still ice-cold, meant that gloves of living metal alone would never work. She had to put them on a hard metal frame. It meant hinges at every joint and complex hinges at the wrists to allow side-to-side motion as well as up and down. With a solid metal frame her finished creations would be far heavier than she had planned. If gloves couldn't exist on their own, a whole suit of living metal would be a nightmare. A *heavy* nightmare.

She put down her metals and oils and kicked her chair in frustration. White-hot pain burst through her booted toes. She hopped on one foot, softly cursing in Tradertalk, Imperial, Hatarese, and Pajunna, until she realized she was being a fool. She slumped into her chair to nurse her wounded foot.

It was her own fault. She had given in to pride. Because she was successful with this stuff, she had thought that she could just wave a hand and get what she wanted with little planning and effort. Had she ever made anything purely of liquid metal? She hadn't. All of her other pieces had included hard metal like iron, brass, and bronze. Her false hands, arms, and legs were liquid metal fixed to iron skeletons.

"As well expect quicksilver to walk on its own," she muttered. Over and over people had warned *Tris* about pride, but Frostpine had never cautioned Daja against it. Why not?

Instead of spending her day in glory, finishing off her achievement, she began the tedious labor of replacing each lump that represented a joint with tiny oiled hinges, using her power under tight control to remove the lump and to solder each hinge into place where the lump had been. Her only breaks had come at midday, for lunch and a swift skating practice, then meditation with Nia when the girl returned home. She'd pretended to be her normal, centered self at meditation: had Nia gotten so much as a whiff of Daja's self-disgust, she would have thought *she* caused it, not Daja's own folly. Daja briefly considered telling the younger girl her mistake, but decided against it. She was vain enough to feel that she didn't want one of her first students to think she was human enough to make a botch of something.

She felt shriveled and grumpy at supper, poking Anyussa's good cooking with an indifferent fork. Nia, too, was silent, listening to her parents talk. Jory was still at

Potcracker's. Frostpine joined them, though he added little to the conversation. He looked exhausted. Daja looked at him with a growing sense of betrayal.

"Why didn't you warn me about overconfidence?" she finally demanded, silencing Kol's and Matazi's conversation about a change in gold prices. "You never lectured me about pride like Niko and Lark always lecture Tris." She realized she had forgotten her decision not to let Nia realize she was human, but resentment overpowered her. "Why not? You let me walk into a mess, you know. I wasted hard work and I feel like a grub, and it's your fault."

"I'm not the only one who knows how to make a sentence last," Nia murmured.

Daja gave her student an I'll-get-you-later glare and turned back to Frostpine. "Well?" she asked again.

Frostpine leaned his head on his arm. "I thought you'd find out for yourself," he informed Daja. "Learning sticks when you get it the hard way." He yawned. "When I've finished my current task, you must tell me what happened. You've worked so smoothly I'd begun to think I'd have to mention pride to you after all. Just to be sure I'd taught you properly, you see."

Matazi tapped Frostpine's plate with her fork, making the delicate porcelain ring. "You. Bed. Now," she ordered. "You're tired and addled."

"Yes." Frostpine left, waving an idle goodbye over his

shoulder. He did not go to the front stairs and the guest rooms, but back to the kitchen.

"He's the most annoying man," Daja announced, still vexed. "Why does he get to be right?"

"He's always been that way," Kol assured her.

"When he told me I'd be happier with Kol than him, I tried to punch him in the nose," Matazi added, startling a gasp of surprise from Nia.

"Worse, he was right." Kol smiled into his wife's eyes.

Matazi blew him a kiss. "Much worse," she agreed.

Nia rolled her eyes at Daja.

"If he gets too smug, tell him a truly perfect person wouldn't get seasick," Kol said without looking away from his wife.

"That's right, he does," admitted Daja, feeling better. "I forgot." Her appetite returned, and she began to eat.

When Ben's father had been alive, the Ladradun family worshipped on the first Watersday of the moon at the temple of Vrohain the Judge, the god who had cut off his left hand so he could never dilute the justice he dispersed with his right. On the second Watersday they attended the temple of Qunoc, mother of the earth and its seed; on the third, they paid their respects to Baion, the cold, white god of killing ice. On the fourth moon they worshipped Eilig, goddess of spring and freedom. After his father's death, Ben and his family still worshipped all four gods each month. It was Morrachane who went less and less to the other temples. When Ben returned from Godsforge's school, he took his mother to worship Vrohain each Watersday, rather than fight with her. He also made frequent offerings at the temple of Sythuthan, the trickster who ruled the immense lake.

The day after Daja's first attempt with the gloves failed, the Ladraduns attended Vrohain's worship. As they left

Morrachane was elsewhere, her copy of *The Book of Judgment* clutched to her chest, her pale-green eyes fixed on some vision of justice and punishment. She looked exalted. The oddest thought wriggled through Ben's mind: did he look like her when he watched a fire?

He snorted. He had nothing in common with her. She would be the first to say so; in fact, she'd been telling the world as much for years.

He did not share her exaltation. Instead he reviewed his plans. Tonight's test of his firefighters had to go without a hitch. For that to happen, he needed to get rid of his mother and go to work.

Just the thought of escaping her, even for a day, sent guilt to nip him. He and his brothers had promised their dying father that they would take care of Morrachane. Only Ben had kept his word, though it got harder and harder. Sometimes he thought the best way to do it would be to put her out of her misery. That was a monstrous thought — he *knew* it was monstrous. Yet he thought it all the same.

Watching the crowd, he saw the white or silver-trimmed hats and long coats of the magistrate's lawkeepers. Of course they worshipped Vrohain, both here and at the shrines in the district stations. A glint of gold mixed with silver caught his eye: the mages who served the lawkeepers were here too. Many lawkeepers and mages nodded to him: Ben was well known to the magistrates' people. He'd trained most in Godsforge's methods of fighting fires and protecting the crowds who came to watch them.

He had not told them that the boardinghouse fire was deliberately set. Just as Ben set fires to test his brigades, he thought of them also as a test of Kugisko's magistrates' mages. They had to be vigilant. They thought the penalty of burning alive was enough to stop anyone from committing arson; it made them lazy. Once people discovered fires were set without the mages' discovering it, their office would have to improve their methods of investigation.

Sooner or later, he knew, someone would realize that his test fires had been set. Sythuthan played tricks on everyone; sooner or later blind accident would make the authorities suspicious. When that happened, Ben would move on, happily, to another city and another set of lessons.

"Don't jam your hands into your pockets," snapped his mother, breaking into his thoughts. "You'll ruin the line of that coat. Do you want us to freeze to death? Let's go!"

Ben fell in beside her, plans tumbling through his head as he rearranged and resorted them.

At home they sat down to midday in the kitchen, where the heat from the stove warmed them. Ben laid the place settings and poured tea for his mother and himself. Morrachane served a four-cornered meat pie with braised cabbage and mushrooms. There were no servants in the house; Morrachane refused to pay the extra coin that any servant expected when asked to give up his Watersday. Instead she cooked like a common householder.

They ate in silence. Ben knew better than to draw Morrachane's attention when her mind was fixed on Vrohain. Afterward, she retired to read her *Book of Judgment* and nap. He cleared and washed the dishes, then left the house. The business was closed. He would be able to finish his preparations uninterrupted.

His workroom was in a corner of the main warehouse garret, secured with two locks and hidden behind empty crates. Inside he lit the stove, then took out his fire-setting device.

He loved working on it. Modeled on a fire-starter designed by Godsforge, it was an intricate layering of materials that would smolder inside for hours before the surface burned and set its surroundings ablaze. Godsforge had drummed it into his students that fires were unexpected; they should always be prepared. To enforce the lesson, he'd arranged with the locals to use his devices to set fires at all hours, calling his students out to fight them. Ben knew he was simply continuing the great man's work.

Working on his present device, Ben longed for the pure study at Godsforge's school. He had recovered from his family's deaths there and even found contentment, only to have it shattered on his return. He was in his mother's house again, for one. For another, he wearied of battles with councils for funds and space to train firefighters, and battles with the men and women who were ordered by their masters to learn from him. It had been worse that summer: the more time between large fires, the harder it was to get the councils' attention. They were as bad as children, longing to play without thought for the future. All he wanted to do was help; all the rest of the world did was fight him. If it wasn't some fur-robed guildsman complaining over the loss of his servants' time, it was his mother squalling about hours taken from the business. Only when he worked on his tests did he feel better. With those he found a way to control his life: the boardinghouse fire had been his second, his own warehouse the first.

Now he put the final touches on the most complex device he'd made. It was worth all his trouble. He must be nowhere near his target when it began to burn, or suspicion might fall on him. By the time the fire broke out of his creation, he would have been home for hours. The fire would destroy all traces of the device, baffling mages and their tracking spells. He had learned that at Godsforge's, too.

Though Watersday was a rest day, the mages in Bancanor House had things to do. After she dressed, Daja went to her lesson with Jory, trading staff blocks and strikes with her, making sure the girl had no time to think, only move. As they practiced, Daja thought that Jory might be working on her own. She was faster, more accurate, her hands and stance surer. Keeping a level head was more of a struggle, but there too she had improved. As they left the classroom, Daja knew that by focusing on movement and not allowing herself to get excited, Jory had already begun to drag her magic inside her skin. The visible flares in the girl's power had begun to flatten and spread over her to coat her skin. It was nearly time to start Jory on the next step as Dedicate Skyfire taught it: the state of waiting for everything and nothing. That would be when their real work began.

At breakfast they found that Frostpine was gone, still chasing his counterfeiter. The capture of those who planned to destroy Namorn's economy was far more important than Watersday rest. The sick needed food, Watersday or not, but Carnoc Oakborn closed his shop. Jory left for Blackfly Bog while Nia and her parents went to the temple of the goddess Qunoc. The Bancanor servants who had the day off were gone. Only a handful rattled around the big house as Daja went back upstairs to her room.

First she prayed to Trader and Bookkeeper, then to the spirits of her family, lighting incense so they would know she still remembered them. Among Traders, to be forgotten was the one final death: memory lasted when the flesh was gone. Daja would make sure that her children, if she had any, would say the prayers for each member of Fifth Ship Kisubo.

She worked on tiny hinges through midday as the tray

of food brought by a maid went cold. Finally she stopped: her last hinge was gone. She would have to go back to Teraud's for a day or two, and trade work for iron forge time. It was time to rest: her back and neck were one solid ache. Her eyes twitched madly when she closed them, a sign that she had been doing too much close work. Time to practice skating.

Daja put on layers of clothes. She didn't try to warm herself: they were good clothes, and after two days of the sharp control and release of her magic, her head spun. She needed to rest her power.

She took the servants' stair down the back of the main house. She could smell supper, all dishes that could be set in covered pots and left to cook through the day. The servants' area was forlorn without the constant clatter, arguments, thumps, and scrapes of a large household. That was Watersday: upperclass servants had almost a full day to visit and to shop, while the handful that stayed received an extra silver argib and another weekday off to balance the scales.

Hearing the soft murmur of voices in the kitchen, Daja stopped to look in. Nia and Morrachane Ladradun sat at a worktable, glasses of tea and a plate of cakes before them, looking through a book that appeared to be sheets of cloth backed in parchment.

"Oh, I like that one," Nia said, pointing. "Look, you can see vines in it."

"That's called Maiden Blessing," Morrachane replied softly. She stroked Nia's hair gently with one knobby hand. "I taught Kofrinna how to make it. She wore an entire veil of that when she married Ben. She was such an adorable girl. I miss her and the children every day."

Daja tried to move on: it was not comfortable to watch Morrachane in a tender mode. Nia saw her at just that moment. "Daja, come see these lace patterns," she called. "Aunt Morrachane brought them for Jory and me. They're so pretty, and some of them are really old."

Daja couldn't refuse without seeming churlish. She glued a smile onto her mouth and sat on the bench opposite Nia and Morrachane. "*Ravvi* Ladradun," she said with a polite nod.

"Daja," replied Morrachane. "Have you been at some work of magic?"

"Tinkering," Daja said, not wanting to discuss her labors with this woman. Once she had made the mistake of biting a sheet of gold foil. Morrachane had the same effect on her. "Is this the lace pattern book you told me about?"

"This one's Maiden Blessing," Nia said, turning the book so Daja could see that the cloth pages anchored samples of lacework, while faded writing on the paper pages described how to make the particular pattern. "This one's Herb Garden, and here's the King's Treasure."

To Daja they looked similar, but she nodded gravely, as

if she understood the niceties. Sandry would have been able to identify each piece separately, she knew. "The book seems old," she commented as Nia turned other pages.

"It was in my husband's family for ten generations," Morrachane said with pride. "Our families come from the old empire, the western side. Books of lace patterns are passed from the bride of each son to the brides of their oldest sons. This was to go to Kofrinna, until the tragedy." She stroked a piece of lace with fingers that trembled. "I'll have to ship it to one of the other boys' wives before I die. It is hard to think of it going to someone I do not even know."

"Please don't be sad, Aunt Morrachane," begged Nia. "Why don't you visit your sons this summer? You could meet your grandchildren."

Morrachane shook her head. "I could not leave the business for so long."

"But Ben's here," Nia pointed out. "And even if you don't visit them, he can still marry again. He's not that old."

Morrachane smiled and cupped Nia's cheek in one hand. "You are a good girl, Niamara Bancanor, and you know your family duty. Vrohain knows I have presented that son of mine with perfectly eligible females, but will he do as he ought?" She folded her lips, her pale-green eyes flashing. "I don't understand how I could have failed with him, but I did."

Daja clenched her hands under the table. She was determined *not* to say that it was hardly a surprise if Ben didn't follow his mother's wishes, not when Morrachane had yet to speak well of him. "I imagine he'll remarry when he gets to it," she said when she got her temper under control. "He seems rather busy keeping the city from burning up."

"That is his excuse," Morrachane said. "He has a gift for making others think well of him. The truth is that he would rather idle with the city's riffraff than serve his family." She looked at Nia, who read the old-style writing on one page, her lips moving silently. Her face, as hard as iron when she discussed her son, relaxed. "Would you like me to have copies of this made for you and Jory?" she asked Nia. "It's no trouble, and I'd like you to have them. Though chances are your hands will be so rough from hammering and sawing that you won't be able to make lace!"

Nia smiled; Daja bristled at the hint of criticism. "I'll just do like Mama does, to keep her work neat," Nia assured the old woman. "I'll make a pair of thin linen gloves."

"Now there's an idea," Morrachane said with approval. "Your mother does have lovely hands."

"She puts lotion on them and wears the gloves to keep the lotion on her skin longer," explained Nia. "I've been thinking about trying that anyway. And then I could make lace without damaging the threads."

"So clever!" Morrachane said with approval. She hugged Nia gently around the shoulders. "I'm glad to see that banging away with rough tools hasn't made you forget womanly interests."

"Oh, look at this one!" Nia said, her eyes wide. "Aunt Morrachane, what is this?" She traced a pattern in old lace, her finger not quite touching it.

So her rough mage's fingers didn't touch Morrachane's precious legacy, thought Daja, cross.

"Well, those are flames or waves, depending on how you look at them," Morrachane answered Nia. "My mother-in-law thought they were supposed to show both sides of womanhood, passion and the ability to flow around obstacles."

Daja had heard enough — did the woman do anything but carp? She got to her feet. "I hope you'll forgive me," she told Morrachane. "There isn't much light, and I need to practice my skating."

Morrachane nodded. Her pale-green eyes did not move from Nia's face.

"Remember, slow is better," Nia said absently, turning another page.

Daja grinned despite her anger with Morrachane. "I have three friends who would tell you I have slowness down to an art," she assured Nia and left the kitchen.

In the slush room she donned coat, scarves, gloves, and even a wool cap so she wouldn't be tempted to use her magic to warm herself. Picking up her skates, she went down to the basin.

"Doesn't do his duty," she growled as she buckled her left skate. "Idles with riffraff. Bangs away with rough tools.

That woman's mouth is so sour she could pickle lemons in it!" She yanked the straps on her right skate so hard they pinched her foot even through her boot. Cursing in Tradertalk, she loosened the strap. "How someone like Ben came from that bitter old shoe of a female . . ."

She stood and thrust herself away from the bench. Unfortunately she did so a little too hard. Across the basin she shot, right into its snowy sides. She pushed herself out of the snow, her face hot with embarrassment. No one was present to witness her humiliation, but she still said aloud, "I meant to do that."

It was like meditation, she realized as she steadied herself on the ice once more. She couldn't think about anything but skating when she skated. She closed her eyes and took deep breaths, thrusting Morrachane from her mind. When her thoughts were filled only with skating, she began again.

Nia joined her after a while. Morrachane had gone home. "You don't like her, do you?" Nia called from the bench.

Daja was practicing turns. "I don't need to like her."

"I feel bad. She's so dreadful to everyone else, and so kind to Jory and me." Nia stood and glided across the ice.

"That's what Jory said," admitted Daja.

"I don't understand it," Nia told her, going into a tight, quick spin. As she slowed she added, "I used to think all the stories about her were just lies from jealous people. Then —

then I saw her thrash a beggar with her driver's carriage whip one day. How can she be so loving to us, and so horrible to the rest of the world? What would make a person grow up that way?"

"I don't know," replied Daja. "I've never seen anyone like her. My Aunt Hulweme was mean to everyone, no exceptions. Great navigator, but a dreadful person. I'm just glad Ben isn't like his mother."

"The whole city's glad," Nia assured her. She grabbed Daja's hands. "Come on. Let's go try the ice in the canal."

"Oh, no," Daja said, trying to pull free. "No, no, no!"

"*Yes,*" replied Nia. "Come on. You can do this."

Much to Daja's surprise, Nia was right. They skated carefully from Bancanor House north to the tip of Kadasep and back. Daja fell only once, where a patch of ice was pitted. Both girls returned to Bancanor House flushed with victory.

Their good feelings carried over into Nia's meditation after they went inside. The younger girl entered the breathing pattern with confidence. Daja watched as her power slid over her skin to coat it in a glowing layer. The emptier Nia's thoughts, the fewer occasions when her power flared away from her skin. She was close to the point where she would be able to handle her power as she did wood.

"Did Camoc give you work for today?" Daja asked as they left the schoolroom.

Nia shook her head. "I asked if I could borrow a book on magic for hard wood, and he grunted. I think it meant yes. He knew I took it, anyway. I read some this morning — I hid it in my hymnbook." She smiled. "Papa saw me, but he didn't say anything. I think he gets bored in temple, too."

Daja shook her head as they separated to dress for supper. After she ate, Daja spent the evening in the book room with the family. She went to bed feeling as if she'd accomplished a great deal that day, despite Morrachane. She was silly to let the woman irritate her, she decided as she crawled under her covers. Morrachane was a sad creature, hated by most, not understanding what a prize she had in Ben. She was to be pitied, not fought.

It was nearly dark when Ben left the warehouse, a rough wool coat and felt boots over his clothes. He wrapped scarves around his head, hiding all of his face but his eyes, and carried his device and a lantern in a basket. Unnoticed he joined the stream of servants returning to their masters' homes, their heads bent against the hard wind that blew off the Syth. Ben appreciated the wind: protecting his face from it, he also disguised his height.

Ever since he had begun training firefighters, he had walked over every inch of most Kugiskan islands, through courtyards and alleys, past middens and wells, around outbuildings and along the tops of walls. He had descended into cellars and climbed into garrets and towers. He knew those islands, including Alakut, better than those who had lived there for centuries.

With that knowledge, he had his pick of sites at which to test his lone Alakut Island brigade — footmen and shop assistants who skipped training a third of the time, to run their masters' errands or simply because they forgot. They needed sharpening up. For this test he had chosen a confectioner's shop on Hollyskyt Way. It was near enough to Ladradun House that his brigade would immediately send for him when the fire started, but not so near that it might draw suspicion on him.

Hollyskyt Way was nearly deserted. The families who ran its exclusive shops weren't deemed good enough to live on Alakut: their businesses were closed for Watersday. There was a houseguest the confectioner didn't know about, a beggar who crept into the cellar to sleep. But she came well after dark, when there was no chance she would be seen.

Ben had seen her, of course. He'd watched the place for two months before making his decision. Now he used her tight-fitting entrance to the shop, feeling his servant's garb catch and pull on its edges. He would lose bits of thread that a magistrates' mage might use to trace the wearer, but that was no problem. He would leave his outer clothes and anything he'd carried behind to burn: mages couldn't use tracking spells on items cleansed by fire. Ben smiled as he dropped to the cellar floor, envisioning those mages like frustrated bloodhounds, looking for a trail that only doubled back on itself.

He lit the lantern and went upstairs, where he set his device in the pantry and lit the fuse. He propped the door open to feed his blaze air, and set empty sacks and jars of olive oil nearby to serve as fuel when the device set the room on fire. He left his basket there as well.

Outside the shop, he removed his coat, scarves, and boots and thrust them into the cellar, making sure his other clothes didn't catch on the edges of the opening. Last of all he blew out his lantern and threw that into the cellar. This area was directly under the pantry: the cloth would be ash, the lantern molten tin by the time the magistrate's mages arrived.

Then he hurried home to be his mother's browbeaten son until his summons arrived. While she fed him her endless scolds and insults, he imagined the shop as it started to burn. Imagination got him through supper and her usual Watersday speech, that it was his fault, his inattention, his stupidity that had gotten her grandchildren killed. He endured it. Some days he wondered if she was right. Tonight he did not: his thoughts were on his test. Once she finished, she ordered him to bed, so he wouldn't waste candles. Ben obeyed. He always did.

The truth was, Morrachane was an inconvenient convenience. In return for service as her verbal whipping boy — he'd put a stop to her real whippings a month before he married — she gave him a place to stay. If he lived alone, there would be a house to manage and servants to oversee, endless boring details that took precious time from his reason to live. He gave his mother his work at the business and someone to blame; she saw to his daily needs. And one day he would repay her for every time she made him wonder if indeed it was his fault that his wife and children were dead.

Going to bed posed certain problems. He'd planned to be reading in his nightshirt when they came, until he realized he had no urge to freeze as he fought a blaze in nightclothes. He set out his things as if he prepared them to wear the next day. He could stuff them on over his nightshirt, perhaps leave the end of the shirt trailing outside his breeches. That decided, he got into his bed and opened a book, Godsforge's *Types of Burn and Burn Healing*. It was nearly impossible to read. Soon they would come. Soon, soon . . .

But the clock kept striking. No one came. He didn't dare go to the garret window that would give him a view of Alakut. If they came while he was there, it would be hard to explain why he watched a fire instead of racing to it.

So Ben waited through a sleepless night. Some of his Alakut brigade arrived in the morning, long after it was over.

"We thought we could handle it," whined the head footman from Lubozny House. "We've trained for weeks —"

"Three," Ben interrupted coldly. "When you bothered

to come. You didn't know enough to put out a brush fire in a park, let alone a shop. "Anyone hurt?"

"A woman who slept in the cellar — she was fried black. And two of us," said an undercook from the Gemcutters' Guildhall. The cook was a big woman, one of the few who came to every training session. "The healers said they breathed smoke. We got them at the Alakut Infirmary. . . ."

Ben yanked on his coat. "Smoke! Were you wearing masks? When I told you smoke is as deadly as fire?" Some glared at him as if it were his fault that they hadn't remembered about smoke.

Ben flung open his door and strode out into the glare of the morning sun on snow. At least his so-called firefighters had brought a large sleigh. They tumbled into it after him and raced to the infirmary, arriving in time for Ben to hold one smoke-stricken man's hands as he died. As his last breath escaped the man's lips, Ben felt a joy so intense that it made him weep. The healers, even the fire brigade, looked properly sober and admiring. They think it's grief, Ben thought, trembling as he fought laughter.

What he'd felt just now was almost too intense to bear. He'd made the rules. He'd told them, they hadn't listened, and two people had paid the price, this fellow and the beggar woman. The fire had killed them for him. He had turned it loose as mages commanded the winds to rescue becalmed ships, and the fire had given him its greatest gift — the power over human life.

The destruction of wood and glass and porcelain was nothing to this, Ben thought. Look at them, after their complaints over the drills and schedule. Let one die — let one of them struggle to breathe until the struggle was too much — and suddenly Ben had their attention. Here was why Kugisko had treated him callously. The stakes weren't high enough.

Gently he freed himself from the man's grip. "I'll look at my other firefighter," he informed the healers. "And then that beggar. What was she doing there? And then I need to see Alakut council. One of you tell them I will meet them in the council hall, by midday."

Healers and brigade trainees alike, they scrambled to do as he ordered. It was amazing, the way dead people changed things.

The joy was less powerful with the second firefighter: the healers said he would live, though his lungs would never be the same. The beggar woman, though . . . again he felt that overpowering thrill. He had done this — Bennat Ladradun, his mother's scapegoat, ignored by the coin counters of the island councils. They would heed him now, wouldn't they?

He rested a hand on the dead beggar's charcoaled ankle, knowing the picture he made, solemn-faced, eyes bright with tears. The firefighters watched him with awe as they fought to keep from vomiting at the dreadful smell of burned flesh.

He drew his hand away, pretending not to notice the black flakes that clung to his palm. "Such a price to pay," he murmured shaking his head. "Maybe we could not have saved this poor creature, but we *might* have saved our own people."

They stood back to let him pass, like a noble, like a king. It was the best morning of his life.

By the third hour of the afternoon, his world was bleak again. The Alakut council had argued, expressed regret, and refused him more funds to train a second brigade, though he explained that one was not enough for the whole island. His brigade, they said, had done poorly at this first challenge. They had to wait and see. They *would* insist that those who were supposed to learn the skills attended training more often.

Ben managed to contain his rage until he reached the warehouse. There, when no one could see or hear, he slammed his hands against the walls. Only fire respected him. The Alakut council, it seemed, required a special lesson. He feared that it would be a frightful one, but they had to learn that fire exacted a frightful price.

10

Sunday night Daja and Frostpine stood on a broad
gallery from which two staircases led to the meeting hall
of the Mages' Society of Kugisko. They held glasses of
mulled cider as they watched the activity below. Kugisko's
mages, dressed in assorted finery, gathered in clusters and
broke apart, greeting colleagues. Daja, too, wore her best, a
Trader-style knee-length coat and leggings in gold-brown
damask trimmed with black braid. No one put on elegant
leather slippers when they had to walk to and from sleighs
as snow fell, so Daja wore polished Kugiskan boots with gold
spirals stamped around the rim. Frostpine, as always, wore
his Fire-red habit over his layers of non-Temple clothes,
but no one could ignore Frostpine, even in this gaudy crowd.
Light glittered from gems and crystals or shimmered over
velvets and brocade. Mages who were not priests or reli-
gious dedicates, Daja had found, tended to peacock in dress
and ornaments.

Masters were accompanied by those students they deemed worthy. The students, their clothes good but plain, struggled to hide awe. Already Daja had seen Camoc, Arnen, and two more young mages she recognized from Camoc's shop, as well as the carpentry- and cooking-mages she had met.

"I don't see Olennika Potcracker," Daja remarked to Frostpine. "I wanted you to meet her."

"Potcracker once told me she cooks for parties — she doesn't go to them," a harsh female voice said behind them. "She's also referred publicly to some of our richer members as parasites. I doubt they'd welcome her."

Daja and Frostpine turned to face the speaker. She was in her early fifties, two inches shorter than Daja, with pale, weathered skin and crows' feet wrinkles around small, dark eyes. Her no-nonsense lips were thin and wind-chapped, her nose a sharp angle thrust straight down from her forehead. Like many older native Kugiskan women she had dyed her hair blonde so many times that it looked like straw. In contrast to her plain looks, she wore a black silk undergown and a sleeveless maroon velvet overgown, both decorated with gold embroideries. The buttons down the front of the overgown were small gold nuggets. She wore a sheer black veil and a round maroon velvet cap over the ragged twists of her hair.

She continued, "I personally think Potcracker is

overgenerous. After all, there are creatures that feed on real parasites, so the real ones do some good. Our wealthier members feed no one but themselves."

"I bless Shurri and Hakkoi for keeping my nature sunny, unlike yours," Frostpine told the woman, naming the fire gods to whom he had dedicated his life. To Daja he said, "Anyone connected with magistrates sees too much of the bad side of things."

"You can hide from it in your pretty temples," the woman said. She measured Daja with thoughtful eyes. "We don't."

"That's why I prefer the pretty temples," retorted Frostpine. "*Viymese* Heluda Salt, this is my student and friend, *Viymese* Daja Kisubo. Heluda's the mage I've been working with lately."

"I'm honored, *Viymese* Salt," Daja told the older woman politely. "I hope the investigation goes well."

"We're close," said Frostpine.

"Don't say that until we have the *naliz* in irons," Heluda advised him. She offered Daja a hand gloved in black lace. A smile softened her firm mouth, though her eyes remained wary. Daja had a feeling that Heluda Salt remained watchful even in her sleep. "I hear many good things about you," she told Daja.

"Then you can't have been talking to him," Daja said, giving the older woman's hand a squeeze and letting go. "He only ever gives me a hard time."

"But it's for your own good," Frostpine said, inspecting the room below again. "I force myself, so you will be strong."

Heluda jerked her head at Frostpine. "Was he always impossible, or has the cold he moans about so often done this to him?"

Daja shrugged: she too could be as wary as a magistrate's mage. "I wouldn't know. He likes to keep me confused."

In the air below, five golden swirls rose, coming together in a whirlwind beneath the huge chandelier. They sparkled as they whirled and spread, until they formed a soaring palace in midair. The watchers applauded. Slowly the illusion faded until only a handful of specks glittered in the air. These vanished, one by one. The last shimmered, faded, then blazed into flaming orange glory as a sun. Then it too winked out.

"It's a Society tradition," Heluda explained to the two southerners. "The illusionists compete all winter, and the Society votes a winner at the last meeting, in the spring. A waste of magic, but nobody listens to me."

"If you earned your living making old men look young and fat women look thin, I should think just doing something pretty would be a relief," Frostpine commented. "Let them have their fun."

For a time they watched the crowd, Heluda naming some of Kugisko's mages and what they did. Daja leaned on the stone rail, listening to her and to bits of conversation that rose from people below.

"— and I said, why not give up doing love potions? If you have to keep moving so jealous husbands and lovers won't catch you —"

"— undersold me by five gold argibs. *Five!* I told him, do that again, and I'll go to the Fair Practices Council —"

A handful of mage-students descended on the tables where food was laid out. Some looked like this was their first solid meal of the week. Daja was grateful that Frostpine was a great believer in the theory that well-fed students worked harder. Many teachers weren't.

"— now that he's got a noble protector, he can afford pearls instead of moonstones for his money-drawing spells."

"His protector's *wife* isn't complaining either, not when her husband's out making money until all hours!" The two who discussed that topic laughed in a knowing way. Daja hated them. Was this what the meditation, work, and study were for, to make rich men richer and supply material for smutty jokes?

"I did all I could." That voice was tearful, female, coming from the stair to Daja's left. "I tried to call rain to put it out, but I couldn't fight the snow. It — it froze. It coated everything like glass." The speaker sniffled.

A male voice murmured something.

"I told them the dangers, that I couldn't warm it enough

to rain, but they *ordered* me to do it. Just trying half-killed me. My head still hurts. My landlord wants me out because the district's angry at me. A man in the crowd broke his leg on the ice." The woman's voice quavered. "And this beggar woman, who always blessed me when I gave her a copper? She was sleeping there after the shopkeeper left, and — and — Griantein shrive me, she burned. They brought her out. . . ." The woman began to sob.

Daja swallowed hard. A fire. They were talking about another fire. She wanted to ask, but it would take more courage than she had to face the weeping mage. A hand gloved in black lace rested on her arm. "A confectioners' shop on Hollyskyt Way, last night. Alakut Island," Heluda clarified, when Daja frowned, not knowing the street name. "Just on the other side of Pozkit Bridge. Lucky for the confectioner that he wasn't good enough to live on Alakut, just to sell his sweets there."

Daja frowned. If she remembered correctly, that was near Ladradun House.

"It could have been worse, then," Frostpine said. He appeared to be absorbed by the view, but it was like him to have heard everything.

"Was Ben Ladradun there?" Daja asked, trying not to seem worried. Frostpine glanced at her with a brief frown, then returned to his survey of the assembled mages.

"No, or things might have gone better," replied Heluda.

"Two of the firefighters breathed in smoke. One won't ever have healthy lungs again. The other died this morning. And it was stupidly done, stupidly. They didn't even think to send for Ladradun, where he lives maybe ten minutes' run away, on the other side of Pozkit Bridge. He only started training them three weeks ago. They should have known they couldn't manage yet. He would have reminded them of the danger from smoke, at least."

Daja's cider was cold, but it wasn't the cider that made her sad. Ben wouldn't blame the novice firefighters — he would blame himself for not being there. There was no convincing someone like him that he couldn't fix everything. It would be worse because the fire had been nearby.

"No one can be everywhere all of the time," Frostpine said quietly, as if he knew what she thought. "He's a grown man; he'll realize that."

"Yes, but he takes fires so personally," Daja pointed out. "He's got this idea in his head . . ."

Heluda cleared her throat. "I was talking to the Alakut magistrate's mages before I got here. They believe this fire may have been set. They're going to work their investigation spells as soon as the site cools — tomorrow, probably."

Goosebumps rippled along Daja's flesh. "Ben and I think the Shopgirl District boardinghouse fire was set too," she said. "Maybe they're connected."

Heluda raised her brows. "The Shopgirl fire was set? This is the first I've heard of it."

"But Ben reported it," Daja said. "Or I thought he did." She couldn't remember his exact words. Had he said he'd done it, or that he *would* do it?

"Then chances are the report's buried on my desk," Heluda replied with a shrug. "I get copies of reports from all the city districts to review — it's hard to keep up, particularly with a major investigation of my own underway." She turned a large, jeweled ring on her finger. "Have you or *Ravvot* Ladradun any ideas on who set that fire?"

Daja shook her head. "I don't know why someone would do such a thing in a city that's mostly wood."

"Oh, there are dozens of reasons to set fires," Heluda said. "The worst we had, a man who'd quarreled with his woman blocked the exits to the Weaver's Guildhall and set it on fire. Two hundred and forty people died so he could tell a journeyman weaver he was angry. I'll send word to the Lord Magistrate's office to have someone look at the Shopgirl site as well as the confectioner's shop. An experienced magistrate's mage will be able to tell if they were set."

Daja raised her eyebrows, wondering if Heluda didn't believe her.

"Just as well to put your own people on it," Frostpine commented. "Your mages see the whole city, not just individual islands. They'll know if there have been suspicious fires elsewhere in Kugisko."

"Hey! Frostpine!" called a tall man below. Over his gray velvet tunic he wore the sapphire-studded chain of the head of the Mages' Society. "Stop monopolizing all the beautiful women. Bring them down so we get a chance!"

Frostpine grinned. He led Daja and Heluda down the stairs opposite to those where the woman had been crying.

"The thing about Master Northice?" Heluda murmured in Daja's ear as they descended. "He honestly believes that we're beautiful. That's why he gets reelected to head the society every year. He sees the beautiful everywhere." She smiled ruefully. "I wish I still could."

In addition to the Society head, Camoc Oakborn met them on the ground floor. He kissed the magistrate's mage on the cheek. "Heldy, you look grand," he told her, eyes twinkling.

She actually smiled up at him; Daja had begun to wonder if Heluda could smile. "As you are handsome," she told Camoc. "Do you know —"

She'd turned to Daja, but Camoc was already offering Daja his hand. "I've met *Viymese* Daja," he told Heluda. He looked at Frostpine and raised his brows.

Daja performed the introductions. "This is my teacher, Dedicate Initiate Frostpine of Winding Circle temple," she said formally. "Frostpine, this is *Viymese* Camoc Oakborn, Nia's teacher."

Frostpine took Camoc's hand briefly. "Of course. I'm glad to meet you."

"It's good to have you here, Dedicate Frostpine," Camoc said. "You honor Kugisko with your visit."

"It's been interesting," Frostpine said casually. "I wanted Daja to get some experience of other smiths' — and other mages' — ways of doing things, if only so she can see mine is best."

Camoc actually laughed at that. Even Heluda smiled. "Have you met Dedicate Initiate Crane there at Winding Circle?" asked Camoc. "We went to Lightsbridge together."

Listening to the men talk of Crane and other mages they knew as Heluda added her own comments, Daja thought that she could almost like Camoc this way. If only she felt better about how he dealt with Nia.

She looked until she saw Camoc's student Arnen at the supper tables, in a group of other student mages. They were eating and talking. Daja walked over to them, taking a couple of anise horn cookies as she waited for Arnen to notice her.

Finally someone told Arnen, "You have a shadow," and snickered.

Daja looked at the speaker — a young man with the pale skin and fair hair of a western Namornese. Was his remark an insult?

Arnen turned and saw her. "*Viymese* Daja, good evening," he said.

"If you have a moment, I was just wondering how Nia's lessons go," Daja replied. "She says the workshop's very busy."

Arnen nodded, his gold earring winking in the

candlelight. "We get frantic days, particularly as Longnight approaches," he said. "But she's no trouble, if that's what you mean."

That didn't sound like anything Daja wanted to hear. "How is she at her studies?" she asked. "Learning runes, oils that work best with wood, and so on."

"Next she'll tell you how to set a peg in a floor, Arnen," remarked the pale young man. "Or how to smooth a chair leg. Little girl," he said to Daja, "whatever tricks you learned down south, you are interrupting adults here. You speak when you're spoken to."

Daja wrapped her right hand around her left. The brass under her palm heated along with her temper. She disliked being sneered at by a jumped-up *kaq* with a maggot's complexion. Since she refused to lose her temper with an idiot, Daja instead remarked. "The basics of mage-teaching are the same whatever one's discipline."

"Shut up, Eoban," said a young woman in the group. "Didn't your mother teach you guest-manners?"

"She's not my guest, is she?" demanded the fair-haired Eoban. "She's just another southerner, come to take the bread from working mages' mouths."

Daja sighed. "Might I speak to you away from the watchman's clapper?" she asked Arnen. A clapper was two flat pieces of wood on a cord, a noisemaker. "I can't hear over its racket."

Eoban pushed her lightly on the chest, forcing her back a step. "Back to your straw hut, wench," he snapped.

Daja looked at him as she thought for a moment, fiddling with a braid. All three of her foster-siblings argued inside her head — not truly, but they'd had so many discussions like this that she knew what they would say. Briar would punch Eoban or wrap him in vines. Sandry would treat Eoban to noble's scorn for a commoner who'd touched her friend. Tris would go so white-hot with fury that she would literally have to find cold water to stand in, so she could nurse a rage headache as water seethed and boiled around her.

Daja simply reached into her tunic jacket and drew out her medallion. She held it up so Eoban would clearly see that she wore the insignia of an accredited mage.

As a student, he possessed no such insignia.

"I have things to do just now," she said quietly, "or I would teach you manners. But I'm busy. You'll have to wait. Touch me again, I won't make you wait long." When she saw him gulp, she turned her back on him and looked at Arnen. "We were talking about Nia."

His eyes flicked to her medallion. Daja had shown it to Camoc, not to him, though she thought Camoc would have mentioned it to him. Arnen met Daja's eyes again. "We started on basic tools today, fixing them and putting edges on the cutting ones," he told her. "She knows a lot for a girl of her background — she says the carpenters who worked around Bancanor House explained things to her." He smiled, a glint of warmth in his eyes. "She doesn't complain as much as *I* did over tools. I mean to start her on basic runes next week. She works hard. She really wants to learn, and I can see she's picking up the meditation skills she needs."

Daja folded her arms over her chest, inspecting Arnen — really inspecting him — for the first time. There was someone here she hadn't seen when Camoc had introduced them. She had noted the young man's artistry, but did not think about what kind of person he was. She'd believed he was like most top mage-students, always running behind the master, with no minds of their own. Now she wondered if she had misjudged those students too. "Will you mind if I check on her now and then?" she asked.

"Master Camoc takes his midday at home and works on papers there for two or three hours," Arnen said. "The shop's at its quietest then."

Daja smiled. Her opinion of Arnen rose another notch. He'd realized her misgivings were with Camoc. "I'll keep that in mind," she promised.

An hour later, Daja saw that Frostpine was struggling to hide yawns. She sent a runner for the sleigh Kol and Matazi had ordered them to take. Their driver was in the kitchens, eating and drinking with other servants who drove those mages who could afford them.

Together she and their driver bundled Frostpine in fur throws and blankets, with hot bricks under his feet, before the driver set the horses forward. Frostpine immediately disappeared under the rug. Daja reached into the earth for warmth, as far as she could, but North Fortress Island was at the Syth's edge. Its icy water made a powerful extra barrier to the heat under the islands. Daja could punch through the water in the canals and even the Upatka River, but here the Syth's size and natural magic was much stronger than she was.

At least the snow had stopped for the moment. Three fresh inches lay on the road that led across North Fortress Island. It hissed under the runners and muffled the horses' hooves.

Daja worked a hand through Frostpine's cocoon until she found his arm. Through their magic she said, *I don't see why they built the Mage Society Hall all the way at the western tip of North Fortress.*

Kugiskan mages were infamous for experiments once, Frostpine replied. *The idea was to get them as far from the city as possible without actually throwing them out.*

Maybe these northerners are smarter than I thought, Daja said. She could feel his body shake with laughter through his cocoon.

The wind picked up sharply as the sleigh raced across Schoolman Bridge onto Odaga Island. Most of the artisans and servant families who served the wealthy of Kadasep and Alakut Islands lived here. Their wooden houses were dark, shuttered against the snow and the wind off the Syth. Only the brass-backed lanterns on Mage Road were lit. No one stayed up late on Odaga, not when they rose at servants' dawn, the cold gray hour before sunrise.

Daja saw pinpricks of light on Kadasep Island, across an intersection of canals from Odaga. More winked along the rocky cliff that was the north point of Alakut Island. A bigger light bloomed next to them, one that grew even brighter as the sleigh approached Bolle Bridge.

Daja yanked at Frostpine's wrappings. His head shot up out of his cocoon like an irate turtle from its shell. "Girl, what are you *doing* to me? We aren't there yet. . . ."

His eyes followed Daja's pointing finger to the fire on Alakut Island. It blazed from a house at the peak of the cliff.

Frostpine lunged forward and tapped their driver's shoulder. "Look!"

The man turned his eyes from his horses to Alakut. "Sythuthan!" he cursed. "That's Olaksan Jossaryk's house!"

Daja and Frostpine gauged the fire. Neither of them spoke for a moment. Then Frostpine told the driver, "You'd better take us there. We might be able to help."

The man glanced back, as if he had a mind to argue. If he did, he changed it, and turned the horses not down the road to Pozkit Bridge, but onto a steeper one that climbed the heights of Alakut. Daja stared at the blaze as they approached it, a strange, idiot thought repeating itself over and over: real or set? real or set? as if a fire deliberately started were any less deadly than those with natural causes.

Frostpine scrambled free of his blankets; Daja grabbed his wrist and threaded warmth through his veins until they were three houses downhill of the blaze. There the driver halted the sleigh.

"This is as close as I can get," he said, apologetic. Other sleighs blocked the street; a crowd had formed ahead. "I have to stay with the horses," he added, even more apologetic.

"You should go back —" Frostpine began as he clambered out of the sleigh.

"The master and the mistress would kill me," the driver said, his voice flat. "Take some of them lap robes. They'll be needed."

Frostpine and Daja each grabbed an armful of quilts and fur rugs, then headed up the street. People stood in the road watching, coats thrown on over nightclothes, belongings thrust into pillow slips, sheets turned into bundles. Servants ranged around the houses on either side of the Jossaryk home and on the opposite side of the street, watching for deadly, floating embers ushered along by the bitter wind. Others formed rough lines to sand piles in kitchen courtyards, passing full buckets to those who fought the blaze. Sand was safer: it didn't freeze to slippery ice. People helped others — wrapped in sheets or blankets, sobbing, soot-marked — through the tangle of sleighs and gawkers into houses farther down the road.

Onlookers moved away from Frostpine's scarlet habit, hardly noticing Daja in his wake. Once the pair entered the main courtyard of the sprawling Jossaryk House — it was nearly a palace — they stopped, panting, and measured what they saw.

The parts of the house that wrapped around the outer edges of the courtyard were one-story extensions. They led to two-story sections that attached to the three-story main house. These extensions would include servants' quarters, storerooms, coops, stables, dairy, and all the other workaday parts that supported the elegant building. They were not yet on fire. Behind those additions the ornately carved and painted main house was half in flames. The hard wind off the Syth struck the rock cliff on which it sat and raced upward, picking up speed and strength until it blasted over the cliff's edge against the face of the house. The fire that burned along the roof's peak stretched toward courtyard and street, thrust almost horizontal by the wind. There would be no saving the house, only the people.

Firefighters stood on the wall around the place with buckets, ready to shout an alarm if they saw clumps of fire blown toward other homes. Men and women hidden under sodden blankets streamed in and out of the extensions, returning with those who were still inside.

"Get the gawkers out of here!" Daja heard a clear voice

order over the roar of wind and fire. "Take the victims inside — they'll freeze in this wind. Tell the neighbors to open their homes — if they balk, come to me!"

Ben stood in the courtyard in the gap between the extensions. The wind whipped the curls that escaped his fur hat; his coat was half-buttoned; one pant-leg hung outside his boot. He directed those who left the buildings with people in their arms. For a moment Daja wondered how he'd known to come, before she realized he probably saw the fire from his house.

Frostpine and Daja went to Ben. "Where can we help?" asked Frostpine. "Tell us what's left to be done."

Ben looked them over. For a moment Daja thought he was angry, or perhaps just vexed. She wondered why, trying to put herself in his shoes. He must be thinking about how to put the most people to the best use. Frostpine and Daja were just two more elements to worry about.

"Do you firewalk like her?" Ben demanded.

Frostpine nodded.

"There's a servants' dormitory on the second floor of this extension," Ben raised his voice over the roar of the flames, "near the main body of the house." He pointed to the upper story of the longest extension, the one to Daja's left. "We're still trying to get them out, but people are afraid to get too close."

"Can't blame them for that," Frostpine shouted. The wind tossed his hair and beard wildly, turning him into some dark, mysterious figure, more a wind spirit than a man.

Daja heard screams inside the roar of fire; her belly clenched. People were dying. She and Frostpine handed their dry throws and quilts to someone, then snatched up water-soaked blankets from a heap on the ground. Ben gave them wet cloth masks from a bucket. Frostpine hesitated, then shrugged. He and Daja suffered less from smoke than most, but they weren't immune. He let Ben tie the mask over his nose and mouth; a woman performed the same service for Daja. Then Frostpine ran through the smoking door with his load of dripping blankets.

II

Ben looked at Daja. He shouted, "The nursery. We haven't brought any children out." He pointed to a second-story window where the other extension met the main house. A woman in a white nightdress leaned over the ledge, a child in her arms. Their mouths were dark Os in their faces; they were screaming. A handful of firefighters maneuvered under the window with an outstretched blanket, yelling for her to jump. The woman tossed the child down instead, then disappeared from the window.

Ben grabbed a huge axe and ran down the courtyard between the extensions, Daja behind him with her load of soaked wraps. He swerved around the firefighters as they tipped the wailing child off the blanket and approached a door on the ground floor near the nursery. First Ben put his palm against it, making sure no fire waited behind the door to burn anyone who opened it. He then tried the latch: the door was locked. Swinging the axe, Ben chopped until the door fell apart, releasing a billow of smoke.

"Try to come back alive!" he shouted over the roar of wind and fire.

Daja grinned at him and ran into the building, stretching her senses out. Her power was of more use than her eyes; she could see, barely, but the smoke made her eyes stream with tears.

The fire was still deep inside the main house, greedily devouring cheap pine and costly teak columns alike. She heard metal scream as it lost the shapes it had held for years. She had some time, but not much, before the blaze reached this extension.

To her right was a stair: someone lay crumpled on it. Daja hesitated, then dumped her blankets, grabbed the victim — a boy — and dragged him to the open door, tossing him outside. Ben was still there: he gathered the boy up with a nod to Daja. She went back inside with relief. Ben had him. Now the boy had a chance to live.

She raced to the stair, grabbed her blankets, and climbed to the next floor, wondering how all this had started. Not in the kitchen, or the back part of the house would burn first. Not in the extensions. In the front of the house, perhaps? A branch of candles knocked over, a hearth fire that popped burning embers onto a silk rug? They might never know.

Perhaps it was set, whispered a thought. Daja shook her head. Who would be cruel enough to stage such a disaster?

She heard screams as she lunged into a hallway from the

stair. Running toward them, she searched for doors on either side of the smoky corridor. Here was the source of the screams, a door on her left.

She felt the press of the oncoming fire; its power flooded her veins. At the end of the hall she saw wisps of smoke curl through a closed pair of double doors that must lead to the rest of the house. How long did she have before the doors blew off their hinges?

No time to think of that. Daja checked the nursery door for heat as Ben had, then thrust it open. Women in nursemaid clothes or nightdresses spun to face her, all but one. She stood at the window across the room, gripping a child by the nightshirt with each hand. She stopped, changed her hold to grab one shrieking youngster by the waist, and hoisted the captive to the open window. A quick shove and he was falling out. The woman seized the next child.

Daja counted heads. There were more than a dozen people here, five servants, the rest children. She thrust blankets at the three nearest women. "Carry one pig-a-back, have the other walk right behind you!" she shouted, grabbing a small child and lifting it onto one maid's back. The woman stared. The child — a boy, Daja thought — wrapped arms and legs around her. Taking an older child, Daja thrust her against the maid's legs and made her grab the woman's nightdress. Then Daja took the wet blanket she'd handed the maid and draped it over her and the children like a cloak, wrapping one of the woman's hands around the blanket's edges so it wouldn't fall off. She put another edge in the woman's free hand and tugged until the servant held a wet fold over her own nose and mouth.

Daja looked at the other women: they copied what she had done as Daja helped. Seeing the children might slide off, she yanked sheets from the cots strewn around the room and used them to tie each child to a woman's back.

There were two more adults, but she was out of blankets. Looking around frantically, Daja saw water pitchers beside two beds. She dumped them on several covers, giving one to a servant woman and wrapping two small boys in another.

"The babies!" cried the woman at the window. "They sleep together and I can't drop them!" She pointed to a small side chamber near her.

Daja shoved the first woman that she had wrapped in blankets at the door. "Go!" she ordered, pointing. "Get them out of here!"

She grabbed a third pitcher of water, dumped it onto a tumble of sheets, and carried the wet linens to the nursery door. She could feel the blaze in the main house advance. She had to slow it down. Freezing for a moment, Daja closed her eyes and threw up the biggest shield she had ever created in her life, a solid barrier the width of the nursery, stretching from the ground floor to the roof overhead, to prevent the fire from going under or jumping over her floor. She placed her shield ten yards into the main house and made it as hard as she could, knowing her real fight would come when the fire reached it.

The cool-headed servant was already in the babies' nursery, bundling up three infants there. Daja followed her inside. "Why so many children here? So many babies?" she shouted as she folded a sheet into a sling.

"Two of us are nursing our own — we've permission to keep them with the *Ravvi's* newest," the woman yelled over the roar of the burning house. She was streaked with soot: working in the open window, she had been in the path of any smoke that entered the room and passed outside. She coughed for a moment desperately, gasping for air as she clutched a small gilt figure of Yorgiry that hung on a ribbon around her throat. "And *Ravvikki* Lisyl had her tenth name-day, with her friends to stay the night."

Using sheet slings, Daja hung one baby off each of the young woman's shoulders. The fire approached her barrier. Once it touched her defenses, Daja's war would begin. She would have to hold it in place or no one would get out alive. If it reached the nursery, the open windows and the corridor leading to the door outside would act as chimneys, pulling fire and smoke down the only exit.

She draped the young woman in wet sheets. "Cover your nose and mouth; keep the babies covered," she ordered, picking up the last child. They went into the main nursery. The women Daja had ordered to get out still waited by the door, too frightened to move.

There was no time to waste breath on curses. Daja gripped her companion's arm. "You're the only one with sense. Lead them out of here — down the hall to the first stair, and outside. Hurry them. Go!"

"But you —" The woman reached for Daja. "You must lead!"

Daja shook her head. "I've got to hold the fire. Get them moving!"

She shoved the woman toward the rest. The servant hesitated, then ran to her fellows, yelling. When they balked she thrust them and the children around them through the open door, harrying them like an overworked sheepdog.

Daja slung the infant she carried on her back, draped a final wet sheet over her as a cloak, then stood at the center of the main nursery as the others left. She faced the wall between her and the main house, listening to her power. The topmost part of it was weak. There wasn't enough to keep the third floor blaze from its hungry advance. She retracted her power there before the fire ate it. A moment after she did so, she heard the third floor shutters overhead smash open under the fire's pressure. Now the roof on that part of the building would burn. On the other side of the wall before her the huge blaze pressed her barrier, leaning on her. She felt her power forced back, inch by inch, until the wall started to smoke. Tiny gray threads worked through cracks in the plaster.

She had kept back some of her strength in case she needed it. That time was now. Daja fell deep into her power and freed it of all boundaries. She dragged her shield to her side of the wall and filled it with everything she had, on that floor and the ground floor. If she held the blaze on the other side of her barrier, the women and children had a chance to reach the outside door below.

Some would die. The air was very hot: water-soaked blankets and sheets would dry fast. As protection against suffocation they were half-measures at best. All she could do was pray to the Bookkeeper that their accounts weren't due. Her task was to pit her strength against that of a blaze that was dining well on a wooden house rich with paints and oils, whipped to white heat by a hard wind streaming off miles of icy lake. She needed her friends for this; she needed Tris, who could help her shove the fire into the icy canals and the cold water death of the Syth. She needed Sandry to weave the blaze into a net that would imprison it. All she had was herself. It would have to do.

The fire roared, a massive tide of heat and destruction. It wanted her to know it was no tame forge fire.

"And you're no forest fire," she informed it, her teeth chattering with fear. "I handled one of those that would make you yelp like a puppy." She did not admit that her friends had lent her their strength, that Sandry managed one woven strip, and Frostpine another. This fire didn't have to know that.

Frostpine — was he all right? Was he putting his will against this thing in the servants' dormitory?

Her barrier wavered: she couldn't think about Frostpine. *NO*, she thought grimly, leaning forward against the blaze's force as she might lean into a high wind. *NO*.

It pressed. Her skin felt taut, as if she were a cooking sausage about to pop. The fire stuck a finger through one gap in the wall, then another, widening them. Daja backed toward the door. She would have to give the fire the nursery to keep it from breaking through in the hall and on the ground floor. She couldn't hold this room, not now.

She eased through the door, still fighting to hold the barrier upstairs and down. Her magic was burning to feed her shield, burning, and running out of fuel.

The barrier on the ground floor swayed. Daja released the nursery barrier and slammed its power into the ground floor protections. The nursery wall splintered as unobstructed flames blasted through.

In the hall, behind her last upstairs barrier, smoke poured around the edges of the double doors that opened into the main house. Their hinges and latches glowed a dull cherry red. Daja retreated from them, one hand on the wall. It was hot. That would be the fire on the roof. She refused to look up. If it broke through over her head, there was nothing she could do.

She found a door-chimney pouring smoke: the stair. She backed into it, then reclaimed her last piece of magic on this story, freeing the blaze. The double doors exploded off their hinges. A column of flame spat down the hall she'd just abandoned. Daja turned, blinded by smoke, descended three steps, and tripped over something soft. She seized the rail, dragging it loose from two sets of bolts to stop her fall and save the quiet child on her back. Her ground floor barrier wavered. Gasping, Daja clung to the rail until her fingers cramped, fighting the blaze's surge against her power. She thrust, scraping all she could from the wellspring of her magic, that had once seemed so deep. Sweating, she jammed hungry flames back, past the limits she had set for them. Only then did she open her eyes, take a hand from the rail, and shake the woman she had fallen over. It was the brave maidservant, the two infants wriggling against her in their slings. Her Yorgiry figure gleamed against her sooty throat. She coughed without opening her eyes.

Daja's ears rang; she trembled from head to toe. Her knees wobbled until she finally sat next to the young woman.

Her choices were bad. She could move, or she could hold her barrier. If she lost the barrier, there would be no place to move to: the big fire would roar up the stairwell like a tidal wave. She clung to her barrier, coughing. Perhaps this was a dream. All would be well if she had a proper, *dreamless* sleep.

She might have closed her eyes then and there, but for the flames' defiance. They thrashed against her grip, fighting her. They were being bad. This blaze had to remember *she* was in control here, not it. Fire could not just run where it liked, she knew that much. And so she gripped it with fading strength, with a smith's iron will.

"Just hold that barrier, sweetheart," a familiar voice croaked in her ear. "I'll do the rest. Don't falter, or there'll be roast mage on Alakut tonight." One powerful brown arm passed around Daja's waist and raised her until she could stand. Frostpine leaned her against the wall. "Stay," he commanded.

He dragged the unconscious maid to her feet. Cursing as he found the babies in their slings, Frostpine moved them until he could drape the woman and her burden over one shoulder. He slipped his free arm around Daja's waist. She knew enough to sling her arm over his shoulders, gripping the maid's clothes with that hand.

"Hang on," Frostpine ordered. Daja heard and obeyed, though nearly all of her attention was now in her battle with the fire. It was very hungry. It sensed wood and flesh beyond her barrier and demanded them in a voice that thundered in her skull. She barely noticed as Frostpine half-dragged her down the rest of the stair, along a smoke-filled hall and outside. They stumbled into the cold. Instantly both mages began to hack smoke from their lungs as the stuff they were supposed to breathe fought its way into soot-filled chests.

Coughing broke Daja's hold on the fire. Frostpine knew

the moment it ripped free. "Move!" he shouted hoarsely as others ran in to grab the maid and the infants. "Move, move, move!" His grip on Daja still firm, he slammed into the others from behind, knocking them out of the direct path to the open door.

A column of fire, blasting with pent-up strength, roared through the opening and out over the snow. If Frostpine hadn't knocked everyone to the side, they would be dead.

Ben and others ran in to help, taking everyone back to the gate. There they turned. The extensions to the house were burning. Smoke rolled from beneath shuttered windows. A moment later the shutters blew off; gouts of fire reached for the open sky.

Frostpine and Daja sat heavily on cold and slushy ground. Ben lifted the baby's sling from Daja's back. With its weight removed, she could lie down. The cold, wet stuff under her felt wonderful on her hot skin. *All* of her hot skin. She opened a smoke-teared eye and looked down. She could see brown arms, a brown side, brown legs. She giggled. Sandry had never expected that Daja might wear her best clothes into a fire, so she hadn't protected them.

Daja glanced at Frostpine. He sat, knees drawn up, resting his head on them. Like her he was naked, his clothes burned off.

"Frostpine?" she whispered, her voice cracking.

For answer he let the arm nearest her fall, until his hand lay over one of hers. *Don't you* ever *scare me like that again,* he told her through their magic. *Especially not for crazy people who build fancy houses all of wood.*

She knew what he meant, but that wasn't what *she* needed to say. *I want to go home,* she told him. Her eyes hurt; she wanted to cry, but she was so dried out she couldn't produce tears. *To Summersea. To our family.*

On the first caravan out of here in the spring, he promised.

She slept, or passed out, and woke in her bed in Bancanor House. It was dark; a pair of lamps burned at a table near the bed where Matazi and Nia sat. Matazi worked on a tapestry frame as Nia read softly to her mother.

"Cedar is for the protection of the home," the girl said, "to ward against lightning or the entry of evil from without. It —"

"Babies?" Daja croaked, and coughed. Matazi came to help her to sit. Jory, who Daja hadn't seen on a stool beside the fire, poured something into a clay cup and brought it over. Nia stood at the foot of the bed, wide-eyed.

Daja sipped from Jory's cup. Onion and garlic exploded in her mouth and Daja began to cough in earnest, hacking and fighting for breath. A clump of some dreadful mess blew from her chest into her mouth.

Matazi put a bowl under Daja's chin. "Spit," she ordered.

Daja spat. Three mouthfuls later, she could breathe without pain. "Your first spell?" she asked Jory.

The girl nodded. "Olennika told me to make her a copy, after I used it on Frostpine," she said. "Only it's not all mine. It was in a family book of cures that Aunt Morrachane gave me. I have to tell her how good it works."

Daja nodded. "Thanks, I think," she told Jory, onion and garlic still burning her tongue and throat. To Matazi she said, "The babies? The maid Frostpine brought out with . . . ?" Her voice trailed off as she read the answer in the woman's dark eyes.

Matazi sat beside Daja in a drift of jasmine scent. "They saved the babies the girl carried," she told Daja gently. "But she died in the courtyard."

"And the baby I had?" Daja whispered. She felt tears rise; her mouth trembled. She wouldn't cry in front of them, she refused to cry.

Matazi shook her head.

"It would've lived if I sent it with someone else," Daja whispered. Tears overflowed for all her refusal to shed them. "I had to stay, to — to hold —" She couldn't bear it. Couldn't bear the thought of that baby suffocating on her back, couldn't bear the thought of that brave maid, who had saved all those children only to die herself. Daja turned facedown into her pillow, and cried herself to sleep.

When she woke again, she saw that she still had company: Frostpine and Nia meditated in a protective circle on the floor. Daja blinked, her eyes stinging in the brilliance of Frostpine's power. Beyond him she saw that Nia's magic was now a steady silver glaze on her skin, still and unmoving.

Quietly she turned onto her side, away from them. The events of Sunday night returned in all their fear and sorrow. Her own natural clearheadedness came with it. Yes, she ought to have sent the baby with someone else: who would that have been? Every adult had at least two other children in charge, and the handicap of water-soaked covers to manage. If she hadn't held the fire, slowing her own escape to do so, it would have broken through on the ground floor and killed everyone inside, including the two babies who had lived while the woman who carried them began to die on the stair.

What had started this disaster — a kitchen fire? Overturned candles, a popping log on a hearth? The gods were cruel, to make such a tragedy from a stupid accident.

Real or set? asked that very determined part of her mind.

Daja bit her lip. She wished the others were here — Sandry, Tris, Briar. She didn't have them, but she did have Frostpine. She could have lost him: they put themselves in danger when they agreed to enter the house. Their magics wouldn't have prevented their being crushed by falling timbers.

The clock chimed downstairs; Nia's eyes popped open. A moment later Frostpine emerged from his trance. "Very good," he told Nia. "You've come a long way." He rubbed out part of the circle. The protections around them collapsed and flowed into his body like a plume of smoke returning to its chimney. He helped Nia to stand, then dragged himself to his feet, using the bed as a crutch. He was stiff.

"You're awake!" Nia said happily to Daja. "Hungry, too, yes?"

Daja sat up. "Starved," she admitted.

"I'll tell Anyussa," Nia said, but for a moment she didn't move, looking at Daja with huge brown eyes. "I could never do what you two did," she said. "Walk into a burning house . . . I couldn't."

"You don't know what you can do till you're tested," Frostpine said. He leaned down and kissed Nia's forehead. "Wait until you are, before you judge yourself."

Nia glanced up at Frostpine and gave him a tiny smile, then left the room, shaking her head.

Frostpine leaned back, hands on hips, stretching. Daja looked at him, worried. His skin was ashy over the brown; his few wrinkles seemed deeper. Did he have more white hairs now, or was it just that she hadn't noticed how many he had before this? "Are you all right?" she asked.

"Better than when they fetched us back here," he admitted. He threw several chunks of wood on the fire and poked up the embers so they would catch. "I had it easier," he said. "Mine were adults. Once I got their attention, they did as they were told. I lost two," he admitted, his full lips pinched. "Old people, stuck in beds. The others would have left them. You don't see people at their best, times like this."

Remembering the women who appeared to stop thinking at all when faced with peril, Daja nodded. "You tried to get them out?" she asked softly.

He went to her wardrobe, opened it, and began to take out clothes. "Smoke got them," he said. "I think they died as I carried them out. Everybody always worries about burns, not smoke. Usually they're dead before they know they're in danger."

Daja looked at the clothes he laid out for her. "I can't put those on till I wash," she pointed out. Someone — Matazi and the girls, she hoped — had cleaned the worst grime from her skin while she slept, since her nightshirt wasn't too dirty, but she smelled of fire, and there was ash in her hair. "I need the steam room." East Namorn lived for its huge, steamy bathhouses. Normally Daja hated the things, preferring nice, clean baths, but right now she felt grime in her pores. Steam would scour it out.

"I'll help you to the steam room after you've eaten," he promised.

"How many died?" she heard herself inquire. She shouldn't ask — she knew she didn't want an answer — but she had to know.

"Twelve," said Frostpine in a dull voice. "Seven dead

right away. Five after, including people who fought the fire. Three more — no one's sure if they'll make it. It could have been worse. They were having a children's party and a supper party, with all kinds of extra servants. Fifty in the house. Olaksan Jossaryk is dead. He saved his wife and supper guests first. The last he was seen, he was on his way to the nursery wing."

"The whole town is exclaiming over the coincidence," Heluda Salt announced from the open door. Anyussa and Jory, each carrying a loaded tray, filed in past her. They put the dishes on a small round table before the hearth. When they finished, Anyussa towed the obviously curious Jory out by the arm. Heluda closed the door behind them. "I see I visited at just the right time," the mage remarked coolly. "We must talk."

"I'm only wearing a nightshirt," Daja said in apology.

"Oh, of course you should wash and dress and put off eating to save me the sight of you in a nightgown," retorted Heluda, amused. "Don't be ridiculous. Once you've helped your daughter give birth to your first grandson, believe me, things like proper dinner wear aren't important."

Daja threw off her covers and stood with a lurch. If anything, she was stiffer than Frostpine. He helped her to one of the fireside chairs. Daja's stomach growled as she saw fresh bread, ham, stewed spinach, and custard. It wasn't Trader cooking or Trader spices, but it smelled just as good right now. "Excuse me," she said. Grabbing a spoon, she got to work on a pork soup with pearl barley and sour cream.

"What coincidence is the town exclaiming over?" Frostpine asked as he poured tea for each of them. He and Heluda took chairs across from Daja.

"Sunday, Bennat Ladradun told the Alakut Island council that the confectioner's shop fire proved he needed more money and more people to train in firefighting. The council said all it proved was that he'd trained those people he had poorly."

Daja looked her question over a mouthful of barley; Frostpine asked it for her. "Yes, but what's the coincidence? There are fires all over the city in winter."

"Yes, but this was Jossaryk House." The magistrate's mage looked from Frostpine to Daja. "I keep forgetting you aren't local," Heluda said wryly. "Chiora Jossaryk is Romachko Skuretty's mistress."

Frostpine and Daja traded baffled looks.

Heluda shook her head. "Romachko Skuretty is the head of Alakut council. The one that turned Ladradun down."

Frostpine grimaced. "I could happily spend the rest of my life without such coincidences."

Daja nodded, inspected her bowl. It was empty, but there were bits of meat and barley and sauce. She tore apart a rye-and-wheat roll and mopped up the rest.

"What of our counterfeiter?" Frostpine asked. "I'm able to go out."

Heluda shook her head. "Our people are sitting on every brass supplier, with spectacles magicked to see through illusion," she told him. "Sooner or later our friend, or his people, will come for supplies. Once we track them home, we'll need you. We may not be equal to a truly powerful illusion-mage who tampers with coins, but my trackers can follow quarry through blizzards. We're fine for now." She drummed her fingers on her chair for a moment before she said abruptly. "I'm here on another matter, actually."

She got up, paced to the door and back, then stopped, frowned, and went to Daja's worktable, where the iron glove forms stood upright. "What in Vrohain's name are *these*?" She leaned in to inspect the forms, then took something from her pocket and screwed it into her right eye. It was a lens spelled for magical vision: Daja could see gleaming silver runes on its rim. "It's been made with magic, but these aren't magical in and of themselves. Are you building an artificial man?" She wriggled one of the hinged fingers.

Daja had started on a plate of *pirozhi* stuffed with salmon and sturgeon. She gulped a mouthful, drank some tea, and said, "They'll be gloves, covered with metal that isn't much affected by fire." She absently rubbed the brass mitt over her left hand. "For Ben Ladradun. I thought it would be good to make him gloves so he can push open burning doors and the like. I *thought* I'd make a whole suit for him, but I need to think about that a while."

Heluda put her eyepiece back into her pocket. "You craft-mages have the oddest ideas," she remarked, shaking her head.

Frostpine cleared his throat. "You said you came about something else. I'm going to expire of curiosity." He picked up one of Daja's rolls, ripped it in half, and buttered a piece.

Heluda walked back to her chair and flopped into it. "Jossaryk House. My people laid the inspection spells as soon as the remnants cooled. The fire wasn't accidental. It was set," she told them.

Daja's fork slipped from suddenly cold fingers, clattering on her plate.

Frostpine sighed. "Have you suspects?"

"Only at least three for each servant and ten for each guest," replied the magistrate's mage. "There's always that many people who wish someone ill, and they all must be questioned. Tracking the firesetter by his traces was a waste of time," she growled. "Whoever did it burned all he used, so what we did find, the fire scoured clean. What's maddening? No one saw him, but he must have done it while guests were arriving for those parties. Look." Clearing a space on the tablecloth, Heluda sketched the ground floor of the house with a fingertip, her magic turning the lines to inklike streaks. "The front of the house, that looks over the cliff? In winter it's closed — it takes the brunt of the wind off the Syth. The servants store whole carcasses — pig, cow, sheep — in it, it's that cold. In summer, of course, it's lovely. Our firesetter broke in there. He walks up the cliff road, which no one uses for the same reason the house's front is closed off — he may as well have been invisible."

"Could you track him on the cliff road?" Frostpine wanted to know.

"He had two pairs of boots," said Heluda. "Our trackers followed one pair down to a fire the hired sleigh men use to keep warm on the Kadasep side of Alakut. None of them saw anyone throw cloth boots into their fire, of course. Then he walked away in clean boots." She grimaced and passed her hand over the drawing. It vanished. "Curse him, rot his teeth, may he drop through thin ice," she growled. "He laid a fuse to a good-sized fire, lit it, and left. By the time anyone knew the front of the house was burning, it was too late to stop it. The winds were like oil on the flames." She looked at Daja. "If you or *Ravvot* Ladradun have any ideas about this *naliz,* let me know. As soon as we've bagged our counterfeiter, this one's mine."

"I don't know what ideas I could have," Daja said. "Ben's the one who's studied all this."

"But you're a mage, and in his company. You —"

Someone rapped on the door and opened it without waiting. It was a housemaid; behind her was a man in magistrate's colors. "*Viymese* Salt, we've got a possibility," he said breathless. "Bought twenty sheets of brass. We tracked him."

Frostpine levered himself out of his seat as Heluda stood. She frowned at him. "Are you up to this?" she demanded. "You look half dead."

"Magistrate's mages, so pessimistic," Frostpine replied, walking to the door. "I prefer to think I am half alive. *And* I know the marks of his power. You need me." Looking at Daja he said, "Rest."

Daja nodded. "Bundle up," she replied, thinking the *kaq* who mucked with money would discover he was no match for Frostpine.

She dragged on a robe, gathered her clean clothes, and doddered down the servants' stairs to the steam room. Once she washed and rebraided her many braids, she slept again. She woke to the clock's chime at midnight and got up, feeling stronger. Someone had cleared the fireplace table of the remains of her supper. Downstairs she went to raid the kitchen. The urge to go out caught her as she piled strawberry preserves on bread. Still eating, she went to the slush room and pulled on her winter clothes. Once that was done, she picked up a torch and her skates, and went outside.

She didn't need a torch: several burned around the basin, though they would be out soon. Daja buckled on her skates, then began to exercise doggedly. She kept one eye on the ice, alert in case her tired muscles decided to give way. Instead, the skating seemed to help both her muscles and her spirits. She speeded up, gliding this way and that across the basin. The icy night air was calm, with no breath of the wicked Syth in it. It was clean and unburdened with soot, ashes, smoke, or smells. It brushed her face like a blessing — a bitterly cold blessing, but a blessing all the same.

12

Despite her skating session, Daja woke at her usual hour, feeling better physically, though sad yet. She had dreamed about the maid, clutching her figure of Yorgiry as she died.

Once dressed, her Trader staff and the staff she used to train with Jory in hand, Daja went upstairs to the schoolroom. To her surprise and pleasure, Jory was there practicing her forms. It had to be boring, but from what Daja glimpsed before Jory noticed her and stopped, Jory had made progress. Her staff movement and hand and feet placement matched the marks Daja had made for them perfectly.

"We're ready for the next step," Daja announced, leaning her staves against the wall. She stepped into an open space and positioned Jory there, then traced the outlines of her feet with a piece of charcoal. That done, she used her Trader staff to draw a protective circle around them both, and raised her barriers to enclose them. She was looking forward to this, she realized. Her protections weren't as strong as usual — Daja hadn't recovered from her efforts at Jossaryk House — but they would hold any power Jory might throw off.

"Stand here," Daja told her. "Eyes forward, your staff in the middle block position. I'll walk around you; now and then I'll strike. Keep your eyes straight ahead. No looking at me, no turning your head, until you actually have to move to block me. Block *only*. No strikes."

"I don't understand," Jory replied. "If I can't follow you —"

"You have to be ready," Daja said. "Open your senses, magic and all. Act only when you must. If you start thinking your foot itches, or your hair needs to be washed, if you want your breakfast, I'll hit you."

"You're going to hurt me?" Jory asked, horrified.

Daja sighed. "Now there's a silly question. No, but I *will* tap you. You have to know you were wrong."

"What if you hit my back?" Jory wanted to know. "I can't stop you then!"

"Trust I won't do it till you're good enough to anticipate it. Now take the position." Daja paced in front of Jory as old Skyfire did with his students. "Stop following me with your eyes. Look straight ahead. Wait. Listen. Relax. Your hands aren't in the right position. Stop winking; I haven't hit you yet. Twitching your eyes won't protect your face."

Jory instantly threw up a high block, expecting a strike

from Daja's remark about her face. Daja tapped Jory's ribs. "Don't listen to what I say," she told her student again, pacing once more. "Forget the cold, or breakfast, or —" Daja shifted her body. Jory's head whipped around; she blocked low, and Daja tapped her skull. "Don't try to outthink me," ordered Daja. "Maybe you can one day, but not today. I'm in my center, in my empty space, and I go where I like." Another high strike. Jory's block glanced off Daja's staff: she was a breath too late. Daja thumped her head lightly.

For an hour Daja walked her staff up and down Jory's body, talking or silent, always in motion. At first it seemed as if she had overestimated Jory as the girl got angry, then sulky, then stubborn. Each time she lost her temper Daja saw Jory's magic flare away from her in spikes. Once, angry, she struck at Daja's head. Daja disarmed Jory, sending her staff flying against the barrier. It bounced back, nearly hitting the girl.

Daja nudged the staff with hers. "Pick it up," she ordered.

"You're not human," Jory grumbled as she obeyed.

"More silliness. Come on, let's go," Daja urged. They began again.

When the house clock chimed, Daja, in the right-hand corner of the younger girl's vision, snapped a middle strike at Jory's ribs. Jory's power swirled and soaked into her skin as she blocked Daja squarely.

Jory's jaw dropped. She looked at the staff, and at Daja.

246

"I did it!" she gasped. "I did it! I — I felt it, it was like, being *everything*."

"Good," Daja said, wiping out part of the circle with her boot and retrieving her power. "But we won't know if you *really* have something until you can do it all the time, not just once."

Oh, *Daja*," moaned Jory, "you sound just like my parents." She ran from the schoolroom.

"Well, there's no reason to insult me," muttered Daja, half offended.

After a hearty breakfast, she returned upstairs to do the physical work of fitting the living metal to the gloves, making sure it was anchored to an iron rod as well as the other pieces. There was just one more thing to do after that, but it had to wait. Simple tasks like protective circles for the twins were easy enough, and she needed no magic to fix the living metal onto the forms. For anything bigger, her magic felt weak and floppy, as her arms might after she lifted something far too heavy for her.

She collected her Trader staff and went down to midday when the bell rang, but she didn't return to her room when she finished. She had things to do that involved no magic, but she wanted to skate. Staff in hand, Daja headed for the slush room. As she passed the servants, they bowed and got out of her way — they'd done so at breakfast too. Obviously they had heard tales from Jossaryk House.

They'll get over it, Daja thought as she donned coat and scarves, picked up her staff, and slung her skates over her shoulder. A few quiet weeks and they'll treat me like a human being again. If only she could hope there would be no more excitement for a few weeks!

Outside, she donned her skates. Gathering her courage, she skated out of the basin, under the bridge, and onto Prospect Canal, balancing the staff in her hands. The canal was as busy as any street with skaters and the large, heavy sleighs that carried supplies, pulled by horses shod for ice walking. Passenger sleighs kept to the dirt streets, owners not liking the expense of ice shoes and the risk to their horses if they were not specially shod.

It was snowing lightly as Daja skated north along Prospect, keeping well to the side. Daredevils raced down the middle of the canals. So did robbers and pickpockets: those good skaters looked to winter as their bounty season. Daja didn't think she could move in the fast traffic in the center. She envied the speeders and liked to watch how they did it, half crouched, skates flashing, swerving around bumpy or uneven areas in the ice. She envied them, but she wasn't about to copy them. Sometimes she had to use her Trader staff to keep herself upright.

Still, she had improved. She negotiated the turn into Mite Canal with no accidents, and slid to a halt at the hired sleigh stands a quarter of a mile north of Pozkit Bridge. Her skates hung over her shoulder, staff in hand, she climbed up to the street. Hollyskyt Way met Jossaryk Place, the road Daja and Frostpine had followed across Alakut on their way to the fire. The sleigh stand was probably the one where the firesetter left one pair of boots to burn.

She knew where she was going now, and she didn't turn back. She had changed in the smoke, and the fear, and the dark. The change wasn't to her magic. It would recover with meditation and rest, more quickly than her spirit would. If she was to make sense of that night and those deaths, if she was ever going to understand the kind of person who would sentence fifty people to death by burning, she ought to see the final result for herself.

Daja walked down Hollyskyt until she found the rising street that followed the edge of the cliff. The sign read FORTRESS VIEW ROAD. It showed little signs of winter use. Daja huddled deeper inside her coat and scarves — she would rather brave the Syth's wind than tap her ability to warm herself for now — and hiked up the steep road.

No blast of lake wind caught her as she walked. The air was cold and still. "Oh, now you're as nice as a kitten," she told it as she toiled upward. "Back when it would have saved lives, you blew your worst."

Her mother always said it wasn't polite to mock other people's gods, and Sythuthan was a notorious trickster. He was not likely to appreciate being scolded. Daja shut up.

Wall after wall showed her blank faces as she passed the

homes of the wealthy. As she approached the summit, Daja found the damage left by fire and the people who fought it. The road was churned and frozen into peaks and dips that made the footing tricky. Once more she used her staff to brace herself. Soot marked the walls of Jossaryk's neighbors. Then she reached Jossaryk House itself. The gate stood open. The wall was intact: the wind had blown so hard that the fire never turned this way. Daja took a breath, resettled her grip on her staff, and walked through the gate.

She had expected to see part of the house — foolish, given the fury of the blaze and the wind. Instead she found no house, its cellars exposed, everything a blackened mess. No wall stood higher than a foot. The ruin stretched before her, complete all the way out to the courtyard where she and Frostpine had collapsed.

How did mages like Heluda do it? How could they tell where this had started, where the evil took root? Daja was a mage, and she couldn't tell. Looking hard, she noticed that the largest section of wall remaining was the front. It was that hard wind, which had thrust the fire into the rest of the house before it had completely devoured the front wall. Against the base of that fragment she saw a huge, old-fashioned hourglass, its brass parts melted to globs, the sand within turned to blackened glass from the heat. Ten yards to her left she saw three whole burned cow skeletons — the staff really did keep meat here in the winter.

Walking around the outer rim of the house filled her with awe for the power of fire. All that remained were parts of things: charred clothes embedded in frozen mud, melted jewelry, a set of false teeth in enamel over metal, more animal bones. The dead were gone by now.

At last she reached the rear wall and its empty gate. Firefighters had removed the wooden doors from their hinges to give easy passage to the street. There Daja turned to stare at the black ruin, leaning on her Trader staff.

In Sandry's last letter, she had written Daja that she'd been forced to kill three murderers before they escaped a trap set for them and killed again. Reading, Daja had thought she could never do such a thing. Now, as she looked at Jossaryk House, she wasn't so sure. Could she kill the one who had done this? Who was she to say what punishment was right? Anyone who used fire this way must be mad beyond question, mad and pitiful. Even if his madness came to evil, he shouldn't be killed for something he couldn't help, only locked up forever.

Another part of her disagreed. What if he escaped his keepers and set more fires? More people would die. And why did she think he was mad? Madmen didn't burn anything mages could use to track them. Madmen wet themselves and talked to the air. They claimed to be gods and rocked in corners. They didn't come and go unnoticed. They didn't watch what they'd done.

That was a new idea, one she didn't like. *Did* he watch? How could he?

And yet, if she had taken such care on a project, wouldn't she want to see it through?

That was evil. It was evil of the worst kind. Such evil would show on his face. The mages would find him. There was no way he could escape capture. Then he would get the traditional penalty for firesetters: burning. His evil would be cleansed. Probably right now the magistrate's mages spoke to people who had seen someone so empty of good it had frightened them.

With that thought to comfort her, Daja hiked back down to Mite Canal. She hoped she would see this firesetter before they burned him, so she would know pure evil if she saw it again.

On the canal she skated faster than she had before, staff tucked into the crook of one arm, trying to leave the bad thoughts in her wake. She drew closer to the canal's center: slower skaters on the edge eyed her nervously as she passed. She almost came to grief, swooping around the rim of Kadasep into Prospect Canal, but quick shoves of her staff against the ice kept her away from those making the same turn. As Bancanor House drew closer on her right, she saw a familiar person skating toward her. Daja couldn't see her face at this distance, but she knew Nia's bright hat and scarves as well as she knew her own. Daja raised two fingers to her lips and blew the earsplitting whistle that Briar had spent an afternoon teaching her, then slid past Bancanor House to meet her waving student. Other skaters grimaced or made rude comments that Daja ignored.

Nia was giggling as Daja reached her. "I see *you're* feeling better," she commented as Daja turned and skated with her. "Only please, don't let Jory hear you do that, or she'll want to learn, too."

Daja shuddered. "Give me credit for some sense." She grimaced: her thighs were aching after a long skating session and her climb to Jossaryk House.

"You've gotten so good at this!" Nia exclaimed as they glided into the boat basin.

"I had a good teacher," Daja said. "Speaking of that, how go your studies? I saw you were reading about wood magic the other night."

Nia beamed at Daja. "Isn't it fascinating? Arnen gave it to me. He assigns me pages to memorize at home and I recite back to him first thing in the morning. That way I work on the physical part at the shop during the day and do book learning at home."

"So you like him," Daja remarked, pleased. It seemed her conversation with Arnen at the Mages' Society gathering had borne fruit.

"He's really clever, once you can get him to talk. If it's just the two of us, he chatters like Jory, but bring in someone else, and he barely speaks." Nia shook her head, smiling. "At first I thought he was a snob," she admitted. "But he's just shy. And I'm learning a lot from him."

They meditated, changed clothes, and met the family at supper. Afterward Daja joined them in the book room, accepting Kol's challenge to a game of chess. As they played, the twins lay on their bellies, Jory in front of the hearth, Nia behind her. Their lips moved as they memorized information from small, leather-bound mage books. Matazi worked at needlepoint. One of the family's dogs lay stretched out between the twins, while the largest of the household cats draped herself across Daja's feet.

The quiet shattered as Frostpine swept in, carrying a drift of outdoor cold with him. He went immediately to one of the big chairs beside the hearth and fell into it. Jory scrambled to her feet and left the room.

Frostpine glanced at the fire: the logs, which had been crackling peacefully, roared into active flame. Daja set three more chunks of wood on the blaze. As she brushed off her hands, she looked at her teacher and raised her eyebrows.

"Done," he replied to her silent question. "Arrested, the whole pack enjoying the governor's hospitality. They don't have heat in the cells, either. Though I doubt they'll be there long enough to really suffer. The governor wants this ended."

"Now that it's done, will you let us know what's kept you

out until all hours?" Matazi asked, choosing a fresh length of scarlet silk for her work. "Or is it still secret?"

"Check and mate," Kol told Daja. She grinned and shook her head. She had a long way to go before she mastered chess.

"I'll tell you later," Frostpine said with a nod at the twins. "For now, you may rejoice that I am among you again."

Daja rolled her eyes. "If you're going to be saucy, I'm going upstairs," she told her teacher. She relented enough to kiss his cheek. "Congratulations," she whispered. "Good work for an old man."

She was preparing the washes she would need to set the gloves on the iron forms when one of the maids knocked on her door. "Excuse me, *Viymese* Daja, but *Ravvot* Ladradun is here and asks if he might see you. He says he knows he is late — he just came from his business — but asks if you would grant him the courtesy."

Daja corked the bottle she was about to empty into a bowl. "That's fine. Show him up, please."

"*Viymese!*" the maid cried, shocked. "A man, in your bedroom? The impropriety!"

Daja raised her brows and waited for the woman to remember she was not exactly a Kugisko maiden. Mages weren't held to the rules of merchant propriety, even young ones. Tris had once remarked crossly that people thought mages had the morals of cats.

The maid looked down. "*Viymese*, forgive me," she said. "I'll bring *Ravvot* Ladradun right away."

Daja picked up a few things and moved her tools around, though it wasn't necessary. She always kept her room neat. She also lit more candles. As she put down the taper she'd used to light them, the maid showed Ben in.

"Shall I bring tea, *Ravvot?*" she asked him. "Cider, pastry?"

"Nothing, thank you," Ben replied. "I won't stay long."

The maid curtsied and left the room, leaving the door open an inch. Daja noticed; her mouth twitched with a smile. It seemed the Bancanor servants meant to look out for her reputation even if she didn't. Her amusement faded when she looked at Ben — he seemed weary. Part of that was fire and candlelight. They cast his face in sharp relief, making its lines deeper, his expression harder.

"I'm sorry I didn't come earlier," he confessed without looking at her. "I wanted to make sure you were all right before this, but the fire wasn't out till dawn on Moonsday. I was helping with the victims until almost noon on Starsday. Someone did tell me you and your teacher were fine." He looked at her with concern. "You are, aren't you?"

"Yes, of course we are," Daja said hurriedly, in the grip of a sudden wild thought. "Ben, who hates you this much?"

He looked at her, his face oddly still. "Why do you say that?"

Daja sat on her workstool to work the idea out aloud.

"You told me you saw it on your way home. I bet if you'd gone home you could have watched it from your upstairs windows. I *have* to think maybe these fires are being set to hurt you. To, I don't know, destroy your name in the city, to make people think your firefighting ideas don't work. Maybe even to drag you into danger."

"Daja, that's a tremendous leap of logic," he murmured. He sat in one of her fireside chairs.

"I'm not so sure. Well, I'm a mage, and they teach us not to believe in coincidences, you see. You've met this person, that's my guess. Can you recall meeting someone who just seemed evil to you? Someone who made your skin crawl? Some you crossed?"

"*Evil?*" he asked.

"Only an evil person would harm others to get at someone else," Daja said flatly.

Ben ran his fingers through his thinning curls. "You honestly believe there are people who are either good or evil?" he asked. "How old are you?"

"Fourteen," she said, frowning. "What has my age to do with this?"

Ben shook his head. "This is the second time I've heard you talk like a young person. Usually I forget you aren't my age. People aren't that simple, Daja."

"Of course he's evil," she said, impatient with typical adult shillyshallying. "Look at what he does. Or maybe it's a she —" She stopped, abruptly. Morrachane? His own *mother?* Teraud's wife had said she whipped her servants . . . no. Morrachane Ladradun would never do something that would mean crawling into houses or walking icy, wind-swept clifftop roads.

So involved was she in thinking, then discarding, the possibility, that she had missed the start of what Ben said now. "— someone tired of being ignored, tired of others trampling on him. Perhaps some rich person treated him with contempt. At least, with Jossaryk House, people will know he *did* something that no one will forget. He would be less, less evil and more — besieged."

Daja stared at him. "It sounds like you're on his side."

"I'm exhausted, Daja, I can't think straight." Ben smiled ruefully. "Mother insisted I work late on the books to make up for my time at the fire. As if numbers are more impor-tant than lives . . . I'll consider what you've said. I certainly have enemies, people who don't want to hear what I tell them, but I doubt very much that any of them would kill innocents." He got up and walked over to her worktable, where the living metal gloves stood on their iron bases. In the flickering candle- and firelight they seemed to move.

"They need more work. Try them on if you like," Daja suggested.

Ben picked one up, weighing it in his hand. "Do I roll up my sleeves?"

Daja shook her head, the beaded ends of her many braids slapping her cheeks lightly. "They're made so you can yank them on in a hurry. They'll be a little big even now, because I made allowance for your coat."

Ben slid on first one glove, then the other.

"I need a few more days to finish," Daja admitted as she watched Ben adjust the fit. "My control over my magic's still weak, after Jossaryk House."

"Was it hard, walking in there?" Ben wanted to know. He turned his hands back and forth, fascinated by the play of light on their mirrored surfaces.

"Fire walking, no," Daja said, eyeing the gloves. The metal's edges had blended seamlessly, so it looked as if she had simply poured it over the forms. "But holding it back, with the wind driving it? That took all I had. Actually, I didn't think I had that much." And it wasn't enough, she thought, her eyes stinging at the memory of the baby who had died on her back.

"Why hold it?" Ben opened and closed each glove hand. "Why not just tell it to stop? To go out?"

"That works with tiny fires, not big ones." She grimaced as she saw the outline of hinges when he made a fist. She had to fix that. The gloves worked, but as a craftswoman she wanted them to look like cloth, and the bulge of iron hinges ruined it. "As long as there was fuel, that fire wanted it. The wind gave it strength. The more it ate and the harder the wind blew, the stronger it got. I wish I *could* have sent it somewhere else or put it out, but I couldn't."

Ben picked up one of the hearth pokers, then one of

Daja's rods. The gloves grasped the thin rod as easily as the heavy poker. Daja watched as he twisted his hands to and fro. Hinging the wrists had been the most difficult part. They had turned out well.

"Doing a whole suit will be hard," she said with regret. "It'll need an iron scaffolding, almost, with hinges and ball and socket joints. It'll be heavy. I'll need all winter to grow enough living metal, and there's iron and brass to buy. And I haven't worked out how you'll see and breathe yet."

He stood in front of the hearth fire, moving his arms inside the gloves. Now he looked at her sidelong. "Are you giving up on me, Daja?"

She frowned, half distracted by planning. "Of course not! I'm just saying it's going to take lots of work."

"People do give up on me," he said quietly, looking at the gloves. "At first they think I'm fine. They admire how hard I work, how I try to teach others, prevent as much harm as I can. . . . But then they say I don't know how to enjoy myself, that I don't spend enough time with people. Then it's I'm obsessed, and they're busy. They find other, easier companions." He slid off a glove and angled it so the light of a branch of candles illuminated the inside. He peered at it. "It wouldn't surprise me if you decided this thing was just too much effort."

His words confused her. What was he talking about? She had meant only to explain the project would take months, not weeks: he *needed* that suit. Ben seemed to mean something else, something that made her uncomfortable, though she couldn't say why. "No. I just don't think you should look for results until spring." Daja sat again on her workstool. "Did Heluda Salt talk to you? About Jossaryk House."

About to put down the glove he held, Ben fumbled and nearly dropped it. He put it on the table and held the second glove up to the light. His hands were shaking.

"They won't break if you drop them," Daja pointed out. "They're up to a lot of work. They won't be of use to you otherwise."

"They're just so lovely it's hard to think of them as strong," Ben replied. He continued his inspection. "You talked with Heluda Salt?"

"She and Frostpine were working on something." She wasn't sure if she could tell him more than that, even if the counterfeiters were captured. "And I met her at the Mages' Society party. She hadn't seen the report about the board-inghouse fire, the one you told the mages was set. Did you tell them? I couldn't remember if you had or if you hadn't gotten a chance."

"I pity this firesetter," Ben said, smiling at Daja. "If Heluda Salt takes an interest, he should hang himself now, or he'll surely burn later."

"Is she good?" Daja asked.

"She's one of the best in the whole empire," Ben told her. "Certificate and advanced certificate from the university at Lightsbridge, crown honors by the basketload — *I'm impressed.*" Reluctantly he put the second glove on the table. "When will these be ready?"

"I should be done by Firesday." Daja looked Ben over, making rough estimates of his height, shoulder breadth, waist, legs, and arms. "Should I bring them to your warehouse Sunday afternoon?"

"Actually, Watersday is better. Come to the house in the afternoon, around one," Ben suggested.

Daja murmured, "Watersday is fine." She grabbed a slate and began to write down numbers. Only the major weight-bearing struts of the iron form need be heavy. Perhaps she needn't use thin iron rods to support the metal at all, but wire cables or even chain mesh . . .

"I'd best go," she heard Ben say.

She nodded absently. "The maid will let you out." She glanced at his head. If she hung the weight from his shoulders, she might create a helm that was also a long sack, a cloaklike bag filled with air. That would solve the breathing problem, if only for short periods. What about living metal coated over a fine mesh? There was still the vision problem to settle, but the suit appeared to be emerging from a tangle of half thoughts and problems.

"You won't let me down, will you, Daja?" he asked.

She smiled quickly at him, still lost in her plans. He would understand her liking for him was true when she created his suit. He just didn't know that mages above all understood what it was like to be obsessed. She was as fixed on her magic — most of the people she cared about were as fixed on their magic — as he was on fire. "I try not to let my friends down," she told him.

When she thought to look up from her notes again, he was gone. She didn't remember that he hadn't said if he'd talked to the magistrate's mages.

I3

Over the next two days Daja continued her staff classes with Jory, who began to grasp the idea of waiting emptiness that would open the door to her power. When breakfast was over Daja continued work on her gift jewelry and on her plans for the living metal suit. As the days ended she would go for a nice, long skate to air out her mind.

The first day she timed her return to meet Nia under Everall Bridge as the younger girl came home from Master Camoc's. The next day she reached Bancanor House as Morrachane dropped Nia off. It seemed that she had "just happened" to be driving past Camoc's as Nia left for the day.

"I feel so sorry for her," Nia confided as she and Daja climbed the stairs to the schoolroom. They stood aside as the two youngest Bancanors, free to play outside after their lessons, raced by yelling at the tops of their lungs. Their harassed nursemaid followed, murmuring apologies as she tried to catch her charges.

When the older girls could hear again, Nia continued,

"She misses her grandchildren. She never sees the families of her other two sons, and . . ."

"She blames Ben," Daja said drily, nodding to the young Bancanors' tutor as he left the schoolroom.

"I wish she wouldn't," Nia admitted, and sighed. "She's so dreadful to him and her servants at the same time she's good to Jory and me."

"That's what Jory says," Daja told her as she closed the schoolroom door. "Now, let's begin."

They settled to their meditation. Nia reached the next step, pulling all of her magic into a small object — she had chosen a pine knot — as Daja had once fitted her power into the striking head of one of her favorite hammers. Supper followed, then an evening in the book room with the Bancanors and Frostpine.

On Firesday Daja left the book room early. Her grip on her power was strong at last. It was time to finish the gloves. She mixed two washes, each blended from different herbs, powders, and oils, then thinned with boiling water. One she applied inside the gloves, the other outside. After that was done, she hung them out the window overnight. In the morning, after her session with Jory, Daja brought the gloves in. A final polish inside and out with a soft cloth, and her creations were finished.

Watersday morning dragged: she wanted to go to Ladradun House. She wanted to see Ben's face when he tried the gloves. The Bancanors and Frostpine went to temple; Daja worshipped at her personal Trader shrine. For the first time in years other thoughts distracted her during prayers for her family and ancestors. She loved it when she created something people could use, not simply admire. This was the first time she had made something that might save lives. She wanted Ben to have it before the next fire broke out.

Midday came and went. Daja finally set out for Ladradun House.

Ben opened the door so quickly after she rang the bell that she had to think he'd been waiting for her to arrive just as impatiently as she had waited for the hour set for her visit. Any odd feelings she'd had after their last, strange conversation evaporated as she noted his blazing indigo eyes and eager face. "Daja, you came! Come in, come in!"

She obeyed with a grin, smelling fresh beeswax, lemon oil, and wool, the smells of a well-kept Namornese house. Ben disposed of her coat, hat, and scarf while she carefully wiped her boots on the coarse mat. She didn't want Morrachane to get annoyed with her son because his guests left tracks on her perfect floors.

"Mother's at a meeting — these merchants have to do some business every day, I think," he told Daja as he led her to his study. A pot of tea and a plate of cakes waited on his desk. He poured the tea out like a good host, but his hands trembled; he was that eager to try the gloves. Daja took them from the satchel and offered them to him.

He slid them onto his arms without a word, opened his small stove and thrust one gloved hand inside, scooping up coals. He dumped them, grabbed a second handful, and squeezed. The coals broke apart in his metal-clad fingers.

"And . . . ?" Daja asked.

He looked up at her, the stove's heat turning his cheeks a feverish crimson. "I may as well be holding sand, or salt. How hot a fire could they withstand?" He withdrew one arm and dug in the fiery coals with the other, stirring them with a gleaming finger, shoving them together in a pile.

"Well, the living metal came about in a forest fire. I suppose maybe if the governor's palace was to burn, they might get warm."

Ben snorted. "Governor's palace? He builds in stone, like the rest of the nobility. He's no fool. I've been trying to convince Mother to rebuild in stone. She says wood is good enough for her neighbors, it's good enough for us." He shut the stove. "I know I'm being rude, but . . . would you mind if I tried these in the kitchen hearth? It's a bigger fire. You can stay here — I won't be long." He didn't even wait for Daja's answer, but left the study at a trot.

Daja smiled, shook her head, and tried one of the cookies — they were very good. So was the tea. She hoped that Ben hadn't dipped into Morrachane's finest supplies. Though the woman did her best to be polite to someone who was Jory's and Nia's friend, she always made Daja feel as if she must have cheated somehow to get her medallion.

Daja had the feeling Morrachane wouldn't like knowing Ben had given her the best tea and cakes.

Bored after a few minutes' wait with no sign of him, she got up to look around the room. A touch of the stove told her it wasn't as badly made as the one in his warehouse office. His books interested her for a moment, as did his pen-and-ink drawings and knickknacks. She tried to keep her attention on those things, but time stretched. They weren't very interesting. Daja found herself standing before the shelves half hidden in the shadows behind his desk. There was the skeleton hand with its molten gold ring. Looking at it, Daja felt the hair stand on the back of her neck. What if it had come from Ben's dead wife?

She shook her head. Where had such a gruesome imagining come from? That was more the kind of nonsensical thing Sandry or Tris might think. There would be something *very* wrong with Ben for him to keep his dead wife's hand. The only thing that was wrong with him was that he lived with his dreadful mother, a mistake any widower could make. That didn't make him bad or cracked enough to keep a piece of his dead wife on a shelf.

She had stared at the hand too long. She forced her eyes to other things: the partly melted soldier, the glass lump, pieces he said he saved from fires he had beaten. Her nostrils twitched: the odor of smoke was stronger than it had been the first time she had seen these shelves.

Her eyes moved higher through the collection. The upper shelves were empty, except . . . Daja blinked. She had thought the shelf on a level with her own face was empty last time. Yet here were three objects. One looked like a half-burned corner piece from a Namornese outer door, carved with good luck signs. One was a scorched glass bowl; its contents smelled like burned sugar. The last was a blackened female figure with a loop on the back, as if it were a pendant. Silver gleamed through cracked gilt. Daja stared at it, memory stirring at the back of her mind like that gleam of silver. She had seen that figure around someone's neck.

Goosebumps prowled her arms and her spine. Was she falling ill? The stench of smoke was thick around this shelf. It made her stomach lurch. That alone was proof that she might be ill, because smoke never made her queasy.

She backed away from the shelves and smashed her thigh into one of the sharp corners on Ben's desk. Daja yelped and bent over, grabbing the hurt muscle, all other thoughts banished in that white-hot burst of pain. I hit it on exactly the wrong place, she thought, exasperated, as her head cleared.

Ben strode back in and grabbed Daja in a hug that lifted her off her feet. "They're incredible!" he cried, putting her down at last. He still wore the gloves. "I've never seen anything like them. No wonder they gave you the medallion at fourteen!"

She wanted to correct him, to say she'd actually been

thirteen, but it wasn't important. His delight in her creation was important. "I'm glad you like them."

Ben grabbed her face, the metal gloves flesh-warm against her skin. Enthusiastically he kissed her first on one cheek, then the other, before he let her go. "Is a whole suit really so much trouble?" he asked.

Any reluctance she felt about the suit evaporated. He did so much for others: she could do this for him. "I started my calculations," she reassured him. "I have the air problem solved, at least for short periods. There's still how you'll see, but we have all winter to thrash that out. If you'll come by Bancanor House on your way home a couple of nights next week, I'll take all the measurements I need."

"Yes, of course I'll come. I never thought I'd be grateful for our long winters," Ben said with a grin. "Now tell me, how did you do all this? Please, I'd love to know."

They were still talking an hour later when the front door slammed. Morrachane had returned. Daja managed to leave without talking to the woman beyond the usual polite exchanges. Once outside, she heaved a sigh of relief. Ben was a good man, maybe a great one, but she didn't like being near him and Morrachane at the same time. Something wasn't right there. She wished she could talk to Ben about his mother. It was strange to think that even though she felt they were friends, she didn't feel able to discuss Morrachane with him. It ran contrary to her last four years, spent with friends she could and did say anything to. It made her feel sad and lonely.

Nia would be home by now. Daja hurried her steps. Maybe they could go skating.

Now that Jory could block most of Daja's strikes without watching her, they began the work of controlling her power. Jory envisioned a jar like those in which spices were stored, trying to draw her power into it as Daja circled her. Each time she tapped Jory gently with the staff, the younger girl was distracted and lost control of her magic. She was cross enough to growl and stamp on the floor when the house clock chimed.

"Calm down," Daja ordered, shaking her gently by one thin shoulder. "You thought you'd never know when I was about to hit you either." Remembering her talk with Ben, she added, "We've got all winter."

Jory sighed as Daja opened their protective circle. "Olennika says you must be a wonderful teacher, because I'm learning really well," she said.

Warmth crept into Daja's cheeks. She had developed a hearty respect for Jory's teacher that one night in the great kitchen. "She did?"

"I'm glad you two think I'm doing well." Jory grumbled, leaning her staff against the wall. "*I* don't notice anything different."

"That's why you're the student, and we're the teachers," Daja said in her loftiest tone.

"And *I* thought full mages were so wonderful they didn't need to tease their students," Jory retorted with a sniff.

"Tell that to Frostpine," Daja suggested. "He's been teasing me for years."

"It's just that Nia does so well," Jory said. "I *see* her getting better. She's turning into a lamp that glows all the time, only I don't think anyone notices."

"Only those who see magic can," Daja pointed out. "You're not used to her getting ahead of you?"

"I didn't say it was a *nice* way for me to feel," grumbled Jory.

Memory suddenly kicked Daja. In their second year at Winding Circle, the four of them had taken classes in anatomy under Water temple healers. Time after time she had watched Tris and Briar answer questions: they always knew the answers. Sandry hadn't cared about being second best, but Daja had.

"Don't worry about how well Nia does," she told Jory more kindly. "You picked a kind of meditation that's more complicated. I don't know if I would have made as much progress in the same time you have, if I hadn't learned the easier way first."

Jory only shrugged, her mouth set in an unhappy line.

Daja scrambled for something to brighten the younger girl's spirits, and found it. "Would you like to try an attack-defense combination for staff fighting? I think we have time."

Jory's eyes lit. "Not magic?"

Daja grinned. "Just combat."

Jory grabbed the staff she'd put aside.

After breakfast Daja returned to Teraud's shop and lost herself in plain work with no issues of magic to distract her. It was relaxing not to have to think of anything but iron as she heated and hammered. When they stopped for midday her muscles were pleasantly warm, well exercised and tingling. Over the meal everyone wanted to know about the Jossaryk House fire. Daja told them as much as she could without going into the grim details. When the journeymen tried to press her, Teraud changed the subject. He caught Daja's grateful look and winked.

Once the journeymen and apprentices had left the table, Teraud leaned back in his chair and fixed Daja with his deep-set eyes. "I hear dat fire was set."

She looked down. She wasn't sure if she ought to speak of that to anyone other than Heluda or Ben.

"Two killer fires on Alakut, after months of no fires bigger dan my forge, except Ladradun's warehouse." Teraud shook his head. "So either the firesprites came back from holidays, or we got a firebug. I ain't never seen no firesprites. I seen a firebug, though. Boy twelve years old, couldn't stop, whatever they done to him. Dey finally burned him after he did a fire killed five people."

Daja shuddered. When she was nine, she had seen a firesetter burned alive. She'd had nightmares for weeks. She couldn't think of a worse death.

"I'll pray the gods dat lawkeepers catch dis one soon," Teraud said, getting to his feet with a sigh. "Nothin' scarier than a firebug. Nothin'."

"I'll pray, too," Daja assured him.

Daja skated home. She was too late to meet Nia: the skies were dark, the lamplighters busy at their work, and shadows lay over the canal ice. Daja stumbled three times on uneven spots, but managed not to fall each time. She was proud of herself as she glided into the basin at Bancanor House. Like Jory and Nia, she had come a good way in a short time.

Frostpine was in Anyussa's kitchen, basking in front of the large hearth as he idly made links of steel wire for mail. Nia sat across from him, dutifully carving buttons.

"Would you mind if I came?" Frostpine asked when Nia stood to follow Daja. "I won't be in the way."

Daja put her hands on her hips. "I could have used your help when I started this," she pointed out, perturbed. Did he want to take over Nia's teaching? Had he seen things Daja had done wrong? If he wanted to take over, shouldn't she be glad that an experienced mage wanted to step in?

Stop that, replied her sensible self. If he thought you

had done badly, he would have mentioned it the night you saw him meditate with her.

"No, you couldn't have used my help earlier," Frostpine said coolly. "When you four were given medallions, it meant you had permission to fumble your way to a teaching style, just as the rest of us did. It was also understood that you knew enough about magic to do so successfully. Most who wear it never have their teachers close enough to oversee when they find their first students, you know."

"That seems careless," Daja informed him.

"Magic so often is," Frostpine reminded her.

Daja sighed. He had to be telling the truth about teaching — he never lied to her. "The schoolroom's cold," she pointed out.

"No, it isn't," Anyussa said. She was basting a roast. "I sent a footman up to build the fire when *Ravvikki* Nia came home."

Daja shook her head at the grinning Frostpine. "Come on if you're coming, then," she said, letting Nia lead the way.

Once their protections were set, Daja and Nia returned to their work as Nia tucked her magic into her pine knot. Frostpine slipped into his own power, keeping it in the small, tight ball it normally occupied inside his chest. His attention was turned inward: he'd simply wanted to meditate. Daja, relieved, concentrated on Nia. Tonight only a double handful of tendrils escaped the younger girl; she pulled each back quickly, her face serene. Daja enjoyed Nia's quiet and Frostpine's solidity so much that she jumped when the clock struck.

"Beautiful," Frostpine said once Nia had gone. "You've brought her along well. You have a knack for teaching."

Daja felt warmth in her cheeks that had nothing to do with the hearth fire. "You really think so?" she asked shyly.

He hugged her with one arm as they went downstairs. "You're patient and steady," he said. "Nia feels your confidence in her. It gives her confidence in herself."

"And Jory?" Daja asked, uncertain. "Did you want to look in on that?"

Frostpine shook his head, his mane and beard flopping. "Too early, too cold, and that girl is much too wide awake at that hour. Besides, old Skyfire knew what he was doing when he taught you fighting meditation."

They had finished supper and gone into the book room when a maid came to say *Ravvot* Ladradun had come to call on *Viymese* Daja. Once more Daja took Ben up to her room; once again Ben refused tea or anything to eat.

"Were you working late?" Daja asked as she began to measure his upper arms, shoulders, neck, head, and waist with a cord.

Ben nodded. "Mother wants an inventory of every fur before Longnight taxes are levied. We haven't gotten the last shipment yet, but she still wants me to start the count."

Between measuring and writing measurements down, Daja sneaked looks at his face. He was pale and sweaty. "Can't we offer you something to eat?" she asked.

Ben shook his head. "My mother keeps supper for me. If I don't eat everything, she says I'm wasting food."

Daja felt rage boil in her belly. "Does she ever have anything *good* to say of you?" she cried. Then she covered her mouth. Only when she was sure of her hold on her temper did she take her hand from her lips. "I'm sorry. I had no right to say that. I apologize."

For a long moment he was silent. Finally he murmured, "It's a strange friendship we have, isn't it?"

Daja stared at him, not sure what he meant. It was an odd thing to say, when *she* thought their friendship was almost like the ones she had with Briar, Tris, and Sandry.

Ben patted her shoulder. "I'd better go. Shall I come tomorrow? Or the next day. I have brigade training tomorrow morning and afternoon. She'll make me stay till midnight to make up the work. The day after tomorrow, then." He hesitated, then asked, "Do you know if the magistrate's mages have anyone they suspect of the Jossaryk fire?"

Daja shook her head. "Do you?"

"No. They questioned me, but I've heard nothing. I would tell you if I had," Ben assured her. "Well, that's the magistrate's people for you — all eager to get information, and entirely mysterious about what they do with it."

He left Daja unsettled and uneasy, though she couldn't

say why. It's not for you to question his life, she told herself as she put away her measuring cord. You can't ask a hero to live like an ordinary man, to rebel against a cold mother or to marry and have a family again.

But he was her friend; he'd said as much himself, in a peculiar way. In Daja's world friends wanted their friends to be happy, and Daja knew Ben wasn't.

He does so much for others, she thought, lighting a stick of incense at her small Trader shrine. Surely he's owed something for all he's paid out.

Moonsday was like Starsday, except that Ben didn't visit. Daja went to bed with the household, though it seemed as if she tossed and turned for hours before she finally slept.

She was in partial darkness. Around her danced the ghosts of flames, pale orange against shadows. The reek of burning wood, hair, and flesh filled her nose. Something clicked and rattled in the dark, coming closer.

Daja struggled, but she couldn't move. The thing that rattled crawled up her body and onto her face. It was a skeleton hand, the metal ring on one finger ice-cold on her nose.

Daja sat up with a gasp. Braids that had dropped across her face as she slept fell away. She grabbed them. Here was a gold piece that she had missed when she removed the decorations from her hair before bed. With a shaky chuckle at her foolishness, she took it off, and put it on her bedside table.

Now she was afraid to sleep. Instead she went to a window and opened the shutters to the icy night. A full moon shone over snow-draped roofs. On the city streets the lamps were pale rivals to the moonlight. Daja hoisted herself onto the broad sill — Namornese walls were thick — and wrapped her arms around her knees. Things were clearer up here in the cold. The fire of emotions always distorted what she saw. In the freezing air she could see without the heat of affection or admiration to blur her thoughts, making them unclear.

She thought about Ben's collection of tokens. He brought them away from fires where he'd done good, he'd said, or that was the sense of it. Unless she was mistaken, though, his recent additions were from fires he could only stop from spreading: the boardinghouse, the confectioner's shop, and Jossaryk House. In his shoes, she would be happy never to be reminded of those fires. Were she Ben Ladradun, the boardinghouse and Jossaryk fires would look like personal failures. The confectioner's shop, when his raw firefighters had done so poorly, would be maddening.

Teraud was uncomfortable with Ben's crusade against fire. Teraud she knew as well as any piece of iron she had ever worked. He was true in every fiber, not a spot of rust on him, and Teraud didn't like what Ben did. Surely Teraud saw that Ben was Kugisko's best defense against what he'd called a firebug.

What did Heluda Salt think of Ben? The magistrate's mage had impressed Daja. How did she see Kugisko's firefighter? What did Frostpine make of Ben? Maybe she ought to find out. Something was not right here. She didn't know what it was, but she could feel it like a faulty weld.

Perhaps I misunderstood, she thought as she closed the shutters. Maybe he chooses a token when he's learned something from a fire. That has to be it. He's a good man, a real hero. I shouldn't let nightmares make me crazy — and perhaps I'd better leave the *pirozhi* with jam and fruit alone too. Rich desserts probably had more to do with the nightmare than anything else.

On Starsday, Ben came to the house well after supper. Daja escorted him up to her room and began the rest of her measurements for his waist, hips, legs, ankles, and feet.

"I won't see you for a while — two weeks at least," he said as she measured and wrote down numbers. "The last fur shipment of the year comes in through Izmolka. Mother has asked that I meet it and escort it back."

Daja stared at him, surprised. "You travel in *winter?*" she asked. "But you could be caught in a storm at any moment."

Ben smiled. "It's not as bad as you think. The empire keeps wayhouses every twenty miles along the merchants' roads — it's never far to shelter. And we always work like this. The best time to trade furs is late autumn and early winter, when the pelts are at their finest."

Daja shook her head as she continued to measure. "Move your legs a bit apart?" she asked. "I don't mean to be rude, but I need thigh measurements."

"Always the last moment you want your old teacher walking in," Frostpine said. Daja jumped at the unexpected sound of his voice, and very nearly measured Ben in an area that would have shocked them both. "We never really got properly introduced at Jossaryk House," Frostpine continued as he came over to them. "I'm Frostpine, and you are the Kugisko miracle worker."

"No miracle worker," Ben said glumly as he clasped Frostpine's hand. "Jossaryk House was a disaster from start to finish. It's a miracle we saved any, mostly due to you and Daja."

"Ah, but it was your organization that saved the other houses and kept the victims from dying of exposure." Frostpine leaned against Daja's worktable.

"Have the magistrates turned up any information about who set the fire?" Ben asked. "I know Heluda Salt is a friend of yours."

"If they have, they're keeping it to themselves," Frostpine answered. "They just asked what I saw. I hear you studied with Pawel Godsforge. We've been corresponding for years. What's he like in person?"

Daja continued to measure, listening to the men talk

about Godsforge. She was glad that Frostpine had come to give Ben a proper adult conversation — she got the feeling Ben rarely talked to people for sheer enjoyment — but she was also concerned. Why had Frostpine come here, tonight? He could have visited Ben at the warehouse, or invited him for tea.

While Frostpine was the most easygoing of the Winding Circle teachers, he made sure that he met any new person in Daja's life. Once a Fire temple novice had begun to meet Daja accidentally on her way home from the forge. After a few weeks of meetings he had persuaded her to walk through private areas of the temple city, where he stole a few kisses. What might have come after that Daja didn't know. The kisses were interesting, but she didn't like it when the novice's hands strayed to her body. She was still trying to decide what to do on the day that they turned down a side path and ran into Frostpine. He asked for an introduction. Then he asked other things as the three of them strolled through the gardens: what the boy studied, where his family came from, if he meant to take vows, how long had he been at Winding Circle, who his friends were.

Daja never saw the novice again except in the training yards or the dining hall. She knew that something had passed between him and Frostpine as they talked, but she had never figured out what. She didn't get quite the same feeling as Frostpine talked with Ben now, but she still didn't know why he was there.

Measuring Ben, she noticed worrisome things. He trembled slightly. It was almost invisible, but as she wrapped her measuring cord around his body she felt it. When she touched one of his hands, it was clammy. He had a faint sour odor, as if he hadn't bathed in a couple of days. The lines around his mouth were deeper than ever. That might be the angle from which she looked at him and the flickering light. He looked like a man who was being hounded by a *yerui*, a hungry ghost — or more likely, a man who was being worked to death. Why did Morrachane drive him so?

"I told Daja I'm off to Izmolka to pick up a fur shipment," Ben explained as Daja measured his feet. "The weather-mages claim we'll only get light snows during that time, but of course you have to treat their predictions with caution."

"Weather's nearly impossible to predict for longer than a few days," Frostpine agreed, though he and Daja knew a weather-mage whose predictions for the next month were always right. "I assume you carry storm-warning charms though."

"Nothing but the best for Ladradun," Ben replied. "Good for half a day's notice of storms. I don't know how Mother can let them out of her sight, they were so expensive, but she always makes me carry them for the last caravan of the year."

Because she doesn't want to lose her precious furs, Daja

thought grumpily as she gathered her cord, slate, and chalk, and got to her feet.

"All done?" Ben asked.

"Just one more thing," Daja promised. She got on a stool and measured the height and width of his eye sockets, from one temple to the other. "In case I work out how you'll be able to see," she explained as she stepped down. His eyes were bloodshot, his skin putty-colored. Like his hands, his face was clammy.

"I look forward to this construction," Frostpine admitted. "Daja, you should write a paper for the Mages' Society when you're done — they love details of unusual workings. Lightsbridge and Winding Circle will want copies, too."

Daja snorted. She didn't need to impress mages she didn't know.

"You won't help her?" asked Ben, surprised. "I assumed . . . As you say, the work is unusual. She ran into trouble with those gloves."

Daja ducked her head, wanting to protest, They came out all right in the end! She was surprised that Ben had made a typical adult mistake, thinking she couldn't manage without an older person's aid. She thought he knew her better.

"Oh, she miscalculated, but that's to be expected," Frostpine replied. "She's the only mage in the world who has this living metal. It means she has to invent magic for it as she goes. I can advise, but the only kind of assistant she needs is one to hold things steady while she works."

Daja flapped a hand at him, grateful for and embarrassed by the praise.

"Besides," added Frostpine, "Heluda says she'll want my help in a few other matters for the magistrate's court this winter. She seems to think I'll turn magistrate's mage at my stage of life. I just hope that between us we'll catch the fellow who's setting these fires."

"You'll do us great service if you can," Ben replied. He looked at Daja. "I must go. I'll call on you when I'm back." He kissed her, right cheek, left cheek. "I'll see myself out." To Frostpine he said, "It was an honor."

"A pleasure for me," Frostpine replied. "I like meeting Daja's friends. She encounters the most interesting people."

Once he had gone, Frostpine picked up an iron glove form, turning it over in his hands. "Your friend doesn't look well."

"No, he doesn't," Daja agreed. "Between fires, and training, and that mother of his, I don't know when he sleeps."

"Kol's heard a rumor, put about by Ladradun's mother, that you're looking for a rich husband, and Ben is your mark." Daja gasped with indignation. Frostpine raised a hand to stop her protest. "I know you, don't forget. So do Kol and Matazi. But there *are* men who involve themselves with young girls, girls younger than you, I'm ashamed to say. And merchant families often marry daughters to men Ben's age and older, because they can afford a wife and family. I had wondered if Ladradun might be looking at you."

Daja stared at Frostpine. Then the humor of it struck her. "Me and Ben?" she asked, amused. "Never mind that he's old —"

"Early thirties is not old!" protested Frostpine.

"Old, and a widower, and — really, Frostpine!" She chuckled.

Frostpine grinned. "All right, I knew I was wrong almost right off, but I had to make sure. You're wise for your age, but you aren't experienced in what goes on between men and women."

"While *you* have too much experience," Daja pointed out. "*One* of us has to be restrained." He'd managed to make her feel weepy: he was looking out for her like a father or a brother.

"*I've* heard no complaints about my conduct," Frostpine informed her wickedly. More seriously he added, "When I find someone to share my bed, I try to ensure that no one gets hurt or lied to. It's another kind of friendship, though not what I'd recommend to someone just beginning to find out what love is."

Daja grabbed a fistful of his beard and tugged gently. "Since I'm not starting that sort of thing, particularly with Ben, you can relax, oh watchful teacher."

Frostpine stretched, like the panther she sometimes

imagined he was. "I don't think he's interested in your body or your heart. But . . ." He combed his fingers through his beard. "Daja, something's not right there," he said at last. There was concern in his dark eyes. "I don't know what it is, but it worries me."

"I think so too, sometimes," Daja admitted. "But he's complicated, Frostpine, and his mother — Bookkeeper, don't log this against me, but I think his mother is a monster. And more than half cracked, if she's talking that way about me and him."

Frostpine hugged Daja to his side. "Maybe it's just as well he's going away for a while. Come down to the kitchen. Anyussa wants victims for some pastry experiments."

Wearing the gloves to help him think, he arrived at something that would be not a lesson but a test, and chose Airgi Island for it. When he'd presented his plans for fire-fighter training, their council decided that he asked too much in funds, people to train, and training time. When his demands were more reasonable, they told Ben, they would be happy to hear him again. They sounded like his mother. Airgi Island had to learn that lessons were always far more expensive than was preparation for the future. Their council had to learn that it was folly to turn Bennat Ladradun and his hard-earned expertise from their doors.

He left home an hour and a half before sunrise and walked to Threadneedle Canal, where he donned his skates. A hard wind cut into those parts of his face not covered by scarves. To avoid it he kept to the walls of first Threadneedle, then Kunsel Canal. He held a lantern on a pole just ahead of him to light his way. A sense for pebbly ice let him skate without accident. The gloves, slung on his back in a bag, would do him no good if he fell, cracked his head, and froze to death. Airgi Island wouldn't learn this necessary lesson.

At least the wind kept lawkeepers and watchmen in their shelters. The crews who leveled canals and moved snow were still locked up for the night. No one saw him glide between islands.

He'd wanted to do this on Watersday, as soon as she'd left him with the gloves. It had taken iron control to keep from rushing straight out to try them. He had to be careful. He wanted to set any fire, without planning, just to watch the sheep scramble and bleat for their lives. That would never do. The gloves meant he had to plan *more* carefully, not less. Cloth, hair, even skin couldn't be tracked by mages if they burned, but magic left traces. The more powerful the magic, the better chance that a trace would remain. Any surface he touched with the gloves must be completely destroyed by the fire.

He'd waited and planned for four, nearly five, mortal days, though he'd thought he would explode with impatience. The trip to Izmolka gave him a reason to be away. He arranged to meet his escort at the Suroth Gate the hour after dawn. If he timed what he did exactly, everyone would believe he was on the road when his newest creation unfolded. It meant he couldn't watch, but no plan was perfect.

In Izmolka, perhaps, he could experiment with the gloves and fire before he came home.

The city's clocks struck the hour before dawn. He stopped at the second stair that led from Airgi to Kunsel Canal and unbuckled his skates. The staff at Asinding Bathhouse wouldn't stir until dawn: he had to be on the ice when they began their day. His prize would heat as they began to shovel wood onto the night's embers, building the fires to heat the huge pools over the furnaces. Once the fires were roaring, his gift would open, its clay outer layer shattered by heat, its thick leather wrappings drying until they burned. When they did, his surprise would explode. The merchant who had sold him five pounds of the new invention called "boom-dust" thought Ben was a farmer, looking for a quick way to clear stubborn tree stumps from his land. In a way Ben had not lied: this boom-dust would clear quite a large piece of land.

The lock on the door through which wood was carried to the cellar was easy to open. He had a set of master keys, granted to him by the governor's council when they'd agreed to let him start training programs. With them he could enter all public buildings — the bathhouses were run by the city, not the island, council.

Inside the cellar, he closed his lantern and put it down, then waited for his eyes to adjust. Gratings in the huge furnace released dull orange light, enough to see by. He found the main furnace door, two slabs of iron with thick iron handles. Attendants used heavy gloves and iron pry bars levered under the handles to drag the doors open. Even with the fire at its lowest the metal was hot enough to cook on. Ben didn't use the tools: they were nowhere in sight. The point in any case was to try out his gloves.

He took them from his sack and slid them on. They fit perfectly over his knitted gloves and the heavy sleeves of his coat. Gripping the iron handle that opened one furnace door, Ben pulled. He'd counted on his size and strength to make up for the lack of a pry bar. They did, though he needed both hands and wrenched a muscle in his back. Slowly the iron door, taller than he was, swung open.

A desert of embers lay in the furnace, heat rippling over them. Reaching into his sack, he brought out his device, a globe twice as big as his head. There was no need to make this one so it would take forever to burn, giving him hours to get clear. The furnace would hatch this egg for him soon. He kissed the dry clay surface and pitched the ball deep into the heart of the glowing embers. He tossed the sack and the lantern in after it.

Overhead a door slammed. Voices echoed against the tiled surfaces of the bathhouse proper. Ben thrust the open furnace door shut, hanging onto it desperately at the last until he eased it to. A slam would bring the sleepy attendants down here on the run.

He stuffed the metal gloves down the front of his coat and climbed out of the cellar. The attendants entered at the far side of the building — he had watched their morning routine for two weeks that fall. He doubted they would hear as he used the axe to smash the lock from the outside. If this entrance survived what was to come, the lawkeepers would think someone had broken in to sleep warm.

He ran to the canal and strapped on his skates, fingers trembling as he secured the buckles. The clay was getting harder and drier on the embers. The attendants would be on their way to the wood stores, to stoke the furnace to wakefulness. Time was running out; the eastern sky was showing red.

He lunged onto the ice. Three strokes and he went sprawling, the price of skating with his mind on other things. He took a breath and forced himself to stand carefully. He'd fallen beside a wood pile. Quickly he cut off his boot covers, pulled them out of his skate straps, balled them around his knitted gloves, and thrust them under a few logs. He always carried a vial of oil and flint and steel in his pockets: he poured the oil over the logs that concealed his clothes, then set it to burn. Then he kept his eyes on the ice and skated off slowly.

Near Joice Point he turned to watch the eastern sky. Those who liked to take steam before work would be lining up at the bathhouse doors. Some might already be inside. Ben sighed. It was hard to judge how long each device took to do its job. Black powder boom-dust was particularly unreliable, though effective when it finally worked.

He heard a muffled thump, then a booming roar. A geyser of water, fire, wood, and who knew what else blew into the sky. Ben's breath caught in his chest as oily black smoke and fountaining water soared above the buildings that stood between him and the bathhouse. It was beautiful. He shook with the need to go back. How much would be left? How many would be alive?

He bit his lower lip until it bled. His eyes stung; he was sweating ferociously. He must not do it. He had to follow his plan. He could not be seen here.

Somehow he forced himself to turn and skate on. He and his escort must be out of the city before word reached Suroth Gate of the disaster on Airgi Island.

On the day Ben left, Daja practiced combat meditation with Jory and puttered about after her bath, repairing jewelry for Matazi's friends and mulling over the living metal suit. She was inspecting a triple chain like a white gold waterfall when she heard loud voices below. Curious, she went to the servants' back stair, closest to the noise.

"All those old fur throws, and I mean *all*. Don't argue anymore, you put me out of patience." That was Matazi, sounding unusually crisp. "Tea, kettles. Yanna preserve us, I've never seen such a thing, never. Aloe balm, all we can spare. Don't stint. Muslin and linen for bandages. Make up beds in the cow loft and the storage rooms – we can take twenty people if they don't mind crowding. Half of Stifflace Street is in flames."

Daja pelted downstairs. Matazi stood in the hall to the

slush room, hands to her temples, as servants hurried to do her bidding. Maids bustled to and fro, building piles on either side of their mistress: the chest of medicines that Matazi kept for emergencies, cheap tin mugs, bowls, and tableware, and bottles of spirits used as stimulants and soothers in open crates. Footmen emerged from a storeroom with rolls of canvas used for shelters over their shoulders; a houseboy followed with a collection of long tent poles.

Daja looked at Matazi. "What happened?" she asked. "Can I help?"

Matazi's dark eyes were haunted. "I was visiting one of Kol's aunts. She lives on the other side of Kadasep. We were to go shopping. We . . ." Matazi's lips trembled. She put her hand over them, trying to compose herself. Maids arrived with more supplies; the footmen carried them outside. "We heard the fire bells, of course," Matazi said. "There's — there's a bathhouse on Airgi Island, a big one, where Stifflace Street and Barbzan Street come together. They said the furnace exploded — it's just a crater now. The whole block around it is burning."

Daja clenched her hands. She didn't want to do this again, but . . . surely it would be better than Jossaryk. And maybe she could send the fire somewhere — into what was left of the bathhouse, that might work.

"Daja? Are you all right?" asked Matazi.

Daja rested a hand on Matazi's shoulder. "If there's fire,

maybe I can help," she reminded her hostess. "Do we know where Frostpine is?"

"Right here." He came from the kitchen, tying his crimson habit over breeches and shirt. "Matazi, we need horses."

By the time Frostpine and Daja reached the fire zone, the blazes were contained inside the streets around the destroyed bathhouse. Most were out, having consumed every house near the center of the destruction. Rather than fight them, now that no one or nothing else could be saved, Daja and Frostpine let them alone. Instead they joined the volunteers who cared for the survivors and moved them as quickly as possible onto sleighs that carried them to hospitals or families who would take them in. Daja and Frostpine labored until mid-afternoon, when the last victims alive were taken away. Now the wagons for the dead arrived. The bodies had been placed in one street under pieces of canvas. The thought of loading them on wagons made Daja's eyes fill with tears. She tried not to look relieved when the lawkeepers ordered them home. They said others would finish up.

They didn't leave immediately. Instead they walked to the deep black gouge in the earth that was all that remained of the bathhouse.

"Shurri defend us," Frostpine whispered, taking the sight in. "Does this look familiar to you?"

Daja nodded. In her first summer at Winding Circle, pirates had attacked the temple city and neighboring Summersea. They brought with them a new, terrible weapon, a substance packed in baked clay balls and lit with fuses. Wherever the boomstones and the black powder they carried hit, they exploded. Their mark was a distinctive sunburst pattern in blackened ground and scorched wood.

"Maybe the furnace blew up, but it was helped along," Frostpine said grimly. "This wasn't an accident." He went to the nearest lawkeeper and spoke to her. As Daja waited for him, something caught her eye. A freak of the explosion had driven a triangle of glazed tile like an arrowhead into a chunk of wood: it was embedded there. She tried to pry it loose, until a thought intruded: Was she doing as Ben did, taking mementoes of a fire?

She released the tile as if it were a viper, wiping her fingers on her coat. Her skin crawled. How could Ben do that? How could he do it even after a fire where he'd saved lives and homes? It was like hoarding pieces of bad luck.

At least he's not here for this, she thought dully. It would break his heart.

Frostpine returned. "Let's go," he told Daja, wrapping an arm around her shoulders. "Someplace where fire isn't the enemy."

The next day, Firesday, Daja could not stay still: if she did, the image of rows of the covered dead haunted her. She couldn't even concentrate on the living metal suit. At last she decided to skate to Alakut Island to visit the fancy stores on Hollyskyt Way. She had forgotten the confectioner's shop, or the hole where it had stood, was there. Seeing the charred gap ruined her desire to look at other smiths' jewelry. Instead she skated to Bazniuz Island. There she wandered the open air markets on Sarah Street, buying her midday from dumpling and grilled meat carts, washing it down with cider. She bought notepaper to write letters on, then new quill pens to write with, and a packet of roasted chestnuts to eat while she wrote.

She even reached Everall Bridge in time to race Nia home: she lost. When Nia teased her as they glided into the boat basin, Daja replied loftily that Nia had taken unfair advantage of her, because she was laden down with parcels. She would have added more, but the sight of the refugee children housed by the Bancanors stopped her. They had gone still beside a snow fort they built near the alley. Daja looked at the packet of chestnuts, still warm in her hand, then offered it to them. One boy accepted it, never taking his eyes off her, then ran back to his friends. Daja and Nia removed their skates in silence. Once they'd left their outdoor gear in the slush room, they went upstairs to meditate.

After they finished, Daja went to her room. A maid found her there. "*Viymese*," she said, bobbing a curtsey, "*Viymese* Salt has come, and requests a moment of your time. She is in the front parlor."

"Doesn't she want Frostpine?" Daja asked, confused. "He's at Teraud's."

The girl shook her head. "*Viymese* Salt requested you."

Daja sighed and went downstairs. The front parlor was not a room for a big girl who was most comfortable in a smithy. The delicately carved and painted furnishings were cushioned in bright yellow and white striped silk; porcelain and crystal figures were on tables and shelves everywhere. The windows were paned in costly glass, and protected by gold and white brocade curtains.

Heluda Salt sat in one dainty chair, looking like a market woman in the empress's sitting room. Her gown was sensible black wool, old-fashioned, with long sleeves. A white blouse with a round collar rose above its neckline. The veil on her strawlike dyed blonde hair was solid, sensible wool like her gown, black, with a tiny white embroidered border. The tea glass in her soot-streaked hands looked simply ridiculous. At her side was a large leather bag that Daja supposed contained her mage kit. It looked just as out of place as Heluda did.

"Don't they use proper mugs around here?" she demanded of Daja.

Wary as she felt, Daja had to smile at that. "No more than they must," she told her guest. "It makes their teeth hurt, or something."

Heluda set her glass on the table next to her. "Daja, I

have news, and some questions. This concerns the explosion and fire on Airgi Island."

"I saw," Daja said grimly. "They told you Frostpine and I think they used boom-dust?"

"They did. I didn't get to the site until this morning — I was out past midnight over a double murder in Blackfly Bog," Heluda explained, and sighed. "Why the idiots didn't just pick up the husband right away . . . it's usually the husband, or the lover." She drummed her fingers on the arm of her chair. "Never mind. The thing is, I've had a chance to go over the area. Most traces of the crime — of the criminal — are destroyed in explosions and fires, of course. But some traces are too strong to be wiped clean by fire. I found traces of your magic."

Daja felt as if her spirit had stepped back to leave her body as a seated shell. Traces of *her* power? She and Frostpine hadn't even tried to stop the fires. All they had done was muscle work, not magic.

Heluda finished her tea and poured herself another glass. "Some of my colleagues wanted to look at you and Frostpine. The sheep-brains thought that since black powder comes from the south, and you two are from the south, and the most suspicious fires began after your arrival, well! The matter was solved. They were going to bring you in for questioning."

Daja wasn't that detached from her body: she felt her

skin creep. Not even law-abiding citizens heard the phrase "brought in for questioning" comfortably. Unless they had a mage skilled in interrogation spells — such mages were usually expensive to hire — lawkeepers used crude, painful means to question people.

"Don't worry. They'll be good little cow pats for now." Heluda smiled, a flinty look in her eyes. "They don't understand character as I do." She sipped her tea. "I want you to take a mage's look at something, though." She reached into her open bag with both hands and pulled out a heavy object wrapped in silk magically treated to protect its contents. Gently she put the object on the table between her and Daja and opened the silk to reveal a curved, twisted iron bar covered in soot.

Daja did not want to touch it. She already knew she wouldn't like what she learned. It was fire-blistered, its shape warped: everything about it made her twitch.

She looked up to find kindness in Heluda's eyes. "If I had another way to do this, I would," the woman told her quietly.

Daja lifted her right hand and held it over the iron. She was trembling. "Must I touch it?" she asked.

Heluda nodded.

Daja laid her plain hand on the iron bar. It was solid — no wonder Heluda had needed both hands to lift it. As she wrapped her fingers around it, Daja was slammed with feelings. She was the bar. Violent force rammed her from behind, blowing her off the vast iron shield she was welded to. Fire raced in her wake. She plunged into cold snow that hissed and shrank from her.

Biting her lower lip, Daja released the iron. Sometimes she felt a thing bearing down on her like a storm just over the horizon. She sensed that now. If she turned the full weight of her power on this piece, curved and twisted half around by an incredible burst of heat, her life would change. She could put it off. She could. She could be safe a day more, a month more. Sooner or later, the accounting demanded in this metal bar would come due and she would have to pay it, but she did not have to do that today.

"Are you done?" Heluda inquired.

Daja shook her head and set her right hand on it. Then she flexed her left hand, feeling the brass that coated it grip her flesh. She reached out, seeing the hand as a stranger might: bright golden metal, dark brown skin, trembling fingers. She laid her metal palm on the twisted bar, and clenched both hands around it.

She was inside the iron *and* on the inside of her own skin. Somehow her hands were bigger. They had strange bumps in the joints. No, they weren't hers, exactly. There was a man in her skin, a big man. He strained to pull the iron bar, his sweat oiling her skin from the inside.

Didn't he understand about the iron stick, the bent one

that men used to open the furnace door at her back? Why didn't he use that instead of hands? The crooked, heavy bar was a quicker, easier way to help her do her job.

He dragged, and dragged, and dragged, until she did as she was supposed to. She drew on the massive iron door that shielded her from the fire on the other side, pulling it until the shield moved, letting a wash of heat pass her. She felt the heat inside the furnace, steady and calm, as it always was during the coldest hours. The fire didn't fool her. She knew how quickly it could roar up when men tossed wood onto it.

The hands that were her and not her let go, leaving a taste of her brass skin on the iron handle.

Daja plunged into the furnace of her power, drawing strength to reach to that image of her brass hands. One of them held a large round thing. That hand tossed the round thing into the furnace. Then both brass hands gripped Daja-the-furnace-door-handle, pushing her and the iron door at her back slowly into place, between the fire and cold air. Daja's brass hands released her iron self and vanished.

As the iron handle, she didn't have long to wait until her people came to open the door at her back. They *never* grabbed her with their weak hands: she would have seared them to the bone. Instead they used the crooked pry bar to lever her and her door open.

They threw wood past her, into the heat, then began to

close the doors against the rapidly growing blaze. There was a *thwap* that made her entire world shudder. A very hard thrust knocked her clean off her door and twisted her around on herself. She blasted through a man's body. On she flew, into the open air and cold snow.

Heluda was talking as Daja pulled free of the iron. Daja barely heard. She tried to moisten her lips with her tongue, but it too was dry. She blindly felt for a tea glass.

"Let me," Heluda said. Picking up Daja's glass, she muttered in Namornese. She went to the door and flung it open to reveal the maid who sat there waiting for any request. "Get me some proper mugs, and a cloth soaked in cold water."

Daja heard those words as if they were spoken at a distance. Her face was numb. A chasm had opened in her belly; she swayed on its edge. In her mind she saw Ben as he knelt before his stove, sifting embers in a gloved hand. She saw a black bone hand with a gold ring, and a half-melted figure of a local goddess. "Not —" she croaked.

"Hush," ordered Heluda. "I don't want anyone to overhear." When the maid returned with a tray, the magistrate's mage took it. "Back to the kitchen," she ordered. "Don't come within a week of this room, understand?"

Heluda closed the door and set the tray on a table. With a hand movement she threw a magical barrier over the door. Then she took the wet, folded cloth and laid it across the back of Daja's neck. The coolness made Daja shudder, and straighten. She had been sitting folded over, as if kicked in the stomach.

Heluda poured tea into both mugs. "Here." She thrust Daja's mug into her hands and folded the girl's fingers around it. "It's not sweetened."

Daja sipped carefully. Hot and strong, the tea burned its way down to that chasm in her belly. She took another sip, then a third, and a fourth. At last she put the mug down and shifted the cloth on her neck, holding the ends against the pulse points under her ears. Like the tea it helped to clear her head, but neither cloth nor tea stopped the quiver of her lips or the sting in her eyes.

"I don't understand," she told the woman. "It — it's iron, and metal can't lie to me, but — it makes no sense."

"I saw the gloves here," Heluda explained. "You smith-mages, you'd no more start a fire to destroy than you would beat a dog to make him vicious. Either I am well past my game and I never spotted you as a danger, or something you made left the mark of your magic on the furnace door. If that piece hadn't blown clear, we might never have picked up the trace of your power. Of your gloves, used by the person you made them for."

"No," Daja said woodenly. She refused to believe it.

"I began to wonder at Jossaryk House," Heluda continued, her voice inflexible. "The fire that came after Ladradun was slighted by the island's council. Burning one of *their* houses — we would have questioned Ladradun at the very least. He was careful. Burning the home of one of their mistresses . . . tricky thinking. In my work, coincidences are suspicious. And Ladradun said he agreed with you that fires were being set. He had to say that, because you had already told me. Otherwise I doubt he'd have drawn the magistrates' attention to it. Ladradun knows every inch of the city. He had the governor's leave to explore as he trained his brigades. And after a long summer with no big fires, a Ladradun warehouse burns. The Bazniuz mages slipped up there. They should have questioned him, and they didn't."

So much didn't make sense, Daja thought. That collection of blackened, foul mementoes . . . "Someone tired of being ignored," he'd said during a very odd conversation. "Are you giving up on me?" he'd asked.

"I won't believe it," she insisted, trying to sound forceful. "He's a hero. He'd never burn a houseful of people because he was angry with someone barely connected to them."

"I'm thinking as he thinks," Heluda replied gently. "You learn how to do that, you've been at this as long as I have. Don't look at him as a friend. Look at him for who he is, Morrachane Ladradun's son. Killers like Bennat, they're sad when they're little, when someone knocks them about like toys, but not when they grow up. The only way we learn how adults act is from the adults who raise us. The children of monsters become monstrous, too."

She leaned forward and held Daja's eyes with her own as

she took Daja's hands in her dry ones. "Morrachane was fined ten times by the island council for beating servants. Her younger sons fled the city as soon as they were able; her husband died young, probably shrieked to death. And Bennat? The first time in his *life* he got kindness and attention was when his family died in an accidental fire. The second time was when people *he* trained saved lives in another fire. And so it goes, burning after burning. People are saved, houses are saved. Councils hear him with respect. He isn't Morrachane Ladradun's idiot burden of a son — she called him that in front of a room full of people — he isn't that when something burns. Except he does his job too well. He's gotten rid of too many fire hazards. People get accustomed to his work, and the number of big fires drops off. Respect, attention — he only gets those if the fires get worse. If there are no fires, well, if he starts one, and saves everybody, there's no harm done, practically.

"So he sets a fire. Then a bigger fire next time, then a bigger one. People die. And he is given a tool that will let him shape huge fires." Heluda stopped. Fumbling in a pocket, she pulled out a handkerchief and thrust it at Daja.

Only then did Daja realize that tears ran down her face in steady streams. "You don't *know*," she whispered. Even in her own ears she sounded weak.

"I think I do," Heluda replied quietly. She pointed to the twisted iron handle. "Tell me I'm wrong. Tell me he didn't use your gloves to pitch something loaded with black powder boom-dust into the furnace, something to protect the boom-dust for half an hour or so. When the morning's business started, his creation exploded, taking the entire furnace with it. Thirty-three dead right now, from the bathhouse and the homes around it that burned. Sixty-eight are in hospitals all around the city. Some won't live. It's his handiwork, isn't it?" She leaned back in her chair and laced her hands over her stomach.

"He's my *friend*," Daja told her.

"He's the fire's friend," was the brutal reply. "It's the only thing he loves."

Daja wiped her face, then ran a warm hand over the linen. When she returned the handkerchief to Heluda, it was dry. "He did it," Daja said. "He used my gloves — gloves I made to help people — he used them to blow people to pieces and burn them alive." A tear rolled down her cheek. She swiped it away with an impatient hand. "I made something good, something bright, and he, he dirtied it. This piece of iron tore through a man's body when the furnace exploded. I *lived* that." She had to stop, and drink her tea, and eat a cookie, and wipe her eyes on her sleeve again. Through it all Heluda Salt waited, drinking her own tea, her eyes not leaving Daja.

As she poured fresh tea, Daja thought of something she had felt through her gloves. "But he wasn't just doing a job that would yield something he wanted. He *liked* it. He was all, all giggly inside. Like a nasty little boy putting a nail on his sister's chair."

"They like excitement, criminals of this stripe," replied the magistrate's mage. "Danger, the risk of arrest, all your senses awake — it's like dragonsalt, or bliss leaf, or wake paste. At first a taste is enough. Maybe the second taste is as good, but the third isn't. You need more. And more after that. Excitement's a drug."

"How could I not know?" Daja asked.

"Because for all you're an accredited mage at fourteen, with the kind of power that most mages whistle for, you're still human," Heluda informed her. "*I* didn't suspect till Jossaryk House, and I've been at this game forty years. Blaming yourself is natural enough, but silly. Blame Morrachane. She made him what he is. And blame him. He knows what he does is wrong, or he'd just burn the first thing he sees. He picks, he works out a plan, and he goes to a lot of trouble not to get caught. He could stop. He doesn't want to." She watched Daja think about this, then asked, "Will you testify against him at the magistrate's court? Will you tell the judges what your power has just told you —" she pointed to the twisted iron — "and what you have observed?"

Daja got up and went over to the window, leaning her face against its icy panes. People passed by on Blyth Street outside the open gates, laughing and talking. "He keeps mementoes," she said, hating herself for the betrayal. "In his study, at home, behind his desk. He said he took them from fires where he accomplished something. I believed him, except . . ." Daja hesitated.

"Except?" Heluda prodded.

"I'm almost positive three are from the fires I know of," Daja said. The pane on which she leaned had gone warm. She shifted to another, taking comfort from the chill of the glass on her skin.

Heluda got up and began to pace, dodging furniture and knickknacks. "I didn't know that. We have him. We have him. We'll need time to work the proper spells —"

"He's gone for two weeks," Daja told her. "More, he said, if the weather isn't good."

"I know he's gone," Heluda said. "I'm using the time to build the case against him." She rewrapped the iron bar and placed it in her leather satchel, then straightened and looked at Daja. "You may discuss this with Frostpine, if you like, but please, no one else. You know how gossip spreads."

Daja nodded.

"Should I have you swear — ?" Heluda asked, then shook her head. "You'll hold your tongue. I've left messages at the southern gates and Ladradun House, that I would like a word when he comes back. All very ordinary, nothing to worry about. If you see him beforehand, don't say anything. His mother is a powerful and wealthy woman. I wouldn't put it past her to help him escape, if only to preserve the family name. We must be very careful."

"I will," Daja whispered.

Heluda came over to rest a hand on her shoulder. "I'm sorry," she said. "Talk it out with Frostpine, but make sure no one else hears." She lifted her satchel with a grimace. "I'll get you word as I can." She left without saying goodbye.

15

It was the most ridiculous thing. Ben and his escort reached the first inn on the imperial road shortly after dusk. They set out at dawn the next day, only to encounter their caravan an hour's ride from the waystation.

"You wouldn't believe it," the foreman told Ben as they all headed back to Kugisko. "The roads to the west are nearly wide open — the mildest winter anyone can remember. We only had to dig ourselves out once, at that turn near Thistledown, where the wind's so bad."

"I can't say I'm heartbroken," Ben forced himself to reply casually. "You saved me a trip." And the chance to experiment in Izmolka, where he didn't need to be so careful. He fumed about that, but he also considered his next Kugisko lesson. Shipquarter Island appealed to him, but there were other places as good, if not better.

He wondered how many had died in the bathhouse fire. Without him to direct the firefighters, he knew they would have lost plenty of the surrounding buildings and their residents as well. The excitement of that spout of flame and smoke had faded so quickly, and he hadn't seen any of the results up close. He'd stop by the remains in a day or so, but it wouldn't be the same. He needed something else. Something where he could show them all what he was made of.

They spent the night in the waystation outside Kugisko's walls. None of the Ladradun riders mentioned it, but all of them looked forward to a last night of quiet before they dealt with Morrachane. At Suroth Gate the next morning they waved to the guards and would have ridden on through — there was no line, today being Watersday — but for the sergeant who ran up to Ben waving a paper. "*Viymese* Heluda Salt asked me to give you this when you returned," she said, offering it to Ben. "It was left just yesterday. If she'd waited a day, she could have spoken to you herself!" She waved them on cheerfully.

Heluda Salt. Something cold blew across the back of Ben's neck as he opened the unsealed note. Its contents were innocent enough:

> Ravvot *Ladradun, I have one or two questions with regard to your observations of the boarding-house fire and the fire at Jossaryk House. I would appreciate it if you would contact me upon your return, when it is convenient. The governor has asked me to attend to these matters, and I will be*

your eternal servant if you could help me handle
the governor. — Heluda Salt

Well! he thought, pleased. A mage who didn't think her spells would show her everything she had to know, that was unusual in his book. She had also given him an opportunity, the chance to lead her investigation in the wrong direction.

Half distracted by his plans, Ben escorted the caravan to the warehouse and watched them unload until he got bored. He tossed the key to his foreman with orders to lock up and return it the next day, then rode home. It was only mid-morning; not only were the streets fairly empty still, but his mother would be at temple, leaving him rare time alone.

Once he reached Ladradun House, he tended his horse, cursing his mother's refusal to keep even one servant there on Watersday. Inside the house was dark and silent. Morrachane never left so much as a single lamp lit when they were out. Ben stopped in the kitchen to gather a few coals in a carry-dish, so he could light his office lamps and build a fire in his stove.

As careful as he was, with only some orange coals for light, he banged into a hallway table. He cursed: the edge had struck his hip, sending a bolt of pain through his leg.

A slight rustle and thud greeted his curse.

"Who's there?" he called.

Silence. Ben stepped quietly into the main sitting room and lit a lamp from his coals, then took his grandfather's sword from the brackets over the icy hearth. Blade in one hand, lamp in the other, breath steaming in the chilly air, he walked down the hall to his study, lightly, so no floorboards would squeak.

His study was empty, though he was sure the sound had come from there. He went back to search the other rooms off the hall without success. Bothered still — he knew what he'd heard, and it wasn't mice — he searched the house, checking their jewel boxes and Morrachane's supposedly secret caches of money. Nothing was missing. He found no one.

His heart still chattered as he set the sword in its place and returned to his study, lamp in hand. Inside he opened the shutters, started a fire, then looked around. There was a folded sheet of paper on his desk, identical to the one in his coat pocket. On the outside of the note he saw a note in his mother's hard hand: *What is this? Why does this woman want to speak to you?*

Ben opened the paper with a finger. It was the same note — polite, businesslike — that the sergeant had given him. He let it close and looked at his shelves and desk. His mother had come here already, he knew that; she did it every time he went away. "Straightening," she called it. He called it poking her nose into his correspondence, drawings, and books, making sure he didn't plan to escape her. It was an insult he'd come to live with, but he was getting tired of it, and tired of her.

He checked his memento shelves last. She never touched those, at least. She said they were disgusting, that she wouldn't dirty her hands with them, but Ben knew why she let them be. They frightened her. He liked that.

He smiled now, remembering her fear, until the smile froze on his mouth. At least three items had been moved. His wife's hand: he'd searched the ashes for hours to collect the remains, but in the end, he couldn't bear to let all of her go into her grave. He'd wired the bones together himself, weeping as he'd done it. Untouched, the wire was enough to hold the hand upright and outstretched. Shift it, and some bones would be knocked out of line. The tips of three fingers had fallen over backward.

A lump of crystal, riddled with cracks, had been replaced curved side up. He disliked the curved side. And the half-melted figure of Yorgiry, taken from the neck of the maid who had saved two infants, had been moved.

Someone had been searching his mementoes. Someone who, in all likelihood, carried an invisibility charm. Someone who had taken nothing, who had only looked. And now Ben had two notes from Heluda Salt — Salt the suspicious, Salt the clever, Salt the *best*. The cold draft across his neck was suddenly a northwester off the Syth.

Well.

As usual, he was ready for whatever the gods threw at

him. His plans for this day were long prepared. The time had come to burn away his old life.

His chief regret was that he would never see that living metal suit, never walk into an inferno as Daja could. At least he had the gloves. He would take care of them and use them to further his understanding of fire.

Everything was ready by the time his mother returned from Vrohain's temple. "You!" Morrachane snapped when she saw him. "Why are you back so soon? How even you could bungle so easy a thing as a simple escort trip —"

"Shut up," he said, cutting his mother off for perhaps the first time in her life.

"How *dare* you interrupt me?" Morrachane's mouth was flat with rage, her eyes poisonous.

Ben shrugged. "I know, Mother. I'm surprised myself. Now that I've done it, though, it doesn't seem that difficult. It's never too late to learn, so they say."

Watersday afternoon Daja was virtually alone in the house. Nia had gone to visit Morrachane. Most of the adult refugees were meeting with the Airgi Island council to discuss what to do next. Eidart and Peigi Bancanor were building snow forts in the courtyard with the refugee children. The servants who had offered to work that day were scattered over the large house. Jory was at Potcracker's kitchen, trying to improve her mastery over stews, while

Matazi and Kol paid calls on friends, and Frostpine and Anyussa visited a winter fair. That left Daja in the book-room, reading Namornese history.

"Daja?" Nia stood in the doorway, pale under her bright red cap. "I think something's wrong at Ladradun House. Aunt Morrachane always expects me at this hour and lets me in, but she hasn't, and — and — I know I'm not sup-posed to do anything with my magic outside protections till you say I can, but I spread it out, my magic? I think there's a fire in the cellar."

Daja raced to the slush room for her coat. Nia followed. Together they ran up the alley to Ladradun House. Behind them came the two youngest Bancanors and their play-mates, curious about what was going on.

Daja and Nia halted at the ten-foot wooden fence that guarded Ladradun House from the rear. Above it Daja saw the roofs of the extensions that included the same lesser buildings as did Bancanor and Jossaryk Houses, and the shuttered windows of the top two stories of the main house.

Nia said wonderingly, "The garret shutters are open."

A look up told Daja that Nia was right. From the dark-ness behind the open shutters, there were no windows to block the wind from coming in.

Daja sent her magic rolling over the big house, and felt the fire in the cellar and kitchen immediately. She grabbed it, trying to hold it, only to sense other blazes, in the cellar on the far side of the house, and in the western extension. Those she seized as well. All of them fought her control.

"Nia! The rest of you!" Daja ordered, inspecting the rear gate, "find the alarm bells around here and start ringing them — ring every one you see. Keep ringing them till a brigade comes! Go!" She and Heluda knew Ben had set the bathhouse fire. Was it possible that another firesetter was loose in Kugisko, one with a grudge against Ben, as she once thought? Because she knew Ben was somewhere between Kugisko and Izmolka. This fire couldn't be his work.

Those thoughts flashed through her mind in an instant. She found the small door the servants used to admit themselves and persuaded the metal latch to open. Inside the rear courtyard she saw why those fires she gripped fought so hard. Every cellar entryway gaped; the doors under them would be ajar, too. That was why the garret shutters were open. He had turned the entire house into a chimney. This was the work of someone who knew fire. This was Ben's doing.

Watersday, she thought as she ran onto the covered rear porch. He picked Watersday, when there might not be a brigade anywhere close, because the servants are off. She beat on the door. Was Morrachane or were any of the servants home?

Nearby she heard bright, urgent peals from the fire

alarm bells that hung at the nearest street corners. A few moments later she heard another bell ring in the distance.

There was no time to be polite. She released the fire in the western extension and gave that part of her attention to the door. Seizing the nails and the hinges, she yanked. The metal flew out of the wood, dodging her politely.

"Ow!" someone cried behind her. Daja pulled Nia aside as the boards that formed the door fell onto the porch. The girl was nursing a cut along one cheekbone: she had been scored by a nail.

"I told you to summon fire brigades!" Daja told her. "Get out of here!" In the part of her that gripped the biggest fires, under and in the kitchen, she felt an errant flame discover a trail of oil. Strengthened, it raced along to find a storehouse of full oil jars, pulling other flames with it. "Nia, you can't come in!" Daja gripped the flames hard and tight, holding them from a bounty of oil by less than a foot.

Nia's face dripped sweat, but her eyes were steady. "You can't search alone — you'll never find her in time," she said. "It's an awfully big house. I know the inside."

Daja groped for something Nia would understand. "I don't think we'll find her alive. Ben Ladradun did this. He's as mad as a rabid rat. She's probably dead."

"We're wasting time," Nia insisted.

Daja drew breath to argue, and felt her hold on the cellar fire tremble. She tightened it. If it reached the oil — she couldn't let it reach the oil. "Let's go," she said. "Hold your scarf over your nose and mouth — wet it, if you get the chance. Feel a door before you open it. If it's hot, don't open it."

The girl nodded, pulled her scarf up over her nose and mouth, and plunged into the house, Daja behind her. They searched room after room, with the exception of the kitchen, where smoke rolled out of the cracks around the doors. Like the cellar fire Daja gripped it with her power; it wasn't going anyplace, but it was foolish to stick their heads in there.

"Aunt Morrachane!" cried Nia. "Aunt Morrachane!" Her courage made Daja feel small. She knew Nia was terrified, but she had forced herself to come in to save a woman she pitied.

Once they'd checked the ground floor, they ran upstairs. "Her bedroom's here," Nia said, running to a closed door. She yanked it open. "Aunt Morra —"

Daja stopped beside her. Morrachane was on the bed, but she would not be leaving with them. She would beat no more servants, torment no more sons.

Nia fainted. Daja barely caught her in time to keep the younger girl from cracking her head. She managed to drag Nia into the hall and to slam the door on that dreadful sight. Then she went to an ornamental jar on a hall table and vomited until nothing came through her raw throat or streaming nose.

Daja's grip on her concentration wavered: the cellar and kitchen fires surged ahead a handful of inches. For a full minute she trembled on the verge of releasing them to wipe away that room and the body in it. Only the knowledge that a fire might spread to the neighboring homes stopped her.

She knelt beside the younger girl. "Nia," Daja said, patting the girl's ashen cheeks. "Nia, please, we have to get out." Was Ben still here or had he fled? Surely he'd escaped.

Nia groaned: she was coming to. Daja wished she had smelling salts to hasten the process. No doubt Morrachane kept —

She stopped that thought where it was. Nothing could make her go back into that room. Instead she slung one of Nia's arms over her shoulders and stood, dragging the half-conscious girl to her feet. The blaze in the cellar was getting bigger, searching for cracks in her control.

She hauled Nia down the back stair, sweating so hard the drops pattered onto the wooden steps. More tendrils of the cellar fire escaped her grip, straining greedily for those oil jars. She released the fires in the wing opposite them. Her quickest escape would be the way they'd entered, which took them past the kitchen. She would need all her strength to hold that and the fire in the cellar just below it.

Something changed: Nia had control over her feet. She trembled, but she took most of her weight off Daja. Relieved, Daja forgot to watch where she was going. She tripped and went sprawling on the ground floor, yanking her support away from Nia. The other girl dropped to her knees with a yelp.

Daja's attention broke as she fell. A rope of flame wrapped itself around a jar of oil below. It shattered; the cellar fire roared.

Terrified, Daja shoved it and the rest of the fire into the earth under the house, down through a crack in the underlying rock. Following the crack, the blaze roared into an underground chamber filled with the unfrozen Syth. The water surged up into the crack, turning to steam as it hit the fire and boiling its way to the cellar. All it needed was the slender path the fire had made: the water's force enlarged it fast.

Daja heard a rumble in the ground. It grew like an onrushing tidal wave.

"Run!" she yelled, scrambling to her feet. She hauled Nia up. Together they raced down the hall to the slush room. They charged out through the ruined door just as the underground part of the lake shot through the crack in the cellar floor. Daja released fires with a gasp of gratitude as the icy Syth sprayed into the cellar, then rammed through its ceiling into the kitchen. Steam from the doused fire blasted with it, smashing the ground floor ceiling, then that on each floor, all the way up through the roof.

In the rear courtyard hands grabbed Daja and Nia as they stumbled into the open. Firefighters had come. Daja sagged: she didn't need to hold any fires. Now people moved back, taking the girls with them, as water dropped from the fountain jetting into the sky. It would turn to ice, Daja knew, but it would also douse the fires.

Someone grabbed her arm. She looked up into Kol's face. "What did you hit?" he cried, pointing to the fountain of water.

Daja grinned at him, foolish with relief. "That's a very strong lake you have out there," she said.

"Let's take them home and call a healer," Kol told someone.

"How did you get here?" Nia asked Matazi as her mother helped her back down the alley.

"We heard the alarm bells," Matazi said. "We were just leaving your grandmother's."

They returned to Bancanor House, where Matazi's calm gave way. She wrapped her arms around Nia, weeping, telling her never to frighten her mother like that again. Kol went for a healer as Matazi wrapped Nia and Daja in blankets and installed them on the book room sofa. Both girls began to cough: Matazi fetched Jory's lung-clearing potion and ruthlessly made them drink it. As they hacked and spat into a matched pair of crystal dishes, Matazi took the youngest Bancanors and the refugee children to raid the kitchen, a reward for their work at ringing the alarms.

As her lungs cleared, Daja retreated into a bubble of muted sounds and sights. Heluda was right. Ben was a monster. Daja hadn't quite believed; she'd thought there must be an explanation, somehow, until she saw Morrachane. Until she felt that blaze, with enough jars of oil there to turn the district into a firestorm. As soon as she pulled herself together, she had to find a lawkeeper. She must talk with Heluda. Ben had gotten wind of her suspicions, but how? It didn't matter. He'd worked it out, destroyed his home, and fled. He'd be miles away, free of everything but his fires. He could be found. As long as he had those gloves, Daja would track him. He must return to settle his debts.

Through her numbness she registered that a healer touched her. His power spread through her and through Nia in a gentle examination.

"Shock," he said when he finished. "You must have been quite frightened." Nia could only shiver and nod.

Daja stirred. She owed Nia something. "She didn't show it," Daja croaked, trying to sit up straight. She gave Nia a tiny smile. "I said that you'd find your courage."

"B-b-but I d-d-didn't," protested Nia. "I w-w-was t-t-terrified."

"Then you're wise," the healer said with approval. "Only a fool isn't afraid inside a burning house." To Daja he said, "Your body will be fine, but something burdens your spirit. Whatever haunts you, tell someone about it." He looked up as Kol came in. "I'll leave a throat soother for these two, but —"

Nia's eyes, bloodshot from smoke, popped wide open.

She grabbed Daja's arm. "Jory!" she cried and coughed. The healer laid a hand on her throat; Nia's voice emerged as a rasp. "Daja, Jory's in trouble!"

The twins had that bond; Daja knew it. Her numbness vanished. She tossed away her blanket and raced upstairs, knocking the healer, Kol, and even Matazi out of her way. Her scrying mirror lay on her worktable. Daja grabbed it and stared into its depths. She saw nothing.

Slowly she took a breath, counting. She imagined worry, fear, and grief rising from her skin like steam. She had to let them go. They would return, but for now they were in her way. Only when she was steady did she open her eyes and breathe onto the mirror's surface.

A blurred image rose from its depths and cleared: Olennika Potcracker's soup kitchen. Every set of double doors that led into the hospital was open; smoke roiled through them and along the ceiling. Jory and the rest of the staff shoved the long tables aside to clear a path for the streams of sick and hurt who escaped the hospital through the kitchen. Olennika Potcracker stood at the door to the cellar storerooms, her face covered with sweat. Daja knew she had to be holding back fire. Now Jory was at the water trough that ran along the rear wall of the kitchen, filling buckets and bowls as people brought them to her.

Ben walked in, a toddler on each hip. He handed them to a kitchen maid, turned, and plunged back through a smoky doorway. He wore the living metal gloves.

Daja thrust her mirror into her belt pouch and left her room. Matazi waited in the hall. "Jory?" she whispered, her eyes wide, her face ashen.

Daja rested a hand on Matazi's arm. "Get Frostpine. He and Anyussa went to some winter fair. Call the charity ladies together. People with sleighs, blankets, everything. Yorgiry Hospital is on fire."

Matazi rattled down the stairs in Daja's wake. Daja explained to no one else, but raced back through the house, to the slush room and her skates. She grabbed two coats and put them on, then added gloves, scarves, and a knitted cap. She would need all her magical strength when she got to Blackfly Bog — she couldn't afford to warm herself on the way.

"Daja," Nia croaked from the doorway. She offered a bottle of Jory's lung-clearing mixture in a hand that shook as if she had palsy.

Daja took the bottle with a nod of thanks and tucked it into a tunic pocket. Then she grabbed her skates and went outside.

She couldn't reach the fire in time to halt it. Silently she prayed that other mages who could help were already on their way. The hospital and kitchen people had a better chance than the victims of Jossaryk House: the fire protections she had seen gleaming on the kitchen walls and ceiling were strong. They might keep the fire back. That was in the hands of the gods and whatever mages got there soon.

Her concern was Ben. He was playing hero, with no one to know that he was the creator of their misery. She didn't understand why he'd done this — did he want one last disaster before he moved on? — but she meant to ask when she found him.

Feeling like an overstuffed doll in her layers, she went outside. People stood in the rear courtyard, warming themselves at a fire as others came and went, patrolling the neighborhood to ensure that no other houses burned. The crowd parted silently before Daja as she strode down to the boat basin and sat to buckle on her skates.

She barely noticed them, her mind fixed on the route she must take. If she followed Prospect Canal under Craik Bridge and around the curve of Bazniuz, that would bring her onto Jung Canal. From there it was a straight skate through the frozen intersection of the Whirligig to the hospital. She didn't know if she had the stamina and strength on skates to make it, but she had to try. Ben owed Kugisko a debt of appalling size. All her life she had believed that everyone paid what was owed, though some required help to balance the books. She had to help Ben pay up.

She stood and glided across the basin with a single push. She tripped at its edge, falling onto her back. From there she could see that the sky overhead was darkening. She had forgotten the early nightfall in this misbegotten country. With a growl she lurched to her feet, then ripped the mitten and glove from her right hand. She would have to use some magic after all. Reaching toward the watchers' fire, she twitched her fingers. A globe of flame rose from it and came to sit in her palm. Holding it up as a lamp, she skated into Prospect Canal.

Word of the hospital fire was not out. People skated here at a leisurely pace, servants on the way home for the most part. Daja glided into the stream of skaters. Most saw her flame globe and got out of the way. Daja noticed them no more than she had the people in the courtyard. Instead she stroked forward, breathing deeply to calm her rattled nerves. A fall on the ice had not exactly given her confidence for this.

She pushed harder, moving into the center of the canal where people raced. On the raised streets along the canal's sides, people were lighting outdoor lamps. Inside the open shutters of wealthy homes, candle- and lamp-light glowed. Here on the ice more and more people carried lanterns. This was the proper use of fire, with proper respect and proper fear. Ben had perverted it.

Her pulse speeded up, her breath came faster. No. She couldn't think about this. If she was to help anyone in Blackfly Bog, she had to skate and only that. She would deal with the rest there. In the meantime, Everall Bridge loomed ahead of her. Lamplighters crossed it, their own globes of light shining in an arch over the canal. Daja raised her fire enough to reveal the ice ahead of her feet, and deepened the stroke of her legs and skates. On she sped, the night air biting the exposed skin around her eyes, the Syth's mild wind cold and raw with moisture. At least her lamp kept her ungloved hand warm.

Other skaters were blurs as she passed. The ice hissed as skates cut into it; laughter and talk met her swaddled ears as muffled noise. Daja leaned forward slightly and tucked her free arm behind her back as the racers did, shaping her body to slice the air like a well-honed knife. This was wonderful. It was like flying. She could have done it forever — except that just ahead Prospect Canal ended between two bridges and the flat eastern side of Airgi Island. She was good enough on the straightaway, but if she attempted the turn under Craik Bridge as experienced skaters did, she might not live to see Blackfly Bog. Reluctantly she slowed. She didn't notice when two fast skaters tumbled and went spinning across the canal on their backs, startled by the sight of a big, thickly robed southerner with a globe of fire in her hand.

She passed under Craik Bridge, weaving among skaters who came from three directions. As she eased into Jung Canal the stream of humanity thickened. Moving onto the open ice, Daja looked up and saw why. Ahead, where the Upatka River split to become Kugisko's canals, the sky was orange. The roof and garret of Yorgiry Hospital were in flames.

Daja thrust hard against the ice, yelling for those ahead

to clear the way. Many were sightseers, but others too were skating hard to bring help. On the street that rimmed Bazniuz Island and on Rider Street, the edge of the Pearl Coast, large and small sleighs alike were in motion, racing toward the hospital, their normally musical bells setting up an urgent clatter.

Daja lowered her head and stroked harder. Her thighs, knees, and ankles set up a first, warning throb. Later, she told them. Punish me later.

Even with more people bound for the fire, Jung Canal was so wide that there was plenty of room at the center. Those few skaters coming toward Daja eased away from the girl with the fire in her hand. She locked her free arm behind her and pushed off in long, steady strokes, cold air freezing the hairs in her nose. An icy thread of it wound through a crack in her scarf to sear her vomit-and-smoke-scoured throat. She clenched her lips rather than slow to adjust her scarf and labored to breathe through her nose. When her hat blew away, she let it go.

At the intersection called the Whirligig she struck a ripple in the ice. Before she could fall, hands caught her free arm and supported the outstretched one, lifting her clear of the bumpy stretch. Two skaters, swathed like Daja in scarves, carried her onto smooth ice and set her down easily. They were gone, speeding toward the hospital, before she could gasp her thanks. Now Daja called her fire globe in through her palm, using it at last to warm herself and to ease her throbbing legs. Yorgiry Hospital was all the beacon she needed: the entire top floor was in flames.

I bet they stored things in the garret, she thought grimly as she wove through the skaters as fast as she dared. Nice, dry things that would burn. I bet he went straight up there.

Rather than battle onlookers, she skated wide around them, headed for the soup kitchen's dock. She glided in between sleighs and people with hand-towed sleds as they lined up on the ice. These picked up as many people from the hospital as they could carry at the dock, and took them to safety.

Silvery light shone. Daja shaded her eyes. A mage of some kind crouched on the muddy ground under the dock. Magic radiated away from her, into the ice. A melted puddle of water on the surface, slippery as grease to skater and sleigh, froze. The mage was a weather-worker, drawing cold from the ground into the ice around the dock. Hot as the nearby fire was, the ice would remain safely frozen for the sleighs.

Watching the mage, Daja hit one of the dock's piers shoulder-first. At least I was almost at walking speed, Daja thought, grinding her teeth against pain. Even through all her layers of clothing, it *hurt*. Worse, she heard the ice-mage cackle with amusement.

She didn't linger. Instead she stripped off her skates, slung them around her neck, and climbed a ladder to the dock. A double line of people stretched between it and the kitchen, handing the sick, injured, and young to the waiting sleighs.

Jory stood beside the open kitchen door. Like every worker in this line she had a wet length of the muslin normally used to strain cheese wrapped over her mouth and nose to strain out smoke. She yelped when Daja hugged her from behind, then gasped with relief as Daja pulled off the scarves that hid her face. "I don't suppose you'd want to get yourself to safety?" Daja asked her.

Jory coughed. "I'm safe right here," she insisted. "*Ravvot* Ladradun's still evacuating the nursery — we need every hand to get the little ones out." She took the scarves Daja offered her and wrapped one around the shrieking, coughing, half-dressed infant that someone passed to her from inside the building. Jory gave Daja's other scarves to the workers on either side; they draped the next two children in them. Daja removed her outer coats and handed them over.

"*Ravvot* Ladradun's dead," shouted a man, giving Jory a last infant. "They said the roof just caved in on the nursery!"

Jory's eyes flooded and spilled over, tears cutting through the ash and soot on her face. Automatically she grabbed the next patient to come out, a man with only one leg, and wrapped him in one of Daja's coats before passing him on down to the sleighs.

"Potcracker's still inside?" Daja asked.

"She's holding the fire," Jory croaked. "Somehow it got

into the cellar storerooms, and the oil jars blew out the back of the kitchen."

"Try to stay alive," Daja told Jory. She plunged into the kitchen thinking, somehow it got there, my eye. Ben likes to mix oil and fires.

16

Olennika stood before a wall of flame where the back of the kitchen had been. The dark-haired mage looked embattled. Her black hair tumbled wildly from its pins. Her sober gown was ripped, charred by debris, and smeared with soot. Sweat coursed down her face. Her black eyes were serene, her hands clasped lightly in front of her. About to yell in her ear — the roar of falling beams, fire, and screaming people was deafening — Daja remembered a way to talk that wouldn't distract Olennika from her barriers on the fire below. She placed her hand lightly on the cook-mage's arm.

As she'd hoped, their shared bond with fire made it possible to speak. *Do you need help?* asked Daja.

Olennika smiled crookedly. *I'm fine — I must hold this so they have another exit for the patients,* she replied. *You'll waste time if you try and hold the fire inside the hospital. There's too much. You'll be overwhelmed.*

334

Remembering Jossaryk House, Daja shuddered. She'd do it again if necessary, but it was like surviving a tidal wave. She didn't want to have to try it twice.

Olennika picked up her thoughts. *So you learned you can't beat everything*, she thought, her inner voice as wry as her speaking voice. *So you found you're human. How sad. Listen to me, girl-mage — as soon as they don't need this exit anymore, I am leaving. I know when I'm against something bigger than me.*

I can help, Daja replied. *There are patients still inside. I'll see if —*

Wait, Olennika said when Daja would have let go. *There is a thing . . . if you're not afraid.*

What? Daja asked.

Olennika's thought flickered, as if she herself doubted. Then she told Daja, *On the far side of the hospital, straight through that door on my left, there's a locked wing. The mad ones are there. Most are docile. We drug them nearly all of the time until the healers see if they can be helped. No one's tried to get them out.*

Daja faltered. Like most people she was afraid of insanity. She saw mad folk everywhere, those whose families were too poor for expensive healing that would bring them happier lives, or those who simply couldn't be helped.

It's all right, Olennika told her. *You might try the second floor —*

Daja was afraid, but she knew what Lark and Sandry would do. *Straight across the building from here?* she asked.

Through the door. Olennika pointed to it. *They'll obey simple commands.* Simple, *mind. I brew the drug myself and I made it that way.*

Daja nodded, then ran for the door they'd discussed and the hall beyond. Large wards opened off either side of the hall, disgorging escapees. She was shocked at how many people were still inside, but at least those who could move were there to help those in trouble. She dodged two girls supporting a very old man and caught a toddler when the woman who carried him dropped the child.

"I'd forgotten they were so heavy," the gray-haired woman said and coughed ferociously. "He's the last of the little ones. Some fellow named Ladradun went in for more, and the roof caved on him. We'll get no more babies out." She accepted the child from Daja and continued on her way.

Daja used her senses to check the fire. The garret and the fourth floor were gone, and most of the third. A full story lay between this floor and the blaze — that was bad. She had to hurry.

At the end of the hall she found a large double door with heavy iron deadbolts to secure it. Above the bolts she noticed a small window with a sliding shutter. Daja opened it and peered inside. Most of those she could see sat on cots, weeping. She prowled. A man with very short dark hair, seeing her face, attacked the door, trying to grab her through the peephole. "Get us out!" he screamed, then coughed. "Out, get us out!"

So the drug doesn't work for all of them, Daja thought grimly. She wrestled the bolts out of the locks, thinking bad thoughts about the workers who hadn't tried to move these people. Then she felt guilty; *she* had hesitated at the thought of dealing with crazy people in a firestorm herself. Grabbing both doors, she yanked them back.

The man who had yelled at her tried to shove by. Daja grabbed his arm and hung on. "If you're awake enough to know you're in trouble, you're awake enough to help me," she snapped.

"The questioners — the governor's questioners — they'll come for me," he insisted, fighting her grip. "They don't dare let me go free with what I know. They'll pry my secrets from my mind and they'll kill me."

Daja thought fast. "Pretend you're a healer," she told him. "They won't notice you!" She took a green worker's robe hanging on the wall outside the ward and threw it at him, then let him go and marched into the room. There were thirty beds. Most of the occupants were the sitting-and-weeping sort. "Come on," Daja said, dragging the closest to her feet. "Walk out of here. Follow the others."

The man stared at her wide-eyed, wringing his hands.

"Go!" Daja cried, shoving him at the door. "Walk out of

here!" She did the same with the next patient, and the next. The fourth was curled up on his bed. He did nothing when Daja shook him.

"He won't budge," said the man who feared the governor's questioners. He stood beside Daja, the worker's robe sagging on his bony frame. "He's that way most of the time. They put a diaper on him. And the others are still here."

Daja looked back. The three patients she had ordered to leave stood at the door, huddled together, bewildered. She looked at her companion.

"Lead them like horses?" he suggested.

Daja grabbed a sheet from an empty bed and cut it in strips with her belt knife. "Why aren't you like them?" she wanted to know.

He shrugged. "It doesn't work the same for everyone. I'm not mad enough, I think. That helps."

Common sense from a madman, Daja thought desperately. This day just gets worse by the minute.

Something on the floor overhead caught fire: she felt the surge as the blaze fed, and the sigh of nails as they melted. Daja thrust a wad of linen strips at her companion. "Tie them together by one hand," she ordered, going to the next bed. "Like a string of horses. Get as many as you can, and lead them out. *Hurry!*" She grabbed the young man in the next bed by his wrist and tied one end of a strip to him. "Get up," she ordered. He obeyed. She seized the old woman in the next bed and pulled her to her feet, then tied one of her wrists to the young man's. Towing them along, she added three more to her string.

The next, a middle-aged man with a head shaved bald, threw himself at Daja, shrieking. He clawed her cheek with ragged nails, then got his hands around her throat. Daja let go of her string of docile patients and ran him into the wall, slamming him against it as she called heat from the fire above into her skin. He didn't notice. She rammed him again and called for more heat until he screamed and let go, waving burned hands. He ran from the room. Daja gasped, coughed, and propped herself against the wall as she sent the heat she'd used back into the inferno overhead. She couldn't worry about that fellow running loose. On the second floor, she felt the ceiling give way. It hit the ceiling over her head; the wall under her palm warmed. The timbers overhead groaned under the weight of burning walls and roof. Smoke leaked through the cracks.

Daja roped five more patients into her string and dragged them into the corridor. From the rolling smoke that filled it came her green-robed madman. Someone had given him a soaked cloth to hold over his nose and mouth. Daja passed him her string of patients and plunged back into the ward.

She had four more roped together when the beams above them moaned a second, longer time. Smoke shot down in streams through cracks that broadened as the ceiling began to tear loose from the walls.

There was no time. She grabbed two more docile patients, one in each hand, and towed them to the wall along with her string of people. With one gigantic pull of her magic she yanked all the nails in the wall to her right from their moorings. They shot across the ward like arrows.

With a magical shove Daja thrust both the iron grating on the sole window and the metal in the shutters over it into the night. She turned, still clutching her patients, and rammed herself back-first into the wall. Planks and cross-beams dropped free like rotten teeth. Daja dragged her six people through the tangle of lumber into the night's cold, then towed them toward the ring of guardsmen who held the crowd back.

Hearing wood crack behind her, she turned, still clutching her linen rope and two patients' wrists. In a slow burst of flames, smoke and embers, the ground floor walls collapsed. The madmen's ward fell in. She thought she heard screams from those she'd been forced to leave behind, but told herself fiercely that was just the fire's roar of triumph. It had won.

People were tugging her hands. She jerked away, then realized they wore the green robes of hospital workers. She let them take charge of her patients.

A second roar: the central part of the hospital collapsed. A third: the soup kitchen. Daja scrabbled in her belt pouch, coughing, and brought out her mirror. She pressed it to her forehead, trying to breathe slowly. What of Olennika? Jory?

Sheer exhaustion made her calm enough to summon an image. When she did, her knees went straight to jelly. Down in the muddy slush of the open ground she went, not caring in the least. In the mirror Frostpine helped Olennika to drink from a long-handled ladle. The cook-mage was wrapped in a blanket; as far as Daja could see, Olennika had fled once her clothes burned off. Olennika looked terrible, but she was alive. Beside them Jory bent over, coughing. Someone thrust a bottle at her: Nia. Matazi and Kol were nearby, helping people into the Bancanors' sleigh.

Relief poured over Daja. For a moment she swayed, wanting to cry.

But she had work to do yet. Grimly she felt in her pockets until she found the bottle Nia had given her at the house. Her stomach rolled in protest as she eyed it, then tried to reject its contents when Daja gulped them down. Two minutes later she was coughing and vomiting, her stomach in revolt against the strong-tasting fluid, her lungs expelling their latest load of soot-black phlegm.

When she was done, she lurched to her feet and walked toward the blazing hospital. A guard yelled for her to come back, but it was a scarecrow-thin figure in a flapping green robe who ran up and seized her arm.

"They say *I'm* mad," the man cried. "You're not even locked up!"

Daja gently pried his hand from her flesh. "You're right, but not like you think you are," she said.

The man blinked. His eyes were large and pale, the color impossible to guess in the flame-lit dark, fringed by long, heavy black lashes. He *looked* like a madman, or a prophet, she thought. "That made my head hurt," he complained.

"I'm sorry. An account has come due. Debts must be settled," Daja told him. "I'll be fine." She patted his shoulder and continued her walk into the hospital's inferno. Once more she was reminded of *pijule fakol*, the fearful Trader afterlife for those who did not pay what they owed. Ben probably deserved to spend eternity in *pijule fakol*, but Daja could not help him escape what he owed in this life if it meant he would burn forever. If she did not stop him now, the Bookkeeper might also log the deaths Ben made with her creations to her account.

With no one else to worry her, she let her magic flow out to open a tunnel through the fire. Within moments her non-Sandry clothes had burned away. Her mirror she tucked into the breastband her friend had made. She wasn't sure how long even Sandry's work could last: firewalking in a small boardinghouse was one thing, the holocaust of the hospital and soup kitchen another. For dignity's sake she hoped she would keep her clothes, but the important thing was to find Ben.

He could have died when the nursery roof collapsed, as she had been told, but she doubted it. At first she had thought that he'd slaughtered his mother, then chosen to kill himself by rescuing children from the hospital he'd set ablaze. She didn't feel that way now. He'd leave a bolt-hole for himself. Ben didn't want to die. He wanted to build more fires, not to become one.

Her path took her into the heart of the inferno. Beams fell all around her; walls caved in. She had to be careful not to get struck — a cracked head would kill her — but the fire itself warned her when a large object was about to fall.

In the center of the blaze she stopped. She held her left hand palm up and let the magic in its living metal pour from her fingers like a waterfall, seeking anything like itself. It rolled through the burning hospital and the ground beneath it, questing like a hound. There, about a quarter of a mile away. She pulled the living metal's power into a ribbon that stretched between her left hand and the gloves she had made. Following it brought her to a trapdoor in a burning storeroom. It was open: she looked down and saw a ladder.

Raising a hand, she called a piece of fire to light her steps. With her free hand she gripped the ladder as she descended. She came to level ground about fifteen feet below the storeroom.

She padded along on bare feet: her boots and stockings had burned as she walked through the hospital inferno. She kept one hand cupped over the fire seed that lit her way. He would get as little warning of her arrival as possible. While she could track him if he kept her gloves — and he would never give them up, even if he guessed she could follow him through them — she would rather finish this now. That he'd betrayed her was bad, but she'd been betrayed before. She could survive it. She could not allow him to use her work to ruin more lives.

The tunnel began to rise. Soon she heard movement, and soft humming. The hum stopped as he coughed briefly, then spat. Daja sucked her light into herself. A cold draft rolled down the tunnel: she was near the surface. On she went, the earth icy under her bare feet. She sent warmth into them to ward off frostbite.

The tunnel flattened, then opened into a small wooden shed. He sat on a bench just outside, checking the fit of a pair of skates by the light of a lantern hung on a hook by the door. She watched as he rebuckled his right skate. With the lamp between them, he couldn't see past its light into the shack.

He wore the fur-lined, embroidered coat of a caribou herdsman from the north, as well as a blond wig in the herdsmen's style. A fat pack rested beside him. She wondered if he'd kept it ready somewhere before this, or if he'd packed after his mother's murder.

He still wore the living metal gloves. It seemed he couldn't bear to take them off any sooner than he must. He'd have to conceal them to flee Kugisko, but he would wait until the last minute to remove them.

She sighed. He jerked around, shading his eyes to see

past the lamp. "Daja," he whispered. "Of course. Of course you would come. Fire is your element."

If she was going to talk nonsense with a madman, she preferred her scarecrow in his borrowed robe. He at least had a heart. "You aren't leaving, Ben," she informed him. "You have accounts to settle. Time to pay what you owe."

"Money-grubbing Trader talk," he retorted scornfully. "You're above that."

"I am a Trader and proud of it," she reminded him. "We know that some accounts are written in blood and can be paid only in that. You have blood debts to settle."

"I owe no one anything," he snapped. "I did them a *favor*. I slaved to teach them how serious fire was. When they were too stupid to learn, I gave them lessons that would stick." He seized his pack, and ran the few steps to the canal, balancing on his skates. Daja let him reach the ice. She even let him set the pack on his shoulders. He was three yards away when she sent heat into his skates. They immediately sank an inch deep into the ice: Ben went sprawling. Daja walked toward him, trying not to slip as ice melted around her own bare feet.

Ben scrambled onto his knees and lunged up again. This time she sent a harder burst of heat into the metal skates, fusing them together. Down Ben fell. When he pushed himself up to see what had happened, she reached for the power in the living metal gloves and smacked her palms together. The gloves fused, shackling Ben's arms from fingertip to elbow.

He fell again, then rolled onto his side to stare at her as she approached. The wig was falling off: he'd cut his red curls short to make it fit better. "Daja, please," Ben said. He'd gone dead white, the shadows cast by the great fire rippling over his pale skin. "You can't do this. You're my friend."

There was nothing she could say to that. Instead she looked toward the hospital — they weren't that far from the soup kitchen dock. People were still there. She took out her mirror and fed it enough heat to make it shine brightly. Raising it, she flashed it at the crowd.

"Do you know what happens if I'm accused of deliberately setting fires?" he asked, as if he thought she still might believe his innocence. "Do you? They'll burn me alive."

Someone in the crowd waved a torch overhead, once, twice. Daja responded with two quick flashes of her mirror. A sleigh turned from the dock and drove toward them.

Daja looked at Ben. "I know they will," she told him. "And I will be there, to pay off my account to you."

Kugiskans wasted no time in bringing an arsonist to trial, not one who had killed over 150 people and injured hundreds more. Four weeks after the destruction of Yorgiry's Hospital, Daja stood before three magistrates and a

packed hearing room to tell of her friendship with Bennat
Ladradun, from their first encounter to their last meeting
on the ice off Blackfly Bog. She listened as Heluda spoke of
her discovery of the garret workroom where Ben had created his devices, and heard the tales of people at the hospital, bathhouse, and Jossaryk House.

Throughout it all Ben sat in an iron cage, built to protect him from the vengeance of those he had harmed. He
stared blankly at his hands without ever looking at anyone.

No one doubted how the magistrates would decide, and
they surprised no one: execution by fire. Namornese law
dictated that a criminal's execution take place on the site of
his greatest crime. The healers and directors of the hospital
refused to allow it: as worshippers of Yorgiry they would
permit no murder, even one approved by the state, on
ground just reconsecrated to life. Bennat Ladradun would
burn to death the week before Longnight, at the Airgi
Island bathhouse.

Nia insisted on going with Daja, though her lips trembled as she announced it: she felt that someone ought to
witness for Morrachane. Daja went because she had
promised Ben she would face what she had done by captur-
ing him. Frostpine came without saying why. He didn't
need to; Daja knew he'd come to help her. Room had been
saved for them at the front of the execution ground. When
they arrived, they found their space was shared by Olennika

Potcracker and Jory, the councils of the islands who had suffered Ben's fires, and the families of the slain. Heluda and the magistrates' mages, wearing black coats with gold and silver trim, stood at a right angle to their group. Before them was the stake, its large base of stacked wood and kindling topped by a platform. Opposite Daja's group, on the far side of the stake, waited the governor, the city council, and the officials who served the courts and the lawkeepers.

Beyond those three banks of witnesses stood the crowds: those who had come to see justice, or just to watch a horrible spectacle. They were oddly quiet as they waited.

Soon they heard the beat of a drum, somber and hard. Up the stairs that led to the canal came the execution party. Ben, in a rough sacking robe, was flanked by the black-robed priests of Vrohain, who oversaw every execution, and their attendant lawkeepers. A condemned prisoner could have a priest of his own faith, but Ben had chosen none. He stared at the ground as he shuffled forward. The loudest sounds were the drum, the flap of cloth in the hard wind, and the clank of the shackles secured to Ben's wrists, ankles, and neck.

The priests helped him up the steps to the platform. They chained him to the stake, then climbed down. Ben stared across the sea of people as if his thoughts were years away.

The drum went silent. A herald read Ben's name, his crimes, and his sentence. Then the priests of Vrohain brought their torches. They thrust them between gaps in the logs into oil-soaked kindling. The kindling blazed.

For a long time nothing changed. Ben stood expressionless. Below him the logs caught, and began to burn. They gave off little smoke, Daja realized: he would not be allowed to suffocate before the fire reached his flesh.

His image quivered as her eyes filled with tears. She suddenly remembered the Ben she had known at first, a rare non-mage who understood fire as she did, someone as eager and alive as any member of her foster-family.

Ben shifted, suddenly, as if he were uncomfortable. He lifted first one foot, then the other. The first darts of flame slid through the boards of the platform. Daja's eyes spilled over and continued to spill. This was the law he'd broken, the death he'd given so many. Surely it was right, to give him that same death?

Suddenly flames ran up his sacking robe. Ben flinched aside, trying to crush the fire out on the pillar. His shackles were too tight. His face worked. In a moment he would scream.

She couldn't do this. She couldn't. She didn't care about the law. Daja jammed her power deep into the ground, past bedrock, into the white-hot flow of molten rock and metal below. She summoned a single, overpowering, burst of heat and threw it all into the fire. Let the Namornese punish her, she thought. She couldn't watch him slowly burn to death.

Then she saw it. The silver fire of directed magic roared out of Frostpine and Olennika. It rushed in a silver thread from Jory. Logs, platform, man, and stake turned into an immense, roaring column of flame that shot thirty feet into the air. For a moment it was so hot Daja's face felt tight; she smelled burned hair close by. The column lasted only a breath of time. Then it vanished, out of fuel. A few black flakes drifted over the spot where Kugisko had decreed Ben would die. Smoke rose in discouraged wisps from the freshly charred ground where the stake had been.

Daja looked at Heluda Salt, defiant, expecting the mage to be furious. Instead Heluda stood with a hand over her eyes, shaking her head. Daja couldn't be sure if Heluda was disappointed or resigned. After a moment it occurred to her Heluda might be both.

Someone in the governor's party was more than disappointed or resigned. A man who wore the gold sunburst of a commander on his silver-trimmed black lawkeeper's coat advanced toward Daja's side of the square, his face dark with rage. He beckoned to a group of lawkeepers. "I want —" he began furiously.

Heluda stepped in front of him and put her hand on his chest. She said something; no one heard what it was. The lawkeeper commander glared down at her and opened his mouth. No sound emerged from it; she spoke again, quietly.

Frostpine tugged on Daja's arm. "Let's go," he said,

beckoning to Nia, Olennika, and Jory. "Heluda will settle him. It's not like their cursed sentence wasn't carried out."

Five months later, word came to Bancanor House that the southern mountain passes were open. A week after that, Heluda, Kol, and Matazi accompanied Frostpine, Daja, their mounts, and three packhorses across Bazniuz Island and over Kyrsty Bridge, all the way to the construction site for Yorgiry's new hospital and soup kitchen. While building had only started a month before, carpenters and masons risking the occasional late snow or ice storm to begin the new project, preparations had been underway all winter. Matazi and Kol had been in the forefront of the fund-raising, with donations from their own fortune so large they had shamed fellow rich Kugiskans into granting large sums. Less wealthy families of the merchant and laboring classes had donated cloth, pottery, cooking gear, herbs and oil for medicines, even food. Daja had sold plenty of jewelry and given the money to the new hospital. She, Frostpine, and Teraud had labored all winter on bolts, door latches, hooks, and endless supplies of nails, as had many other smiths. Carpenters set aside wood; weavers made blankets and sheets; herbalists and healers compiled medicines by the vatload.

Now the travelers, Kol, and Matazi sat on their horses, looking at the busy scene before them. Masons labored in cellars and on ground floor hearths as carpenters framed the inner wards and outer walls. The soup kitchen was in business already. Olennika presided over a line of cauldrons from which exquisite smells drifted. Jory, wearing a single plain gown like her teacher, her skirts and petticoats hanging just an inch below her knees, dumped an armload of chopped turnips into a kettle and walked over to them, her calf-high boots squelching ankle-deep into black mud with each step.

"You're supposed to use those board walkways, you know," her father pointed out. "That's why they laid them down, after all. It's not called Blackfly *Bog* for nothing."

"Oh, Papa, it takes forever to get anywhere that way," Jory complained. She stopped beside Daja's horse, a hand on Daja's booted ankle. They had said their important goodbyes while trading staff blows that morning, but Daja had wanted to see her in her element, in the life she was making for herself. To Daja Jory said, "You betrayed me. You turned my meditation over to *her*." She pointed an accusing finger at Heluda Salt, who only grinned wolfishly down at her.

"*And* she can give you a fight with a staff," Daja told her cheerfully. "She'll keep you humble." Trader, log it, she thought, I'm starting to talk like Frostpine.

Jory grinned back, teeth flashing against creamy brown skin. "I have Olennika for that," she said. "I don't think I can stand two humbling teachers."

"All I know is, you'll need them," retorted Daja.

"Come back soon," Jory said quietly. "We'll really miss you." She glanced at the top of a frame wall: Nia straddled it. She was dressed like her twin in a short gown and boots, except that her sensible dress was maroon, and Jory's was blue. As Arnen, seated opposite Nia, drilled openings through two connected beams, Nia thrust pegs into them and hammered them in. Without looking away from her work, she raised her mallet and waved it, then drove the latest peg home. Two weeks after Arnen got his mages' certificate, he had opened his own shop, taking over Nia's meditation as well as her carpentry instruction with Camoc's and Nia's approval.

"I'll come back when I can," promised Daja. She had said her goodbyes to Nia as well, talking with her until late the night before.

"And Nia will write," said Jory. "She's better at it than I am."

Olennika's voice echoed over the clatter of hammers on wood, nails, and stone. "If they aren't going to dismount and help, tell them to go away, Jorality." She had a crow-harshness to her tone now, a lasting reminder of the night when she had kept her part of the hospital safe until everyone who could escape was gone. "Those flatbreads won't put themselves to bake!"

Jory looked at the bundled-up Frostpine. "When he comes out of his cocoon, tell him I said goodbye," she said cheekily. She trudged back to Olennika through the mud, ignoring the plank paths.

"You *can* come out," Matazi told Frostpine. He sat in multiple layers of habits and clothes, a heavy fur hat on his bald crown, two pairs of gloves on his hands. "Breathe some air," urged Matazi. "It's good for you."

Frostpine swiveled his head to glare at her from his layers like an irate owl. "That air is cold, wet, and *moving*," he informed her.

"That's the green wind of the Syth," Kol said with a smile. "Smell it. Damp earth, growing things — spring is on its way."

"On its way, maybe. Here, no," grumbled Frostpine. "I love you both dearly, but I am going to find some real spring. The kind that's actually *warm*."

Matazi leaned over and kissed Daja's cheek. Kol rode over to do the same. "Thank you for our girls," Kol told her. "For setting them on their proper road."

Daja smiled shyly at both of them. "That's what Traders do — we find roads, and we follow them. Trader and Bookkeeper keep your balances high and your debts low."

She looked at Heluda, who said, "If the two of you ever get tired of this smithing nonsense, I could make fair magistrate's mages of you."

Daja chuckled and shook her head. "I think the smithing nonsense is in our blood." She reached across the gap between them and poked Frostpine with the end of her Trader's staff. "Come on, old owl," she told him. "I'll find you the way to springtime."

"Gods be thanked," Frostpine replied with feeling. They set their horses forward on the road south.

ACKNOWLEDGMENTS

With heartfelt thanks to my good geometer, Richard McCaffery Robinson, who maps with such style and accuracy (unlike the author), to my lovely and besieged editrix Kate Egan, who bears so patiently those frantic calls begging indulgence for yet another delay, to my agent Craig, my husband Tim, and my friend Raquel, who supply me with badly needed grounding. I don't think readers always know how much people other than the writer add to books in terms of ideas, fixes, corrections, additions, and general wet-blanketing for authorly hysteria, and they should. Very few books are made strictly by the efforts of one person, even if that person is the only one getting paid.

NOTES

Calendar used in most lands in which these books are set, including major holidays.

January	*Wolf Moon*
February	*Storm Moon*
March	*Carp Moon*
	Sunborn (spring equinox)
April	*Seed Moon*
May	*Goose Moon*
	Wild Night (Beltane)
June	*Rose Moon*
	Midsummer (summer solstice)
July	*Mead Moon*
August	*Wort Moon*
September	*Barley Moon*
	Coldborn (autumn equinox)
October	*Blood Moon*
	Dead's Night (Halloween)
November	*Snow Moon*
December	*Hearth Moon*
	Longnight (winter solstice)

Days of the week:
Sunday
Moonsday
Starsday
Earthsday
Airsday
Firesday
Watersday

ABOUT FUR

I know the use and mention of fur in this book is going to draw howls of dismay from animal lovers, and in our time, I howl with them. (I wear leather because at least the cow gets eaten — we do use everything, and I am a carnivore.) These days in the western world there are so many substitutes to keep us warm that I prefer that the fur remain on the person whose skin it is.

BUT.

My worlds are set in times and places where those alternatives aren't available. They are set in times very like our Middle Ages, and in those times, those who could afford it wore fur to keep warm (and without things like central heating, insulation, and storm-proofed windows, people got a lot colder a lot quicker). Keep in mind that this is fiction based on human history, and that not everyone believes and prefers the same things as the author.

ABOUT THE AUTHOR

*TAMORA PIERCE is a full-time writer whose fantasy books in-
clude* The Circle of Magic, The Circle Opens, The Song
of the Lioness, The Immortals, *and* The Protector of the
Small *quartets. She says of her beginnings as an author that
"after discovering fantasy and science fiction in the seventh
grade, I was hooked on writing. I tried to write the same kind
of stories I read, except with teenaged girl heroes — not too
many of those around in the 1960s."*

In her Circle of Magic *quartet, Ms. Pierce introduced
the four unforgettable mages-in-training who are now four
years older in* The Circle Opens — *Sandry, Briar, Daja,
and Tris. She began the new quartet at the urging of her
many readers, who encouraged her through letters and e-mails
to explore the mages' lives further. She chose their next turning point to be when they each acquire their first students in
magecraft.*

Ms. Pierce lives in New York City with her husband, their three cats (Scrap, Pee Wee, and Ferret), two parakeets (Zorak and the Junior Birdman), and a "floating population of rescued wildlife." Her Web address is www.tamora-pierce.com.

Read on for a special
sneak preview of Book Four
in The Circle Opens quartet,

Shatterglass.

Tharios, *capital of the city-state of Tharios*
On the Ithocot Sea

The short, plump redhead walked out of the house that
belonged to her hostess and looked around, her air that of
someone about to embark on a grand adventure. She shook
out her pale blue cotton dress and petticoats, then wrapped
a collection of breezes around her chubby person as someone else might drape the folds of a shawl before she went to
market. The breezes came obediently to her call, having become so much a part of her in the girl's travels that they no
longer rebelled. They spun around her black cotton stockings and sensible leather shoes, raced along the folds of
skirt and petticoats, slid along the girl's arms and over her
sunburned, long-nosed face. They swept over the spectacles
that shielded intense gray eyes framed by long, gold lashes,
and twined themselves over and along her head. They followed the paths of her double handful of copper braids, all
pinned neatly to her scalp in a series of rings that left no

end visible. Only two long, thin braids were allowed to hang free. They framed either side of her stubborn face.

With her breezes placed to her satisfaction, guardians against the intense southern heat, the girl whistled. The big, shaggy white dog that was busily marking the corners of the house whuffed at her.

"Come *on*, Little Bear," ordered Trisana Chandler, known to her friends as Tris. "It's not really your house anyway."

The dog fell in step beside the girl, tongue lolling in cheerful good humor. His white curls, recently washed, bounced with his trot; his long, plumed tail was a proud banner. He was a big animal, his head on a level with Tris's breastbone. Despite his size, he wore the air of an easy-to-please puppy as effortlessly as the girl wore her breezes.

Tris strode down the flagstone path and out through the university gates without so much as a backward glance at the glory of white stucco and marble that crowned the hill above the house. She thought that the university, called Heskalifos, was fine, in its own right, and its high point — the soaring tower known as Phakomathen — was pretty, but there were perfectly good universities in the north. She was on her way to see the true glory of Tharios, its glass-makers. Let her teacher, Niko, join their hostess, Jumshida, and many other learned mages and apprentices in their long-winded, long-lasting presentations on the nature of any and all vision magics. Tris, on the other hand, was interested in the kind of visual magic wrought by someone who held a blowpipe that bore molten glass on its end.

At one of the many side entrances to the grounds of Heskalifos, Tris halted and scowled. Had Jumshida said to turn left or go straight once she was outside the university enclosure?

A girl her own age stood nearby at a loading dock, emptying the contents of a trash barrel into the back of a cart. The muscles of her arms stood out like steel cables. Though she was clearly female, she wore her hair cut off at one length at ear level, and the knee-length tunic worn by Tharian men. She was also extremely dirty.

"Excuse me," Tris called to her. "Do you know the way to Achaya Square?"

The girl picked up the second barrel in a row of them and dumped its contents into her cart.

Tris cleared her throat and raised her voice. "I *said*, can you tell me the way to Achaya Square?"

The girl flicked her eyes toward Tris, then away. She dumped her empty barrel next to the others, and picked up a full one.

Well, thought Tris. She can hear me; she's just being rude. She stalked over to the cart. "Don't you people believe in courtesy to visitors?" she demanded crossly. "Or are all you Tharians so convinced that the world began here that you can't be bothered to be polite?"

Though the barrel she had taken to the cart was still half full, the girl set it down and fixed her gaze on Tris's toes. "You *shenosi*," she said quietly, using the Tharian word for foreigners. "Don't they have guidebooks where you come from?"

Tris's scowl deepened. She was not particularly a patient girl. "I asked a simple question. And you can look at me if you're going to be snippy."

"Oh, it's a simple enough question," replied the girl, still soft-voiced, her eyes fixed on Tris's no-nonsense shoes. "As simple as the way is if you just follow that long beak of yours. And I'll give you some information for nothing, since you're obviously too ignorant to live. You don't talk to *prathmuni*, and *prathmuni* don't talk to you. *Prathmuni* don't exist."

"What are *prathmuni*?" demanded Tris. She chose not to take offense at the remark about her nose. It was not her best feature and never had been.

"I am a *prathmun*," retorted the girl. "My mother, my sisters, and my brothers are *prathmuni*. We're untouchable, degraded, *invisible*. Am I getting through that thick northern skull yet?"

"Why?" asked Tris, curious now. This was far more interesting than a simple answer to her question. "Why should a *prathmun* be those things?"

The girl sighed, and rubbed her face with her hands, smearing more dirt into it. "We handle the bodies of the dead," she told Tris wearily. "We skin and tan animal hides.

We make shoes. We take out the night soil. But mostly, we handle the dead, which means we defile whatever we touch. If you don't move along and a *giladha* —"

"What?" asked Tris.

"One of the *visible* people," replied the girl. "If they see you talking to me, they'll demand you get yourself ritually cleansed before you go anywhere or do anything. Now will you go away?" demanded the *prathmun*, impatient. "You'll get cleansed, *shenos*, but I'll be whipped."

She said it so flatly that Tris believed her. She walked two steps away, then asked without turning around, "What's *shenos*? And how do you tell who's a *prathmun*?"

"A foreigner is *shenos*," retorted the *prathmun*, dumping the rest of her trash barrel into the cart. "And we all have the same haircut and the same kind of clothes, and straw sandals. Now *go*."

Tris followed the road that lay straight before her, the direction the *prathmun* had indicated with such flattery. "Niko said I'd find some of the customs here barbaric," she informed Little Bear when she was out of earshot of the *prathmun*. "I'll bet you a chop for supper this is one of the ones he meant. Whoever heard of people not being people just because they deal with the dead?"

Once she reached Achaya Square, Tris found the Street of Glass easily enough. Reading about Tharios on the way here, she had formulated a plan of exploration with her usual care to detail. She would start at the foot of the street where most of the city's glassmakers kept their shops, beginning with the smaller, humbler establishments near the Piraki Gate, and work her way back to Achaya Square until her feet hurt. She meant to spend a number of days at the shops that caught her interest, but first she wanted an overview. Tris was the kind of girl who appreciated a solid plan of action, perhaps because often her life, and her magic, was in too much of an uproar to be organized.

As she walked, she looked on the sights and people of Tharios with interest. Buildings here were of two kinds, stucco roofed with tile — like those in her home on the Pebbled Sea — or public buildings built of white marble, fronted with graceful colors and flat-roofed, with corners and column heads cut into graceful lines. The Street of Glass and Achaya Square fountains were marble or a pretty pink granite. Statues carved from marble and painted to look lifelike stood on either side of the paved stones of the road. It was all very lavish and expensive. Tris might not have approved, but her view of people who spent so much on decoration was leavened when closer inspection showed her soft edges on statues and public buildings, and fountain carvings worn almost unrecognizable by long years of weather. Tharios was an old city, and its treasures were built to last.

The Tharians themselves were a feast for her eyes. The natives ranged in skin color from pale brown to black, and while their hair was usually black or brown, many women used henna to redden it. Men cropped their hair very short or even shaved their heads altogether. Ladies bundled their hair into masses of curls that tilted their heads to the appropriate, sophisticated, Tharian angle. The *prathmuni,* male and female, sported the same rough, one-length cut Tris had seen on the girl she spoke to. All *prathmuni* wore a ragged, dirty version of the knee-length tunic worn by Tharian men. Tharian women dressed in an ankle-length, drape-sleeved version called a *kyten.* In summer these garments were cotton, linen, or silk, with sashes or ribbon belts twined around waists and hips. On top of the tunic or *kyten* upper-class Tharians also wore colored stoles, each of which indicated the wearer's profession. She knew that mages here wore blue stoles, shopkeepers green, and priests of the All-Seeing God red. Beyond that she was lost. No matter what color the stole, it was usually made of the lightest cotton, or even silk, money could buy. The Tharians looked cool and comfortable to Tris.

Since the *prathmun* girl had called her attention to shoes, Tris noted that better-dressed Tharian men and women generally wore leather sandals that laced up to the knee. Many of the poorer residents went barefoot. This wasn't as risky as it might be anywhere else: Tris saw *prathmuni* collecting trash and cleaning the streets on nearly every block.

Though Little Bear was content to stay with his mistress, Tris's breezes were not. They roamed freely around her, tugging at curls, tunics, *kytens,* and stoles, exploring people's faces, then returning to Tris like excited children gone for a walk with a favorite aunt. They brought scraps of conversations about trade rates, fashions, family quarrels, and political discussions from all around her, pouring those scraps into her ears. She half-listened, always interested in local gossip.

Some conversations mentioned her. A few of the Tharians she passed had discovered her way to stay cool. Perhaps her breezes wouldn't have been noticed if the air were not perfectly still. The only winds outside Tris's circle of influence were those made by handheld fans and those roused by pigeons in flight from uncaring feet.

Tris sighed, and drew the breezes closer to her. People continued to stare as her dress and petticoats stirred in different directions. She ignored them. It was too hot to give up her fresh air so a number of stuck-up southerners weren't made nervous. If they were as clever as they claimed, they'd find ways to hold breezes of their own, Tris told herself.

She had a number of breezes tied up in knots of thread back at the house. Perhaps she could peddle some at the market, and make a bit of extra money. There were two more moons of summer to go, and the problem with city walls was that they tended to keep out the wind. She ought to be able to sell a knot, or two, or three, for pocket money. She would ask Jumshida how to go about it.

On she walked, planning and observing. She passed between shops filled with wonders: vases, bowls, platters, glass animals in a multitude of colors and sizes. In the shops on the Achaya Square end of the Street of Glass, windows were made of small panes of glass, treasure troves in and of themselves that gave a watery, rippling shape to the beautiful objects behind them.

Mingled with the higher-priced glass was glass that had been spelled in some way. Magical charms and letters in the sides and rims of pieces, suncatchers magicked to catch more than just sun, rounds of glass imbued with magic to capture and hold an image in them, all glinted silver in Tris's vision, showing her the work of the glass mages of Tharios. It was for this reason that she chose to start among the poorer shops, those more likely to sell plain glass and few charms. Tris knew she would spend most of her time later among the glass mages, comparing notes and learning how they practiced their craft.

Closer to Labrykas Square the shops had ordinary, shuttered windows, with the wares arranged on shelves to tempt passersby. Tris lingered at one and another, admiring the curve of a bowl or the blue-green hue of a cosmetics bottle, but she always made herself walk on after a moment. She was determined to start at the very bottom of the glassmakers' pecking order.

As Tris approached Labrykas Square, the first public square beyond the Piraki Gate, her breezes carried a conversation to her. "— a disgrace!" someone cried. "One of the riffraff, murdered and left in the Labrykas Square fountain like, like so much trash!"

"It will take a powerful cleansing to purify the fountain again," a woman replied soberly. "Surely the All-Seeing God will take offense against the district for the defilement —"

"The district? I think not!" retorted the first speaker. "It's obviously the work of some *shenos* who respects nothing and no one. The All-Seeing knows that no Tharian would commit so foul an act."

"The Keepers of the Public Good will put a stop to it," the woman said with the firmness of complete belief. "They have —"

The breeze had not caught the rest of the discussion. Tris shook her head as she walked on. Someone is murdered, and all these people care about is the purity of the square? she thought, baffled. *That's* pretty heartless.

North Fortress

8

d

Odaga

1

2

Central Fortress

Alakut

6

b

3

a

2

4

1

Least Fortress

3

c

f

Kadasep

e

d

h

i

Baznius

Shield

8

4

j

s

l

a

e

7

9

Airgi

m

Pearl Co

The SYTH

Less Ship=
quarter

Greater
Shipquarter

Suroth Gate

0   ½   1   2 mil

© 2002 Ian Schoenherr

KUGISKO

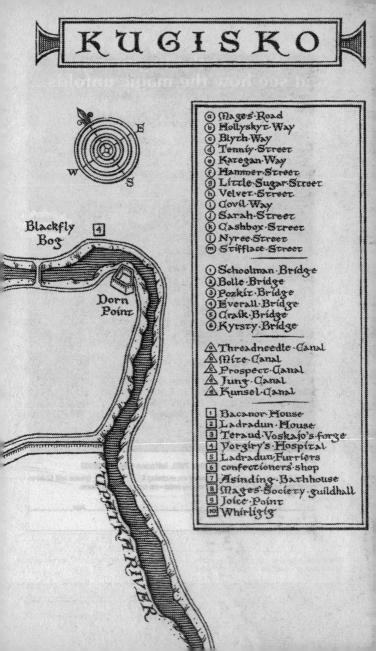

Blackfly Bog

Dorn Point

UPITKA RIVER

a) Mages·Road
b) Hollyskyt·Way
c) Blyth·Way
d) Tenny·Street
e) Kategan·Way
f) Hammer·Street
g) Little·Sugar·Street
h) Velvet·Street
i) Covil·Way
j) Sarah·Street
k) Cashbox·Street
l) Nyree·Street
m) Stifflace·Street

① Schoolman·Bridge
② Bolle·Bridge
③ Pozkit·Bridge
④ Everall·Bridge
⑤ Craik·Bridge
⑥ Kyrsty·Bridge

△ Threadneedle·Canal
△ Mite·Canal
△ Prospect·Canal
△ Jung·Canal
△ Kunsel·Canal

① Bacanor·House
② Ladradun·House
③ Teraud·Voskajo's·forge
④ Yorgiry's·Hospital
⑤ Ladradun·Furriers
⑥ Confectioners·shop
⑦ Asinding·Bathhouse
⑧ Mages·Society·guildhall
⑨ Joice·Point
⑩ Whirligig

DATE DUE

FEB 0 3 2009	
DEC 0 7 2011	
APR 2 3 2013	
APR 2 3 2013	
JAN 2 1 2015	
FEB 1 5 2018	
MAY 1 5 2018	
JUN 0 5 2018	